Last DRAGON STANDING

RACHEL AARON

Dear Reader,

There is no way to write a blurb for this final book without spoiling all of the others. Suffice it to say, mysteries resolve, dragons war, pigeons abound, and no one is safe as Bob's grand plan finally comes to fruition.

But the Great Seer of the Heartstrikers isn't the only one whose schemes are nearing completion. The Nameless End is coming, and even the machinations of the world's most brilliant dragon seer might not be enough to stop it. As everything comes crashing down, it's up to Julius to prove what he's always known: that seers can be wrong, and Nice Dragons don't always finish last.

PROLOGUE

700 years ago, somewhere in South America.

On a night in late summer, on a beach somewhere along the Pacific coast of South America, Brohomir and Amelia sat together in the sweltering heat with their feet dug into the cool, wet sand, watching the waves crest in the moonlight.

As usual, Amelia was drinking from a bone flask full of something that smelled slightly of coconut and strongly of alcohol. Brohomir, however, had nothing. He hadn't eaten or drunk anything in days in preparation for tonight. Now that they were finally on the threshold, though, he found he was having trouble asking his sister to begin.

"You don't have to do this now," Amelia said quietly, her amber eyes shining in the dark. "You said it was centuries in the future. A lot can happen between now and then. There's no shame in waiting."

"No help, either," Brohomir replied, digging his hands into the sand. "But I see the vision every night now, Amelia. There's no escaping it. I *have* to do something."

His sister took another sip from her flask. "What do you see?"

She'd asked him before. He'd *told* her before, but while Brohomir desperately didn't want to talk about it, he could never deny Amelia anything.

"I'm in a ruined city," he said quietly, tilting his head back to look up at the endless stars above them. "At least, I think it's a city. It's so big, I can't be sure. The buildings look as tall as mountains."

"The future is full of marvels," Amelia replied with a chuckle. "Too bad it gets wrecked." She frowned. "Was it one of us?"

"I don't know," Brohomir said. "The death vision isn't like my others. There's no path of decisions, no trails to follow. It's just a moment sliced in time. I don't even know how I got there, but he's already waiting for me."

He could see it perfectly even now. The Black Reach stood over him, a long black shadow silhouetted by the strange orange light shining from something unseen behind him. "He kills me after that."

"If that's all it is, we'll just have to make sure I'm there too," Amelia said proudly. "The Black Reach is the Death of Seers, not the Death of Amelias. I won't let him touch you."

"But you *are* there," Brohomir said. "I can't see you in the vision, but I can smell you close by. There's another Heartstriker as well. One of our brothers."

"Which one?"

He shrugged helplessly. "I don't know. His back is to me, so I can't see his face. I don't actually think he's been born yet." Brohomir smiled. "He strikes me as very young."

Amelia snorted. "So, useless."

"Not useless," the seer said. "The vision is only for a moment, but in that moment, I know he's important. Maybe the most important."

"He can't be *that* important," Amelia said bitterly. "The Black Reach still kills you."

"He does," Brohomir said, voice shaking. "He kills me, Amelia. I see it happen over and over, but what's truly terrifying is that my death isn't actually the worst part."

"What's worse than dying?"

He took a shuddering breath. "The thing in the sky."

His sister scowled, but Brohomir didn't know how else to explain it. There were no words, no names for what he'd witnessed floating above the scene of his death, but every time Brohomir saw it, fear cut straight to his bones. It was even worse than when the Black Reach cut him down. That was merely the end of him. The thing in the sky was the end of everything.

"I have to stop it," he whispered, reaching out to clutch her hand. "It's over for all of us if I don't."

"Fair enough," Amelia said. "But are you sure this is how you want to do it?" She nodded down the beach at the multiple feet of portal calculations she'd drawn in the hard-packed sand. "I was there when the Black Reach found you. I heard him say that he only kills seers who break his rules, but that's exactly what we're planning to do. If this actually works, you could be sealing your own fate."

"If I don't do this, we're *all* dead," Brohomir said firmly, pushing to his feet. "But it's all right, Amelia. I've seen the future, and I have a plan. I'm not going to die, and I swear on my fire I won't let you die, either."

Amelia grinned at him. "If you say so, I believe you," she said, standing up as well. "Shall we get this over with?"

When Brohomir nodded, Amelia tossed back the last of her fermented coconut. Properly braced, she dropped the empty flask in the sand at her feet and lifted her hands in front of her, curling her fingers in the empty air like she was preparing to rip open a curtain. When every knuckle was hooked at the correct angle, the air in front of her lit up as a searing lash of Amelia's magic struck the empty space above the surf, sundering the dark as she ripped the world apart, opening a hole into emptiness itself.

"I can only hold it for five minutes!" she yelled over the wind that began howling past them out into the blackness on the other side of the portal.

Brohomir nodded and pulled his alpaca wool jacket tight, filling his lungs with air as he stepped off the nighttime beach and into the true dark of the space between worlds.

The moment he crossed the portal threshold, all sound vanished. He could still see Amelia behind him, her black hair whipping wildly around her strained face as she fought to hold the doorway open, but there was no more wind or sound. Just the empty dark, stretching out to infinity around him.

"Right," Brohomir said, speaking the word out loud even though the only voice he could actually hear was in his own head. "Let's try this."

He closed his eyes and looked down the shining river of all the possible futures. It only took a second to find the one he'd marked: a particularly bloody future where Bethesda decided to kill her way into one of the European clans instead of laying eggs to create her own. That was *definitely* not a twist of fate Brohomir wanted to suffer through, so he happily ripped it out, plucking the silvery line from the weave of possibilities with a deft mental hand. When it was free, he held it out, waving the future through the dark like a lure in front of him.

It wasn't a sure thing, but Brohomir had chosen this night very carefully. He'd scoured his futures to find the time, the place, even the exact right spot on the beach that had the highest chance of success. He'd stacked his odds as high as they would go, but it still felt as if he'd been waving forever before something finally turned to look.

He didn't know how he knew. The emptiness here was different from any he'd ever experienced. He couldn't see, couldn't feel, couldn't sense in any of the usual ways, but he didn't need to. It was impossible to miss something that huge coming toward him, its tendrils reaching out greedily to pluck the dangling thread of possibility from his fingers.

The moment the future left Brohomir's control, it vanished. Not just that one thread, but all the choices and coincidences that had led up to it. An entire line of possibilities simply ceased to be as the thing in the dark nudged him, forcing a question into his consciousness, though not in words. This was merely an impression of exchange, a request to know what Brohomir wished in return for the future he'd given.

"I want you to listen to me."

Just like before, there was no sound. The words were only in his head, but the thing in the dark turned, its presence growing larger still, as if it were moving closer. There was still nothing to see, but the bigger it got, the more distinctly Brohomir could feel it looming around him, a creature the size of eternity with a body made of cold, dead chains.

"I know you," he said as the chains settled around him. "You are the Nameless End that devoured our old world, the one the ancient dragons called the Final Future."

The darkness surrounding him roiled in fury. How dare he name her? She was what remained when all possible futures were gone. She had no name, no constraints! Only endless hunger, and Brohomir was a tasty beast of many futures. She remembered the dragons he spoke of. Those fools had traded her their entire plane in return for temporary victories, feeding their own end. The memory soothed the Nameless End's anger, and she eased closer to Brohomir. Maybe this one would be foolish too?

"I'm often foolish," Brohomir replied with a smile. "But I'm not here to offer myself as sacrifice. I'm here to make you a deal."

The Nameless End's chains rattled eagerly. A future?

"Everyone gives you futures," Brohomir said dismissively. "I've brought you something infinitely better."

Impossible. What could be better than a future?

Brohomir placed a hand against his chest. "Me."

The Nameless End's confusion flooded through him. What would she want with something like him? He was tiny and finite, insignificant. If he hadn't been her only source of food for millennia, she wouldn't have bothered focusing her attention finely enough to speak with him. The chains crept closer, prodding Brohomir's mind with their terrifyingly final-feeling tips. Maybe he was delusional?

"I prefer imaginative," Brohomir replied, flashing her his most charming smile. "It's true that I am nothing compared to a power like you, but gifts are not valued by size alone. You've eaten the futures of countless planes, including my old homeland. But in all those timelines, all those lives you've vicariously experienced, there's one thing you've never had."

The thing in the dark was growing annoyed with the cocky dragon. She was the end, the one path that remained when every other possibility was spent. All of time would eventually belong to her. What could he possibly have that she did not?

"A life of my own."

The Nameless End turned away, but the dragon wasn't finished. "It's true you'll eventually own all futures," he said quickly. "But only *after* they're done. The only timelines you get are ones where there are no surprises left, no uncertainty, no tension or wonder. Just the wrapped-up life stories of beings who mean nothing to you where every crisis is already resolved and every end is already known." He shook his head. "That has to be *amazingly* boring."

The Nameless End did not get bored. She was what she was.

"Ah," Brohomir said. "But have you ever tried being something else?"

What a stupid question. What else could she be?

The dragon grinned. "Mine."

The Nameless End paused.

"This place is a nothing," Brohomir went on, looking around blindly in the dark. "Everything here is already dead and done, assuming it ever was, but *my* world is still in motion. There are still surprises there, things yet unknown. I can share them with you."

The chains curled in interest. How?

"Come with me," the dragon said, putting out his hand. "Come back to my plane as my consort and ally, and I will give you a front row seat to the most marvelous show you've ever seen. Something more spectacular than all the other eternities you've eaten, because unlike those stale, dead histories, *my* story is alive. The future I'm offering you is still being written. It might end in tragedy, but we won't know until we get there, because until the present becomes the past, *anything* is still possible. That's what I have that you do not, and it's what I want to share with you."

Brohomir stretched his hand out further. "Be surprised with me," he beckoned. "Everyone else trades you futures they don't want in exchange for sure bets, but *I'm* offering to share my present, which is still infinitely possible, and thus infinitely better. So leave this dull emptiness and run away with me. Come and live all the things you've only seen in other people's finished stories, and when it's over, you'll have had something that no one else has ever cared enough to give you: a life of your own."

He was panting by the time he finished, his lungs gasping for the air he knew had to be still rushing through the portal behind him even if he couldn't feel it. He wasn't sure how much time he had left, but he didn't dare look back at Amelia. Even if he couldn't see it, his eyes stayed locked on the place in front of him where he could feel the Nameless End watching in wonder.

No one had ever offered her anything like this before.

"I'm an out-of-the-box thinker," Brohomir said proudly. "Anyone can give up a future, but there's only one present, and I'm offering to share mine with you. I can't promise it will always be pleasant, but it'll never be boring, and so long as I live, you will never be alone."

He felt the Nameless End's temptation like a shiver around him. She *was* very lonely. All ends were, but it couldn't be that simple. The little creature would not offer something so precious unless it wanted a very great boon in return. What did it want?

"There's an End coming to my plane," he explained. "I don't know when or how yet, but I know it arrives during my lifetime. If I'm to beat it, I need an ace of my own. I came here thinking that was you, but now that you're in front of me, I realize I was thinking too small. I don't just need you to come back with me to beat another Nameless End. I *want* you to come with me, because I'm lonely too."

That was far more personal than Brohomir usually liked to go, but he only had one shot at this, and the truth was always more compelling than a lie.

"I'm a seer," he said. "Every time I meet someone, I can't help but see their death. I see all the ways they could betray me, even if they never do. That's why seers go mad. When you're always evaluating every possibility of every individual you meet, it's impossible to interact with others like normal dragons do. But you're different. You have no future as I know it, so when I look at you, all I see is this." He waved his hands at the darkness. "Emptiness. Nothingness." He sighed. "Do you know what a relief that is? How beautiful you are?"

The Nameless End flipped her tendrils. That was foolish. Endings could not be beautiful or ugly. They simply were.

"I disagree," Brohomir said with a smile. "I think you're marvelous, and impending apocalypse aside, I'd very much like to have you with me. I think we'd be good for each other. I think you'd be good for me."

Already, he could feel her calm in his mind, helping him focus, which was an enormous relief. He'd seen what life as a seer would do to Estella, and it had terrified him to the point where getting dumped by the most beautiful dragoness he knew he'd ever meet was almost a relief. The shadow of that same madness and paranoia was always lurking when he looked at his own future, but in the new timelines where the Nameless End was with him, the stain was lessened, or missing entirely.

That gave him enormous hope, which was why, even though he knew his time here had to be almost up, he didn't step back toward the portal.

He moved closer to her instead, walking into her tentacles with his mind open in the hope she could see what he saw.

"Come away with me," he whispered. "Share my present until it becomes past, and so long as I live, I swear, we will never be alone."

The words shook. This was his final gamble, but it seemed to work. He could actually feel the Nameless End in his head now, her vast presence sliding over his thoughts like silk over a topographical map, followed by a question.

What should I be?

"Anything your heart desires," Brohomir said, his heart leaping even as the portal behind him started to cave. "It's your life. So long you spend it with me, I will be happy."

The Nameless End's touch brushed over his mind one last time, then one of its continent-sized tendrils reached out to touch the palm of Brohomir's outstretched hand, leaving him holding something heavy and fragile. The moment he had it, Brohomir clutched the precious object to his chest and whirled around, diving through the portal seconds before it collapsed. He landed hard in the sand on the other side, skidding to a stop beside Amelia, who was heaving on her back under the stars.

"What part of *five minutes* did you not understand?" she gasped. "I almost died!" She gulped down several more lungfuls of air before turning her head to look at him. "At least tell me it worked."

Instead of answering, Brohomir opened his hands to show her the small egg-shaped object.

"What's that?"

"I have no idea," he said giddily. "But the Nameless End agreed to come with me, so I assume it's—"

He stopped as the object began to shake. It cracked wide open a second later, the mottled shell splitting apart as a wet, ugly, spindly hatchling forced its head through.

"What the—" Amelia recoiled in horror. "*That's* a Nameless End?"

Brohomir nodded, his green eyes wide with wonder.

"What's it supposed to be? A chicken?"

He breathed in deeply. "Smells more like pigeon to me."

His sister looked scandalized. "I risked death and worse to help you bring the *Final Future*—the death of our home plane—into this world, and it's a *pigeon?*"

"Don't call her that," he snapped, cupping the newborn chick in his hands. "She can be whatever she likes." He smiled. "I think she's beautiful."

And she *was*. The scope was much smaller, but when he looked at the bird in his hands, he saw the same stunning emptiness he'd witnessed in the void. She had the same calm as well, staring up at him with black eyes deeper than any mortal animal could possess. As Brohomir stared back, he felt the tiny tendrils of her chains spreading like roots through his mind, tying them together. When she was anchored deep, she spoke again in his mind, only this time, the words came out in an actual voice.

I'm here, she said, her new tone excited as the baby pigeon looked around. *When do we begin?*

"Right now," Brohomir said, scrambling to his feet. "Come on, Amelia!"

Amelia rolled her eyes, grumbling under her breath about the dangers of physical exertion after performing miracles as she pushed off her knees, brushed the sand from her trousers, and starting jogging down the moonlit beach after her brother.

CHAPTER ONE

Julius woke to the alien feeling of absolute contentment.

He was still in his old room in the DFZ, squeezed into his narrow twin bed with Marci cuddled up against his side. He had no idea what time it was, and he didn't care. If his arm hadn't been falling asleep, he would never have moved again. He was trying to ease the offending limb into a different position when Marci's brown eyes fluttered open.

"Sorry," he whispered.

Marci just smiled and rolled over, flattening herself against his chest with a contented sigh. Julius sighed too, running his now freed hand up her naked back with a shiver of wonder. He'd been here for all of it, but it still didn't seem real that Marci was here with him, whole and alive again. She didn't even have a scar, a fact that he knew firsthand after the rampant nakedness of the previous hours.

That thought made him blush beet red. But while he'd been able to ignore the obvious questions during the rush of getting the person he loved most back from the dead, this wasn't something he could put off much longer. Now that the initial out-of-his-mind joy at getting Marci back had faded to a more manageable level of extreme happiness, Julius's number-one concern was *keeping* her. It felt like bad form to question a miracle, but he'd sworn he was never letting her go again, and if he was going to make good on that, then he needed to know exactly how this miracle had occurred.

"Marci?"

"Hmm?"

Julius tightened his arms around her. "How did this happen?"

Her lips curved in a mischievous smile. "I'm pretty sure you started it."

"Not that," he said, turning even redder. "I meant this."

He brushed his fingers over the place on her unmarked back where General Jackson's shot had passed through. He could still see the horrible wound in his mind: the smoking edges, the way scarlet blood had spread like spilled ink across her shirt. The memory of her death was one he'd never shake no matter how long he lived, so now that it was suddenly undone, he couldn't relax until he knew.

"Is this real?" he whispered, clutching her. "Are you really back?"

She laughed. "Do I need to prove it to you again?"

"I'm serious."

He must have sounded it, because Marci stopped laughing. "That's a complicated question," she said, pushing up on her elbow so she could look him in the face. "The short answer is yes, I'm back, and I'm human. A mortal, just like I was before, only minus the holes."

She smiled down at her healed chest like that was a joke, but Julius was shaking. "How?" he asked again. "Last I checked, humans didn't come back from the dead."

"Not normally," Marci agreed. "But it's amazing how flexible the rules get when multiple immortals need your help. Amelia always intended to bring me back with her, but Raven was the one who did the actual hauling. He flew me back from the other side so I could reclaim my body and do my job as Merlin."

Then Julius owed Raven a debt he could never repay. "Could he do it again?" Because if people could be brought back from the dead, then the greatest problem of falling head over heels in love with a human had just been solved.

"If you mean 'Are you immortal now?' I'm afraid the answer is no," Marci said, shaking her head. "Happy as I am that it worked this time, the whole 'rise from your grave' thing was the product of highly unique circumstances that probably shouldn't be repeated. But don't worry. I'm not planning on dying again any time soon."

He kissed her in thanks for that. Then he kissed her again, just because he could. He was about to kiss her a third time when Marci started in with questions of her own. "What about you? How did you end up in the DFZ with the Dragon Emperor of China? And why does Chelsie have a baby now? I wasn't gone *that* long."

"The baby's not actually new," Julius said, racking his brain to think of a shorthand way to explain what had happened with Chelsie and the Qilin, or Chelsie and Bob. He couldn't come up with one that made any kind of sense, though, so he wound up telling her the whole story of Chelsie's ill-fated journey to China and the fallout that had haunted his clan for the last six centuries. Marci listened raptly all the way through, though her eyes got really wide at the end.

"So the Qilin thanking you was what caused that golden hammer thing at the end?"

"I don't know about a hammer," Julius said, confused. "But it was definitely a luck bomb."

Marci shook her head rapidly, making her short hair fly. "No way. Bombs are bad things. This was an enormously *good* thing. When we were in the Heart of the World, Amelia kept saying that Bob had warned her not to let any of us charge into the fight until we got his signal. Trouble was, she had no idea what that signal would be. We were about to go anyway—because things were getting *really* bad—when we felt this huge surge of amazing dragon magic, and suddenly everything went right." She grinned. "That must have been *you!* Bob clearly knew it was coming too, which was why he told Amelia to wait. He knew we'd need imperial levels of magical good fortune on our side to make everything work."

The mention of his brother's name made Julius flinch. "I'm not so sure Bob is on our side anymore."

"What are you talking about?" Marci said, incredulous. "He and Amelia planned this whole thing. The fact that I'm alive and with you right now is mostly due to him."

"He's also why you died in the first place," Julius said angrily. "I'm not arguing with the results, but his methods are not good, Marci. Bob used us all. He let Chelsie and her children suffer for six centuries. He could have ended it all at any time just by telling Bethesda to stop. Mother always listened to him."

"Would Chelsie, though?" Marci asked. "You just told me it was her idea to keep her children locked in the mountain so they'd be safe from the Qilin. Even if Bob had freed them all early, she still wouldn't have let the Fs go for fear of her ex. Don't get me wrong. I agree it was all terrible, but I don't think anyone was trying to be cruel. It just sounds like a lot of desperate dragons trying to do the best thing in bad circumstances. But while he's definitely pulled some sketchy stunts, I *know* Bob is on our side. Amelia trusted him with her life *and* death, and she doesn't trust lightly." She shrugged. "We just have to have faith that Bob knows what he's doing. He *can* see the future, after all."

"I've never questioned that," Julius said. "I'm just worried about what he's willing to do to the present to get there."

"Well," Marci said, snuggling closer. "If this is Bob's chosen timeline, I've got no complaints. It sucked for a while there, but now I'm back, Amelia's back, and Chelsie's free and reunited with her boyfriend, which will hopefully make her less snappy. We've even got a bona fide lucky dragon on our team! That's a huge deal, because the way things are looking, we're going to need all the luck we can get."

She glanced over her shoulder at the window, where the rainbow glow of the rising magic was still shining like the Northern Lights through the lowered blinds.

"What are we going to do?" Julius whispered, pulling her closer. "I couldn't follow all your theory talk last night, but I know visible magic rising from the ground like backward snow is *not* good."

"Actually, the magic itself is fine," Marci said. "It's not like we pumped the system full of new power. This is just the magic the ancient Merlins stole from the rest of the world finally flowing back to where it belongs. I always meant to return it. Not in one big blast, of course, but while this situation sucks in the short term, over the long haul, I think this will actually turn out to be a very good thing."

"*Is* there going to be a long term?" Julius asked quietly. "Not to be a pessimist, but everything Amelia and Raven said about the Nameless Ends made it sound like our only hope was to stop Algonquin from falling into despair, and we didn't. We failed. There's no way to know how much since we're trapped in the house until the magic clears up, but I can't imagine Algonquin's been idle. She's probably bringing that thing into our world right now. How do we face that?"

"The same way we face everything else," Marci said, smiling down at him. "How many times have we done the impossible, Julius? We are *always* punching above our weight class, and yet we *always* pull it out in the end. This time will be no different. Our enemy might be a giant creature that eats worlds, but the only thing he's eaten so far is Algonquin, and she's small potatoes these days." She pointed at the glowing window. "The magic is back! We've got two Merlins with fully amped Mortal Spirits. We've got Raven and Amelia and a bunch of really scary dragons, not to mention a legit *luck god*." Marci flashed him a grin. "I bet we kick that Nameless End's butt."

That statement was so ludicrously overconfident it bordered on delusional, but the optimism was just so *her,* Julius couldn't help but grin back. He'd missed her so much. Just like always, Marci was ready to go. Ready to fight beside him against anything, and he loved her for it.

He kissed her then, pulling her down to him with the desperation that still hadn't gone away. She kissed him back just as fiercely, wrapping her arms around his neck. He was losing himself in the wonder of having Marci all over him again when someone knocked.

They both froze, turning in unison to look at the door, which was still locked. That wouldn't mean much to a dragon, but dragons didn't usually bother with knocking. Julius was working up the will to ask who it was when Emily Jackson's voice filtered through the wood.

"Sorry to interrupt," she said, not sounding sorry at all. "Raven and I are calling an ops meeting. Be downstairs in five minutes."

Julius bristled. It was a perfectly reasonable request, but her tone still irked him. He might be a Nice Dragon, but that didn't mean he took orders from humans. Especially not the one who'd shot Marci in the back.

"Who put her in charge?" he muttered as Emily's footsteps vanished down the stairs.

"She *is* a general," Marci reminded him, climbing out of bed, much to his dismay. "Being in charge is her default. General Jackson's no fool, though. No one interrupts a happy dragon unless they have to. If she's pushing, there's a reason, which means we need to get moving." She tapped her bare foot on the moving rainbows the magic from outside was casting across his scuffed wooden floor. "Can't hide in here forever."

Julius would have been happy to stay in this sheltered room with Marci until he died, but she was right. They'd had a reprieve, but now it was time to go back to the real world, so Julius hauled himself reluctantly out of bed and began climbing into his clothes as slowly as he could. Marci was done way before he was, dressed in one of his sweatshirts and what had been her favorite pair of jeans. She'd also dug up a spare plastic bracelet to replace the ones she'd melted, and while Julius didn't see any spellwork written on the inside yet, the chunky pink band made her look like herself again.

When he was finally decent in jeans and a long-sleeved T-shirt, he kissed her one last time, wrapping his hand around hers as they unlocked the door and headed downstairs to jump back into the fight.

• • •

Marci clutched Julius's hand the whole way down, clenching her jaw to keep from grinning. It was hard, but they were in the middle of what could be a world-ending event, and she was the Merlin. Grinning like a lovestruck idiot was *not* allowed, so she forced herself to keep her eyes off of Julius—whom she could *touch* now, anytime she wanted—and on the stairs ahead of them, where Fredrick was waiting at the bottom.

Now there was a dragon she did not understand. From Julius's story, Marci was pretty sure Fredrick was the dragon equivalent of the crown prince of China. Someone needed to tell him that, though, because he was still acting like Julius's butler. He even had the younger dragon's jacket in his hands, which he held out for Julius to put on as soon as they reached the bottom of the stairs.

Julius looked as awkward as Marci felt, but he let Fredrick put the jacket on him anyway, probably because the house was freezing. It was November in Detroit, and they hadn't run the heat in days. Even global warming couldn't take the edge off that chill. They were lucky it wasn't snowing actual frozen water instead of just magic.

When Julius was properly attired, Fredrick handed him a sword that looked like a tooth. It was the same kind of blade Fredrick wore at his own side, a Fang of the Heartstriker.

Julius took the blade with a shocked look. "How did you get this?"

"The Diplomat's Blade is far more forgiving than the Defender's," Fredrick said with a smile. "You dropped it when you went after your mortal. I thought you would need it, so I picked it up. It didn't transform for me, of course, but it was courteous enough to allow me to carry it in its sleeping form. I would have given it back to you earlier, but I didn't wish to interrupt."

From the smirk on his face, Fredrick knew *exactly* what he would have been interrupting. Marci smirked back, but Julius just turned red again, though that didn't stop him from reclaiming Marci's hand the moment the sword was belted around his waist. "Where's everyone else?"

"Waiting for you in the kitchen," Fredrick replied. "They wanted to start earlier, but I refused to let them begin until you arrived, sir."

He hid it well, but Marci swore Julius winced at the "sir." "Thanks, Fredrick."

The F beamed. "You're welcome, sir," he said proudly. "And happy birthday."

Marci whirled toward Julius with a gasp. "You didn't tell me it was your birthday!"

"I completely forgot," Julius said, looking bewildered.

A lot had been going on, but... *"How do you forget your birthday?!"* Marci cried, gaping at him. "So you're twenty-five now, right?"

He nodded, a smile spreading over his face. "Same age as you."

Two months ago, Marci would have considered having a dragon boyfriend who was the same age as herself slightly disappointing. Now, though, she was too happy just having him to care. "Happy birthday," she said, rising up on her toes to kiss his cheek.

He blushed again, lifting their tangled hands to his lips to kiss the back of her fingers before turning them down the hall that led to the kitchen. "Shall we go hear the bad news?"

She motioned for him to lead the way, clamping down on the grin that was threatening harder than ever to take over. It was serious game face time now, but when they walked into the kitchen, the sight waiting for them was comically surreal.

There were three dragons and two spirits sitting at their kitchen table. Chelsie had her human-shaped daughter in her lap, brushing the girl's fine black hair with her fingers while the toddler struggled to fit an entire personal pizza into her mouth. The Qilin was right beside them, looking as perfect as ever, his golden eyes full of happy wonder as he watched his child eat. On the other side of the table, Amelia was tipped back in her chair, deep in conversation with Raven, who was perched on her shoulder. The only ones who weren't sitting down were General Jackson, who was pulling another round of frozen pizzas out of Marci and Julius's tiny electric oven, and Myron, who was standing in front of the back door, staring through the window at something behind the house. The disconnect between the powers in front of her, any one of which could be considered a national threat, and the cozy domesticity of the scene was so bizarre, Marci didn't even realize they were two short until she noticed that Myron was standing alone.

"Where's the DFZ?" she asked, alarmed. And for that matter. "Where's Ghost?"

Just the fact that she had to ask made Marci feel like a failure. She'd been so busy with Julius, she'd completely forgotten about her own spirit, which she was pretty sure made her the worst Merlin ever. She fully expected Myron to call her on it too, but the older mage beckoned her over instead, pressing a finger to his lips with one hand while he tapped against the glass of the back door's window.

When Marci looked out, she saw why. The stretch of dirt behind the house was filled with the same haze of multicolored magic as everywhere else, and bounding through the glowing drifts like kids in the snow were the Mortal Spirits. They were both in what Marci had come to think of as their "casual" forms—Ghost as a cat, and the DFZ as a large rat—and they were clearly having the time of their lives. Ghost actually flipped over as she watched, rolling on his back through the magic like a normal cat would in a field of catnip. The DFZ was just as bad. She hopped through the magic with happy squeaks, her beady orange eyes gleaming with sheer delight every time she landed in the soft, glowing piles.

"Well," Marci said, grinning despite herself. "At least someone's having a good time."

"More than a good time," Myron replied, his chest expanding as he took a deep breath. "Can't you feel it? It's like they're reborn."

She *could* feel it. She'd been so happy herself these last few hours, she hadn't noticed, but now that she was looking at him, Marci realized she could feel the Empty Wind's joy like a wave in her mind. Power was pouring into him, filling the emptiness at last. For the first time since she'd found him latched to that poor old cat lady's chest, the god of the Forgotten Dead felt *alive*, and it was beautiful. So, so beautiful.

"I can feel her delight," Myron whispered, reaching up to wipe the suspicious wetness from his eyes. "It's... I don't have words, honestly. I've never been this happy, and I'm only experiencing a reflection."

"Of course they're happy," Marci said. "This is how they were always meant to be. Ghost was around before the drought, but the DFZ is new. She's never had proper levels of magic before. No wonder she's celebrating."

The rat changed shape as she said this, shifting back into the androgynous-looking human girl Marci had seen before. But though the spirit still looked like anyone you might see on the city streets, she was no longer dressed in black. The clothing she manifested this time was a riot of color as bright as the neon in the DFZ Underground's most garish party districts. Even through the glow of the magic, she was shining, and the longer Marci looked at her, the more certain she became that— even if it had happened by accident—this was the right thing.

"*If* we're all here."

The stern voice spoke right in her ear, and Marci turned to see General Jackson standing behind them, tapping her makeshift body's scrap-metal fingers impatiently. "Myron?"

"Right," the mage said, clearing his throat as he pulled a piece of paper out of the pocket of his rumpled jacket. "Since we're all in this together, General Jackson and I have decided to share information to increase our odds of survival. Over the last eight hours, we've been on the phone with UN Central Command, my lab back in New York, and various other magical institutions all over the world."

"I'm just shocked the phones are working," Amelia said, winking at the Qilin. "Lucky break."

"*Very* lucky," Myron agreed. "There is absolutely no reason we should have internet access here in the DFZ, but we do. That's hardly the strangest thing that's happened in the last twenty-four hours, though, so I'm not even going to question it."

"Enough about how you got the information," Chelsie growled. "What's going on out there?"

"Everything and nothing," General Jackson said, walking over to pick up the two personal pizzas that were cooling on the stove top. She placed one down in front of Julius and one down in front of the seat he'd squeezed in next to his, which was apparently for Marci. "Eat," she ordered. "This will take a few minutes, and there's no reason you have to be hungry during them."

The general didn't have to tell Marci twice. Now that pizza was on the table, her body was reminding her loudly that it hadn't eaten since before she'd died. She practically dove into her chair, trying not to burn her tongue as she stuffed a slice of cheap, and surprisingly delicious, pepperoni pizza into her mouth.

"Good, isn't it?" Amelia said. "I didn't think there was any food left, but then I found a pile of those in the back of the freezer." She wiggled her eyebrows at the Qilin, who was starting to look uncomfortable. "That's lucky break number two. Now we just need to stumble onto your forgotten tequila stash and we'll have a grand slam!" She turned her grin on Chelsie. "Can you kiss him or something? We need another luck blast so I can get a drink."

"Amelia," Chelsie said in a low, deadly voice, "shut up."

The Spirit of Dragons lifted her hands helplessly and motioned for General Jackson to continue.

"Moving on," Emily said irritably. "As Sir Myron predicted, the breaking of the Merlins' seal has created a global crisis. As the epicenter of the breach, the DFZ was hit the hardest, but we have reports of dangerously elevated magic levels all over the globe."

"Dangerously?" Julius said. "How dangerously?"

"That depends on where you were when it happened," Myron said. "Not everyone was lucky enough to have a warded bunker nearby. But high as they are, the elevated magic levels probably won't be fatal to healthy individuals. Highly unpleasant, certainly, but not deadly. The danger General Jackson refers to is more of a long-term problem." He glanced at the glowing particles drifting up from the ground outside. "This is actually quite similar to the night magic first returned, only stronger. How *much* stronger varies depending on the local ambient magic, but the numbers I've seen generally seem to be clocking in at two to three hundred percent higher than normal."

"But that still shouldn't be more than humans can handle," Marci said with her mouth full. "We didn't make new magic. Everything that's here now was here before the drought, and humanity handled it fine back then."

"We did," Myron admitted. "But while the raw amount is the same, the majority of the magic back then would have been tied up in natural systems, not dropped on people's heads all at once. We don't know if the world has ever experienced a flood of this magnitude before, but we can say for certain that no living human has ever been doused with this much free-floating magic. Unless they were able to flee to a warded location, as we were, new manifestations are inevitable."

Julius went pale. "Manifestations?"

"He means new mages," Marci explained. "The night the magic came back, a whole bunch of people with the right combination of genes were suddenly able to use magic. Most of those burned themselves out in the first hour. Another good chunk went crazy. Only a few could actually handle the change. It was only later, when mages started being born naturally and growing into their powers slowly, that magic stopped being a death sentence."

"And you're saying we're going to see that again," Julius finished with a frown. "But isn't everyone who could be a mage one already?"

"Everyone that we're aware of," Myron said authoritatively. "But we've never been able to pin down the exact genetic combination that gives people the ability to consciously control magic because the range is too enormous. Half the human population has at least one of the markers for magical potential. It's been theorized that those people failed to become mages not because they lacked the fundamental ability, but because magical levels were simply too low for them to access. Now that magic is shoving its way down their throats, however, that could change."

"We might see a whole new wave of mages!" Marci said. "Assuming they don't all go nuts first, of course. But everyone knows magic is real now, so the transition should be much smoother this time around."

"That's good for them," Emily said. "But the situation right here and now is anything but. We have no official measurement devices left in the DFZ, but from the visual clues, Myron's estimated that the magical levels here are much higher than the rest of the world's."

"At least a thousand percent higher than normal," Myron agreed. "Maybe more."

"And that's why we can't go outside," Raven finished, turning on Amelia's shoulder to give the frolicking forms of Ghost and the DFZ outside the evil eye. "True mortal spirits might be big enough to roll such power off their backs, but the rest of us are grounded. Even I can't fly in a storm like this."

"*Nothing* can fly," the general said angrily. "I've been on the horn with our air base in Canada since six this morning. They can't get anything within fifty miles of the DFZ due to the magical interference. Planes, jets, helicopters—they're all useless. Even the satellites can't see through the glare of magic rising off this place, and that's a problem, because without eyes, we can't see what Algonquin's doing."

"So send one of the Mortal Spirits," Chelsie suggested. "They're clearly not having a problem, and we need information."

"I've tried," Myron said. "But I'm afraid my spirit is not in the correct mindset to… that is, with the current environment…"

"He can't ask them because they're high out of their minds," Amelia finished. "They're so drunk on magic right now, they don't know which way is up, the lucky bastards."

Chelsie gave her sister a flat look. "I'm surprised you're not out there with them."

"I would be if I could," Amelia said, her voice pained. "Alas, like Raven, I'm too much of a hybrid to actually enjoy the current situation. If I went out there, I'd be squished as flat as the rest of you. Not exactly a useful scout."

Myron turned to Marci. "I was hoping you'd have more luck with Ghost. He's been in magic like this before, and he seems more disciplined.

Whenever I ask her to help, the DFZ just laughs and tells me to come out and play."

Marci understood the importance of what he was asking, but interrupting Ghost's pure joy felt wrong to her. This was an emergency, though, so she reached out reluctantly with a mental hand to tug on her connection to the Empty Wind. The moment she touched it, a flood of happiness washed her under. Ghost's hands followed, clutching her mind and tugging on her to come out and bathe in the glorious magic with him. It was so intoxicating, she actually stood up before she realized what she was doing.

"I don't think he's doing any better than the DFZ," she said, gently prying herself out of her spirit's delirious grip as she sat back down. "But the fallout has to be almost over. What time is it?"

"Noon," General Jackson replied.

Marci blinked. She'd known she'd lost track of time in Julius's room, but she didn't think they'd been in there *that* long. They hadn't even gotten to the house until eight last night, which meant... "We've been experiencing magical fallout at the visible level for *sixteen hours?*"

"I told you it was severe," the general said. "But all these worries are secondary to the threat of the Nameless End."

"You refer to the thing from beyond the planes," the Qilin said, his perfect face worried. "The devourer of worlds Amelia was telling us about earlier."

"*One* of the devourers," Amelia corrected. "There are as many Nameless Ends as there are endings. I'm not sure which specific flavor of destruction Algonquin's hooked up with, but if he was crafty and patient enough to get this much of himself into a healthy plane, he's not going to stop until he gets the rest. According to Raven, Algonquin was the only one holding him back. Now that she's freaked out, I have a feeling we're going to discover exactly what sort of end we're up against."

"I fear the worst," Raven said sadly. "Algonquin would never barter with something that couldn't get her the total new beginning she needs to return this world to the spirits. If the Nameless End plays her fair, he'll scrub every living creature off the face of our plane. If he's playing her for a fool, which is what I suspect, he'll eat her and use her vessel as a platform to eat everything else, leaving our reality an empty husk."

"Then we have to stop him," Marci said. "I know Nameless Ends are serious business, but the fact that we're here having this conversation proves that he hasn't gotten enough of himself inside our plane to start the carnage yet. If the only thing he's eaten so far is Algonquin, then we're still sitting pretty. She might have been the biggest spirit around sixty years ago, but she's nothing these days. I mean, look at us." She waved her hand across all the fantastic, beautiful, stupidly magical creatures sitting at the table. "We're packing a *lot* of firepower, some of us literally. If it's all of us versus Algonquin-plus-one, that's not even a contest."

"Assuming we *can* fight it," Emily said. "We're still talking about a being who lives in the void between worlds. We don't know what it's made of or how it works. We don't even know if we can hurt it."

"Actually, I think Marci's onto something," Amelia said, tapping her sharp nails on the table. "As strong as Nameless Ends can be, this one's still an interloper. The Nameless Ends are scavengers. They prey on the weaknesses of dying planes, not healthy ones. The only reason this one was able to get inside at all is because he tricked Algonquin into letting him use her as a foothold. You can't kill a Nameless End because they're forces of the universe, but if we can find a way to dislodge him from Algonquin, we'll destroy his anchor to this world. Once that's gone, the natural defenses of our otherwise healthy plane should be able to force him back out with no further help from us."

"Like a body defeating an infection," Marci said, nodding. "That's fantastic. All we have to do is defeat Algonquin, and our problem's solved."

"But Algonquin's already defeated," Raven said sadly. "That's how this started. She's already given up and turned her water over to that *thing* because she'd rather die than lose. We can't beat her any lower than she's already gone. I don't even know if she's alive anymore, and I didn't think spirits *could* die."

The table fell silent as he finished. Marci poked her empty plate, trying to think of something that might turn this around. Then, out of nowhere, Amelia said, "We could wait for Bob."

Chelsie snorted. "*That's* your plan?"

"It's been my plan my entire life," Amelia said stubbornly, lifting her chin. "You think he didn't know this was coming? He's a seer. He's been working on this for centuries."

"Okay," Chelsie said, crossing her arms in front of her daughter, who'd fallen asleep in her lap after she'd finished her second pizza. "What's his plan, then?"

Amelia bit her lip. "I… don't know," she said after a long pause. "Knowing your future changes it, so he couldn't tell me anything past my death, but I *know* he'll come through. He's never let us down before."

Chelsie looked away. "Speak for yourself."

"Would you knock it off?" Amelia growled. "Your secret's out, Chelsie. We all know that mess in China was entirely your own making. You've been blaming everything on Bob for centuries, but he wasn't the one who panicked and bolted. Bob could have just let the Empress Mother kill you, but *no*. He pulled a miracle out of his ear and got Bethesda to China to beg for your life. It's thanks to him that you're still alive to hold your grudge. How can you be so ungrateful?"

Chelsie opened her mouth to retort, but Fredrick beat her to it. "Ungrateful?" he snarled, moving away from Julius to stand behind his mother. "Brohomir left us to be Bethesda's slaves for *six hundred years*! He only cares about his future, not about those who suffer to create it!"

Marci leaned back in her chair. She'd never seen the normally quiet F this angry. Amelia was looking uncharacteristically pissed off as well, with dangerous curls of smoke leaking out from between her lips. The atmosphere in the kitchen was getting so tense, Marci was considering preemptively ducking under the table when Julius suddenly stood up.

"You're both wrong."

The whole kitchen turned to look at him. His time as clan head must have done something, though, because Julius didn't even flinch at all when all those predatory eyes landed on him. He just stared back, and when he spoke, his voice was steady and sure.

"Bob's not nice," he said. "But he's not evil, either. He's not like Bethesda, who steps on dragons for the joy of feeling taller, but he's also not afraid to crush us under his heel if that's what he feels he needs to do to guarantee the future he wants. Like Fredrick, I don't think that's right, but it also doesn't mean that Amelia is wrong." His green eyes flicked to Marci. "As someone very smart told me earlier today, Bob's the reason we're in a lot of these messes, but he's also the one who made sure we got out, *and* he's the one who brought us all together here."

"How can you be sure of that?" Fredrick asked angrily. "No offense, Great Julius, but we're cowering in a hovel while an enemy we may not even be able to fight is coming to power above our heads. If this was truly the work of a seer and not mere chance, where is our advantage? Where are our weapons and our armies? Why would Brohomir put us through all of this just to leave us stranded and desperate now?"

"I don't know," Julius said. "But I'm *certain* this is Bob's work, because she"—he pointed across the table at General Jackson—"is the Phoenix, and Bob told me ages ago that I would have lunch with the Phoenix on my birthday." His face split into a smile as he turned back to Fredrick. "Don't you see? This is *all* Bob's plan. Yes, we're trapped, but we're trapped *together*. All of us are here in this house because of Bob's meddling. He's the one who arranged to bring Marci back from the dead, *and* he's the one who finally fixed our troubles with the Qilin."

"Both of which were problems *he* caused," Chelsie growled. "I'm not going to praise him for wagging the dog."

"Did he?" Julius asked, turning to face her. "Did Bob tell you to run from the Qilin? Did he tell you to lie when Xian asked you why?"

Chelsie's answer to that was a deadly glare, and Julius sighed. "I'm not trying to poke at old wounds. I'm just saying that Bob isn't always the total villain you make him out to be. There's no question he's run roughshod over all of us, but you know as well as I do that he's been building toward something huge for a long time now, and I can't think of anything bigger than the end of the world."

He smiled then. A big, warm, dazzling grin that made Marci's breath catch in her throat. "I have faith in my brother. I don't always understand what he's doing or approve of how he does it, but I don't believe for a second that Bob moved heaven and earth to bring us together—from China, from eggs that were never supposed to hatch, from death itself—only to drop the ball at the end. Whatever's coming, Bob *has* a plan, and we're part of it. There's just no other explanation for how we all ended up here. That's why I think, if we want to survive what's coming, we need to put aside our anger and help him make it work."

Fredrick opened his mouth to argue, but Chelsie raised her hand. "I believe you, Julius," she said quietly. "I can't forgive him for all the years he left us to rot, but I believe you when you say that this is Bob's doing. Even accounting for the Qilin's fortune, this whole situation is simply too improbable not to have a seer's fingerprints all over it. Also, if the Nameless End eats everything, Bob will die too, and he's much too selfish for that. But if this *is* all part of Bob's grand plan, what does that mean? What did he bring us here to do?"

"Work together," Julius said, looking pointedly at General Jackson. "All of us. The dragon clans, the UN, spirits, Merlins—we've all got our backs against the same wall. If we're going to survive, we have to join forces."

"And do what?" Myron asked. "The magic outside might not be deadly, but it'll still knock any of us out cold before we make it three feet. Maybe dragons would fare better, but I don't see how we're supposed to work together when half of us can't leave the house."

"We'd make it more like ten feet, but the general idea still holds," Amelia agreed. "Magical fallout is no joke. It'll take you down in a heartbeat, and it'll burn the entire time. But the good news is I think the magical crash is affecting the Nameless End as well."

"How do you know that?" General Jackson demanded.

"Because, as Marci already pointed out, we're not dead yet," Amelia said. "It's been sixteen hours since Algonquin kamikazed herself into the Leviathan. It takes time to eat your way through five Great Lakes, but not *that* much time. I bet the Leviathan is just as stuck as we are. That buys us some wiggle room."

"How much?" Julius asked.

"Not enough," Raven said, hopping off Amelia's shoulder to perch on the windowsill. "Heavy as it looks, the fallout's actually been getting lighter for a while now. In my unprofessional and unresearched opinion, I'd say we have an hour, maybe two, before we can safely go outside."

"Then we need to get to work," Marci said, standing up.

"I thought we just agreed to wait for Bob," Amelia said.

Marci rolled her eyes. "We can't just sit here doing nothing until a dragon seer shows up and tells us what to do."

"It worked last time," Amelia said with a shrug.

"Only because he told you it would," Marci pointed out. "Do you have any instructions for this crisis?"

The dragon spirit shook her head, and Marci spread her hands. "There you go. Maybe Bob will show up with a plan of action to save us all, but until then, I say we listen to Julius and pool our resources to come up with a plan of our own, because we don't have time to mess around."

"I agree," the Qilin said, rising to his feet and turning to Julius. "You have the full support of the Golden Empire. My dragons are already on their way here. We will help you fight the Nameless End in whatever way we can."

Julius blinked. "Um, that's fantastic, but how do you know they're coming? I only said we should work together a minute ago."

The Qilin shrugged. "Because I want them here, and when I want something, my luck generally makes sure I get it."

"Really?" Marci whistled. "Dude, that is a *crazy* power."

The Golden Emperor shrugged again, but Julius was grinning from ear to ear. "I think I see how this is supposed to work," he said excitedly, turning to Fredrick. "You've got Chelsie's old Fang. That means you can cut to any Heartstriker, which gives our clan a way into the city as well. Between the Heartstrikers and the Golden Empire, we'll have half the dragons in the world fighting together against a common enemy. That has *never* happened before!" He smiled even wider. "Don't you see? This has to be Bob's plan! This is why he had us jump through all those flaming hoops! It was so we'd all be here at the right place and the right time with the trust and the tools necessary to fight together against the Leviathan!"

"It does make sense," Marci admitted. "But weren't you the one who always said it was foolish to try to guess a seer's intentions?"

"What else could it be?" Julius asked. "He got you here too, along with General Jackson, Raven, and Amelia, plus the Mortal Spirits. That gives us the Merlins, the human UN, and both types of spirits. Between all of us, every sentient magical force in the world is represented. We're even stuck in the same *house*. If that's not a seer's doing, I don't know what is."

"You make a good point," Fredrick said, frowning down at his Fang. "I suppose I should start bringing in the rest of the clan, then?"

"Not yet," Amelia said quickly. "The magic's better than it was last night, but it's still waaaaaaay too unstable for teleportation. If you try to cut anywhere, you might end up slicing off your own head."

"And we need a better idea of what we're up against," Julius added. "The Golden Emperor can command his dragons however he likes, but I'm only one vote on the Heartstriker Council. If I bring Bethesda and Ian into this, and they see the Leviathan as an unwinnable fight, they might decide to take their chances underground instead. We may only get one shot at this, which means we can't bring anyone else into this fight until we have some kind of idea of how we're actually going to win."

"Assuming we *can* win," Myron said glumly.

"We have to assume that," Marci said. "Otherwise, what's the point of fighting?"

"*Thank* you, Marci," Julius said, flashing her a smile. "Our first hurdle is to figure out how to get out there and take a look at the problem. Once we know what we're actually up against, we can put our heads together and figure out how to beat it, because there *has* to be a way. Bob wouldn't have gone through all the trouble of bringing us together if we didn't have a chance."

"Then why doesn't he just tell us?" Emily said, glaring at him. "Everyone goes on and on about how powerful dragon seers are, but what's the use of all that power if they never *tell* you anything?"

"Because knowing the future changes it," Amelia snapped. "Seriously, Phoenix, pay attention."

"Bob won't tell us his move until he's played it," Julius agreed. "But the fact that we're on the board he's set up means that move is already in play, and we're part of it. The only thing he's ever told me since the beginning is to be myself, and this is what I think we should do. If I really am the seer lynchpin everyone keeps telling me I am, that should be a pretty good indicator of which way we need to push for success. And even if I *am* wrong about all of this, how can us working together be a bad idea? The forces sitting around this table represent the combined strength of our plane. If anything we have is capable of beating the Leviathan, it's this."

He placed his hand down on the center of the table with a *thunk*, and Marci held her breath. She'd seen Julius do his thing enough now to know this was his big push to get everyone on the same side, and it seemed to be working. All around the kitchen, heads were nodding. Even Chelsie looked convinced, and Amelia had been on board from the beginning. The only holdout was General Jackson, who was looking at Julius as though she wasn't sure what to make of him.

"You truly are a very strange dragon," she said at last. "I have no interest in trusting humanity's survival to one of the enemy's seers, but I'm in no position to turn down allies. If you can get me the world's two largest dragon clans and a promise they won't eat my soldiers, we'll work with you. I've already put in a call for backup from the UN's headquarters in New York, as well as our field offices in Chicago and Toronto. The moment the magic clears enough for aircraft, we'll have helicopters, gunships, battle mages, everything but tanks. I'll have to warn my people not to shoot at the dragons this time around, but if this is going to be as bad as I fear, I don't think target confusion will be a problem."

"We'll help too," Marci said. "I mean, obviously *I* was going to help, but I'm formally offering my assistance as the First Merlin, which I'm pretty sure means I speak for Myron as well."

"I was already in through the UN," the older mage said stuffily. "But if it makes you feel important, feel free to claim me."

This time yesterday, Marci wouldn't have claimed Sir Myron Rollins if he'd been the last mage on earth. But his words to the DFZ last night and his steadfast efforts to protect the world from magical disaster had raised him a great deal in her opinion, enough that she met his grumbling with a smile. Julius was smiling too, beaming at her with a happiness that lit him up from the inside out, and no wonder. He'd brought everyone together, which was all Julius ever wanted to do. To pull it off so quickly now, when so much was at stake, he had to be feeling on top of the world. Maybe it had only worked because they were stuck on the rails of Bob's plan, but Marci was proud of him anyway. She was proud of *all* of them, because they were finally going to fight back.

After so long spent scrabbling in the dirt, so many defeats, they were finally going to end this. She still owed Algonquin for what had happened in Reclamation Land, and for Vann Jeger. Now, though, everything was coming up aces. They were going to finish Algonquin and end her stupid, reckless idea of a super-weapon Leviathan once and for all. Marci was already imagining armies of dragons backed up by fighter jets soaring through the sky when something hit her ward so hard it nearly knocked her over.

She grabbed the table, fighting to stay upright as the wrongness rolled through her. It was gone a second later, leaving her blinking in pain and surprise. Amelia looked equally shocked, her amber eyes wide as she jumped to her feet.

"Anyone else feel that?"

"Feel what?" Julius asked, looking at Chelsie, who shook her head.

"I felt it," Myron said, putting a shaking hand to his forehead. "Someone just did something awful to the magic we wrapped around the house."

"They tied it in a knot," Amelia snarled, stomping out of the kitchen. "A very *good* knot at the end of a very *good* spell."

"But that's insane," Marci said, scrambling after her. "Good or not, casting a spell in magic this thick is like throwing a lit match into a sea of gasoline. Who in the world would be stupid enough to risk—"

She didn't get to finish, because at that moment, a giant sphere of ice materialized in their living room, landing with a thud on the hardwood floor. Cold rolled off it in waves, dropping the temperature of the house ten degrees in an instant. Marci was still gaping in surprise when the outside of the sphere exploded into ice dust, releasing the winter cyclone of fury that was Svena the White Witch.

CHAPTER TWO

"_W_**here is she?"**

Julius darted behind Amelia. Or at least, he tried to. His sister had been right in front of him a second ago, but now she was nowhere to be seen, leaving him standing face-to-face with a deadly-angry Svena, her blue eyes glowing like radioactive cobalt through the icy mist of her arrival.

As the frost began to settle, Julius realized the new clan head of the former Daughters of the Three Sisters looked… odd. She was still horrifically terrifying, but the effect was mitigated by the ridiculously fluffy white shawl she wore over her shoulders. It was so big, he didn't even see Katya until the other dragoness moved, looking both embarrassed and determined as she stepped up to stand beside her sister. Even that was strange, though, because though Julius could only see two new dragons in his home, he smelled a lot more. His brain had already identified fourteen unique scents, and the fact that he only knew the location of two of them was sending him into a panic. Where were the others? Was this an ambush?

But as his eyes darted frantically around the room in search of the hidden dragons, Svena's giant white shawl began to twitch. It moved again when he snapped his attention back to her, and Julius suddenly realized the fluffy white wrap draped over Svena's shoulders wasn't actually a wrap at all. They were dragons. *Tiny* ones.

Little serpents the size of dachshunds were clinging to Svena's body with their tiny claws. Each one was covered in an identical coat of fluffy, snow-white down, which was why they'd looked like a solid mass at first.

Once they started moving, though, Julius counted a dozen at least, and every one of them was staring at him, their suspicious eyes as large and inhumanly blue as Svena's.

"Oh my god," Marci said beside him, pressing her hands over her mouth. "Are those... Are you covered in *baby dragons?*"

As always, Svena ignored her. "*Where is the Planeswalker?*" she yelled in Julius's face.

"I-I don't know," he stammered. "She was right here a second ago, but—"

Svena whirled on her heel and stomped to the nearest door, blasting it off its hinges without even pausing to try the knob. When that turned out to be the bathroom, she turned and blasted the door to the broom closet. The little dragons squeaked in alarm as wood went flying, and Katya jumped forward to catch them as they fled from their furious mother.

"Sorry," Katya said as she frantically gathered all the wiggling whelps into her arms. "She's been like this ever since we saw the news. We left as soon as the magic stabilized enough to allow teleportation. I tried to make her wait, but..." She trailed off with a helpless shrug, backing into the living room to make room for the crowd that was now pouring out of the kitchen into the hall.

"What is she doing?" Chelsie snapped, shoving her way to the front just in time to see Svena blast the door off the stairs to the basement.

"Looking for Amelia," Julius said frantically, watching in dismay as yet another part of his house was pulverized into splinters. "I don't know what happened! Amelia was right here just a second ago!"

"Oh, for the love of—" Chelsie handed her own daughter to Fredrick and stepped forward, lifting her voice in a roar. "*Amelia!* Stop hiding, you coward! Get out here and face the consequences of your actions like a dragon while there's still something left of Julius's house!"

The words echoed through the building. Even Svena paused her campaign of destruction, her delicate ears twitching as she listened. She was about to head upstairs when Julius felt something sigh deep inside his fire, then the air in front of him flickered like a mirage as Amelia reappeared.

"Svena!" she said in a bright, false voice. "How nice of you to… um… drop by."

The words rang hollow in the silence that followed. Then, slow as a glacier, Svena turned to face her. The cold moved with her, making Julius shiver. Even Katya scrambled out of the way, taking the pile of baby dragons with her as she fled into the hallway to take shelter behind Julius and Marci, leaving Amelia and Svena facing off alone in the empty living room.

"You," Svena whispered, the word leaving her lips in a puff of frozen smoke. "You were *dead*. I saw it. Brohomir killed you!"

"He did," Amelia said. "But I can explain—"

"*Explain?*" Svena roared, sending a wave of frost across the floor. "We nearly went to war over you! How did you just *come back?*"

With every angry word, the freezing magic in the room grew sharper. Even Amelia flinched, and one of the white whelps on Katya's shoulder bailed entirely, jumping off to land on Marci's back. Julius's heart froze as the tiny dragon made contact, but though she stumbled when it hit her, Marci didn't fall. She didn't even look scared. Quite the opposite. Her eyes were sparkling when she looked over her shoulder at the little dragon climbing up the back of her sweatshirt. "Julius…" she whispered, running her palm gently over its downy head. "It's so *fluffy.*"

Julius's response was to bolt for the kitchen, returning moments later with a pair of oven mitts. "Here," he said, thrusting them onto Marci's hands. "You're going to need these. And try to keep away from its mouth."

Marci nodded, but she still hadn't torn her mesmerized gaze away from the tiny dragon clinging to the back of her shoulders. "Sooooooo fluffy."

He sighed and pulled the oven mitts down more tightly. When he was satisfied she wouldn't lose a finger, he turned back to the standoff going down just a few feet away.

"What are you?" Svena demanded, the frost at her feet rippling as she took a step toward Amelia. "You don't even smell like a dragon anymore. You smell like *him*." She pointed at Raven, who'd flown up to perch on the stairwell banister, where he'd have a better view. "What did you do to her, creature? *Where is the Planeswalker?*"

Amelia rolled her eyes. "For fire's sake. It *is* me, ice queen. If you want proof, I can tell the story of that night back in the twelve hundreds when I got you so drunk off fortified wine casks that you ran off and saved the capital of Slovenia. Or if that story's too well-known, I could tell everyone about the time you got a crush on a human fisherman and asked me to cover for you to your sisters while you two ran off behind his boat to—"

"Okay, shut *up*, I believe you," Svena said frantically, her pale cheeks flushing a very slight pink. "But that still doesn't explain how you're here."

"Come on," Amelia said with a chuckle. "Surely you don't think a minor inconvenience like death could stop someone as amazing as me?"

"A *minor* inconvenience?" Svena repeated, clutching her fists. "You were *ash*, Amelia! I saw it happen! The human we put your fire into was dead as well. Your flames were *gone*. Dragons don't come back from that."

"I know," Amelia said proudly. "But that doesn't apply to me, because I'm not a dragon anymore. *I* am a *god*."

She spread her arms with a flourish, but Svena just huffed. "What does that matter? Any dragon worth the name has been worshiped as a god at one point or another. Even your tacky mother tricked the Aztecs into offering her blood sacrifices."

"Don't confuse *me* with Bethesda," Amelia said, insulted. "And I'm not talking about human worship. I'm an actual superior being. Here, see for yourself." She thrust her hands at the white dragon's face. "Look at my magic. Does that look like normal dragon magic to you?"

Svena narrowed her eyes. "Of course not. We've already covered this."

"And I'm *trying* to answer your question," Amelia said, her face splitting into a grin. "I've transcended, Svena! I didn't just cheat death. I drop-kicked it! I *asked* Bob to kill me so I could travel with Marci through mortal death into the Sea of Magic. Once there, I conquered and devoured the nascent Mortal Spirit of dragons and took its power for myself, forever tying all dragon magic to this plane." Her grin turned manic. "Do you get it now? I solved the non-native reduction problem you've been working on for the past five centuries! *Me!* You always called my interest in humans a narcissistic obsession, but it was through *human magic* that I finally solved the biggest magical problem of our species! The one even *you* couldn't crack! *I* did that, and now I'm the first dragon ever to become truly immortal by merging with an effectively infinite magical source, which means I have finally and officially *won*. Our rivalry is over. There is absolutely nothing you can do to beat me now. Even if you did manage to kill me, I'd just come back like any other spirit and laugh in your face." Her expression grew unbearably smug. "Face it, frosty, you've *lost*."

Amelia cackled after that. A loud, cringe-worthy guffaw of pure bad sportsmanship, and Svena began to shake. Julius stepped back at the sight, moving to shelter Marci with his body against the inevitable explosion that came from rubbing defeat in a proud dragon's face. But as he opened his mouth to call his sister out for unnecessary levels of gloating, he realized Svena wasn't shaking with rage.

She was crying.

"You *idiot!*" she roared. "*I thought you were dead!*"

"Well, yeah, I was," Amelia said, looking confused. "It was the only way to make everything work. But I was always planning to come back."

"I didn't know that!" Svena cried. "You turned to ash in front of my eyes." Then before anyone could move, Svena reeled back and launched a trash-can-sized ball of ice at Amelia's face. "*How dare you do this to me!?*"

Amelia didn't have time to do more than look surprised before the attack smashed into her, blasting her across the living room and into the couch, which exploded in a shower of wood splinters and synthetic cotton filling. The stuffing hadn't even finished falling before Svena was on top of her, tossing the ice boulder away with a wave of her hand so she could grab Amelia by the shoulders and slam her into the floor so hard the boards cracked.

"You were the only one left I could talk to!" she shouted. "The only one who remembered what dragon magic actually meant! You were a brash idiot with no sense of subtlety, but you were *mine*. My idiot, my enemy, my friend! You belonged to *me*, and you let that smug bastard of a seer take you away!" She slammed Amelia into the floor again and then dropped down herself, her face vanishing behind the long sweep of her ice-blond hair as she buried her head into the crook of Amelia's shoulder. "Did you even think of what it would be like for me, you stupid, selfish snake?"

She was sobbing by the time she finished, her whole body heaving as the giant hunk of ice she'd thrown at Amelia melted into a puddle. Pinned to the ground, Amelia shot a panicked look at Julius, but he just shrugged. It wasn't that he didn't have sympathy. It was just all for Svena. Amelia and Bob had done this to her as much as they'd done it to him, and as nice as Julius was, he didn't move an inch to save his sister from the consequences of her recklessness.

"Okay, okay," Amelia said at last, awkwardly patting Svena's shaking shoulders. "I know egg-laying makes dragons emotional, but—"

She cut off with a gulp as Svena's hands wrapped around her throat.

"But perhaps I didn't go about this in the *best* way," she finished, eying Svena's sharp claws nervously despite her much vaunted new immortality. "I'm back now, though, so everything's cool. All's well that ends well, right?"

"All is *not* well," Svena snarled, sitting up with a glare. "You hurt me deeply, and I want an apology. A real one, right now, or I will never speak to you again."

"Oh, come on!" Amelia cried. "What are we? Five?"

Svena set her jaw stubbornly, and Amelia clonked her head back down on the floor with a groan. "Fine," she muttered, rubbing her hands over her face. "I'm sorry."

The white dragon did not look satisfied. "Promise you'll make it up to me," she demanded. "A life debt good for one favor of my choosing."

"No way!" Amelia shouted. "I've already admitted I was slightly in the wrong here, but you're crazy if you think that means I'm giving you an open-ended favor."

It *did* seem like overkill, but Svena wasn't budging. She just sat stubbornly on Amelia's chest, glaring down at her as the silence grew colder and colder until, at last, the new Spirit of Dragons sighed. "All right," she growled, lifting up her hand. "If it will make you *stop*, then I swear a life debt to make this up to you with a favor of your choosing."

"Done," Svena said immediately, grabbing Amelia's offered hand. The moment their fingers touched, dragon magic slammed down on the room like a falling guillotine. One favor was relatively small for a life debt, but Amelia's new status must have given the spell extra bite, because Julius wasn't even tangentially involved in the agreement, and the magical spillover was still strong enough to make him gasp. Even Marci looked uncomfortable, rubbing her own hands together as if they hurt. Svena, however, looked deeply satisfied, her lips curling into a smug smile.

"Apology accepted," she said as she rose gracefully to her feet. "You always did grovel beautifully."

"Shut up," Amelia growled.

"Why should I?" Svena replied, looking down at her with a superior smirk. "I just put myself back on top."

"*What?*" Amelia shrieked, shooting to her feet. "That did *not* count!"

"It absolutely counts," Svena said with a toss of her hair. "Everyone just heard a self-proclaimed god apologize and agree to grant me a boon in exchange for the mercy of my forgiveness. Including the Golden Emperor, apparently." She arched an eyebrow at the Qilin, who was standing behind Julius in the hallway. "I think we've all just seen who has the real power here."

"You little faker," Amelia growled, her face furious. "That was *extortion!*"

"I faked nothing," Svena said angrily. "I was legitimately wronged! If you'd told me ahead of time it was a ploy for power, I would have understood, but did you do me even that small courtesy? No! You let me think you were *dead.*"

"She held a beautiful funeral for you," Katya said sadly. "Full honors at sea, same as she'd do for one of our sisters."

Svena nodded, crossing her arms over her chest. "You hurt me truly, Planeswalker. A life debt is the least I could demand for the loss of my greatest rival. Not that you deserve my forgiveness after rubbing my pain in my face." She turned up her nose. "I should have let you dangle. See how *you* like being left alone."

To Julius's amazement, Amelia laughed at that. "Like you could," she said with a smile. "I admit it, you played me good, but I should have known you were bluffing. 'Never talk to me again,' my tail. You couldn't even wait for the magic to settle before you came running." She nodded at the baby dragons still clinging to Katya and Marci. "You even brought your poofballs."

"I couldn't leave them behind," Svena said haughtily. "I know how little you Heartstrikers understand proper parenting, but a *responsible* dragoness doesn't leave her whelps alone for a moment during the first month."

"Are you sure they're whelps?" Amelia asked, stepping out of the wreckage of the couch to get a better look at the little dragon on Marci's shoulder. "They look more like feather dusters to me. But if you're back to insulting my mother, all must be forgiven. And speaking of forgiveness, you owe Julius a new sofa. And a lot of new doors."

"They do *not* look like cleaning implements!" Svena cried. "They are an entirely new sort of dragon! A hybrid of my clan's shape and snow-white coloration with the Heartstriker's feathers." She held out her arms to the little dragon perching on Marci, and the whelp almost knocked the mage over leaping back to its mother, much to Svena's delight. "They will be unspeakably beautiful," she said proudly, cradling the fluffy white whelp in her arms. "And my eldest daughter here, the first born after Estella's death, will be the next seer."

She said that so proudly, Julius had to look away. The Empress Mother wasn't the most trustworthy source, but unless Bob had stolen Chelsie's egg and then waited around for half a day before hatching it, he was pretty sure that his new niece was older than Svena's babies by at least a few hours. That meant Chelsie and the Qilin's daughter, not Svena's, would be the next seer. Not that he was going to tell Svena that. Chelsie had clearly had the same thought, because she motioned for Fredrick to scoot her currently human-shaped child back into the kitchen, out of the white dragon's sight.

Such a simple ruse should never have worked on a dragon as old and ruthless as Svena, but it did remarkably well, likely because no dragon of any experience would expect to see a whelp that young in human shape. She'd probably assumed the little girl was just a snack for later, if she'd cared enough to notice her at all. A macabre thought that Julius was surprisingly willing to roll with if it kept Svena from blowing up on them again. There'd be time to tell her the truth of what Bob had done later, assuming they survived. To make that happen, though, Julius was going to need all the friends he could get.

"If it makes you feel better, Amelia didn't let any of us in on her plans, either," he said, stepping out of the hall to keep Svena from looking down it. "We thought she was dead too. I'm just glad we're *all* happy to have her back."

"I don't know why you'd think it would make me feel better to know I was treated like a *common* fool," Svena said with a huff. "But I suppose this does remove the cause for friction between our clans."

Julius perked up at once. "Does that mean our alliance is back on?"

Svena considered that for a moment. "I don't see any point in continuing my hostilities toward Heartstriker. This was entirely the Planeswalker's fault, and she's already sworn to pay."

She finished with a snap of her teeth at Amelia, who rolled her eyes. "Don't let her fool you into thinking she's doing you a favor, Julius. Svena's the one who freaked out and broke her oaths."

"I did *not* 'freak out'," Svena said angrily. "I did what I thought was best for my clan given the information I had available. Now, of course, I realize I might have been overly hasty, but the laying of eggs is extremely taxing on the body. Add in the trauma of seeing my best enemy murdered in front of my eyes, and I may have... overreacted in certain decisions. But that's all behind us. Amelia has begged and been granted my forgiveness, and now I feel it is in the best interest of both our clans to normalize relations again."

"We'd like nothing better," Julius assured her. "The world is going a bit crazy, and we all need our alliances now more than ever."

"You certainly do need me," Svena said, petting the fluffy white dragon in her arms absently. "I suppose I should call Ian."

"He'd love to hear from you," Julius said, smiling at Katya in relief. The youngest Daughter of the Three Sisters currently had her hands full with Svena's other children, all of whom were fighting each other in their rush to get back to their mother, but she managed to give him a thumbs-up. He was returning the gesture when a knock sounded on the front door.

Everyone jumped. Even Raven looked perplexed, shifting his talons on the wooden banister. When Julius crept over to look through the peephole, though, the tall, black-haired figure standing on the other side was one he probably should have been expecting.

"Good evening," the Black Reach said in a soft voice from outside. "May I come in?"

Julius had no idea. "*Can* we open the door?" he whispered to Marci.

"I can nudge the ward aside for a sec to let him in," Marci whispered back, rising up on her tiptoes to look through the peephole as well. "But should we? That's the dragon from the throne-room fight, the one you told me is actually... um..." She glanced over her shoulder at the others, who were watching the two of them curiously. "I give up. Is this still a secret?"

Julius wasn't sure if it ever had been. He didn't know how many dragons knew the Black Reach was actually Dragon Sees Eternity, Construct of the Future, or if it even mattered. All he cared about was that the dragon outside was Bob's death unless he did something, which he was pretty sure he hadn't. Other than figuring out that Bob had brought them all here together, Julius hadn't spotted—or foiled—a single one of his brother's plans. He didn't want to, either. He thought getting everyone on the same page in one place was a very *good* idea. Certainly not something he wanted to disrupt, but he couldn't just leave the Black Reach standing outside in the magical fallout forever.

"Open it," he whispered.

Marci frowned. "You sure?"

"No," Julius said. "But it's not as if he couldn't bust his way inside if he wanted to. At least this way we keep our ward intact and stay in control." As much as anyone could be said to be in control when seers were involved.

That thought caused a sour feeling in his stomach, but Marci had already pulled a marker out of her pocket and started rewriting the spellwork she and Myron had scribbled all over the inside of the newly repaired front door. Half a minute later, she grabbed the deadbolt and flipped it, cracking the door open just enough to let the Black Reach into the house.

He came in silent as a shadow, brushing the glowing magic off the black silk sleeves of his ancient Chinese tunic as Marci slammed the door shut behind him. "Thank you," he said politely.

"Who's that?" Svena said, glancing at the Qilin. "One of yours?"

The Golden Emperor shook his head, which was a shock. As ruler of all Chinese dragons, Julius had assumed the Qilin had some sort of claim over the Black Reach as well. But Xian looked as confused by this as Svena, which, now that Julius thought about it, was the biggest surprise of all. Svena had been Estella's closest sister. If anyone here should have known the Black Reach on sight, it was her, but she didn't seem to recognize him at all.

"Estella was petrified of her death," the Black Reach said before Julius could ask. "She did not speak of me. As for the Golden Emperor, I stayed away from him, as all seers must. Even before dragons fled to this plane, the Qilin's magic caused distortions in the future. We avoid him at all costs."

He shot the golden dragon a dirty look as he finished, but Julius still didn't understand. "If you've always avoided him, why are you here now?"

"Because I must be," the Black Reach said, folding his arms in front of him. "The time has come. I am here for Brohomir."

A sharp gasp went up from all the dragons, but Julius almost laughed in relief. Maybe he *had* done something right, because he could say in all honesty, "Bob's not here."

"That's all right," the Black Reach replied. "He will be."

"He won't," Julius said angrily. "I've already figured out his plan. We're all in position to fight the Leviathan. He doesn't need to be here." And he definitely wouldn't come if he knew the Black Reach was waiting, which he must. "He won't come."

"He doesn't have a choice," the Black Reach said, meeting Julius's determined scowl with a sad look. "He *must* come, because you are here. You are the point around which his entire life's work revolves, and now, fittingly, you will be his end." He smiled, a cold turn of his lips that didn't touch his eyes. "I like things to be fitting."

Julius didn't know how to respond. He wanted to shout that the seer was wrong, that Bob would never be stupid enough to walk into such an obvious trap, but that was a trap of its own. He'd learned long ago that seers didn't lie. They didn't have to. They were the only ones who saw the entire board, but unlike everyone else in the house, Julius had changed his future before. He'd beaten Estella when every vision of the future said it was impossible. He could beat this too. But just as he was opening his mouth to say so, he was knocked off his feet by an enormous crash as something very large going very fast collided with his house.

$$\bullet\ \bullet\ \bullet$$

Three minutes earlier, Brohomir, Great Seer of the Heartstrikers and topic of much conversation, was standing in the bed of the once swollen Detroit River, digging the point of his Mage's Fang into the too-dry mud and muttering to himself like the madman most dragons assumed he was.

"Not good. Not good, not good."

A coo sounded a few feet farther down, and he jogged over to his pigeon, who was drinking from a small pool left in the hollow of a long-abandoned oil drum. The only water left in the entire riverbed.

"This is not good," Bob said again, scrubbing his hands through his long black hair. "How much water does she have left in Lake Erie?"

His pigeon shrugged her wings, but it didn't matter. Bob knew exactly how much water was left in every Great Lake because he'd already seen this future a thousand times. He'd seen *every* possible incarnation of this day, enough to know that this wasn't the one he'd been hoping for.

"Very not good," he muttered, pulling out his phone to glance at the clock on the tiny greenish screen. "Looks like we're stuck on a faster-than-preferred track. It's going to be tight."

The pigeon hopped onto his shoulder with a reassuring coo, and he turned to kiss her feathered neck. "I suppose it had to be late, didn't it? I promised you a grand adventure, and no grand adventure has ever ended with time left on the clock."

That was supposed to be a joke, but he couldn't keep the tremble out of his voice as he raised his head to look at the shadow above them. The pigeon looked as well, her dark eyes ancient and calm.

We are big from your perspective, aren't we? She tilted her head. *How interesting. I've never seen an End from this perspective before.*

"I told you I'd show you new things," Bob said, craning his neck as he tried to spot the Leviathan's end.

There wasn't one. The devil Algonquin had bargained with took up the entire sky, blocking out the sun behind an endless expanse of matte black shell and thousands of beady insect eyes. Below the giant body, thousands of whipping tentacles were hard at work, sucking up every bit of the remaining water from Algonquin's lakes. One actually dropped down beside him as he watched, descending from the sky like a long, undulating pipe to suck up the small puddle of water his pigeon had just been drinking from. When it was done, the tentacle moved on, its bulbous tip digging through the riverbed like an anteater's snout as it hunted for more water to absorb. Bob kicked the black flesh as it went past, earning himself a bruised toe for his efforts.

"Time to go," he said, taking one last look at his bloody clothes. The scarlet jacket had been one of his favorites, but it was getting a bit frayed at the edges, which was why he'd decided to wear it. A duel with Chelsie was a fine way for any garment to go out. Between his shoulder and the bloody finger holes his furious sister had put in the front, the jacket was definitely done, so Bob didn't spare it another thought as he changed to his true shape, shredding the once beautiful clothing to ribbons as he flapped into the sky with his transformed Fang of the Heartstriker sitting across his claws like gauntlets, protecting him from the swirling, glowing magic below.

"Hop on!" he called to his pigeon, who was struggling to keep up with his much bigger wings. "We've got to move fast. I've already seen every way this ends, and if we don't stick millimeter-tight to the schedule, this whole thing could blow up in our—"

He cut off with a pained grunt. Behind him, absolutely silent, the tentacle he'd kicked had suddenly whipped back around. Bob had calculated the chances of the monster noticing such a tiny blip as minuscule, but he clearly hadn't given the Nameless End enough credit, because the black appendage curled up into the air like a coiled whip to smack him out of the sky.

If he'd been human, the blow would have killed him instantly. As a dragon, it merely sent him rocketing toward the ground, crashing through the broken Skyways and into the roof of what had been one of the last intact buildings left in the DFZ.

CHAPTER THREE

Julius grabbed Marci and dove, rolling them both out of the way just in time to avoid the hunks of splintered wood. The dragon came in like a meteor, shooting straight through the attic and the second floor right above their heads before landing with a crash in the gravel driveway out front. It was still rolling over and over when Julius felt the familiar burn of Marci's magic snap like a broken rubber band. The ward, he realized numbly. The ward protecting the house had been broken, which meant...

"*Ghost!*"

Marci screamed the name beneath him, and suddenly, the spirit was there, but not as Julius remembered. This was no fluffy transparent ghost cat. It wasn't even the shadowy figure of the faceless Roman legionnaire that seemed to be the Empty Wind's preferred combat form. This was a giant. A mountain of a man eight feet tall who blew in on a wind even colder than Svena's ice. His dusky flesh was still dark, but it was no longer shadowy or see-through. Quite the opposite, the spirit now looked even more solid than Julius himself. With so much magic crammed inside him, Ghost had a weight to him that no living thing could match. Julius could actually feel his own magic bending toward the spirit like metal shavings toward a magnet as Ghost held up his hand to stop the flood of iridescent power rising up to swallow them.

He also stopped the collapse of the house, which, now that there was a dragon-sized hole blasted straight through the middle, was no longer structurally stable. The chimney fell over as Julius watched, leaving a gaping hole in the side of the living room. He was looking up to make sure the roof wasn't about to follow suit when he saw Marci's spirit looking down at them.

As always, the Empty Wind's face matched his name—an empty helmet with two blue-white glowing eyes floating like fireflies inside—but here, too, something was different. It wasn't just shadows in there anymore. This was a deeper darkness. Staring into it, Julius could almost feel himself being forgotten, as if his bones were already crumbling dust. It was horrifying, but he couldn't force himself to look away. He was trapped in the sudden realization of his own mortality, the truth that even a dragon like him would eventually die and be forgotten. They would *all* be forgotten, and—

Marci reached up and slapped her hands over his eyes, breaking the spell. Julius collapsed into her the moment the darkness let him go. He was still gasping when he heard her yell at Ghost. "I thought that only worked on the other side!"

"So did I," replied a thousand empty voices.

"Well, can you tone it down or something?"

There was a long pause, and then the freezing wind began to slack off. "Sorry," Ghost said in a far more normal—but still incredibly creepy—voice. "It's just... I've never had this much magic before. It's *incredible.*"

"I'm sure it is," Marci said, dropping her hands from Julius's eyes. "But as a wise man once said, 'With great power comes great responsibility.' I don't mind you stuffing yourself full of magic, but please don't send Julius into an existential crisis. I just got him back."

"Sorry," the spirit said again, and then his voice brightened. "I stopped the magic."

"I saw," she said proudly. "And caught the house! A-plus job on both, by the way. Just keep up the good work until Myron and I can reestablish the ward."

"I can hold it for as long as you need," Ghost said, his empty voice a bit too joyful for Julius's comfort. "It's just like it was back in the Sea of Magic, but even greater. I can fly here, Marci. I can feel the dead all over the world. They call to me, and I can help them now. I can help them *all.*"

"And we will," Marci promised as she helped Julius back to his feet. "But right now, we have to focus on the immediate concerns, like what hit our roof."

She turned to look through the shattered front of the house, glaring at the giant dragon that was still lying in the long gouge he'd put in their gravel driveway. From the feathers, it was obvious the culprit was a Heartstriker, but Julius had never seen one so colorful, aside from Bethesda herself. Even covered in insulation and drywall dust from the house he'd just destroyed, the dragon looked like a giant bird of paradise. His feathers were a riot of tropical greens, reds, purples, golds, and rich blues. Heavy bone gauntlets encased the delicate scales above his clawed feet, the transformed evidence of a Fang of the Heartstriker. Despite all this, though, it wasn't until the pigeon swooped down through the hole the dragon had left in the spiraling Skyways overhead that Julius finally realized exactly *which* Heartstriker he was looking at.

"Bob?"

The beautiful dragon shook the dust from his feathers and rolled over, pulling himself out of the crater to smile down at Julius. "In my defense," he said, "that was not the entrance I'd planned."

"Not the entrance you..." Julius trailed off as his hands clenched into fists. "*What are you doing?*"

"Trying to make a smooth recovery," Bob replied, looking around until he spotted something in the dark. "Ah-ha!"

He reached out and snagged a backpack hidden under the edge of the on-ramps. "I stashed this here months ago, in case of just such an emergency," he said, unzipping the bag delicately with his long claws to pull out a set of perfectly folded clean clothes. "I'd intended to fly in, of course, not crash, but I'm actually only a few feet from where I'd planned to—"

"*Brohomir!*"

The name came out in a roar, making even Bob jump as Chelsie stormed out of the broken house. She crossed the dirt in record time, stopping right in front of the bigger dragon's enormous claws with a look of pure murder. "What game are you playing now?"

"At the moment?" Bob held up the folded clothes. "Attempting to get dressed so we can have a proper conversation. I can't have my grand entrance spoiled by distracting nudity, and trust me, my nudity is *highly* distracting."

"Distracting is all you do," Chelsie snarled, but she turned her back just the same. Smiling down at her, Bob's dragon disappeared in a puff of smoke and rainbow feathers. When he reappeared a few moments later, he was wearing a pair of ripped jeans and buttoning a Hawaiian shirt over his still-healing chest. "Is Amelia here?"

"Where else would I be?" Amelia called, picking her way through the debris toward them. "It's good to see you," she said, pushing Chelsie aside so she could hug her brother. "But seriously, how long were you planning to make us wait? I was getting sick of—"

Whatever she'd been about to say was lost in a squeal as Chelsie's daughter—who'd been hiding with Fredrick in the kitchen the last Julius knew—burst out of the ruined house and charged full speed at Bob. She leaped on him a second later, knocking him back into the crater when she hit his chest like a rocket. He hugged her back with a laugh, keeping his fingers clear of her excitedly snapping teeth.

"Yes, yes, I missed you too," he said as he rolled them back to his feet. "But this isn't the time for games, little ratter. Now run back to your mother." He lowered his voice to a stage whisper. "You're making daddy jealous."

The Qilin did *not* look happy to see his youngest daughter, who'd only just begun to let him touch her, fawning all over the seer. His scowl deepened further when the whelp ignored the order, choosing instead to clamber onto Bob's back like a monkey. He wasn't the only one who looked upset, either. Svena and Katya had come out of the destroyed house as well now to see what the fuss was about, and the moment the White Witch saw the child clinging to Bob, her blue eyes widened in a look that made Julius's blood run cold.

"Bob," he said quietly, taking a nervous step toward his oldest brother. "I don't think this is a good time for—"

"It's the only time," Bob said, the laughter leaving his voice. "This might not be the way I'd planned to kick things off, but everything I see says we're still on course, which means this might be all the time I have left."

"There is no more might, Brohomir," replied a deep voice.

Julius whirled around just in time to see the Black Reach step to the edge of the now-roofless front porch. "I gave you more chances than you had any right to expect, but no more." The oldest seer lifted his chin to look down his long nose at Bob. "This is the end."

The finality in his voice made Julius's stomach clench. "It can't be," he said desperately, taking a step toward the construct. "How is this the end? Everyone's still alive, and we're all here together. We can beat Algonquin!"

"I'm not here for what could be," the Black Reach said dismissively. "I'm here for what *will* be." He lifted his eyes, looking over Julius's head at the taller dragon standing on the edge of the crater behind him. "This is your very last chance, Brohomir. Turn back now, and you may yet have a future."

"If I turn back, there's no future for anyone," Bob said, his voice shaking for the first time Julius had ever heard. "I've looked down every possible path millions of times. This is the *only* way." His green eyes narrowed. "And you know it."

The Black Reach released a long breath, and Julius's hand dropped to the Fang at his hip. He wasn't even sure what he meant to do with it—if there was anything he *could* do against a power like the Black Reach—but he refused to stand by while his brother died. To his surprise, though, the Black Reach made no move to attack Bob. He just held out his arms.

"If you're intent on destroying yourself, at least give me the next seer," he said. "It's too early for her to see the end that awaits her."

It was a reasonable request, but Bob made no move to comply, and why would he? Even if he hadn't adored the whelp clinging to his back—which he obviously did—it was clear he didn't mean to give the Black Reach anything. The oldest seer had to know that, so why bother to ask? Julius was still wondering when a sheet of ice flew across the ground to bind Julius's and Bob's legs to the ground. That was when he understood. The Black Reach hadn't made the request for the baby seer's sake.

He'd said it for Svena.

The White Witch was standing in front of the porch with her infant daughter clutched in her hands. The white whelp was squirming, but her mother didn't seem to notice. Svena's eyes were fixed on the little girl clinging to Bob's back. The human child who wasn't actually human at all.

"What are you talking about?" she demanded, holding out her daughter. "*This* is the next seer."

"No," the Black Reach said. "What you hold is merely a child. That"— he nodded at the golden-eyed dragoness clinging to Bob—"is Estella's replacement. Brohomir hatched her from a dud egg using Amelia the Planeswalker's fire thirty minutes before you laid your clutch." He shook his head. "I'm sorry, Svena of the Three Sisters. I'm afraid you lost before you began."

His lips curled as he finished. It was a tiny motion, barely more than a twitch, but Julius had been watching powerful dragons all his life. He knew a pulled trigger when he saw one, and from the way Bob was struggling to free his legs from the ice, so did he.

"No," Svena whispered as frost began to form in the damp air around her. "*No.*"

By the second *no*, a strange expression spread over Bob's face. On any other dragon, Julius would have called it panic, but seers never panicked. He was still trying to figure out what it meant when Bob snatched Chelsie's daughter off his back and tossed her at the Qilin a split-second before a wall of ice took him off his feet.

Standing right beside his brother, Julius felt the cold of the ice as it flew by, but he was miles too slow to do anything about it. The blow had already slammed Bob into the spiral of Skyway on-ramps that sheltered the house, sending his sword—the Magician's Fang—flying off into the darkness. Julius held his breath as the cement guardrails cracked, waiting for Bob to pop back up to his feet as he always did...

But not this time.

When the ice released him, Bob fell hard, landing facedown in the gravel at the start of Julius's driveway. When he finally pushed himself up, blood was running from his mouth. He was still wiping it away when

Svena lunged at him, her hand already raised as the icy bite of her magic filled the air.

"Svena, *stop!*"

The white dragon froze, her blue eyes flicking to Amelia, who was running to Bob's side faster than Julius had ever seen her move. "Back off," she snarled, smoke curling from her lips as she put herself between the white dragon and her brother. "Brohomir is under *my* protection."

"He stole my seer!" Svena roared at her. "My clan's legacy! He played me for a *fool!*"

The killing rage in her voice was enough to make Julius cower. Even Amelia looked nervous, glancing warily down at the thick carpet of frost that now coated the driveway and everything around it. "I know it hurts," she said, melting the ice from her own feet with a flick of her fingers. "But he had his reasons."

"*Reasons?*" Svena cried. "He stole from us!"

"He did," Amelia agreed. "But you're just going to have to let it go, because the only way you're getting to my little brother is by going through me, and we both know you can't."

That wasn't bravado. Amelia was simply stating fact. Now that they were standing face-to-face, even Julius, who was terrible at judging dragon magic, could feel the power gap between them. But despite being hideously outclassed, Svena showed no fear.

"You see, this is why we're not actually friends," the white dragon said bitterly, glaring at Amelia with hard, hurt eyes. "A *friend* would not allow this crime to go unpunished. But it doesn't matter. I don't need to beat you to win."

The Spirit of Dragons snorted. "How do you figure that?"

Svena's lips curled in a vicious snarl. "I invoke life debt. You will not interfere with my fight until the Seer of the Heartstrikers is dead."

Amelia's eyes went wide, but it was too late. The moment the words left Svena's mouth, the Planeswalker's own blazing magic closed on her like a bear trap, binding her in place. After that, all Svena had to do was step around her to stand triumphantly over Bob, who was still pushing himself up off the ground.

"I suppose it's too late to say it wasn't personal?" he asked, giving her a weak smile.

Svena's answer was to kick him as hard as she could, aiming her delicate pointed shoe right at the spot in his chest where Chelsie had clawed him. He shifted at the last second to avoid the worst of the damage, but the blow still sent him slamming back into the on-ramps. It wasn't until the cement barriers cracked completely, though, that Julius finally realized Bob wasn't faking. He was so used to the seer's tricks, it hadn't even occurred to him that this might not be part of his brother's plan until he heard Bob's ribs snap. When he moved to help him, though, an iron hand landed on his shoulder.

"Don't get involved," Chelsie growled, her green eyes hard as stones as she watched Svena advance.

"But he'll die!" Julius cried.

"Better him than you," the Qilin said quietly, stepping up beside them with his arms wrapped firmly around his youngest daughter, who was still desperately trying to get to Bob. "The White Witch is one of the most dangerous dragons in the world. Even I would not wish to tangle with her when she's this angry."

"Amelia's the only one who could have done it safely," Chelsie agreed, tightening her grip on Julius. "Now that she's locked down, our chances of stopping Svena are nil to zero. Even if we could win, though, I wouldn't get involved. Bob brought this on himself. He always knew she'd never get her seer, but he let her think she'd won for his own benefit." Her eyes narrowed. "He deserves everything he gets."

Julius couldn't argue with that logic, but just because Bob deserved it didn't mean it was right. "He's still our brother!"

"And I was his sister!" Chelsie snarled, her voice shaking with old anger. "But that didn't stop him from letting Bethesda make me a slave, did it? He put us *all* on the block, and for what?" She looked over her shoulder at the Black Reach. "His stupid plan didn't even work."

"Only because he didn't get a chance to finish!" Julius said frantically, turning to look her in the eyes. "Are you really going to stand here and let him die?"

"He's a thousand-year-old dragon," Chelsie said with a shrug. "Let's see him act like one for once. He picked this fight. He can finish it."

Something was *definitely* going to be finished in the next few seconds. Svena had already hopped up onto the rim of the broken cement crater Bob had made when she'd kicked him, standing over him with painfully cold magic pouring off her like a fountain. The frost on the ground was arctic-thick now, transforming the drab dirt and dingy concrete of Julius and Marci's hideaway into a pristine blanket of white save for the places where Bob's blood had stained it bright red. There was an awful lot of red, actually, and Svena reveled in it, leaning down to scoop up a handful as she gloated over her fallen enemy.

"What's the matter, fortune teller?" she asked, tossing the bloody snow in his face. "Forgot how to dodge now that I'm no longer handicapped by pregnancy and your horrible desert?"

"What is it with your family and grudges?" Bob muttered, his face tight with pain as he finally managed to sit up. "But surely you must see that this is ridiculous. I had the advantage last time. There's no shame in—"

"This won't be like last time," Svena hissed as her ice climbed the broken ramp behind him. "I've cold and water in plenty here, while you have nothing. Even your pigeon has abandoned you."

She was right. After the first chunk of ice had hit Bob, his pigeon had fluttered to safety. She was now perched on a tilting piece of the house's roof, which was only still standing because Ghost was holding it up. Julius held his breath as he watched her, waiting for something to happen, but the pigeon just sat there cleaning her feathers as if she really was the dumb bird she'd always appeared to be. He'd always assumed Bob's pigeon was special, but maybe he was wrong. Maybe his brother really *was* just crazy.

Either way, in that moment, two things became painfully clear: Svena was going to kill Bob, and no one was going to stop her. Svena's grievance was running the hottest right now, but every dragon here, and most of the mortals as well, was someone Bob had used terribly. Even the Qilin had been played, ramped up by Bob and his mother and then broken to weaken Algonquin and empower Amelia. As for Julius, he'd been a pawn too many times to count. From the moment Bethesda had kicked him out of his room, he'd danced on Bob's string. He'd been a tool, a puppet, a domino Bob had knocked down and set back up over and over and *over*. He should have hated his brother for that. For using all of them with no care for whom he hurt. And yet...

And yet...

"Here it comes," Chelsie said as frost began to gather in Svena's raised hand. "Look away, Julius. This is going to be—"

But Julius was already gone.

He'd never been a particularly strong dragon, but he *was* a fast one. Julius used that now, darting out of Chelsie's hold before she realized what was going on and sliding across the thick sheet of ice to throw himself in front of Bob, flinging his arms around his brother seconds before the avalanche of razor-sharp dragon magic crashed down. He squeezed his eyes shut, clinging to Bob as he braced for the death that never came. Instead, the freezing air went still, falling into a silence as deep as midwinter before Svena's frustrated voice growled, "What are you doing?"

Julius's heart was pounding so hard, it took him several seconds to form the words. "Saving my brother."

Without releasing his hold on Bob, he cracked his eyes open to see Svena staring down at them through a haze of frosted magic with a look that was half fury, half utter disbelief. "Are you out of your mind?" she cried, grabbing Julius with a hand so cold it burned. "*Get out of my way!*"

The order was laced with magic that hurt even more than her grip, but Julius bore the pain and clutched Bob more tightly, looking her right in the eyes.

"No."

Svena's lips curled in a frigid sneer. "If you think I am soft like my sister, you are fatally mistaken. I have no problem going through you if that's what it takes." She lifted her hand again, and the magic above them sharpened to a deadly point. "Last warning, little Heartstriker. *Move.*"

Julius had been threatened by enough dragons to know that wasn't a bluff, but he still didn't let go. He just sat there, kneeling on the ice with his arms around his brother's neck and his eyes on Svena. It was a pointless resistance. His body wouldn't even slow the ice before it crushed them, but that didn't matter, because this wasn't about winning. It was about Julius and the fact that no matter what Bob had done, he couldn't stand by and watch his brother die.

When it was clear he wasn't going to move, Svena shrugged and started to bring her hand down. But then, just as the glacier's worth of frozen magic she'd gathered was about to release on top of them, another body appeared in front of Julius's.

"*Svena!*" Katya cried, grabbing her sister's hand with both of hers. "Stop this!"

Svena was so surprised, she actually took a step back. "What are you doing, Last Born?" she roared when she'd recovered. "Move!"

"No!" Katya roared back, planting her feet firmly on the bloody ice in front of the two Heartstrikers. "I don't care what you do to the seer, but I will not let you harm Julius! He's the one who saved us from Estella!"

"That debt was paid," Svena snarled. "This is diff—"

"This is greater than debts!" Katya said angrily. "Julius is my friend and yours. Since we met him, he has done nothing but stand by our clan. Even after you broke the pacts, he was reasonable and fair. He could have branded you an oath breaker and thrown our whole clan down in shame, but he didn't. He understood and accepted our weaknesses. Now he's fighting for his brother as you once fought for me, and you're too snow blind to see it!"

"Brohomir stole our seer!" Svena yelled, her voice echoing to the crumbling Skyways. "He killed my enemy and stole our legacy!"

"So what?" Katya snapped. "We all know you were never really going to kill Amelia, and you were the only one who wanted another seer in the clan anyway. The rest of us were looking forward to making our own decisions for once."

Svena stared at her in horror. "So you're just going to let him get away with this? Let him take what is ours?"

"It's only stealing if we care," Katya said, crossing her arms over her chest. "Way I see it, we dodged a bullet. You remember how crazy Estella was at the end. Brohomir's not even half her age, and he has a complex emotional relationship with a *pigeon*. Why would we want to invite that lunacy back into our clan? Your daughter might not see the future, but she'll still be every bit as clever, strong, magical, and ruthless as you are. Let that be enough, Svena! Take that blessing and go, because if you're going to stand here and obsess over the Seer of the Heartstrikers, then you're as bad as Estella. Especially when we've got such bigger problems."

Katya lifted her arm to point at the hole Bob's crash had left in the spiral of on-ramps that formed the ceiling of the hidden house's urban cavern. Julius hadn't had time to even glance at it during the chaos. Now, though, he followed Katya's motion out of habit, lifting his eyes to the sky. Or at least, where the sky should have been.

Julius sucked in a breath. Being stuck in the house since yesterday, he'd heard a lot about the crisis they were facing, but he hadn't actually laid eyes on it until this moment. Now, doom was all he could see. An endless expanse of it, complete with a black shell, beady black eyes the size of blimps, and writhing tentacles that filled the sky from horizon to horizon.

"Is that…?" He swallowed. "Are we seeing…?"

"We are," Bob whispered, his body as still as the ground beneath them. "That is the Nameless End."

There was no laughter in his words now. No jokes, no smugness, nothing that made him sound like Bob. The voice whispering in his ear might as well have belonged to a stranger, but Julius just shivered and clutched his brother closer. "You have a plan, right? You can beat it."

"I have a plan," Bob assured him. "But first…" His voice dissolved with a quiver as he nodded in front of them. "This is it."

Julius had no idea what Bob was talking about. All he saw in front of them were Katya and Svena, but while Katya was exactly where she'd started—standing in front of Julius with her finger stabbed up at the monster who'd taken over the sky—Svena looked like a different dragon. Maybe Katya's words had gotten through, or maybe she'd had the same reaction to the Leviathan's new form as Julius had, because she no longer looked ready to kill. She looked terrified, her fair skin even paler than the frost on her fingers as she stared at the death floating over their heads. She was still gawking when Katya grabbed her arm and pulled her to the side, away from Bob and Julius. This should have been their chance to escape, but when Julius tried to get up, Bob pulled him back down.

"What is your problem?" Julius whispered frantically. "We need to go!"

"There's nowhere *to* go," Bob replied, clutching his brother. "Look."

He nodded again at the space in front of them. This time, though, when Julius turned around, Katya and Svena were gone, leaving nothing between them and the Black Reach.

The oldest seer hadn't moved an inch since the fight began. He was still standing on the steps on the ruined porch, watching silently. Julius was trying to figure out what had changed to make Bob so spooked when the shattered light above their front door miraculously flickered back to life. It was very bright—security grade at Marci's request—but due to the damage, the bulb was hanging down by a wire, dangling from its fixture directly behind the Black Reach.

With the bright-orange light behind him, the Black Reach was now little more than a dark silhouette. The glare did funny things to his shadow too, throwing it out like a dagger across the white frosted ground, down the frozen driveway, and over the bloody, cratered ice to touch the tips of Bob's shoes. A simple shadow, that's all it was, but between the ice, the dark, and the Black Reach's height, it looked as though someone had painted a line on the ground. A long, black arrow, pointed directly at Bob.

"Julius," the seer said, his voice little more than air. "Do you remember when I told you that a seer's first vision is always their own death?"

Julius nodded, scooting away from the shadow's edge.

"This is it," his brother whispered. "*This* is what I saw all those centuries ago. The ice, the shadow, you and me. This moment, right now." He looked up at the monster in the sky and swallowed. "My last moment."

The air changed as he spoke, growing sharper. *Final.* It was a little like when Julius had used Dragon Sees the Beginning's black chain to beat Estella, only now, instead of every chance miraculously working out in his favor, Julius felt like a train car on rails. There were no more choices, no more chances. Every detail—him and Bob, the Black Reach,

Marci and the others, Ghost holding up the collapsing house, even the spirals Svena's frost left in the air—was part of a static picture, the backdrop of a stage where every line was scripted. Every moment that passed was just another dot on the line leading to this moment, and now that they were finally here, there was nowhere left to go but forward to the end.

"I'd hoped Svena would kill you," the Black Reach said as he walked down the steps. "There was a high probability, but once again, you skate through on the most unlikely of chances."

"It was never unlikely if you knew what I know," Bob replied, his voice only shaking a little as he patted Julius on the head. "My brother has a very good track record for miracles."

The Black Reach said nothing. He just kept walking through the snow, his steps crunching across the frozen dirt until he was standing over them like a sword.

"You should be proud," he said. "In all my years as guardian, I've never been forced to act so directly. I much prefer to arrange things so that seers die from the consequences of their actions, as Estella did. But you have evaded every payback, sidestepped every threat that you created. No matter how many dragons you step on, you keep getting away with it." He tilted his head. "If the situation were less dire, I'd be tempted to let you keep going, if only to see how long you could maintain this insanity. Alas, you have not left me that luxury. *I* am now the one left with no choice, Brohomir, and I cannot permit you to do what we both know you're going to do."

"What's he going to do?" Julius asked.

Both seers looked at him, and Julius fought the urge to roll his eyes. "I *don't* know the future," he reminded them. "Bob's not perfect by any stretch, but he's always come through for us in the end. Now we're up against an enemy we can't understand who might destroy everything. Bob says he has a plan to stop it, but you won't even let him say what it is. Why? What could Bob possibly do that would be worse than *that*?"

He pointed at the black shape of the Leviathan that filled the sky. When the Black Reach failed to answer, though, Raven filled the gap.

"Because Bob has the other one."

Julius jumped as the spirit swooped down to land on the bloody ice beside them. "There's more than one way for the world to end," Raven said. "Algonquin was foolish enough to let herself be infected, but she wasn't the only one. There's another interloper here."

He glanced pointedly at Bob's pigeon, who was still perched on top of the wrecked house, but Julius was having trouble following. "Wait," he said, putting his hand to his suddenly throbbing temple. "Wait, wait, *wait*. You're telling me this whole thing is about Bob's *pigeon*?"

"That is *not* a pigeon," Raven cawed. "I don't know why it chose that form, but it's no animal or spirit, nothing of this reality."

"It is an End," the Black Reach agreed, his voice trembling with rage. "The same End that ended our true home ten thousand years ago. The Final Future."

"Now, now," Bob said, holding out his hand to the pigeon, who immediately fluttered over to him. "It's not polite to name the Nameless."

Julius ducked as the bird swept in to land on Bob's arm, scooting as far from his brother as he dared to get away from the pigeon who apparently wasn't so harmless after all. "*That's* a Nameless End?" When Bob nodded, his eyes grew wide. "But what—how did you get—"

"I wasn't tricked into letting her in, if that's what you're implying," Bob said, turning up his nose. "My ladylove isn't a lawless glutton like Mr. Dark-And-Broody up there, and I'm not a fool like Algonquin. I invited her to join me here, and I'm continually delighted that she agreed."

His pigeon cooed happily, but the Black Reach looked angrier than ever. "And that is why you must die," he growled. "That *thing* you claim to love is the extra-planar monster who ate our race's eternity! The ancient dragon seers fed her potential timelines in exchange for certain ones until there was no future left at all! I should have killed you the moment you decided to bring her in, but you had not yet used her power, which meant my hands were tied."

"Why?" Julius asked, careful not to look at Bob. "Not that I want you to hurt my brother, but if he'd already brought in a Nameless End, well… that seems pretty damning."

"Oh, it was," Bob said. "If he made decisions like Chelsie does, I'd be centuries dead. But the Black Reach isn't like the rest of us. He's not even really a dragon. He's Dragon Sees Eternity, a construct created by our ancestors to be judge, jury, and executioner. With powers that vast, the rules governing his actions had to be very strict, and the strictest of all is that he's forbidden from killing a seer until they actually break the rules."

"Why?" Julius asked. "I mean, that seems a little late."

"Because the future is never set until it becomes past," the Black Reach said firmly. "So long as there is even the slightest chance remaining that they will take another path, I cannot move against them. That is why I send every seer a vision of their death at my hands. I want them to know what is coming in the hope that they will choose differently and be spared."

"But they never do, do they?" Bob said. "Because anything a seer decides to cross you over is something they're willing to die for. That's not a decision you go back on."

"I've seen the future you're willing to die for," the oldest seer growled. "That's why I'm here. It's bad enough that you brought the death of our old plane into this one, but I allowed it because consorting with a Nameless End is not the same as using one. This, however, I cannot permit. I will not allow any seer to repeat the mistake that destroyed our world!"

That certainly sounded dreadful, but Julius's original question still hadn't been answered. "But what is he planning to do?" he pressed, frustrated. "You go on and on about how it's the worst thing ever, but no one has actually explained what Bob's supposed future-crime is."

"*Thank* you, Julius," Bob said, glaring up at the Black Reach. "At least *someone* has the decency to actually ask about my plans before condemning me."

"I don't ask because I already know them," the seer snapped. "No one has time for your grandstanding."

"But this *deserves* grandstanding," Bob argued. "It's the second cleverest idea I've ever had."

The Black Reach growled deep in his throat, but Bob had already focused all of his attention on his youngest brother. "I saw this coming before anyone else," he said, pointing at the Leviathan in the sky. "This scene was my very first vision. It took me a while to understand what I was looking at, but I was blessed with a very clever and well-traveled older sister, and together, we figured it out. A Nameless End was coming. Normally, that would be that. After all, how does one defeat an all-powerful being from beyond our understanding? Answer: with *another* all-powerful being! And I knew how to find one."

"Because it destroyed our old home," the Black Reach growled.

"It's called learning from the mistakes of the previous generation," Bob said haughtily, but Julius was shaking his head.

"I'm sorry, Bob," he said, voice shaking. "But this sounds insane. You're talking about making a deal with the force that destroyed our old home!"

"Technically, we destroyed it ourselves," his brother said. "She didn't make us sell out *all* of our futures. We did that. Leviathan's current actions aside, Nameless Ends aren't usually aggressive. They don't plot to destroy planes. They're scavengers, not hunters."

"As a scavenger, I take offense at that," Raven cawed. "They are the ends of worlds!"

"They are forces of nature," Bob snapped. "No more good or evil than the rest of us. What they *do* have is power on a planar level, and that was what I needed."

He lifted his head to the sky again. "I've spent my entire life looking as far as I could into the future, but no matter how many millions of potentials I examined, they all ended here." He swept his hand over the broken Skyways, the ruined house, the Leviathan in the sky, and the Black Reach standing like a dark memorial in front of it all. "For centuries, this moment has been my event horizon. The hard line where all the branching streams of my future ended." He ground his teeth. "I couldn't stand it. I was determined to find a solution, but how do you keep going past something that ends everything by its definition? That was the question I had to answer, and like any good seer, I found it in the future itself."

"But you just said all futures ended," Julius said, confused.

"They did," Bob replied with a smile. "For me. But contrary to popular belief, I am not the center of the world. Time continues after my passing, and though I couldn't see it, I knew that somewhere in the infinite stream of the future beyond my death, there *had* to be a timeline where we survived the Leviathan."

Julius's breath caught. "Did you find it?"

"In a manner," Bob said. "My original goal was to find a way to stop the Leviathan from coming into our world at all, but by the time I had my first vision, he was already on his way. Believe it or not, this timeline is the one where we had the most time to prepare, and you wouldn't believe the hoops I had to jump through to get even these sixty years. I was practically helping Algonquin at times to keep her delusion going for as long as possible."

"But you *did* find a way out," Julius said hopefully. "A way we survive."

"I did," Bob said, his smile fading. "Though whether you'll like it is another matter."

The way he said that made Julius's stomach clench. "What are you going to do?"

"What he should not," the Black Reach snarled, lifting his hand, but before he could do whatever he was about to do, Julius put up his own.

"Please," he begged. "Bob's my brother, and I owe him my life. If he's going to die for this, I at least want to know why." He glanced over at the others, who were still hanging back. Well, Marci looked like she was trying to get to him, but Chelsie had a firm grip on her arm. Amelia was still bound by her own magic, but the Qilin, Fredrick, and the others were all behind her, watching the Black Reach with wary eyes. "We all deserve to know. All of us have been Bob's pawns without knowing why. If he's going to explain himself, we deserve to hear it."

The construct cast a nervous look at the sky. In the end, though, he lowered his hand, motioning for the watching dragons to step forward. Marci was there in an instant. The dragons approached far more slowly, but eventually they gathered, forming a semicircle facing Julius and Bob. Even Svena and Katya came forward. Svena still looked ready to murder the seer of the Heartstrikers, but her curiosity at finally hearing what this was all about must have been stronger than her need for vengeance, because she stood with her arms crossed and her magic pulled in, waiting for him to speak.

"You really were my best decision, Julius," Bob whispered, letting out a tense breath.

"Just keep it short," the Black Reach warned. "*If* you can."

It was a sign of how serious this was that Bob didn't even have a comeback for that. He just turned to his new audience and began talking in a quick, intense voice.

"You're all veterans of the seer game now. You know how we manipulate individuals into choices that nudge future events in our favor, but what you might not know is just how limited we are when it comes to seeing and manipulating futures not directly related to ourselves. That's why Estella had to resort to using chains when she tried to meddle in Heartstrikers' affairs. She was attempting to control pawns that were not within her purview."

No one seemed to like being called a pawn, but Bob was clearly on a timer, so they didn't interrupt.

"For this particular problem, I found myself in the same boat," he went on. "It wasn't enough to merely discover a future that didn't end with the Leviathan eating us. I also needed the means to secure it, which were far beyond what I had available as a mere Seer of the Heartstrikers." He glanced down at Julius. "Since it happened on another plane, I never saw exactly what Dragon Sees the Beginning told you, but I'm sure he explained that the exchange rate on buying futures is terrible."

"He did more than explain," Julius said. "He showed us firsthand. When Marci and I were in the dragons' old plane, I had to buy a future where Estella didn't kill us. It was just five minutes, but it cost a lot."

"Certainty always does," Bob said, nodding. "It takes an absolutely enormous amount of potential futures to buy even one guaranteed outcome. But Dragon Sees the Beginning didn't actually sell you anything. He's only a construct, a tool. He can't actually trade futures. He merely used the knowledge of past seers to act as a broker for the one who could." He nodded at the pigeon on his shoulder. "Her."

"Wait," Julius said, voice shaking. "So you mean when we were in the dragons' old world, when I made the trade for a chain of guaranteed events to defeat Estella, I was actually dealing with a *Nameless End*?"

"There's no one else who could have done it," Bob said with a shrug. "That's her End. She's what remains when every choice is made, the point all the streams of the future eventually flow to, the end of time itself. And before you ask how the end of time can be here now, know that our way of seeing time is very much limited by our perception. We experience time as a line because that's how we live it, but Nameless Ends aren't bound by such strict measures." He smiled proudly at his pigeon. "My lady exists simultaneously in all times at once. That's how she's able to trade one future for another, because from her point of view, all possible futures are already done. If we want one instead of another—say, survival instead of death—she can find that possibility, pluck it out of whatever hole it was languishing in, and shove it in front of us so that—from our limited perspective—that future becomes the only path. But this sort of heavy lifting requires an enormous amount of energy. Energy that she creates by consuming other timelines in bulk, until—"

"Until there's nothing left," Julius said angrily. "That's what happened to our old world. The ancient seers were so bent on securing the timelines they needed to beat each other, they let her consume *all* of their futures."

Bob nodded. "Ironically shortsighted, wasn't it?"

"If you understand that, why are you repeating their mistake?" the Black Reach growled.

"Because it's better than the alternative," Bob replied, his head snapping up to glare at the construct. "There are futures where I don't use the Nameless End, and you don't kill me, but in every single one of them— *every single one*—I die. Sometimes I make it an hour, sometimes I make it four, but every one of them is fatal, and not just for me. Everything in this world dies when the Leviathan wins, which he does in every future I can see where you don't kill me. That means if there *is* a way we get out of this, it can *only happen* if I ask the Nameless End for help, because I've seen every path where I don't, and they all lead to the end of the world." He cupped his hand gently over the pigeon's wings. "Given those odds, I'll take my chances with her."

"And do what?" Marci asked, stepping forward. "What future are you buying?"

"The best there could be," Bob promised. "I've been studying the events leading up to this day for nearly all my life. I knew that if there was a future where we lived, I'd have to buy it, but I couldn't see past my death, which meant I'd have to make my purchase sight unseen. But unlike us born seers, my lady isn't limited by chance. I can only nudge the events back and forth between likely possible futures, but she sees everything. Any event that could happen, she can make happen, so since I was going to be bringing the Death of Seers down on my head anyway, I figured I might as well go for broke and buy the best future I could possibly imagine. One where *everyone* lived happily ever after, including me."

"How is that possible?" Julius asked. "You just said that every future where you lived culminated in the end of the world."

"You're absolutely right," Bob said. "It *wasn't* possible by everything I could see, but again, I can only see what's partially likely to happen. There are billions of practically impossible futures I can't see simply because they're so unlikely, but she can." He stroked his pigeon again. "She sees every way time can bend, no matter how impossible. All I had to do was tell her what I wanted, and she found it. The only downside was the cost. As you might imagine, turning impossibility into certainty is *ghastly* expensive, and with only the futures of Heartstriker to work with, I simply didn't have enough. I needed more. I needed *everyone*, every single dragon that exists. There was no way to get all those futures under my control through the usual ways—no dragon has ever united all the clans in the history of our kind—so Amelia and I hatched a plan to do it *magically.*"

He smiled at his older sister. "As the Spirit of Dragons, Amelia is now intimately connected to every dragon's fire, and I'm connected to her as her beloved brother." He swept his hand at the gathered dragons. "The moment she became a spirit, you all became part of my matrix, and your futures became mine to trade."

Svena began to growl deep in her throat, but Julius was too shocked to pay it any mind. "*That's* why you killed Amelia?" he cried. "So she'd be the Spirit of Dragons and give you the ability to sell our futures? What about restoring our race's connection to the native magic of a plane? What about giving us a home?"

"Oh, well, that was good too," Bob said. "But eyes on the prize, Julius. *Everything* I've done—hooking you up with the human who would become the Merlin, placing you at the top of our clan, reuniting the Qilin with his old flame and then breaking him to weaken Algonquin before restoring him so Amelia would have the luck she needed at the right time to claim her place as spirit—it was all a play to bring us to *this* moment. This one particular crossroads in time where every dragon's future is mine to manipulate, which should be just enough sway to purchase the one future in which *we don't die.*" He held his hands up with a flourish. "I will now accept your praise and adoration."

Silence was his only answer.

"I can see why the Black Reach wants to kill you," Svena said at last. "You're worse than Estella. At least she only sold her own future. You've sold us all!"

"Considering that every other path led to *death,* I don't see how you have cause to complain," Bob said testily.

"But she has every right," the Black Reach said, his normally calm voice shaking in fury. "Death is not the only end, Brohomir. You and I would have no quarrel if all you'd done was bring all dragons under your influence to manipulate the species toward a beneficial future. That's just good seer work. But that's not what you've done. For all your machinations, the future you've chosen is still so unlikely as to be functionally impossible. To ensure it, you will have to feed every other potential outcome to the Final Future, which means that even though lives will be saved, they will not be lived. By trimming every branch of the future but one, you will destroy our free will. Dragons will live on, but our choices will mean nothing. No matter what we decide, there will only be one path forward. Yours."

Silence fell again, harder this time. "Is that true?" Julius asked at last, looking up at his brother.

"It's not a perfect solution," Bob said, his confident smile slipping. "But what else was I supposed to do? I've spent my entire life looking down millions and millions of futures in my search for a way to beat

Algonquin's Leviathan, and every single one ended in death. My death, your death, the death of my family and friends. Everyone I knew or cared about, including me, had no future past this point unless I did something, so I did." He looked up at the Black Reach. "I know I'm breaking your rules, but I'm doing it to save the future of the race *you* were created to protect. That has to count for something."

The eldest seer shook his head. "Good intentions do not excuse the crime. Every seer I've ever killed thought they were doing what had to be done. You are no different."

"But that's ridiculous," Bob argued. "I'm not Estella, trading my soul for petty vindictiveness. We're talking about the end of the world. *Our* world, right now. The scale alone should—"

"No different," the Black Reach repeated, pulling himself to his full impressive height. "Selling potential futures was how we destroyed the only true home our race has ever known. It does not matter if you are buying one life or millions, the mistakes of the past *must not* be repeated."

"So you would let us die?" Bob snarled. "You would rather let Algonquin's tantrum destroy us than bend on this one issue? Have you even *looked* at the future I chose?"

"I have," the construct said. "And I can admit that it is good. Far better than I expected of you, to be honest. But a lovely prison is still a prison, and yours only saves dragons."

"Dragons were all I could control," Bob argued. "Even I couldn't get my claws in the futures of the entire world."

"But what are we without the world?" the Black Reach asked. "In your future, we survive, as does Amelia as our spirit, but everything else gets eaten down to the bedrock. Humans, spirits, plants, animals, they're all gone. We'll be stranded in a wasteland no bigger than what remains of the dragons' old home without even the free will to choose how we will rebuild." He bared his teeth. "Can such a future really be considered better than death?"

"Yes," Bob snarled. "Because we'll still be *alive*. There will be new problems, but at least we'll be around to worry about them. If we stick to your hard line, everything we know will end."

As if to prove him right, the ground began to rumble. Deep in the magic, something was shifting. Thanks to Amelia's new connection, Julius could feel it in the base of his fire. Marci must have felt it too, because her face turned ashen.

"Hoo boy," she said, shaking her head. "I think Big and Ugly up there just bit into something critical."

"He must be reaching the end of Algonquin's physical water," Raven said, flapping up to the shimmering barrier where Ghost was holding the magic at bay. "I'm going to check the Sea of Magic to see how much time we have left. Phoenix?" Emily snapped to attention. "Get our forces into position. If we get a chance to move, it's going to have to be fast. And as for *you*..." Raven turned his sharp beak toward Bob. "Our bargain still stands. Do what you must, but don't forget what you promised us."

Bob nodded, but the spirit was already gone, vanishing with a shimmer into the dark.

"What did you promise him?" Marci asked Bob.

"That I would save his world," the seer replied with a smile. "Raven is very civic-minded. He'll do anything to save his plane, even if it means working with a dragon against his fellow spirits."

"Then he was cheated," the Black Reach said bitterly. "You sold him something you knew you could never deliver."

"I knew nothing of the sort," Bob replied, staring his death in the face. "You're right that this ends in a wasteland, but a wasteland is still better than *no* land. If dragons survive, some part of this world must as well, because otherwise we'd have nothing to stand on. And if the land is still there, there's a chance the spirits will rise again. A *chance*, that's all I promised, but when you're an immortal spirit, a chance is all you need. We mortals aren't so fortunate. If we don't take the future into our own hands, we're doomed."

"We are doomed either way," the Black Reach growled. "Better to die with this world than repeat the fall of the last."

"How can you say that?" Bob cried. "You're the Construct of the Future! You were created to do *exactly* what I'm trying to do: preserve our future."

"You can't preserve the future by repeating the past."

"I'm not repeating the past!" Bob shouted. "I might be breaking the letter of your law, but when it comes to the spirit, our goals are the same! You've been working for ten thousand years to protect dragons from themselves. You've fought as hard as you could within the limits of your purpose, not just to stop rogue seers, but to make us better as a species. You've bent over backward to foster peace and end the in-fighting that has torn us down for so long. The future I mean to buy does all of that, *and* it keeps everyone from dying! How can you kill me for it?"

"Easily," the Black Reach replied, his voice final. "You knew the price, Brohomir. You were warned countless times, but no more."

He lifted his hand, which no longer looked like a hand at all. It was a dragon claw, an enormous one every bit as huge and deadly as Dragon Sees the Beginning's. But where his brother's talons had been as white as bleached bone, the Black Reach's claw was as dark as the shadows that surrounded them. And it was in that moment, that second that seemed to stretch on forever, that Julius finally realized the Black Reach had never been more than a shadow himself. He truly was a construct, a carefully pieced-together mask created to hide the truth of what he was. Death. The final end no seer—no matter how clever or justified or righteous—could avoid.

"You have made up your mind, Brohomir," the construct said in a deep, sad voice. "And I see no more futures where you change it, which means the time has come. Now tell your brother to move aside and accept what you have made inevitable."

Bob took a sharp breath, his hands tensing on Julius's shoulders, but whatever he was working up the courage to say never made it out, because Julius spoke first.

"No."

CHAPTER FOUR

The word rang through the cold air like a shot. Everyone beneath the broken spiral of on-ramps held their breath as Dragon Sees Eternity's eyes narrowed.

"What?"

"No," Julius said again, putting his arms out so that he was blocking Bob. "I'm not letting you kill my brother."

The construct's giant claw flicked down, the point stopping less than an inch above Julius's head. Terrifying as that was, though, Julius had been threatened by giant dragons many, many times. He couldn't stop his flinch, but he didn't move out of the way, which seemed to anger the Black Reach more than anything else.

"Why are you doing this?" he snarled. "Your *brother* has done nothing but use you!"

"He has," Julius agreed. "But he never tried to hide it. For all his other faults, Bob's been up front that I was his tool since the very beginning, and he's never forced me to do something I didn't already want to do. In fact, the only time he ever tried to give me a direct order was when he told me not to free Chelsie, and I did it anyway. You call me a pawn, but the choices that brought me to this spot were always my own. That makes this my problem as much as Bob's, but it doesn't excuse you." His eyes narrowed. "You stand there and accuse Bob of ruining the future, but he's the only one who saw this disaster coming and tried to *stop* it. You're a seer too! You knew this was coming. Where's your solution?"

Dragon Sees Eternity frowned, but even though he'd asked the question, Julius was rolling too hard to stop. "At least Bob was trying!" he cried. "He used us, sure, but unlike Bethesda or Estella or anyone else who's called us pawns, Bob takes what *we* want into account. I'm sure he didn't have to help me achieve my dream of changing our clan to get what he wanted, but he did. He helped me and believed in me when everyone else in the world thought I was a failure. It's because of him that I'm standing here as a clan head instead of cowering in my mother's basement."

"You think he did that for you?" Dragon Sees Eternity scoffed. "He was manipulating you. He abused your compassion by playing the kind brother so you'd defend him, exactly as you're doing now."

"I'm not defending him because I was manipulated," Julius said. "I'm refusing to let you kill my brother because *he's my brother.* Gregory treated me way worse than Bob has, and I didn't let him die either, because killing doesn't fix *anything.* When will you stubborn snakes get that through your skulls?" He flung his hands up at the blacked-out sky. "The world is ending! *Literally!* We should be working together to fight *that,* not wasting what little time we have left fighting each other. That's how we got into this mess and lost our old home in the first place! Seriously, what is *wrong* with you?"

In hindsight, lecturing an ancient construct of dragon magic several thousand times older and bigger than he was probably wasn't the brightest idea, but Julius didn't care. He was so sick of fighting the same fight again and again and *again.* Especially with the Black Reach, who, of all dragons, should have known better.

"You told me back at Heartstriker Mountain that you were sick of watching history repeat itself," he said, leaning toward the construct. "Why can't you see that you're doing the same thing? You saw this coming. You *knew* Bob's back was against the wall, but did you help him? Did you even try to work with him to find a solution that *wouldn't* get him killed? No. You just watched from a distance and judged. You didn't even act until it was too late."

"I did act," the construct snapped. "I gave him warning after warning—"

"Warnings aren't the same as help," Julius said stubbornly. "If you really are the guardian of our future, then you should be helping us shape it, not just smacking down every seer who steps out of bounds. I don't like Bob's solution any more than you do, but at least he has one. Your answer to this seems to be to kill a seer who can't fight back and then leave us all to die in the tentacles of an unbeatable monster that *you* never thought to warn us was coming!"

He was growling by the time he finished, the words coming out in angry curls of smoke, which, if Julius had been calm enough to pay proper attention, would have made him jump. He *never* breathed smoke, but then, he'd never been this angry before. It was as if everything he'd fought against since he'd realized he *could* fight had finally come to a head in this one terrifying moment, and Julius was determined to beat it back once and for all, even if he had to use his own head to do it.

"I'm not moving," he said, wrapping his arms around his brother. "Bob might not be right, but neither are you. I don't know if there *is* a right answer, but I'm certain murder isn't it. So if you want to actually try something new, put your giant claw away, and we'll talk this out like reasonable dragons. But if you're determined to kill my brother for a crime he hasn't committed yet and only planned to attempt because he saw no other way to save us, you'll have to go through me to do it. I know I'm not enough to stop you, but I'm not moving, and you can't make me."

Julius wasn't actually certain of that last part. If Dragon Sees Eternity's true form was anywhere near as big as that claw made him look, the construct could easily pry Julius off Bob and send him flying. He was still determined to try, though, so he held tight, clutching his oldest brother with all his strength. But while Julius fully expected that rash decision to be his last, he did *not* expect Marci to suddenly appear in front of him.

"What are you doing?" he hissed, heart pounding in terror.

"Same thing you are," Marci said, reaching up to shove the Black Reach's giant claw away from Julius's head. "Taking my last stand. I'm still not entirely sure what's going on, but I did *not* just come back from the dead to lose you over *Bob*. No offense."

Bob spread his hands to show that none was taken, but before he could actually say anything, the ice around them turned to steam as the dragon magic binding Amelia broke.

"Finally," the dragon spirit growled, glaring at Svena as she stomped over to stand beside Marci.

Julius gaped at her. "You too?"

"Of course," Amelia said, cracking her knuckles. "Bob and I have been partners in crime since before he could fly. He couldn't tell me exactly how this would go down because of that whole 'knowing the future changes it' problem, but I knew it would come to a standoff eventually." She nodded at Dragon Sees Eternity. "He *is* called the Death of Seers."

The construct growled in frustration. "So you're going to let your sister die for you as well, Brohomir?"

"I'm not dying for him," Amelia snarled. "I'm fighting *you*. You might be a construct built by my ancestors, but I'm the first dragon ever to blend with the magic of this plane. I'm something you've *never* seen before, pal, and Marci here's the First Merlin. She keeps monsters bigger than you for pets."

"Yeah!" Marci said, her face lighting up. "This is *our* world! We say who lives and dies around here. I'm not a fan of letting Bob put my future on rails, but I'm a *big* fan of avoiding the end of the world, and I think Julius makes a very good point. We'll never get anywhere new if we keep playing by the same old rules."

"Took the words right out of my mouth," Amelia said with a grin. "These are crazy times, and crazy times call for crazy plans, not the same old hard line. Isn't that right, Chelsie?"

Julius jumped. He hadn't even realized she was there, but the moment Amelia said her name, Chelsie appeared beside them. She had a long piece of broken metal in her hands that she was holding like a sword, and her face was a sour scowl, as though she couldn't believe it had come to this.

"Don't take this the wrong way," she said, shoving her way past Amelia to stand in front of Julius. "I'm not on Brohomir's team, and I refuse to participate in the hell he calls a future, but I owe Julius more than can ever be repaid." She pointed her makeshift sword at the Black Reach. "If you swing at him, I will swing first, assuming Fredrick doesn't beat me to it."

The words weren't out of her mouth when a cut opened in the air directly behind Dragon Sees Eternity, and the familiar curved blade of a Fang of the Heartstriker slid through the hole to rest on the construct's back. A heartbeat later, Fredrick followed, stepping through the portal he'd made with the confidence of someone who'd been doing this for decades rather than a day. It wasn't until he slid the edge of his Defender's Fang up to the construct's neck, though, that Julius finally realized what was going on.

Dragon Sees Eternity was completely surrounded. Everyone facing him was doing so for their own reasons, but, like a triggered trap, the moment the Black Reach had turned his claw on Julius, all their disparate elements—dragons, humans, spirits, even the Qilin, who'd moved in to support Fredrick—had suddenly snapped together into one powerful whole. Even Svena and Katya had stepped forward, though Svena mostly seemed to be trying to keep her little sister in place. Ghost was there as well, his grave-cold magic filling the air to bursting as he prepared to fight at Marci's command.

If it hadn't been so terrifying, the joy of seeing everyone working together for his sake would have made Julius cry. But while he was fighting back emotions, the Black Reach didn't seem bothered in the slightest. He wasn't even looking at the deadly force surrounding him. He was just standing there, staring at Bob with a sad, sad look.

"Is there no depth you won't stoop to, Consort of a Nameless End?" he asked bitterly. "You've built something truly amazing, a web of real connection built on trust and friendship instead of fear. You could change the world with power like this, and you're throwing it away on a desperate, selfish bid to save your own skin."

"Am I?" Bob said, letting go of Julius as he rose to his feet.

"That question insults us both," the construct said irritably. "You know as well as I do that I can kill everyone here. Your forces are children, not even in their mid-thousands. I am a weapon forged from the combined magic of the greatest dragons of our old world. My fire could consume all of theirs without even noticing."

That sounded suspiciously like bluffing to Julius. The Black Reach had the advantage in age and power, but there was only one of him versus a *lot* of them. To his surprise, though, Bob nodded rapidly.

"You are stupidly powerful," Bob agreed. "No living dragon can challenge you, but that's the most beautiful thing about this. We don't have to beat you."

The Black Reach arched an eyebrow. "How did you come to that conclusion?"

"From you," Bob replied, leaning closer. "You were the one who taught me that the future is never set, old friend, but you wouldn't know it from how you act. We seers get so focused on what's ahead, we often forget that the most important decision is the one right in front of us. We forget that *we* make decisions too. We are part of the stream of time same as everyone else, and just as you told me only minutes ago that I could still choose to change my fate, you have a choice as well."

"*You've left me no choice!*" the Black Reach roared, pointing his claw at the pigeon, who was still sitting placidly on Bob's shoulder. "You deliberately sought out the force whose only purpose is to break the *one rule* I've ever given you! I am the guardian of the future she exists to destroy! What *choice* do I have?"

"A very simple one," Bob said. "You can decide *not* to kill me."

A visible wave of anger rolled through Dragon Sees Eternity, but Bob wasn't finished.

"I've known you nearly all my life. In all those centuries, I've learned that the thing you hate the most isn't seers who break your rule. It's *us*." Bob pressed his hands against his chest. "Dragons. You've been guarding us since we first fled to this plane ten thousand years ago, watching helplessly as we made the same mistakes over and over and *over* again. You used to complain to me about the endless clan wars filling the future with death everywhere you looked. It got so bad that you moved to China. *China!* With *him!*" He pointed at the Qilin, who looked insulted. "You loved to travel, but you sequestered yourself in rural China for centuries because the Qilin's luck kept it relatively peaceful. *That's* how much you hated dragons. You would rather constantly unpick the knots the Golden Wrecking Ball's luck put in your plans than deal with the pointless violence of the normal clans anymore. But I'm changing that."

Bob put his hand on Julius's shoulder. "I found a dragon who didn't think like the others, and I put my entire clan under his care. I built Heartstriker into an empire bigger than any dragon clan this world has ever seen, and then I gave it all to him. But the best part—the *best part*— was that after I put Julius on top, he kept it without my help. He was able to stay in command because he understood what you lost faith in long ago: that dragons are not always defined by our lowest common denominator. That we are all different, and that we are just as capable of compassion, reason, and understanding as any other intelligent species. I didn't manipulate him into being that way, either. Quite the opposite. Julius is Julius *despite* his environment. He's living proof of his own concept, *your* concept, and the moment I realized that, I knew I'd found the lynchpin that would let me break the cycle you've always hated."

"Break the cycle," Dragon Sees Eternity repeated skeptically. "Brohomir, you just put him in power. He hasn't even done anything yet."

"*Au contraire*," Bob said. "Julius has changed our clan more in these last two weeks than Bethesda managed in a thousand years. I may have set up the board, but he's the one who played through. He changed our clan from a dictatorship to an elected Council structure in a matter of days, and he did it without killing. He reconciled our war with the Qilin without bloodshed as well, and repaired our relationship with the Daughters of the Three Sisters. His human also just became the first Merlin, which means we have a real shot at peace with the native species of this plane for the first time since we arrived and started eating them. *And* it was through his great and selfless service to the Qilin that my sister Amelia received the stroke of magical luck she needed to become the Spirit of Dragons, solving our greatest magical problem on this plane and giving us a new home."

He pulled Julius closer. "It's true I pointed him at each of these events, but my brother was the one who actually made them happen. Together, our efforts have reordered the world into a more peaceful, more cooperative, *nicer* place where the old draconic ideas of might-makes-right, take-what-you-want, step-on-everyone-else are finally seen for the barbarism they always were. *That* is the future Julius and I have built, and even after I sell everything else to buy the one timeline where we aren't devoured by the Nameless End, *that's* the future that will remain. It can be yours too, Black Reach. All you have to do is make your own decision not to kill the key players, and you can finally have what you've always wanted: a better dragonkind."

By the time he finished, Julius's head was spinning. He hadn't realized just how much they'd changed until Bob had spelled it out. But while he was feeling awestruck by everything they'd achieved, the Black Reach looked more furious than ever.

"So that's your final play?" he spat. "Bribery? I deny my purpose and spare your life, and you'll give me a future I won't hate?"

"It's not *bribery*," Bob said, insulted. "It's incentive. And I'm not asking you to defy your purpose. Why do you think you were tasked with making sure no seer ever sold a future again? It wasn't because selling possible futures is inherently bad. Let's not forget that seers were doing it for eons before the end. The only reason it was forbidden is because dragons got irresponsible and sold *everything*. That's where we messed up. *That* is the mistake you were made to prevent, but I'm not doing that. I'm not selling timelines to gain an advantage over another clan or make myself a king. I'm trading millions of futures where we *die* for the one where we get to *live*. That's all it is. Not a horrible crime, not a sellout, but a carefully planned shot at survival with a good dragon at the helm."

He put his hands on Julius's shoulders. "That's the choice *I* made, Black Reach. Now, I'm giving it to you. You can enforce the letter of the law and kill me simply for the act of trading a future. Or you can honor the *actual* reason you were made and help me save our species before fear of one End dooms us to another."

He finished with a smile, but Julius was close enough to feel the truth. Bob looked confident, but his heart was pounding so hard Julius could feel it through his coat. He didn't even breathe while the ancient construct considered what he'd said, which was a problem, because Dragon Sees Eternity thought for a long, long time. Then, finally, the Black Reach lowered his arm, his impossibly giant claw shifting back to a normal hand as it fell to his side.

The moment it was clear he wasn't going to raise it again, Bob collapsed on the ground.

"Bob!" Julius yelled, dropping down beside him. "Are you okay?"

The seer burst out laughing, grabbing his brother in an enormous, joyful hug. "Julius!" he cried, rolling back and forth. "We did it!"

"Did what?" Julius croaked, because he hadn't heard the Black Reach say anything.

"We *lived*!" Bob yelled, letting him go at last so he could grin wildly into his face. "Don't you see? This was my death. I was supposed to die just now, but I didn't! I'm alive!" The grin fell off his face, replaced by a look of dumbstruck wonder. "I'm the only seer who's ever beaten the Black Reach."

"Don't get cocky," the construct growled, crossing his arms over his chest. "Just because I've decided to give you a chance doesn't mean I won't change my mind later."

"No, no, no," Bob said quickly, waving his hands. "I am the *epitome* of humility. But..."

He trailed off, fighting so hard to hide his grin, Julius was surprised he didn't pull a muscle. "I knew it would work! I *knew* it. Every seer tries to avoid their death. We all have the vision, and then we all drive ourselves crazy trying to beat the Black Reach at his own game. I spent a good century making the same mistake before I finally figured it out: you can't beat him. He's a construct, a magical supercomputer. No born dragon can ever hope to match that. For a while, I was convinced the whole situation was hopeless, but then I realized that didn't matter. I didn't need to beat him at his own game. I just had to make sure that, when the time came, my solution would be *so good,* so in line with his own desires, the Black Reach wouldn't be able to bring himself to kill me. I knew I couldn't stop his sword, so I focused on removing his will to swing instead, and it worked! It *worked,* Julius! I'm still alive, and it's all because of *you*!"

He hugged Julius again, his chest heaving with what could have been laughter or sobs or both. "I *knew* I was right to choose you," he said, his voice rough. "I knew you'd pull it all together in the end!"

It certainly had come together, but Julius still wasn't entirely sure what he'd done.

"Wait," he said, pushing his brother back to arm's length. "So all that stuff you set up—overthrowing our mother, changing the Heartstriker clan, making Amelia a spirit, freeing Chelsie and F-clutch—wasn't actually to help the clan or make a better world. It was so *you* wouldn't die to the Black Reach?"

Bob snorted. "Is there a nobler cause? He was going to kill me. Of course I did everything I could to prevent it! All those other things were just positive externalities… which I'd always planned from the start," he added quickly at the Black Reach's cutting look. "I'm sure a better dragon would have put the world peace stuff first, but as I keep telling you, Julius, I'm not a better dragon. You're the nice one, which is why *you*—not me—had to be the lynchpin. No one else would do, because no one else would be foolish enough to spare Bethesda, or to form a council when he could have taken the Heartstriker clan for himself. No one else in our family would have worked with Katya instead of bringing her in, or won the trust of a human mage dedicated enough to become the First Merlin."

He reached out to pinch Julius's cheeks. "That was all you, you darling boy, which is why I never told you to be anything but yourself. You were already the Nice Dragon I needed you to be. The only problem was you were *too* nice to use your power. If I hadn't been constantly applying pressure, you would've happily run a magical pest control company in the DFZ until Algonquin's purge caught you. But I knew you had the potential to be a lever large enough to move the world. Once I'd tested your conviction to be sure you wouldn't break, I got you into position and used you exactly as you needed to be used, and just look how marvelously it all turned out!" He hugged Julius again, almost crushing his ribs. "I am a *genius*!"

"So much for the epitome of humility," Chelsie said, reaching down to save Julius from Bob's stranglehold.

"I'm the epitome of many things," the seer replied, releasing Julius reluctantly. "So," he said, sitting back on his heels. "What do we do now?"

Everyone gaped at him.

"You mean you don't know?" Julius cried.

Bob shrugged. "I am unquestionably brilliant, but no seer can see past their own death. All my visions of the future ended thirty seconds ago."

"What about your plan to keep us alive?" Svena demanded. "You owe me my survival at least after I so benevolently spared you."

Amelia snorted at her. "Benevolent my tail. You couldn't bring yourself to kill Julius any more than the rest of us."

"For your information, I was going to go *around* him," Svena snapped back. "I am perfectly capable of stabbing Brohomir full of ice without putting a scratch on Julius Heartstriker. However, Katya's words make me consider the larger picture, and I decided killing your cut-rate seer was no longer worth my time."

"Whatever you need to tell yourself," Amelia said, shaking her head at Svena before turning back to Bob. "But seriously, what *are* we going to do? I don't like the sound of a single future with no free will, but I'll take it if that's the only choice. I didn't fight my way out of death just to get killed again the very next day."

"My original plan is still an option," Bob said, lips curling into a smile. "But it might no longer be the *only* option."

"What do you mean?" Marci asked, glancing up at the Leviathan, who looked exactly the same. "What changed?"

Brohomir turned to grin at the Black Reach. "He did. By making a decision he never would have made before I intervened, the Black Reach kicked off a cascade of shiny new futures. There are so many possibilities in front of us now, I don't even know where to start, so unless you want me to sit here for a few days while I follow each new path to its conclusion, you'd do better to ask him." He nodded at Dragon Sees Eternity. "He's the seer supercomputer."

That was the best thing Bob had said yet, but when Julius turned hopefully to the Black Reach, the construct's face was dour.

"My decision to spare Brohomir has indeed created a host of new possibilities," he said. "Unfortunately, none of them improve our situation. We are still under siege by a Nameless End, a power that acts on a planar level. It's not something we can simply defeat."

"But *do* you have a plan?" Svena said, butting her way forward. "I agree that Brohomir's idea to lock us all in a static future was unacceptable, but it's the height of foolishness to shoot down a strategy unless you have an alternative."

"He has to have something," Amelia agreed, moving to stand beside her best frenemy. "He's the guardian of the future, and there's not much future to guard if we're all dead."

Both dragon mages glared at the construct, but where any sensible creature would have cringed before their combined fury, the Black Reach merely looked annoyed. "I have not been idle," he said irritably. "I saw this coming as Brohomir did and prepared accordingly, but though I am and always shall be the better seer, even I can't work miracles. Brohomir's plan was desperate for good reason. There are no good options in this scenario, and while I was not so insane as to court a death of planes"—he shot the pigeon on Bob's shoulder a nasty look—"I'm not certain you'll like my solution any better."

"I knew you had a plan!" Bob blurted out. When everyone looked at him, he shrugged. "I knew he had a plan. What kind of guardian of the future doesn't plan for the future?"

"If you knew the Black Reach was planning something, why didn't you go with that instead of messing with our lives?" Marci asked irritably.

"Because I didn't know what his plan was," Bob said. "I'm supposed to be dead right now, remember? And I don't see how you have room to complain. You came out of my plans very well, Miss One-in-a-Million-Chance-Merlin."

Marci put her hands up in surrender at that one, and the Black Reach sighed. "I would encourage you not to get your hopes up too high. As I said, I did make arrangements for this inevitability, but even I wouldn't call them salvation."

"Our options right now are death by Leviathan or spending eternity trapped on Bob's string," Chelsie said with a shrug. "What could be worse than that?"

Instead of answering the question, the construct reached into the pocket of his silk jacket and pulled out a golden orb the size of a softball. A *very* familiar golden orb filled with flecks of golden foil that glittered like tinsel in the glow of the broken porch light.

"*Hey!*" Marci cried angrily. "That's my Kosmolabe!"

"A powerful and useful instrument," the Black Reach agreed, rolling the delicate ball between his fingers until the spellworked gold foil that covered the orb's interior fluttered like leaves in the wind. "I've been angling for this one in particular since I saw Estella bringing it into her plans a decade ago. I would have taken possession of it sooner, but the mage who was most likely to become the First Merlin was quite attached to it. The emotional impact of removing it would have sent inconvenient ripples through a very delicate phase of my plans, so I decided to wait until a more appropriate opportunity presented itself."

"You mean until you could steal it," Julius said, unexpectedly angry. "I knew you took Marci's bag! Did you think about the emotional impact that would have on *me*?"

"Why did you even want it?" Chelsie asked at the same time.

"Isn't it obvious?" Amelia growled, crossing her arms over her chest. "Why does anyone *ever* want a Kosmolabe?" She narrowed her eyes at the construct. "He's going to run."

The Black Reach said nothing, but he didn't have to. Now that Amelia had spelled it out, the plan made perfect sense. Why stay in a world that was about to die if you didn't have to? There was even a precedent since fleeing through a portal was how dragons had arrived on this plane in the first place. The only thing Julius didn't understand was why the Black Reach was only doing it *now*.

"Aren't you a little late?" he asked. "If you've known about the Leviathan for as long as you claim, why didn't you start evacuating everyone weeks ago? Even with Amelia and Svena here for teleports, there's no way we can possibly get everyone out before..."

He trailed off. The Black Reach still hadn't said anything, but again, he didn't need to. The answer was right there on his face.

"You never planned to save everyone, did you?"

"No," the Black Reach said quietly, looking down at Bob. "The reason Brohomir's appeal worked so well on me is because he was right. I was created in our species' moment of greatest regret. It was only through the absolute destruction of our home that the old clan heads, including your grandfather, the Quetzalcoatl, finally understood the damage their selfishness, greed, and constant war had wrought. In their sorrow, they created my brother to watch over the grave of our old home and myself to make sure nothing like this would ever happen again. You would think that after such a colossal failure, dragons as a species would *learn*, but it took barely a century before the fleeing clans were right back at each other's throats." He shook his head. "I was created to guard our future, but when I looked ahead down the stream of time, all I saw were the same mistakes repeated endlessly. After ten millennia of trying and failing to correct our course, even I, a construct built in hope for a better future, was forced to accept that dragons would always be conniving, selfish, violent beasts incapable of caring about anything but their own self-interest."

"That's not true," Julius said fiercely. "Sure some dragons are like that, but not all of us. Look around! You're surrounded by dragons who prove the stereotype wrong."

That was meant to be an argument, but the Black Reach nodded excitedly. "Exactly," he said. "You are an extraordinary group that represents everything I've always hoped dragons could be. Why do you think I allowed Brohomir to gather you all here?"

Julius felt as if he'd just been punched in the stomach. "What do you mean 'allowed'?"

"I am the world's greatest seer," Dragon Sees Eternity said solemnly. "As I told you back in your mountain, the only thing I couldn't see was Brohomir's motive. His moves—what he did, how he did it, what he was going to do—were always perfectly clear. I saw him gathering all of you together as clearly as I see you standing before me now. I saw no reason to stop him, though, because he'd already chosen the pieces I myself would have selected, including a brand-new seer." He smiled over his shoulder at Chelsie's daughter, who was peeking out at him nervously from behind Fredrick. "Truly, I couldn't have arranged a choicer group of dragons for our second try at a new beginning."

The Black Reach held up the Kosmolabe. "This world was chosen at random and in haste, but with the compass of the Kosmolabe and my knowledge of what was coming, I was able to search at my leisure until I located the perfect hospitable plane. A place where we can survive the Leviathan *and* keep our futures under our control. Those of you gathered here—Svena and Katya of the Three Sisters, Svena's children, Julius and Chelsie of Heartstriker, and I suppose Brohomir now as well.

Also Xian the Qilin and his eldest son, Fredrick, and of course the new seer—you are all dragons who've proven you can overcome the inherent evils of our race. Once I move you to a new plane, you will become the foundation for a reborn dragonkind."

Julius had no idea what to say to that. His sister, however, had plenty. "Your invitation list is missing a pretty big name there, buddy," Amelia growled. "Where am I in all of this?"

"You were not included," the Black Reach replied. "You are a selfish alcoholic who was willing to risk the fire of every dragon and this world's entire magical system in your quest for personal power. Even if you were less typically draconic, however, I couldn't take you with us because you are now a spirit, bound to this plane. The same goes for you." He turned to Marci. "You are a Merlin, a human whose magic is inextricably linked to a concept of this world. You can visit other planes, but you cannot survive without this one, which I'm afraid means you can't come with us."

"I didn't want to go, anyway," Marci said stubbornly. "I'm not running like a coward and leaving everyone else to die!"

"Me, neither," Julius said, taking her hand. "I'm not going anywhere Marci isn't. And what about Justin and Ian and all the other Heartstrikers? Don't they deserve to live?"

"It's not about who deserves life," the Black Reach said angrily. "It's about who is *best*. I could not put this plan into motion until after I'd done my duty and punished Brohomir, but I wouldn't have chosen differently even if I'd had centuries. You are all the absolute best candidates to ensure my desired outcome. I don't need anyone else."

"Then you'd best come up with a B-list, because I'm not going, either," Svena snarled. "I will not abandon my sisters to Algonquin's tantrum now that we're finally free of Estella and our mothers."

"I, too, will not run," the Qilin said, his beautiful voice as steady and immovable as bedrock. "I am an emperor, the pillar of twenty clans. I will not abandon my subjects, or the rest of F-clutch. They are all Chelsie's and my children. I will not leave them behind."

"Nor will I," Fredrick snapped. "Those are my brothers and sisters. We just got free. I haven't even told them who our father is yet, or that we have a new sister."

75

Everyone started talking after that, the whole group launching into all the reasons they couldn't, wouldn't, and shouldn't run away. It was starting to get deafening when Bob's maniacal laughter broke through the din.

"What are you cackling about?" Svena demanded.

"Nothing, nothing," Bob said, trying and failing to get a hold of himself. "I'm merely appreciating the irony. The Black Reach chose all of you for salvation precisely because you were the sort of good, compassionate, responsible dragons he's always dreamed of having. But now that the chips are down, you're all *so* responsible, no one will take his out." He laughed again, turning to grin at the Black Reach. "Surely you saw this coming?"

"I did," the construct said. "But I've also foreseen every one of them will take my offer in the end. Responsible they might be, but there's a line between doing what is right and throwing your life away for no reason, which is what they will be doing if they dawdle much longer."

All the arguments cut off like a switch after that. "What do you mean?" Marci asked.

"He means there's no way out of this corner," Bob said. "Not unless we're willing to pay for it." He smiled sadly at the Black Reach. "I'd really hoped you had something brilliant up your sleeve. Some miraculous plan that would save everything at the last second. Alas, you do not, but I think I actually like this outcome better, because it proves I was right. If even the great Black Reach has been forced to cut and run, that means I really did find the only future where we survived."

"No one claimed you were incorrect," the Black Reach said irritably. "I wish I did have something brilliant, but we're dealing with a Nameless End. Survival of any kind is the best we can hope for against a foe like that."

"If that's the baseline, then my way was better all along," Bob pointed out. "At least in my plan, everyone lived."

"If the future you'd saved for us could have been called living," the construct growled. "Your plan would leave us puppets. My way, fewer survive, but they are the best dragons this world has to offer, and their futures would still be full of possibilities."

"Would we even be dragons anymore?" Bob said, his voice growing heated. "Your Brave New World of Nice Dragons wouldn't even include our spirit." He crossed his arms over his chest. "I appreciate you adding me as your plus-one at the last second, but if my sister can't come, I'm not interested. Your salvation sounds boring beyond belief."

Terrible as things were looking, Julius couldn't help but smile. He *knew* Bob would never give up Amelia. He just wished they had another choice.

"Well, I don't like any of it," Marci said, echoing his thoughts. "Is there a plan C?"

The two seers frowned in unison. "Nothing I can see," the Black Reach said.

"Me neither," Bob said, running a shaking hand through his long black hair. "It gets pretty dark, doesn't it?"

"Quite," the Black Reach agreed, peering into the Kosmolabe. "Whatever we decide, though, we'd best do it quickly. If the Leviathan gets much bigger, this plane will soon become too fragile to support our end of the portal, and then we really will be trapped."

As though to prove his point, the ground began to shake, causing Amelia to gasp in pain.

"What is it?" Julius asked.

"Same old, same old," she replied, her voice shaky. "Just the unpleasantness of having an extra planar interloper rooting through your metaphysical insides. He hasn't tried to take a bite out of me yet, though, so I think we've still got time."

"How do you figure that?" Marci asked. "A Nameless End in your insides sounds pretty serious."

"Oh, it's serious," Amelia said. "He's forcing his way into our plane like he's getting paid by the inch, but he hasn't actually started devouring it yet. Probably because he's not done with Algonquin."

"I'm sorry," Julius said, confused. "Tell me again why he has to finish Algonquin first."

"Because she's his cover," Amelia explained. "Remember, this is still a healthy plane. Normally, a Nameless End couldn't squeeze more than, say, a pigeon-sized amount of themselves through the barrier. Algonquin cheated the system sixty years ago by letting the Leviathan live inside her water. By using her magic to hide his true nature, he was able to get a lot more of himself inside our plane than he should have. Now that she's given up, he's eating her wholesale, but it's still not triggering the plane's defenses because, technically, he's still undercover. He won't have to hide much longer, though. Once he finishes eating Algonquin— and I mean *all* of her, as in magic, lakes, rivers, the works—he'll be so big, the barrier won't be able to kick him out anymore. Once he doesn't have to worry about getting the boot, he'll be able to eat the rest of us at his leisure, and our plane will end."

That was the grim picture Julius had been worried about since the beginning, but hearing his sister describe the details now gave him a spark of hope. "You're certain he hasn't finished eating Algonquin yet?"

"Absolutely," she said. "If he had, we'd all be dead, which was the entire point of that explanation. Pay attention next time."

"I have been," Julius said. "I just wanted to be sure, because I've seen how Algonquin moves around between her lakes. She literally *is* her water, so if some of that water still exists, then some part of her must still be alive as well!"

Amelia glowered. "I know that tone in your voice. Don't bring your optimism into this, Julius. Raven knows a lot more about spirits than I do, and he's convinced Algonquin is gone."

"But how can she be gone?" Marci asked. "She's an immortal spirit. You were just bragging to Svena that you could come back from anything now. Why shouldn't that same standard apply to Algonquin?"

"Because she's got a Nameless End inside her!" Amelia yelled. "Emphasis on the *End*."

"But she can't be ended yet," Julius said excitedly. "Because if she were, we'd all be dead, as you just said. Since we're *not* dead, we have to assume that some part of Algonquin is still alive."

"Okay, fine," Amelia said. "Maybe a bit of her is still hanging around being crazy. What does that matter? This whole thing was her idea. We're in her end game. Even if you could reach her, it's not like she's going to change her—*hey!*"

Julius sprinted away, not even bothering to stick to human speeds as he jumped onto the railing of his broken porch. He jumped onto the collapsing roof next, clambering over the broken shingles until he was right at the edge of the hole Bob's landing had punched through the second and third stories. He was about to make a leap for what was left of the Skyway overhead when Marci yelled his name.

"What?" Julius yelled back.

"I said, 'Don't cross the barrier!'" Marci shouted. "Ghost is the only thing holding back the magic. If you leave his protection, you'll get squished!"

That was a terrifying thought, but this couldn't wait, so with a final bracing breath, Julius jumped as high as he could. For a moment, he thought he was going to miss completely and land face-first on the ground three stories down. But then his fingers caught a piece of steel rebar sticking off the edge of the broken concrete. He hung there for a moment, swinging back and forth as he caught his breath, and then he hauled himself up onto the cracked overpass, pushing his body right to the edge of Ghost's protective bubble.

It *hurt*. Julius had been in strong magic before, but nothing like this. The rising power might have looked like multicolored snow, but it felt like molten lead. Even with the barrier, magic pounded over him like a storm surge. Standing under these conditions felt blatantly impossible, but Julius couldn't see anything from where he was crouching, so he forced his body to move, breathing out puffs of his own fire as he stoked his magic against the hammer that was still crashing into the world. It took forever, but finally, he made it to his knees, which was good enough to see what he'd come up here to see.

The city was absolutely silent around him. Smoke still rose from a few of the buildings that had been on fire last night, but the common sounds of the city—the horns and car alarms, the rumble of trash trucks and buses, all the clatter of people living their lives—had vanished. Even the birds were gone from the sky, leaving nothing except the Leviathan.

The Nameless End hung over everything like a storm front, his black body stretching as far as Julius could see in all directions. Below his floating bulk, huge tentacles hung down like streamers, their tips plowing through the dry riverbed and the empty basin of Lake St. Clair as they searched for every drop of Algonquin's water. There had to be thousands of them, but apocalyptic as it looked, the news wasn't all bad. With so many buildings down, Julius could see all the way to the edge of Lake Erie, and while most of the once Great Lake looked depressingly like a drained bathtub filled with dead fish, there was still a pool of water reflecting the Leviathan's shadow in the far distance, its muddy surface rippling in the breeze.

"Julius!"

He looked over just in time to see someone land beside him, and then the horrible weight of the burning magic lifted as Amelia grabbed his shoulders. "Hey," she said, looking him over with a worried frown. "Are you all right?" When he nodded, she smacked him. "What were you thinking, running up here without protection? You could have spent your last hour alive knocked out cold!"

"I didn't know we had portable protection," he said, looking up in wonder at the radiant shimmer of the magical bubble Amelia was holding over them like an umbrella.

"Neat trick, huh?" his sister said with a grin. "I copied it from Ghost. I can't make mine as big as his yet, what with the whole I've-only-been-a-spirit-for-less-than-twenty-four-hours thing, but I'm still pretty stoked about my progress." She looked around with a grimace. "So what did you bolt up here for? I hope it wasn't something stupid."

"It's not," Julius promised, pointing at the puddle of water in the distance. "Take a look at that."

Amelia winced. "Not much left, is there?"

"Actually, that's a lot more than I'd hoped," he said. "If I can still see Lake Erie, we still have a chance."

"A chance to do what?"

Julius smiled and jumped back down, falling a good fifty feet to land in a crouch beside Marci. She'd barely recovered from the shock when Julius shot up and grabbed her shoulders, his hands shaking with wild hope as he said the magic words.

"I have an idea."

CHAPTER FIVE

Marci had a feeling she knew where this was going, but she asked anyway. "What sort of idea?"

Julius grinned down at her. "I'm going to talk to Algonquin."

She'd known it.

"*Talk* to Algonquin?" Amelia cried, jumping down beside them. "Seriously, that's your plan?"

"Why not?" Julius asked. "She's the reason all of this happened, and she only gave in to the Leviathan because she thought all was lost. There's still water in her lakes, though, which means we've still got a chance to convince her that's not the case. It might not even be that hard. This is basically a suicide, but vengeful as she is, I'm pretty sure Algonquin doesn't actually want to die any more than we do. If we can find a compromise, something she can live with, I'm betting she'll change her mind and choose survival. Once she does that, she'll withdraw her protection from Leviathan, and the plane will kick him out, just like Amelia said."

The Spirit of Dragons pressed a hand to her forehead. "No offense, Baby-J, but that's the most Julius-y thing you've ever said."

"It's ridiculous," General Jackson added, striding over to join them. "Do you know how many times we've tried to negotiate with Algonquin? It's impossible. She will not listen."

"That was back when she still had an ace up her sleeve," Julius argued. "Things are different now. I've lived in the DFZ. I know how deeply Algonquin loves her lakes. She's been watching the slow destruction of everything she loves for sixteen hours now. If she was ever going to be open to changing her mind, this would be the time, but she can't listen if no one's there to talk."

"Fair enough," the general admitted. "But how do you propose we get to her? The Leviathan is drinking her down as we speak, and we're still stuck in this bubble."

"I don't think he's going as fast as we feared, though," Julius said excitedly. "The river and Lake St. Clair are gone, but if the other Great Lakes are anything like Erie, we've still got a chance. Before he left, Raven said we had two hours tops before the magic dropped enough to go outside. If the Leviathan doesn't finish her off before then—and at the rate he's going, I don't think he will—we can go out there and buy time to find Algonquin and convince her to stop her monster for us."

"Buy time?" Svena asked. "How does one buy time against a Nameless End? What do you intend to do, talk it to death?"

Julius smiled. "I was actually thinking of something more traditional. We can fight it."

"*Fight* a Nameless End?" Amelia said. "Like, with claws and fire?" When Julius nodded, she threw her hands in the air. "That's it. You've officially gone from crazy optimistic to plain old crazy."

"Just hear me out," Julius said. "I'm not saying we should fight the Leviathan himself. That *is* crazy. He's the size of the entire sky. But we don't actually need to defeat him. We just need to stall long enough to convince Algonquin to do it for us."

"Stalling, huh?" Marci said, tapping her fingers thoughtfully on her bracelet. "You mean like make a distraction?"

"I was actually thinking we should go for the tentacles," Julius said. "That's how he's sucking up her water. If we start cutting them off, it's bound to have some effect."

"Assuming they *can* be cut," General Jackson said grimly. "I've fought the Leviathan before, and while I was able to damage him, he always healed immediately. The thing above us is infinitely bigger and stronger than the shadow we faced in Reclamation Land. He may not be vulnerable at all now."

"I bet he's vulnerable to dragon fire," Amelia said with a smoky grin. "I've never fought a Nameless End, but until he's big enough to haul the rest of himself in through the barrier, that thing is ninety-nine point nine percent Algonquin. That makes him spirit magic, and I know for a fact that spirits burn."

"It's true," Svena said cruelly. "I've sent several back to their domains myself. They always burn so prettily." She looked up through the hole in the Skyways where one of the Leviathan's tentacles was passing overhead. "I could burn that."

"But could you burn enough?" Chelsie asked. "Julius just said the Leviathan was the size of the entire sky. Given the number of tentacles I've already seen above us, we're talking about thousands of targets spread out over hundreds, maybe thousands of square miles. That's too much even for you, White Witch."

Svena growled deep in her throat at the implied weakness, and Julius quickly jumped in. "We don't have to get all the tentacles. Again, we're just trying to slow him down, not cut him off entirely, and we don't have to do it with only the dragons we have here." He turned to the Qilin. "You said your clan was already on its way, and Fredrick can bring in the rest of the Heartstrikers with his Fang. That's a *lot* of dragons if we all work together. More than enough to keep the Leviathan from drinking the last of Algonquin long enough for me to get a chance to talk to her."

"Which I still don't think will work," General Jackson said. "I like the idea of burning tentacles to buy time, but the end goal of your operation is fundamentally flawed. We could buy you a year, and it still wouldn't make a difference, because no matter what you say, Algonquin will not listen."

"How do you know that?" Julius demanded.

"Because Algonquin *never* listens."

The sudden booming voice made Marci jump. She hadn't even heard him coming in, but Raven was suddenly right on top of them. The true Raven, landing on the muddy ground beside them in all his huge, feathered glory. In this form, his head rose even taller than the Black Reach, and his flight feathers were as long as Marci's leg, each one shining with a black rainbow sheen like oil on water. He actually looked like a god for once, but his magnificence was undermined by the very mortal look of terror in his black eyes.

"I take it things on the other side didn't go well," General Jackson said grimly.

"They didn't go at all," Raven replied, shaking his huge head. "Algonquin's not in her vessel."

"What?" Marci cried. "But that's impossible. Spirits are defined by their vessels. It's what gives you guys your shape. How can she not be there?"

"I have no idea," the spirit said. "But I know Algonquin's shores below the Sea of Magic almost as well as I know my own, and she's not there. Nothing was, except that thing's vile tentacles."

"Wait," Amelia said, her voice shaking. "You're saying he's got tentacles *inside* a spirit vessel? As in at the bottom of the Sea of Magic?"

"He's got tentacles everywhere. The other side's filthy with them, and that's not the worst of it." The Raven Spirit swung his huge beak toward Julius. "I heard your plan through my Emily's ears. Your idea of talking to Algonquin is utter rubbish. She's never listened to anyone who says things she doesn't want to hear. She's certainly not going to start with a dragon. Not even you, Julius Heartstriker. I am well aware of your reputation for turning enemies into allies, but this is beyond even your powers. In case her wholesale slaughter of your kind a few days ago in the DFZ wasn't clue enough, Algonquin hates dragons only slightly less than she hates Mortal Spirits. Even if you could somehow miraculously push through that millennia-old resentment, it wouldn't matter, because you *can't* talk to her. Not where she is."

"Where is she?" Julius asked.

Marci was wondering the exact same thing. She still didn't buy Raven's story about Algonquin not being in her vessel. Spirits were *always* in their vessels. The hollows at the bottom of the Sea of Magic were the cups that held the magic that made them sentient. Even during the drought, they'd been in there, asleep. Algonquin's vessel was the outline of her soul, as much a part of her as her water. If she wasn't inside, where else could she be?

"There," Raven said, looking up at the darkness that filled the sky. "The Leviathan isn't just consuming her lakes. He's consumed *her*. She's withdrawn completely inside him, and there's no way we're getting her out."

"There has to be a way."

"Not without getting eaten yourself," Raven said. "I know. I just tried. Why do you think I'm in this shape?" He lifted his massive head. "When I realized what had happened, I tried to bash my way inside, but he's armored himself in Algonquin's magic."

"Then you should step aside and let someone bigger try bashing," Amelia suggested.

"It's not just a problem of power," Raven snapped. "Out here, the Leviathan can't eat us until he's finished off Algonquin and gotten big enough to fend off the planar defenses, but the inside of his shell is his turf. It's like being in a spirit's vessel. He controls everything within his own domain, which means he can eat you at any time without worrying about tipping his hand to the rest of the plane, and as I just learned, his teeth are very sharp."

Raven lifted his wing, showing them the huge chunk that had been bitten out of the top. "That's why your plan isn't going to work," he went on, turning back to Julius. "The Leviathan might not be done sucking up her water, but Algonquin's finished. She's not technically dead yet because of the way spirits work, but she's buried herself so deep inside her End that she might as well be. Even if you could somehow beat your way to her, the Leviathan would devour you before you could say a word."

Julius's face crumpled, and Marci's heart went out to him. "It was a good plan," she whispered, reaching out to squeeze his hand.

"Parts of it are *still* a good plan," Amelia said. "I was never on board with talking to Algonquin, but burning tentacles is still very much on the table."

"Agreed," said General Jackson. "We all die the moment the Leviathan finishes off what's left of Algonquin's water, so slowing the draining of the lakes should be our number-one priority. I've already got every military jet in North America on standby. Add in Heartstriker and the Golden Empire, and we should have enough air supremacy to stop those tentacles cold."

Raven shifted his huge clawed feet. "Not to be a naysayer, but I don't think that's going to be enough. When I was trying to find a way inside, I got a look at just how big the Leviathan's body actually is. I couldn't do a fly-by in the real world due to the still out-of-control magic, but I did nip into the Heart of the World to take a peek through Shiro's scrying circle."

Marci had forgotten all about that. "Of course!" she cried, smacking her forehead. "Why didn't I think of that?"

"Don't feel bad," Raven said. "I have infinitely more experience with being tricky than you do. Anyway, the point is, I finally got a clear look at our enemy's new guise, and it's *big*."

"How big?" Emily asked.

"Apocalyptically," the spirit replied, scratching a quick map in the frozen dirt with his claw. "The Leviathan's body spans the entire Great Lakes region. There's tentacles from the tip of Lake Superior all the way to the eastern edge of Lake Ontario. The water alone is over ninety-five thousand square miles of territory, *and* he's covering the land in between as well. That's seven states with a sky full of giant flying End Times. Not squirrelly little East Coast states, either. Midwestern ones."

Myron put his head in his hands. "Then we're finished," he said quietly. "Even if everything was ready to go right now, there's no way we can guard that much territory."

A horrible silence fell after that. Everyone, even Amelia, was looking at the ground. The only ones who didn't look as though they'd just heard the drums for their own execution were the seers. Bob didn't even seem to be paying attention. He was just sitting on the ground with his eyes closed, the lids fluttering rapidly as his eyes moved behind them. Marci dearly hoped that meant he was searching the new possibilities for an outcome where they didn't all die, but he could have been lucid dreaming for all she knew. The Black Reach, on the other hand, was standing to the side with his arms folded as if he were merely an impartial observer to the end of this drama, which, considering he could leave at any time, Marci supposed he was.

"We can still run," the construct said when the silence had stretched too long.

"*You* can run," Amelia snarled. "We're still screwed."

"No one needs to run," Julius said firmly, turning to smile at Marci. "We've got the best minds on the planet working together. We can figure this out."

Marci blushed at the implied compliment, which was as sweet as it was inaccurate. She'd become Merlin because she had the right attitude for the Heart of the World, not because she was a particularly brilliant mage. That was Myron's job, and he looked just as stumped as everyone else. It wasn't that she didn't have her moments, but for all of her academic aspirations, at the end of the day, Marci was just a regular old Yellow Pages mage. Aside from Ghost, the bulk of her actual experience with magic was in curse breaking, wards, and banishing obnoxious minor spirits like the female tank badger she'd pulled off her and Julius's last paying client before—

Marci froze, eyes going wide. "What about a banishment?"

Amelia arched an eyebrow. "What *about* a banishment?"

"You can't banish a Nameless End," Myron said at the same time. "They're not spirits."

"That doesn't matter," Marci said, her voice trembling in excitement as she pointed at the black shape in the sky. "The whole reason that thing is able to be in our plane is because Algonquin's been hiding it. If that's true, then it doesn't matter if the Leviathan himself is a spirit a not. He's relying on Algonquin's magic to keep himself hidden, and Algonquin *can* be banished."

"That makes a surprising amount of sense," Raven said, turning his head. "Myron, you're our expert. *Could* we banish it?"

"In theory, I suppose it's possible," Myron admitted grudgingly. "But it won't work in reality. There's a reason Algonquin was never banished. She's just too big. The circle required to suck all the magic out of the Great Lakes would encompass the entire northern hemisphere, not to mention the mages you'd need to actually use it."

"How many mages?" Emily demanded.

Myron thought for a moment. "At least a hundred thousand, which is ninety-nine thousand nine hundred and fifty-two more than the current world record for largest casting team." He shook his head. "It's not a bad idea, but it simply won't work on this scale."

"Not if I did it your way," Marci said. "But I'm not talking about a draining banishment." Her lips curled in a smirk. "I'm talking about dropping the hammer."

Myron's eyes grew wide, and then he pressed his palm to his face. "You *can't* be serious."

"Why not?" Julius asked. "What's the hammer? And why can't she be serious about it?"

Marci opened her mouth to explain, but Myron beat her to the punch.

"There are two methods of banishing spirits from the physical world," he said authoritatively. "The most common is a draining banishment, which is where you trap a spirit in a circle and suck out its magic until it either surrenders or can no longer maintain a physical form."

"That's what I used on all our spirits back when we had our business," Marci explained.

"Precisely," Myron said. "Draining banishments are a staple mage tool because they are a safe, reliable, and highly effective method of controlling spirits. Also, draining banishments don't require you to have any magic on hand beyond whatever was needed to trap the target initially. Since you're sucking power *out* of a spirit, the process is always a net positive for the mage, which is fortunate because you often need that magic to fix whatever disaster inspired you to banish that spirit in the first place."

"But that's not what she's talking about doing," General Jackson said.

"No," Myron said, shooting Marci a dirty look. "Miss Novalli is referring to the second type of banishment, colloquially known as a 'hammer banish.'"

"Why?" Julius asked.

"Because that's exactly what it does," Marci said, taking over the conversation before Myron talked them out of the idea she hadn't even explained yet. "The whole point of a banishment is to reduce a spirit's magic to the point where it's no longer a threat. Draining banishments do that by sucking magic out, but hammer banishments do the opposite. They work by hitting spirits with *so* much power, their own magic is blown to bits. It's like throwing a rock into a puddle. Get a big enough rock with enough force behind it, and you can knock every drop of water out of that sucker, leaving the puddle dry."

Raven grimaced. "That doesn't sound pleasant."

"Oh, it's horrible," Marci agreed. "It also takes an enormous amount of magic, which is why most mages never do it. But if you *can* land a hammer banish, it works instantly, which is its key advantage here." She glanced at Julius and Chelsie. "Remember when we were fighting Vann Jeger, and it took me forever to banish him?"

"How could I forget?" Chelsie growled. "We both nearly died multiple times."

The Qilin turned to her in wonder. "You fought the Death of Dragons?"

Chelsie nodded as if that was no big deal, but Marci didn't miss the smug smile she was struggling to hide. Neither did the Golden Emperor, who seemed to be falling in love all over again.

"Anyway," she moved on. "That's the downside of a draining banish. Vann Jeger was only a fjord, but I still pulled on him as hard as I could for over half an hour without making a dent in his magic. Assuming being consumed by the Leviathan hasn't changed her size, Algonquin is *much* bigger. Even if we could somehow get a hundred thousand mages working together, the Leviathan would probably kill us all before we drained him down to anything like a reasonable size. If we use a hammer banish, though, we won't have to touch his magic at all, which means he won't see it coming until the hammer lands on his face."

"But how are you going to get that much magic?" Myron asked. "A hammer banish requires at least an exponential square of the magical mass of the target. Cubed, if you want to be sure. Where in the world are you going to get that kind of power, and where are you going to put it?"

"Um, dude," Marci said, pointing at the glowing magic that was still rising from the ground beyond Ghost's barrier like a snowfall in reverse. "I don't think magic is going to be a problem. As to where to put it, that would be an issue if we didn't already have access to the biggest magical circle in the world."

Myron looked confused for a moment. Then his eyes lit up, and Marci knew she had him. "The Heart of the World," he said, his voice trembling with excitement. "Of *course*, it held all the magic in our plane for a thousand years. Assuming we could repair the seal, it would hold the magic necessary for a hammer banish, no problem."

"So you're saying it would work," General Jackson confirmed.

"If we can gain access to the Heart again and fix the circle, it's definitely possible," Myron said. "But even if we could pull it off, I still don't know if it would do any good. Even the hardest banishment is only temporary. You're just sending a spirit back to the Sea of Magic, not destroying it permanently. All the Leviathan has to do is gather up enough magic to become corporeal again and he'll pop right back in."

"If he were a normal spirit, sure," Marci said. "But as everyone's gone to great lengths to point out, he's *not* a spirit. He's just hiding inside one. He doesn't have a domain or a vessel or any of the normal stuff spirits have to catch them when they fly apart. If we banish all his magic, he'll have no power left and nothing to hide what he really is. Best case scenario, we explode Algonquin's magic, the Leviathan's left naked, and the plane kicks him out like it always should. Worst case, we still disperse all the magic he's gathered, which means he has to spend time picking it up again, maybe a *lot* of time. The bigger a spirit is, the longer it takes them to re-form after a banishment. I'm sure that cooldown is shortened now that we're up to our necks in magic, but we're still putting time back on the clock. That's not small potatoes considering the death of everything we know might only be a few hours away."

"Fair point," Myron admitted grudgingly.

"Of course it is," Marci said. "You think I didn't think this through? Small banishments and curse breaking were how I paid my way through college. You just worry about fixing the Heart of the World. I'll take care of the rest."

"Oh you will, will you?" Myron said suspiciously. "And how do you intend to gather that much magic before the Leviathan eats us all?"

"I've got a plan," Marci said confidently. "You just make sure you've got your end."

Myron looked highly skeptical, but Emily just nodded. "That's settled, then. We'll banish it."

"Hold on," Svena snapped. "You can't just say what we'll do. I don't take orders from humanity's dragon slayer."

"Too bad," Emily replied dryly, crossing her scrap-metal arms over her chest. "Because so long as our Merlins are the ones with the plan, humanity's holding the cards right now."

"Would you both knock it off?" Marci said. "We're all in this barrel going over the waterfall together, don't forget."

"I forget nothing," Svena said. "And I did not say your plan was bad, just that I would not take orders." She glanced up at the Leviathan. "You will need time to pull this off, yes?"

Marci nodded. "Not as much as we'd need for a draining banishment, but it'll still take a while to repair the circle and get the magic together."

"How long?"

"To repair a catastrophic break in the greatest piece of spellwork architecture the world has ever known?" Myron blew out a long breath. "I'd have to do the math before I could—"

"More than an hour?"

When he nodded, Svena turned to stare at the Phoenix with un-nervingly predatory ice-blue eyes. "Humans do not have all the cards, it seems. If you are going to do this, you will need our help."

"I thought you'd already agreed to help."

"*They* agreed," Svena snapped, waving her hand at Julius and the Qilin. "But I alone speak for myself and my sisters."

Emily heaved a long-suffering sigh. "What do you want?"

"Complete immunity for my clan from the UN's dragon hunts," Svena said without missing a beat. "And no more shipping through the Siberian Sea. That is my private territory, and the vibrations from the cargo ships disturb my magic."

"Really?" Julius said. "You're worried about this *now?*"

"I can't make Russia give up its northern trade lanes," Emily said at the same time. "I'm general of the UN's Anti-Dragon task force, not queen of humanity."

"If we help save the world, I see no reason why our demands cannot be met," Svena said stubbornly. "I'm promising you the most magical dragons in the world. Surely that's worth some international leverage."

Emily ground her teeth. "Fine," she said at last. "I just hope for everyone's sake you're not all talk."

"You have not begun to see what we can do, tin soldier," Svena replied, lifting her chin. "My sisters and I were burning spirits to ash back when your kind was still farming dirt with rocks. We will show that black slug what it means to trespass on *our* plane."

Katya nodded rapidly at that, clutching Svena's fluffy hatchlings in her arms. Amelia, however, looked less impressed. "How are you going to do that?" she asked. "Not to dig up old grudges, but you couldn't beat *me*. What chance do you think you'll have against Big and Ugly up there?"

"Why must you always be so literal?" Svena snapped. "I didn't mean *I* was going to beat him. As the Phoenix just pointed out, that's the humans' job now. All we need to do is stall the creature. For that, we need dragons, and I know how to get us dragons."

Amelia scoffed. "Where from? Because unless you've got a few hundred more puffball whelps you haven't mentioned, your clan's a little short to be making promises like that."

"*Please*," Svena said. "Only your mother confuses children with power. I was referring to this." She reached out to poke Amelia in the breastbone. "You're the one who set herself up as a god. Start acting like one."

Marci had no idea what that meant, but Amelia was staring at Svena as if the white dragon had just shown her magic for the first time. "She's right."

"Of course I'm right," Svena said. "I've always been the brains to your brute strength. That's how our relationship works."

"Shut up," Amelia said, but her face was a huge grin as she turned to face her brother. "You need dragons to slow the Leviathan? I can get you every single one."

"That would be amazing," Julius said. "But how? Can you open portals straight to dragons now?"

Amelia sighed. "Sadly, no. I'm not that awesome, at least not yet. But I am connected to every living dragon's fire, which means I know where everyone is, and I can talk to all of them."

"Great," Chelsie grumbled. "Of all the dragons, you're the one with the megaphone."

"You won't be complaining when we save your feathers," Amelia snapped. "I might not be able to bring in the dragons I call, but I don't have to. As she just proved by teleporting through a magical disaster, we already have the best teleportation mage in dragon history right here with us."

"Flattery will get you nowhere, Planeswalker," Svena said with a sniff. "But feel free to go on."

"I'd rather you show me yourself," Amelia said, turning her grin on Svena. "You started this plan. Here's how we'll finish it. I can locate any dragon, and I know you can teleport anyone anywhere if you know where they are."

Svena jerked back so fast that that her daughter, who was sleeping on her shoulder, nearly fell off. "How do you know that?" she cried. "That knowledge is top secret, the hidden weapon of my family!"

Now it was Amelia's turn to look smug. "It *was* secret, until I read it in your fire."

"*What?*"

Amelia placed a hand on her chest. "Hey, god here, remember? I see you when you're sleeping, I know when you're awake. I know if you've been bad or good, so do what I say, for goodness' sake!"

Svena clenched her jaw. "First, that doesn't even work with the song. Second, Santa Claus is *not* a god, so your comparison isn't just stupid, it's also incorrect. Third, this whole thing is invasive and disrespectful. I never gave you permission to read things out of my fire!"

"I can't control what I see," Amelia said defensively. "I just looked, and there it was. What was I supposed to do, not see it? Besides, this was your idea."

"My idea was for *you* to do the shuttle service!" Svena roared. "Do you know how much magic teleportation takes? I just laid a full clutch of eggs! You can't expect me to teleport hundreds of dragons thousands of miles through magical fallout!"

"You're the one who's always claiming to be the greatest dragon mage in the world," Amelia reminded her. "It's put up or shut up time. Your secret's already out, so we might as well use it not to die. And speaking of not dying, we need to get on that, because we're racing against an unknown timer, and we've been standing around talking for, like, three days."

They'd been here for thirty minutes tops, but the point must have been well made because, after several angry huffs of icy smoke, Svena threw up her hands. "Fine. But this is *not* over, Planeswalker! I want to know exactly what you've seen of my abilities, and then I want to know about everyone else's."

Amelia snorted. "What happened to 'Oh Amelia, how could you? That's so invasive and disrespectful!'"

"It was," Svena said. "To *me*. I don't care if you disrespect the operational security of other dragon clans. That's just good intelligence."

"Whatever you need to tell yourself," Amelia said, turning to give Julius a wink. "Ice Queen and I will handle the dragon delivery. Can you get Heartstriker here on your own, or should I pull them in too?"

Julius looked at Fredrick, who nodded. "We'll take care of Heartstriker. You and Svena bring in everyone else."

"Not my clans," the Golden Emperor said. "As I said before, they should already be on their way, and I wish to speak to all of them before this begins."

"Just make it quick," Amelia said. "I know you're luck incarnate, but we're on a schedule here."

With that, she walked over to join Svena, who was already staking out a large section of dirt in what would have been Marci and Julius's front yard if they'd had a yard. Or a house anymore.

"I guess that takes care of that," Julius said nervously as he turned to Marci. "We'll get everyone together and stall the Leviathan for as long as we can. How long do you think it will take you to line up what you need for the banishment?"

"That depends on how quickly Myron can work and how much help I can wrangle," Marci said, glancing at General Jackson, who was already back on the phone as Myron whispered frantically into her free ear. "But I promise we'll go as fast as we can."

"I know you will," he said. "You always do your best." He looked down at her for a long moment after that, his inhumanly green eyes nervous, like he wanted to say something else but couldn't. She was about to tell him to just spit it out when Julius swooped down and kissed her.

Even after last night, the move took her by surprise. She was so used to walking a narrow line on her feelings for Julius, she didn't know what to do with herself now that it was all out in the open. But Marci had always been a quick study, and she got with the program in a heartbeat, wrapping her arms around his neck as she kissed him back. She was getting even closer when a cleared throat made them both jump, and Marci whipped her head around to see Myron waiting a few feet away.

"If you don't mind," he said, tapping the cracked face of his wristwatch.

Marci felt her face turn beet red, but she didn't apologize. Instead, she kissed Julius again, holding him close one last time before she reluctantly stepped away. "Good luck."

"You too," he said, giving her the thousand-watt smile that only came out when he was *really* happy. "We can do this."

"We can do this," Marci agreed as Myron pulled her away. She was still staring at him wistfully when the UN mage grabbed her shoulder and yanked her around.

"Ow!" she said, smacking his hand away. "What gives?"

"Everything's going to give if you don't pay attention," he said angrily. "This is the end of the world, not romance time with other species."

"If I waited until the world wasn't ending, I'd never see Julius at all," Marci snapped. Still, Myron had a point. "Okay," she said, sneaking one last look at Julius before she put on her serious face. "What are we doing?"

"You tell me," he said. "You're the one with the plan."

Again, fair point. "Right," she said, scrambling to regather the thoughts Julius had just scattered. "The first thing we need to do is get back to the Heart of the World." She paused, frowning. "Um, how *do* we get back to the Heart of the World?"

"I usually just follow my spirit," Myron said with a shrug. "The DFZ seems to be able to travel freely between both sides. For you, though, I have no idea."

That made two of them. "Stay right here," Marci said, backing up toward the house. "I have to have a quick meeting."

"Make sure it's *very* quick," Myron said, raising his voice in warning. "You put yourself at the center of this, Novalli. If you can't pull it off, we're in trouble."

They were in a lot more than that if she couldn't figure this out, but Marci wasn't afraid. She wasn't entirely sure of the details yet, but after everything else she'd been through, Marci was positive she could pull this off too. She didn't have a choice. Failure was not an option, so she shoved the nagging doubts out of her mind and ran up the broken porch steps toward her spirit, who was still valiantly holding up the barrier that kept the rampant magic from cooking them all.

CHAPTER SIX

Chelsie stood at the edge of the wreckage that had been Julius's front porch, holding her daughter close as the two of them observed the chaos. Fredrick had already left, cutting his way to DC, where Justin, Conrad, and most of the other Heartstrikers were gathered. She'd offered to go with him as backup, but Fredrick had refused. This was his job now, not hers, and he wasn't going to make her do it even one more time.

If it hadn't been such a sweet sentiment, she would have told him what a stupid idea it was to go alone into a bunch of nervous, prideful dragons who still thought he was a servant and rally them for war. But while he'd framed it as something he was doing for her sake, Chelsie knew her eldest son, and the hard set of his jaw had told her the refusal wasn't actually about her at all. Showing up with a Fang and a declaration of war was Fredrick's first big chance to prove himself among the Heartstrikers as a dragon, not a servant. That wasn't something she dared to mess with, so she'd just let him go, staying by the Qilin's side as everyone else scrambled to do their part. She was about to suggest they move closer to Amelia and Svena in case a fight broke out—with those two, it was always a possibility—when she spotted Bob walking toward them

As always, seeing her eldest brother put her on high alert. Even when they'd worked together under Bethesda, she'd long considered the Seer of the Heartstrikers to be her most dangerous enemy. For all Julius's assurances, Chelsie still wasn't sure that was no longer the case as Brohomir stopped in front of her.

"I hope I'm not interrupting family time," he said brightly, giving them both a dazzling smile before turning to the Qilin. "You have a phone call."

Xian looked rightfully suspicious. "But I don't have a phone."

"That's all right," Bob said. "I do, and it should be ringing right... about... *now*."

Sure enough, something in his pocket began to jangle, and Chelsie rolled her eyes as he pulled out his ancient, battered, brick-shaped Nokia. Bob's phone was so old, it didn't even have augmented reality. It didn't even have a *touch screen*. He texted using the buttons like a savage. But for all its shortcomings, the antique apparently still worked as a phone, because when Bob hit the button to accept the call, the male dragon voice on the other end came through clear, loud, and angry.

"One moment," Bob said into the speaker before holding out the phone to the Qilin. "It's for you. A very pleasant fellow named Lao."

The emperor's golden eyes went wide, and then he grabbed the phone from Bob, clutching it to his ear as he began speaking rapidly in Chinese. His cousin replied in kind, his angry voice rapidly transforming into one of great relief as he finally talked to his emperor again.

"How did Lao get *your* number?" Chelsie asked as Xian stepped away to conduct his call in private.

"I gave it to the Empress Mother," Bob said flippantly, as though that were a perfectly normal thing to do. "He probably got it from her."

Chelsie clenched her fists. For a moment, the urge to gut her brother was back strong as ever. But then, as if he could feel her anger building, Julius shot her a worried look from where he was standing beside Amelia on the other side of the dirt yard, and Chelsie forced herself to let it go.

"For the sake of family harmony, I'm not even going to ask what kind of treason you and Fenghuang were cooking up together."

Bob shrugged. "It was a mutual sort. She was as much my pawn as I was hers. But that's water under the bridge now, and you know I never look at the past."

"Because you can't stomach it?" Chelsie asked, giving him a cold look. "I couldn't either, if I'd done what you've done."

"If I spent as much time wallowing in the past as you do, my tolerance would be low too," Bob shot back, and then he sighed. "Let's not quarrel, Chelsie. Julius wants us to be friends."

"Julius wants everyone to be friends," she snapped, getting a tighter hold on her daughter, who was desperately trying to get to Bob. "He should get used to disappointment."

"He's very used to disappointment," Bob said, grinning at the baby dragon. "He just refuses to expect it. That's what makes him stronger than the rest of us."

He held out his arms, and Chelsie sighed, releasing her grip on the whelp, who immediately leaped at her uncle.

"There's my favorite girl!" Bob said, throwing the child high into the air before catching her one handed. "You really should name her."

"She's had a name for years," Chelsie said as Bob tossed her again.

"Really?" He looked genuinely surprised. "I never saw that." He smiled at the little girl. "I hope it's something grand. Seers need grand names, or we just end up labeled by our epithets. Look at poor Estella. She had a perfectly lovely name, but it was too normal, so everyone just called her 'The Northern Star,' including her. Do you know how awkward it is to get clandestine invitations from 'The Northern Star?' Not that I got many of those once she realized I'd never be her pawn."

Chelsie rolled her eyes, "And *Brohomir* is better?"

"Much," Bob assured her. "No one ever calls me by common nouns and verbs. I am always myself, which is a lovely thing to be." He grinned at the little dragon, who was already snapping at him to make him hurry up with the next throw. "So what's her name?"

Chelsie reached out to shut her daughter's snapping mouth. The bad habit had to be trained out early, before her jaws got big enough to do real damage. "Felicity," she said as Bob tossed the little girl up again.

The seer looked so shocked, he nearly missed the catch. "An *F*?" he cried. "*Really?* Don't get me wrong, it's a lovely name, but if you were going to stick with Bethesda's system, you should have gone for an A."

"I didn't choose it because of Mother's stupid system," Chelsie snapped, grabbing her daughter back before Bob could toss her again.

"I wanted her to have a happy name. Maybe it will help her lead a happier life than the rest of us." She threw the whelp up into the air herself, launching her almost all the way to the top of Ghost's barrier as the little dragon squealed in delight. "Also, all of her siblings have F names, and I didn't want her to feel left out. Or for the others to feel I favored her over them."

"How thoughtful," Bob said, watching Chelsie toss the little dragon higher and higher. "You really are an exemplary mother. I should send you a card."

"Shut up."

"I'm serious," Bob said, and for once, he actually sounded it. "I didn't enjoy hurting you, Chelsie."

"Could have fooled me."

"I didn't," he said again. "I hated what I had to do, but it was the only way I saw to save you."

"At the beginning, maybe," Chelsie said bitterly. "But what about later? I can see sticking me under Bethesda's boot in a pinch, but that didn't make you leave me under it for *six hundred years*."

"That was the only way I saw to save the rest of us," Bob replied, his face falling. "I know you think I'm the villain, and from your point of view, I suppose I am. But everything I've done I did for our greater good. And for the record, I always meant to make it right. In the future I made for us, you spend ten thousand years as the golden apple of the Qilin's eye. Surely that's worth a few centuries of unpleasantness?"

Chelsie caught her daughter with a silent glare, setting the laughing whelp on the ground to catch her breath before turning to face her brother head on. "You don't get to tell me what our suffering is worth," she growled. "You weren't on Bethesda's chain with us. You weren't there at all. You were always off in the future, leaving those of us in the present to clean up your messes. Ten thousand years of happiness is the least you can offer for what you put us through, especially since it's not certain we'll live past tonight."

"The future is never certain," Bob agreed. "I was going to make it that way, but now that we're thirty minutes past my pre-marked expiration date, I'm afraid the future has changed too much for my guarantee to be good anymore."

Chelsie blinked. "What does that mean?"

"It means the one-in-multiple-billions future I was planning to trade all others for is gone, vanished into the streams of time with all the other timelines from before I convinced the Black Reach that killing me would be shooting himself in the foot. We're in a new world now, with new futures. Ones I don't know. But while most of those are very dark, I know we'll get through this."

"How?" Chelsie asked, arching an eyebrow. "Got another trick up your endless sleeves?"

"No," Bob said with a sad laugh. "I'm afraid my tricks and sleeves ended half an hour ago. Frankly, I'm still celebrating the fact I spotted Lao's phone call in time to make a cryptic comment and maintain my reputation."

Chelsie rolled her eyes. "Then how can you say you know anything?"

"Because Julius isn't the only one I needed to be himself," Bob said, smiling down at her. "Every dragon, spirit, and human in this yard is here because I wanted them to be. Not because I foresaw they'd be useful at any one specific time, but because I *knew* them. I know you too, Chelsie. A lesser seer, one with more limited vision, would have connived and blackmailed you to bring you to this point, but I didn't need such blunt tools. All I had to do was choose goals that aligned with your own, and you went after them all by yourself. That's what separates a good seer from a great one, and it's why I'm not worried now. I don't need to see the future to know that we *will* get through this. Because I see you, and if you can't do it, it can't be done."

That was the most sincere compliment Bob had ever given her. Maybe the *only* sincere compliment. But while Chelsie didn't doubt that her brother was telling the truth, something about what he'd said still didn't sit right. "If that's how you feel, why do you still have her?"

She nodded at the pigeon sitting on Bob's shoulder, and he raised his hand protectively, cupping his fingers gently around the bird's feathered head. "She's for me," he said quietly. "My ace in the hole, especially now that I no longer know exactly where all the holes are. The cost of her help will be painfully high now that we've moved past the future I'd picked out, but there may come a time when cost doesn't matter. Besides," he turned up his nose, "a consort never abandons his lady. What kind of dragon do you think I am?"

Chelsie had a lot of answers for that one. She was about to give him the full, blistering rundown when Xian suddenly came back, his gold eyes bright as he told them to make room. The Dragons of the Golden Empire were coming in for a landing.

• • •

Julius watched Bob and Chelsie's conversation with growing dread. It wasn't that he didn't like that they were finally talking—he was *ecstatic*—he just had no confidence it would stay that way. He knew firsthand how infuriating Bob could be, and the seer had only manipulated his life. He'd stomped on Chelsie's, and from the look on her face, she wasn't ready to let it go.

But fortunately, and *very* surprisingly, Bob didn't seem to be antagonizing her. He actually looked sincere, almost apologetic. Not that he would ever *actually* apologize—he was too much of a dragon for that—but it was a marked detour from his normal behavior. Julius wasn't sure if that was because the seer was off his script now or if Bob really did feel bad about what he'd put Chelsie and her children through, but whatever the reason, he was glad of it. One of his biggest motivations for agreeing to take over his clan was the chance to end Bethesda's culture of violence, something that would be a lot easier if members of his family would stop trying to kill each other. He didn't think they were there quite yet, but talking instead of hitting was definitely a step in the right direction. He just wished everything else were going as well.

At that, Julius's attention jumped back to the other source of his anxiety: Marci. She was standing beside Ghost in the ruins of their house. They were too far away for him to hear what they were saying, but Marci looked upset, which, of course, upset him. He wanted to go over and ask what was wrong, but he didn't want to hover or make her think he didn't trust her to do her job. She was the Merlin. He'd seen her do the impossible more than anyone else here, but that didn't stop him from worrying. The stakes were just so high, and there were so many things that could go wrong on every front.

For example, Fredrick wasn't back yet. Julius presumed he was still in DC, talking to Conrad, Justin, and the others, but he could be facing off against Bethesda for all Julius knew. Not that he could do anything about that if it was true, but the combined stress was enough to make a dragon crazy. Especially since the one part of the plan to stop the Leviathan that Julius *was* actually involved with wasn't currently going anywhere.

Since he couldn't actually help Marci with spirit stuff, Julius had volunteered to help Amelia and Svena bring in the other dragon clans. Seeing as they'd already agreed to work together, he'd assumed they'd get right to the portal making or magic circles or whatever it was they did. But other than moving to a relatively flat portion of Julius's dirt yard, neither Amelia nor Svena had done anything except stand around staring at each other like enemies on the field of combat. No one had actually attacked yet, but they'd been at it for a good ten minutes now, and with the Leviathan growing more solid by the second, Julius wasn't sure how much more they—or he—could take.

"Should we do something?" he whispered to Katya, who was standing next to him with Svena's fluffy whelps clinging to every limb.

"Nothing we can do," the dragoness whispered back. "They always do this. Don't worry, though. With mouths and egos as big as theirs, the silence won't last much longer. Just let them posture. One of them will crack soon enough. You'll see."

Neither of the two dragon mages looked anywhere near cracking to him, but Katya had more experience with Svena and Amelia's unique dynamic than Julius did, so he kept waiting, hopping nervously from foot to foot until, when he was close to cracking himself from the stress, Amelia finally spoke.

"Let's hear it," she drawled, cocking her head at Svena. "How does this super teleportation spell of yours work?"

"That is classified information," Svena said. "This spell is a treasure of our clan, the work of centuries. The fact that I've agreed to use it for you is sacrifice enough. I'm not going to hold your hand and guide you through the casting as well."

Amelia glowered. "You know I could just look through your fire and find out for myself, right?"

"You could *try*," Svena said. "But you've never understood half my spells. What makes you think you can grasp the workings of my greatest masterpiece?" Her smirk turned cruel. "Also, before you go rooting through my private thoughts like a pig, remember that street goes both ways. You step where you are not welcome, and I'll shove memories at you that you can't unsee. I have some *very* interesting recollections of events in our youth that you were too drunk to recall, not to mention images of Ian that a sister would never want to—"

"Okay, okay," Amelia said, putting up her hands. "No need to drag out the nuclear ordnance. I was only curious."

"I think the word you're looking for is 'greedy,'" Svena replied with a huff. "Just because you're the Spirit of Dragons doesn't mean all our treasures are yours. If you come for me, I will fight you, and when my opponent is a self-styled god, I see no reason to fight fair."

"You've never fought fair," Amelia grumbled. "But fine, whatever, do it your way. So long as the teleporting gets done, I don't care if you make the circle out of orphan hearts."

Svena looked confused. "What are you talking about? The hearts of children without parents are no more magical than the hearts of any other child, which is to say not very magical at all. You know perfectly well that humans are a vastly inferior source for—"

"For the love of—it was a *joke*," Amelia groaned. "Just cast your spell before Julius has a conniption."

Both dragons looked at Julius, who blushed. He hadn't realized his nerves were showing that badly, but since he had their attention... "We *are* in a hurry. So please, if you wouldn't mind..."

"I don't mind at all," Svena said, walking into the large, clear patch of dirt beside the crater Bob had made when he'd come in. "Amelia's the one wasting time digging for other dragons' treasure. Greedy snake."

Amelia could only shrug at that one, but Svena wasn't looking at her anymore. Her ice-blue eyes were fixed on the ground as she carefully paced off a length of dirt between the wall of cracked on-ramps and the broken house. When she'd walked out a circle that was roughly forty feet in diameter, she held out her hand.

"Katya."

Katya sighed and began plucking the fluffy white baby dragons off her body. "Can you hold them for a moment?"

Before Julius could answer, Katya shoved the entire clutch at him. He was still struggling to keep the squirming whelps from hitting the ground when Katya ran over to take position on the opposite side of the circle from her sister, biting her lip nervously as she held out her hands. She'd barely gotten them up before Svena stomped over and started correcting her form, smacking the younger dragoness's limbs until they were in positions that—to Julius at least—looked only marginally differ-ent from how they'd been at the start. It must have been a critical mar-gin, though, because Svena nodded and walked back to her spot, raising her own arms in a graceful arc until they were a mirror image of Katya's.

"Just like we do at home," Svena said, breathing out a long plume of ice-pale smoke. "Now."

The word was barely out of her mouth when both dragonesses brought their hands down, and the circle Svena had made in the dirt with her footsteps exploded in blue-white fire. The blast that rolled off it hit Julius like a bucket of frozen seawater, and he wasn't the only one. The ghostly flames lowered the temperature of the entire cavern by a good twenty degrees, making everyone except Ghost shudder. Lacy frost was creeping across the ground in curls when Katya stepped back to cede the ignited circle to her sister, who looked smugger than Julius had ever seen her.

"And *that* is how it's done," Svena said, casting a superior look at Amelia, who was openly gaping. "With a proper magical education and attention to form and detail, even a fire-deaf dragon like Katya can assist in creating masterpieces. You would do well to take note, Planeswalker." She turned back to the circular inferno of freezing flames in front of her. "Now that the initial base is ignited, all I need is a name and a loca-tion to grab any dragon from anywhere on this plane, *including* from behind wards."

Amelia looked impressed despite herself. "For real? Wards too? So you can just grab anyone at any time?"

"It would hardly be useful otherwise," Svena said proudly, her blue eyes brighter than ever as they reflected the dancing flames. "This is the greatest work of my clan. I was the primary architect, but we all did our share, and that cooperation is reflected in its power. It is an unbeatable strategic weapon, a spell capable of grabbing any dragon, anywhere. The only one we could never get was Brohomir, but only because he always saw it coming and moved."

"And me," Katya said, walking over to take the whelps back from Julius. "It's written into the base magic of the spell that members of our own clan can only be teleported if we're willing. That was the price of my help. Otherwise, Estella would have ripped me back home every time I escaped."

"There are a *few* limitations," Svena admitted grudgingly. "It takes at least two of us to make the initial circle, and I have to be one. It's also enormously draining. Given that I just laid a clutch of eggs, I shouldn't have been able to make it work at all, but there's so much free-floating magic around right now, I don't have to worry about collapse, which makes things much easier. Also, Amelia's connection to our fire might have given Katya and me a tiny boost, which pushed us over the edge."

"Right," Amelia said, rolling her eyes. "So what you're saying is your amazing treasure spell is a giant pain in the butt that you're only able to cast because I'm helping you."

"I could cast it any time I liked!" Svena snapped back. "It would just require a few months of set up. With proper planning, though, it is an unstoppable weapon!"

"Then why'd you never use it?" Amelia asked, crossing her arms over her chest.

"Because once we did, everyone would know we had it," Katya explained. "If the other clans knew we could grab any of them at any time, they would unite against us. We'd be enemy number one for the entire world, and even we couldn't stand against that."

Svena scowled at her sister while Amelia began to howl. "Some super weapon! You can't even use it without putting a target on your own clan!"

"Which is exactly why I did not wish to reveal it *now*," Svena growled. "There will be no putting it back in the bag after this, but it's too late to turn back." She looked pointedly over her shoulder at the Qilin's arriving dragons, who were so busy gawking at the ring of blue-white fire, they almost missed their landing. "The whole world will know soon enough, so we might as well make it count." She glanced at Amelia. "Whom am I grabbing first?"

"Whoa, whoa, whoa," Amelia said, putting up her hands. "You can't just start plucking dragons out of their strongholds! All we'll get is a bunch of terrified, angry lizards, which is more harm than good. We gotta warm them up before we bring them in."

"And how do you propose to do that?" Svena asked snidely. "Send them a letter?"

Amelia's lips curled in a smirk of her own. "Not quite."

She stepped up to the edge of the flaming blue circle, and her body began to flicker, her edges rippling in the cold wind coming off Svena's roaring magic like a candle flame. Then, in a wink, she was gone entirely, replaced by the same dragon made of fire Julius had seen when she'd first come back from the dead. He was still gawking at her flaming wings when Amelia's voice boomed through his fire, filling his head with the burning bite of her magical teeth.

Hear me, serpents of the Earth, she said, the words throbbing like a physical force inside his chest. *Your new god speaks! I am Amelia the Planeswalker, the Spirit of Dragons. As you've all felt since last night, our racial fire is now connected to the magic of this world. No longer are we wanderers, refugees in a foreign land. With my life, I have won us a new home, but you must fight to keep it. The Lady of the Lakes has sold us to a Nameless End, a force of absolute destruction from beyond our plane. To avoid extinction, we must dig deep into the magic of our new world and come together as one force against our common foe.*

That sounded pretty inspiring to Julius, but Amelia wasn't finished. *This is not a request,* the Spirit of Dragons boomed, her magic gripping his flames like a fist. *If you refuse to fight, then you are not worthy of our new power. Just as I connected all of you to the magic that is now flooding this world, I will cut you off, leaving you a fireless worm. You will be even lower than we sank during the drought, while those around you who answered my call will be bathed in my power. If you do not wish this to be your fate, accept Svena the White Witch's hand when she reaches for you, and she will bring you to me. Once we are all assembled, I will explain how we will beat back this invader and defend our new home.*

She finished with a flourish, cutting off with a jab so sharp, every dragon in the yard coughed out a puff of smoke. Even Svena's squirming whelps went still, their blue eyes wide as they stared in awe at Amelia, who looked incredibly pleased with herself.

"Little overdramatic, don't you think?" Svena said, glaring up at the dragon spirit.

"What's the point of being a god if you can't be dramatic?" Amelia said, fluffing her flaming feathers. "And you can't deny the results. My head is already full of voices. They're falling over themselves to volunteer!"

"You can't call that 'volunteering,'" Julius said. "You threatened to take away their fire if they didn't obey! That's extortion."

Amelia laughed out loud. "Sorry, Baby-J! If you want dragons *now*, this is how we get them. But feel free to apologize for my rudeness when they arrive if it'll make you feel better."

"I'm not going to apologize," Julius grumbled. "I'm just saying you didn't have to go for the throat right out of the gate."

"Spoken like a true Nice Dragon," Svena said, sharing an eye roll with Amelia before turning back to her freezing circle. "Once again, whom am I pulling in first?"

Amelia's flaming eyes moved rapidly, searching through the empty air as though she were studying something very complicated that no one else could see. "Let's start with Fading Smoke, the Dragon of Gibraltar. He's raring to go."

"You mean old Arkniss?" Svena wrinkled her nose. "You really did get everyone."

"Beggars can't be choosers," Amelia said. "And we're going to need every dragon we can get."

As though he'd been waiting for his cue, the Leviathan chose that moment to send a tentacle straight over the hole Bob's crash had punched in the Skyways. Watching it go past was like having an ocean liner sail over their heads. Even Amelia's fire dimmed slightly when the shadow crossed her. When it was gone, both dragons turned back to the teleport circle with new urgency.

"Getting Fading Smoke now," Svena said quietly, her pale face tight in concentration. "Make room."

Julius didn't realize that last part was for him until the dragon came flying out of the freezing flames. He was impressively big, a heavyset European dragon with thick armored black-and-green scales, amber eyes, leathery wings, and a mouth full of shining teeth and black smoke. He landed with a crash in the dirt right on top of where Julius and Katya had been standing before they'd managed to jump out of the way, and the moment his claws touched the ground, he started yelling.

"*What is the meaning of this?*" the old dragon roared. "Planeswalker! How did you..."

His booming voice trailed off as he looked around at the cavern, which was now *very* crowded. The ruins of Julius's house were completely overrun with the Golden Emperor's dragons. The Qilin was still in human form, probably because his giant golden dragon wouldn't have fit inside the cavern, but it was still unquestionably him. Likewise, Svena's identity was obvious, and Amelia was a giant dragon made of fire. Even to Julius, who was used to sudden gatherings of powerful dragons, it was an impressive sight. For a newcomer like Fading Smoke, it was enough to render him speechless.

"I see you weren't exaggerating," he said, much more calmly this time as his reptilian eyes rolled up to take in the Leviathan filling the sky overhead. "I will tell my sons to follow at once. Who is in charge?"

The Planeswalker pointed a burning claw at Julius. "He is."

Julius and the giant dragon exchanged a look of mutual disbelief. When they turned back to Amelia, though, she was already calling out their next target to Svena, who yelled at both Fading Smoke and Julius to move. They obeyed at once, pressing themselves into the wall as Svena brought the next dragon through, this one in human form but looking no less upset than Fading Smoke had been. She also started by demanding to know what was the meaning of this and who was in charge, only to fade off when she saw the army of dragons and the monster in the sky.

She was still staring at it when Fading Smoke hooked her shoulder and pulled her over.

"They say he's the leader," he growled, nodding at Julius when the new dragoness—whose human form was tall, dark skinned, and incredibly striking—smacked his claw away. "But who is he?"

Both dragons looked at Julius then. Fortunately, being stared down at by bigger monsters was something he'd a lot of experience with at this point, and he managed to stare back without flinching. "I'm Julius Heartstriker, and I promise I'll explain once everyone is here. Meanwhile, please change into your human forms and go wait with the Qilin. We have a lot more dragons coming, and there won't be room below the barrier if everyone's their true size."

He pointed at Ghost's barrier, which was still protecting them from the thinning—but still present—magic. Fortunately, that plus the Qilin plus the monster overhead was a combination that worked miracles. Despite the painfully obvious fact that Julius was by far the smallest and weakest dragon here, neither of the newcomers questioned his request. They simply nodded and shuffled over to pay their respects to the Golden Emperor, leaving Julius alone beside the portal to greet the next confused, angry dragon who came barreling through Svena's ring of freezing fire.

CHAPTER SEVEN

Even with dragons rapidly filling the urban cave that sheltered their broken house, the Empty Wind towered over everything. Over the course of what had happened with Bob and the rest, he'd expanded his barrier to cover the entire cavern. His shadowy form had grown with it, leaving him so tall, he could easily touch the top of the spiraling underpasses. That was actually where his hand was now, the giant palm pressed flat against the same spot in the roof where the hole to the Sea of Magic had been inside Marci's death. Considering what she was here to ask, the coincidence made Marci shiver, drawing her spirit's attention as he appeared beside her.

"Whoa," Marci said, hopping back as Ghost—in a new but still completely solid and real-looking body—materialized next to her. "Nice," she said, looking back and forth between the towering giant and the regular-sized Empty Wind at her side. "So can you just multiply yourself now?"

"I've always been able to do this," the Empty Wind replied, his glowing eyes glancing up at the massive version of him. "I just never had the magic to waste on it before. I have so much power now, though, I can divide myself however I like."

To prove it, a ghostly cat appeared in the Empty Wind's arms, his glowing blue eyes smug as he flicked his tail at Marci. Amazed, Marci held out her hands, and the cat jumped over to her, purring deep in his transparent chest as she petted his soft, freezing head. "This is *so* weird."

"The word you are looking for is 'useful,'" the Empty Wind said as the larger version of himself above adjusted his grip. "I can do many useful things now. Things I haven't been able to do in a thousand years." He closed his eyes. "I feel whole again."

Just like back in the kitchen, Marci felt his happiness vibrating down their connection like a plucked string. Beautiful as it was, though, they had no time to bask in the glow. "I'm really happy for you," she said. "But if you've sobered up from your magic binge, we need to talk strategy. Myron and I have cooked up a plan to banish the Leviathan, but I need to get back to the Sea of Magic to do it. Can you just take me there now that you're all souped up? You know, open a portal or something?"

She finished with a hopeful smile, but though she couldn't see the Empty Wind's face inside the shadows of his helmet, she could *feel* him frowning.

"No."

"Why not?" Marci demanded. "The DFZ can take Myron any time he wants. Look, she's doing it now."

Sure enough, Myron had finished his discussion with the general and Raven and was now talking to the DFZ, who still looked a little loopy. A few moments later, the city spirit nodded and grabbed his hand. The moment she touched him, his body fell unconscious to the ground beside a closing manhole that hadn't been there a second ago.

"See?" Marci said, turning back to Ghost. "I'm not generally a fan of leaving my mortal shell just lying around, but that's pretty convenient. Why can't we do that?"

"Because I'm not her," Ghost said irritably. "This entire city is DFZ's domain. So long as Myron is inside her borders, it's easy for her to pass his soul back and forth across the barrier, but I have no such physical domain. My realm is the Forgotten Dead. I had to cheat to get you through before since, though you were dead, you were not forgotten. Now you're neither, and that means I cannot pull you through."

"What about that thing you did before?" Marci asked. "Remember back in Reclamation Land when you yanked me inside the black-and-white world where I was a spirit voice and you were real? That was inside your domain, right?"

"I took you inside my *magic*," Ghost corrected. "But while I was able to hide you as I hide myself on this side, you were still in your physical body, and physical objects cannot enter the Sea of Magic. To get you across safely, I have to separate your soul from your body. If I had a physical domain like the DFZ does, it wouldn't be a problem, because we are gods within our own spheres. But the Forgotten Dead isn't a place like a city. There's nowhere your physical body can go that is totally within my purview, and without that absolute level of godly control, I don't know how to separate your magic from your body without killing you."

Marci swore under her breath, squeezing the cat version of Ghost in her arms so hard he hissed. "Then we'll just have to find another way," she said stubbornly. "Because I'm not dying again. I've got a fantastic dragon boyfriend, a super-powered spirit, and Sir Myron Rollins as my Merlin understudy. I've never had so much to live for, and Raven already told me my return ticket wouldn't be stamped again. There *has* to be some other way to get there. The Heart of the World is basically the Merlins' central office. We're clearly meant to work there, and I can't be the first Merlin with a nonphysical concept as my spirit. There has to be another way in."

"I suppose you could become forgotten," the Empty Wind suggested. "That would give you a foot inside my domain without ending your life, though I'm not sure how you'd manage it."

He glanced over her shoulder at Julius, and Marci sighed. "Yeah, I don't think that's going to work." She frowned, biting her nails as she thought the problem through. "The living body is really what's at issue here. If we could manifest your domain somehow, figure out a way for me to physically walk into the Forgotten Dead, then you could pull me over just like the DFZ does for Myron, right?"

"I think so," Ghost said. "But I've never done anything like that, and I have no idea how I would. The closest thing I can think of are the temples humans built for me back when I was worshiped as a god. But that was long before the drought, and those places are all dust now. I don't think I could even find where they were anymore."

He finished with a helpless shrug, but Marci was staring at him in awe. "You were worshiped as a god? Like, with priests and stuff?"

"Occasionally," he said, shifting uncomfortably. "They were not kind forms of worship. I reveled in the power at the time, but you would not have liked them."

"You *are* a face of death," she said. "I can imagine things got kind of bloody. But that doesn't bother me. I've always known what you are. I'm just impressed at how much you can remember now."

"I remember everything," he said, his voice wondrous. "The more magic fills me, the more I can recall. I can remember events from thousands of years ago like they were yesterday, and I'm still uncovering more. It seems endless."

"You're the manifestation of humanity's fear of being forgotten," Marci said, nodding. "I imagine you're pretty old. But this is awesome! In all those memories, did you ever have another Merlin?"

"No," the Empty Wind said at once. "You are the first and only. That I know for certain."

"Crud," Marci muttered. Not that she wasn't flattered to be Ghost's first, but she'd *really* been hoping he'd had a previous Merlin so she could pick his brain and discover how her predecessor had made the jump to the Sea of Magic. Unfortunately, it looked as though she was going to have to forge her own path, but Ghost's comment about temples had gotten her thinking.

"You might not have a physical aspect to your domain, but the Forgotten Dead *do* have places. The whole reason you rose in the DFZ is because this city was packed with forgotten corners where people have died unnoticed. If we went to one of them, do you think you could take it over long enough for me to step inside?"

Ghost jerked back in horror. "You mean *create* Forgotten Dead?"

"No, no, no!" Marci said quickly. "I'm just saying that if we went somewhere where there happened to be a lot of Forgotten Dead, and you did your job by bringing them peace, then the whole place would be filled with your magic. I've seen the wind you can whip up when you take souls into yourself to carry to the other side. If we both happened to be standing in the same place when you did that a lot, do you think you could just, I don't know, scoop me up too?"

Her spirit thought long and hard. "I suppose it's possible," he said at last. "But—"

"Possible is good enough for me," Marci said, turning around. "Let's go! We're on a hard timer, and we've got a lot of city to cross. I'm just going to go tell Julius what we're up to real quick, and..."

She trailed off, her sneakers crunching to a stop on the frozen, muddy ground. Should she tell Julius? It certainly felt like the right thing to do, but he was still jumpy from her last temporary bout of death. If she told him she was going to the Sea of Magic again, even if she made it clear that dying wasn't part of the plan this time, he'd freak out, and Marci didn't want to do that to him right now. The cavern was already half full of dragons, and Amelia and Svena were still going full tilt. Everyone had switched to their human forms to save room in the suddenly cramped underpass, but Marci could still feel the predatory menace like a knife in the air. Julius was already looking harried as he struggled to wrangle the constant stream of new, angry dragons. The last thing he needed was for her to throw a bomb like this at him. Maybe... maybe it would be better if she just snuck out and explained it to him later.

That sounded like the kinder thing, but as Marci turned to slip around the back of the house, she ran face-first into something warm, solid, and smelling vaguely of smoke.

"Ow," she said, rubbing her nose. When she looked to see what she'd bumped into, though, confusion turned to anger. "Don't do that!" she snapped, glaring at Bob, who'd appeared from nowhere to block her way. "Shouldn't you be off groveling to all the family members you've wronged?"

"No one has that kind of time," Bob said flippantly. "And is that any way to talk to a wise dragon who's come to give you some advice?"

Marci had had more than enough of Bob's "advice," but it seemed stupid to ignore a seer, even a not-up-to-snuff one like Bob, so she waved for him to go ahead.

When she gave him the go-ahead, Bob leaned down to her eye level. It was almost certainly her imagination, but Marci could have sworn his expression softened as he whispered, "Don't leave without saying goodbye to Julius."

"Why?" Marci asked, breath stopping in her throat. "Is something going to happen to him?"

"Lots of things," Bob replied, straightening back up with a shrug. "But I'm not telling you this because I foresee disaster. To be honest, I haven't had a chance to look down your future yet. I just happened to spot you hesitating just now, and as a loving brother, I felt compelled to intervene. Maybe it will matter, maybe it won't, but you should say something to Julius in either case, because he'll be insufferable if you don't."

"It won't be that bad," Marci said, lowering her eyes. "He's busy. I don't want to put him off his game by making him worry."

"You didn't see him while you were gone," Bob said. "Trust me, there is *nothing* you could say to him right now that would upset him more than you vanishing without a word. Just go give him a hug or something. He'd love it, and this cavern could use a little positive energy."

He looked over his shoulder at the tense clusters of waiting dragons, but Marci still wasn't convinced. "Are you sure this is about Julius and not you?" she asked, crossing her arms over her chest. "Because every other time you've told me to do something for Julius, it's been for *your* plans."

"Julius *is* my plans," Bob snapped, his voice surprisingly angry. "How many times do I have to spell this out? Julius. Is. My. Lynchpin. He's the fixed point around which aaaaaaaaaaaall of this"—he waved his hand at the dragons, the spirits, the humans, and everything else that was packed into the cavern—"revolves. Without him, everything would fly apart, including me. You just saw that power in action with the Black Reach, so I don't think my sticking up for Julius's mental well-being is suspicious. I need him to be at his best now more than ever, and that doesn't happen when he's tearing out his hair in worry over *you*." The seer looked away with a huff. "Honestly. I'm starting to wonder which of us is actually his significant other."

Given the hell Bob had put Julius through, the urge to call him on his concerned-brother act was almost undeniable. The only reason Marci didn't was because he really did look upset. The seer was normally such a flake, it was hard to take anything he said seriously, but the anger in his eyes was real enough that Marci was willing to give him a pass, just this once. Also, it wasn't as if she'd wanted to sneak off without her kiss.

"All right," she said. "But just so we're clear, this butting-into-my-relationship thing is a one-off event. I've seen the damage your 'help' can do, and I'd rather take my chances with the blind future."

"A fair criticism," Bob said, reaching up to pet the pigeon that was roosting in his long hair. "Just be careful not to die. I don't know if I'll be able to swing another resurrection."

Marci frowned. "Do you foresee me dying?"

The seer turned away with a flippant wave. "Outlook hazy. Try again later."

Rolling her eyes, Marci hoisted her freezing cat—Ghost number two now that his normal-sized body had vanished back into the huge one holding up the barrier—and tromped out of the wreckage of their house toward Svena's frost-fire circle, where Julius was still directing newcomers.

• • •

Julius was starting to feel extremely overwhelmed.

Once they got rolling, Amelia and Svena summoned dragons at whirlwind speed. In the past twenty minutes, hundreds had come through the icy portal, leaving the dirt yard around his wrecked house packed. At this point, the artificial cavern below the on-ramps was even more crowded than the Heartstriker throne room had been during the vote. Unlike the crowd back home, however, these dragons were *not* all from the same family, and tensions in the cramped space were running high.

Those who could had separated themselves by clan. As promised, the Qilin's dragons—at least the ones he'd brought with him to New Mexico—had flown in on their own, sheltered from the magical fallout by Lao, who was apparently no slouch sorcerer. Those who'd stayed behind in China came in via Svena's portal, which meant the entire might of the Golden Empire was now on display, and taking up a good half of the available space. The only dragon missing was the Empress Mother, whom Julius had been informed was not welcome in this endeavor, which was perfectly fine with him. If he never saw the red-eyed old snake again, it would be too soon.

The other clans were less impressive but still formidable, especially since some of the smaller clan heads had refused to put on their human shapes amid so many enemies. Julius was trying to convince a particularly stubborn old dragoness that she would be much more comfortable in her human form, or any shape that didn't take up such a large amount of room, when he caught the beat of Marci's quick footsteps coming up behind him.

As always, the sound made his heart leap. He bowed out of his conversation as fast as he could and turned around just in time to smile at her as she came to a stop. "Everything okay?"

"No," she said, glancing at the blacked-out sky. "But nothing's more on fire than it was half an hour ago, which is all we can ask right now."

Julius couldn't argue with that. "Is your banishment plan still on track?"

"I think so," Marci said. "Myron's already gone to the Heart of the World to start repairing the containment circle. I'm leaving to join him right now."

Those words were enough to stop his heart. The last time Marci had gone to the Heart of the World, she'd died.

"Don't worry," she said before he could panic. "I'm taking a nonlethal route this time."

"Good," he said with a relieved breath, though nothing could stop his hands from shaking. "I won't keep you, then, but how long do you think it will take you and Myron to set up the banishment?" He looked over his shoulder at the packed cavern. "Everyone will be here soon, and I want to be able to tell them how long they'll need to fight."

Marci bit her lip. "I'm not sure. Myron's the only one of us who's worked with the Heart of the World's spellwork before, but we're talking about fixing a blowout in the most complicated spellwork assembly ever constructed. Even if he's just patching what's already there, I don't see how he could possibly manage it in less than four hours, and that's being really optimistic."

Julius looked away to hide his wince. Four hours was a lot to ask, especially since they didn't yet know what the Leviathan was capable of. For all he knew, they'd be lucky to last ten minutes.

"I'm sorry," Marci said, wringing her hands. "I know that's not what you wanted to hear, but—"

"It's fine," he said, forcing a smile. "I told you we'd hold him back, and we will. Four hours or forty, we'll buy you the time you need or die trying." Because if they couldn't, they were all dead anyway.

"Please don't say that," she begged. "We'll do this as fast as possible, I swear. Myron's one of the best mages in the world, and ancient spell-work is his area of expertise. If anyone can patch that hole in record time, he can."

"You don't have to reassure me," Julius said, smiling at her. "If you say it'll work, that's all I need. In the meantime, we'll do our part. We've got more firepower here than I've ever seen. We'll keep the Leviathan high and dry for as long as you need to bring that hammer down."

That was a ludicrously optimistic statement, but it was worth it to see Marci smile. "They should call you the Flatterer Dragon," she muttered, her cheeks flushing bright pink as she brushed her short hair behind her ear. "I just hope you're right. Even with this many dragons, you've a lot of ground to cover."

Julius shrugged. "All we need to do is blast tentacles out of the sky before they reach Algonquin's water, and if there's anything dragons are good at, it's blasting." He grinned. "Justin's going to have the time of his life."

"At least someone will be happy," she said, looking down at Ghost, who was somehow both a cat in her arms and a giant figure holding up the barrier over their heads. "I've got to go. We've got work to do on the other side, and Ghost and I still have to figure out how to get me over there without dying."

Julius's heart skipped several beats. "But you just said—"

"I know," Marci interrupted. "And I meant it. I am absolutely *not* dying again. I haven't entirely figured out how to do that yet, but there has to be a way. What's the point of being a Merlin if you can't get to your special clubhouse?"

"But—"

"I'll be *fine*," she said, reaching out to take his hands. "I've already got a great idea, but I need to get going if I'm going to pull it off in time."

"I know you will," Julius said, tightening his hands in hers. Then, because he could now, he pulled her into a hug. "You're the cleverest, hardest-working person I've ever met," he whispered into her hair. "You'll make it work, I know it."

Marci didn't reply. She did something much better. She hugged him back, squeezing his chest until his ribs creaked. Finally, after almost a full minute of holding him as tightly as she could, Marci let go reluctantly, looking up at him with the stubborn determination that had made him fall in love with her in the first place. "We're going to beat this."

"We are," he agreed, pressing a kiss to her forehead. "You'd better get going."

She nodded and turned to go. Then, suddenly, she darted back in again and rose up on her toes to kiss him on the lips. Julius was still reeling in surprise when she hurried off, waving over her shoulder as she jogged away. Dazed and happy, Julius waved back, watching her weave through the crowd of dragons with a painfully huge smile on his face. He was still grinning like an idiot when a wistful voice spoke right next to his ear.

"I'm never stealing her away from you, am I?"

Julius jumped and whirled around to see Amelia standing beside him, watching Marci's back with open envy. "It's *so* unfair," she muttered. "The First Merlin of the new age, in love with a dragon who can't even cast a spell." She shook her head. "Such a waste."

"*I* don't think it's a waste at all," Julius said, irritated. "What are you doing over here anyway? Aren't you supposed to be helping Svena?"

The Spirit of Dragons shrugged. "She said she didn't need me anymore. We've gotten pretty much everyone. The only dragons left are the ones she already knows, her family and allies and whatnot. Once she pulls those in, we're done."

"Done?" Julius looked around in confusion. "How can you be done? There are only a few hundred dragons here."

Amelia gave him a flat look. "Julius, how many dragons do you think there are?"

He opened his mouth to say thousands but stopped because he realized he didn't actually know. His mother had lectured them all their lives about the threat of the other clans, so he'd always assumed there must be a lot, but he'd never heard a hard number. To be fair, there *were* no hard numbers for the dragon population since most clans kept their true size secret to obscure the actual extent of their power, or lack thereof. He hadn't even known exactly how many Heartstrikers there were until they'd held the vote, but still, there *had* to be more dragons in the world than this.

"Sorry to burst your bubble," Amelia said when he told her as much. "But we're a species on the decline. A surprising number of us escaped through the portal to this plane, but the attrition since has been brutal. Between the clan wars and the infighting, dragons have been dropping like flies for the last ten centuries, and with the notable exception of Bethesda, we just don't breed fast enough to keep up."

"So this is it?" Julius said, looking at the crowd in the cavern, which now seemed pathetically small.

Amelia nodded. "It was a shock for me, too. I'd always suspected most clans were smaller than they pretended, but it wasn't until I plugged myself into everyone's fires that I realized just how bad the problem had gotten. Counting Svena's whelps, there are only five hundred and thirty-two dragons in the world right now, and most of them are already here."

Julius sucked in a worried breath. When he'd promised Marci they'd keep the Leviathan back, he'd assumed he'd be working with a much bigger force. What they had here didn't even look like enough to cover the DFZ and Lake St. Clair, let alone the five *actual* Great Lakes. But just as he was getting worked up, Julius realized he was being an idiot. He wasn't looking at all the dragons. There was still one major clan missing. One he'd never thought he'd miss.

"Where's Heartstriker?"

CHAPTER EIGHT

"**R**emember," Fredrick said, clutching his Fang in his hands as he looked around at his gathered brothers and sisters. "We only have one chance at this. Julius is depending on us to bring the clan. Whatever happens, we must uphold that, but we will not return as servants. Agreed?"

The others nodded, their newly revealed golden eyes resolute. It was a sight to behold. Before he'd left, Brohomir had pulled Fredrick aside and handed him an envelope containing step-by-step instructions in Amelia's hand for how to break Bethesda's green-eyed curse. It was the same spell the Planeswalker had cast on him, but while Fredrick was no mage, his brother Ferdinand was. He'd cut straight to him, and then they'd cut to each of their siblings in turn, breaking the curse as they went.

Being free of the last vestige of Bethesda's control over them felt as good as Fredrick had hoped, but he hadn't expected *all* his brothers and sisters to share the Qilin's eyes. In hindsight, though, Fredrick didn't know how it could have been otherwise. They were the children of the Golden Emperor, the most magical dragon to ever live, with a fire that had been carefully tended for hundreds of thousands of years. Of *course* his mark would be on all of them, even if his luck was not.

But Fredrick had no need for luck. With his siblings beside him and their real mother's Fang in his hands, he could make their future himself. This was just the first step, and Fredrick meant to step big, motioning for the others to take position behind him in the sterile, cement-brick underground hallway. When all his family was in place, Fredrick nodded at his sister Frieda, who was standing in front of the heavy steel doors at the hallway's end.

The moment his head moved, Frieda hauled back and kicked the doors open, knocking both off their hinges and clearing F-clutch's way into the bunker deep below the Heartstriker compound in the District of Columbia, where all the rest of the clan was waiting.

They were *all* there, too. Fredrick had known they would be. His new sword knew where every Heartstriker was, but it was still intimidating to see so many green eyes turn to look at him. Every Heartstriker in the family except for Bethesda and Ian—who were still at the mountain—and Julius, Amelia, Chelsie, and Bob—who were already in the DFZ—was packed into the warded bunker hidden below David's Washington, DC, mansion. Conrad himself was standing on the riser at the front, addressing the army of dragons he'd gathered to fight the Qilin's invasion.

The moment he had the clan champion in his sights, Fredrick started looking for the second most dangerous target, but the other knight of the Heartstrikers found them first, stepping out from behind the door Frieda had just kicked down with his Fang drawn and his teeth bared.

As always, Justin came out ready to fight. He stopped in surprise when he saw who it was, and then his mouth curled into a dismissive smile. "It's okay," he announced, lowering his sword. "It's just the Fs." He tilted his head at Fredrick and the others. "Where have you guys been? And what's wrong with your eyes?"

"Nothing," Fredrick said calmly as his siblings fanned out to form a wall behind him. "They've simply returned to their natural color."

That should have been the bomb drop of the night, but Justin didn't even seem to be listening. He was too busy gawking at the Fang of the Heartstriker in Fredrick's hand. "Where did you get that?" he demanded. "*Where's Julius?*"

"He's fine," Fredrick said, lifting the blade. "This isn't his sword. It's Chelsie's."

"I know that," Justin snapped. "You think I wouldn't recognize the sword that stabbed me in the back? I want to know why *you* have it, and why aren't you at Julius's side? You're supposed to be looking out for him! What are you doing here?"

"I would like to know that as well," Conrad rumbled. He jumped down off the riser, and the rest of the clan parted like water as the giant dragon made his way to the back of the room. "I ordered everyone to gather here two days ago so we could prepare to take our mountain back from the Golden Emperor. You were exempt since you were watching Julius, but the rest of your clutch is still part of the family. Like every Heartstriker, you were all expected to appear when summoned, but only Frieda showed up." The champion's hard green eyes narrowed. "If this is rebellion, Fredrick, you picked a bad time. I can't afford to be lenient when so much is at stake."

"It is not a rebellion," Fredrick replied, jaw clenching. "It's true we have little reason to love Heartstriker, but Julius risked his life to prove that we are all family, and him we will never betray. He is the reason we are here now. Julius asked me to bring you all to the DFZ so that you may fight for the clan against Algonquin's End."

"Is that it?" Justin said, chuckling. "If that was all you wanted, why'd you kick the door down?" He waved at the dragons behind him, whom Fredrick now realized were all fully equipped for battle. "We're already ready to roll. You didn't have to get all gangster about it."

"I didn't think you'd be so prepared," Fredrick admitted. "I'd heard nothing, so—"

"You didn't think we would cower from a fight, did you?" Justin said, insulted. "What do you think we've been doing here? Having a party? We've been prepping to take back Heartstriker Mountain for the last thirty-six hours! We were just about to head home and kick some golden butt when we heard Amelia's voice in our fires." His eyes dropped again to Fredrick's sword, and a grin spread over his face. "*Now* I get it. You're here to bring in the cavalry! Julius sent you here with Chelsie's dimensional can opener so you could ferry us to the DFZ, didn't he?"

"He did ask me to bring you, yes," Fredrick said, his voice growing hard. "But before I take you to join the others, my siblings and I have a requirement that must be met."

Angry whispers rose from the crowd of watching dragons, many of whom were looking at Fredrick in the way he knew all too well: the disdainful glare that said he was wasting their time. That he was lesser, not even a piece on their chessboards. Seeing it now made his jaw clench. That look was why he'd had Frieda kick down the door, and he would not leave again until he'd wiped it off every one of their faces.

"Heartstriker has treated my clutch as slaves from the moment we were born," he announced, his voice shaking with six centuries of suppressed fury. "Julius Heartstriker won us our freedom, but your thinking has not adapted. Now that I am one of the Fangs of the Heartstriker, I will not allow that to continue." He raised his sword for everyone to see. "Before I take you to the DFZ to join the fight, each of you must swear on your fire to treat my clutch the same as any other in the family from this point forward."

He'd waited all his life to say those words, but they were met with laughter. Some dragons looked merely amused, while others mocked him openly. Justin was rolling his eyes, but Conrad looked dangerously insulted, reaching for the large Fang lashed to his back with a look of cold malice.

"You dare waste our time with this?" the champion growled. "Amelia was very clear. *Every* dragon is needed to defeat this enemy. As the greatest clan in the world, we should be leading that charge."

"And our fires will be snuffed if we don't show up," added a dry voice as David pushed his way out of the crowd. "Amelia will do it, too. She's never cared about anyone except Bob, and she doesn't make empty threats."

Conrad nodded. "Time is already short. If we fail to answer the summons, not only do we risk our fires, we cede our place at the top. They will call us cowards!" He bared his sharp teeth. "You are gambling with our honor, and you dare to ask for our respect?"

"We are not asking for respect," Fredrick snarled, stepping forward to meet the tall knight eye to eye. "All we want is to be Heartstrikers, same as any other! I was just in the DFZ. I know *exactly* what is at stake, but I also know that the end of the world is the only thing big enough to make you stubborn snakes *listen*. If we Fs did our part and quietly obeyed, things would just go back to how they always were the moment the crisis passed. Now, though, you *must* listen to us, and that is why, before we go anywhere, I want a binding promise from each of you that

F-clutch will no longer be treated as servants, but given the same rights and deference granted to any other dragon in this family."

"Why should we give you anything?" Conrad demanded, crossing his massive arms over his massive chest. "You say you want to be equals, yet you come to us like enemies with threats and demands. But your blade is empty, eldest F."

"Quite," David agreed, holding up his sleek black phone. "We've been hearing about Svena's portal from other dragon clans for the last half hour, so if you were counting on playing the 'I'm your only way' card, that ship has sailed. We don't need you to get to the DFZ."

"You don't," Fredrick acknowledged. "But we don't need you, either."

He opened his hand, letting his Fang fall to the bunker's cement floor. The sword landed with a crash that made everyone flinch, even Conrad. But though it was still rocking loudly against the hard floor, Fredrick made no move to retrieve it.

"I picked up that sword for Chelsie's sake," he growled. "But that time is passed. We are happy to fight for a clan that accepts us, but if you can't promise that, then my siblings and I will leave Heartstriker."

"You can't do that," Justin snapped. "No one leaves the family unless they get kicked out."

"Try and stop us," Fredrick snarled back, drawing himself to his full height. "Can you not see what's standing in front of you? We are no longer sealed dragons. We're Fs, the largest of Heartstriker's remaining upper alphabet clutches! In the whole clan, there are only ten dragons older or bigger than we are. Nine if you don't count Amelia, whom I'm sure no longer considers herself a Heartstriker. But there are *twenty* of us, full-grown dragons ready to fight."

He blew out a line of smoke, letting Conrad see just how big he was beneath his human mask. And he was *big*. As the eldest son of the Qilin, Fredrick was well aware that he was much larger than he should have been given age alone. The rest of his clutch was the same, but none of them had had any idea of their true size because of the seal. Yet another thing Bethesda had stolen from them. That time was over, though. This was a new age, one where *they* had the power, and while the timing was unfortunate, Fredrick refused to let another minute pass without forcing the rest of the clan to acknowledge that.

"You are the Champion of the Heartstrikers," he said, tilting his head up slightly so he could glare at Conrad. "You value the power and prestige of the clan above all else. I'm sure you can find your way to the DFZ without my help, but do you want to? Because we have no end of places we can go as free dragons. If you want Heartstriker to remain the top clan in the world, though, you need us."

By the time he finished, Conrad was growling so loudly he was shaking the cement. It was a terrifying sound, because as big as Fredrick was, Conrad was bigger. Putting him on the spot like this was a dangerous gambit, but Fredrick and his siblings had all agreed they'd seize this chance with both hands or not at all, so despite the sweat trickling through his black hair, Fredrick held his ground. But then, just when the knight looked ready to call his bluff, David stepped in front of him.

"We'll take it."

Conrad jerked back, glaring down at his younger brother, but the draconic senator from New Mexico waved the look away. "Now's not the time to be inflexible, Conrad," he said, flashing Fredrick a smooth smile. "If you think about it, we're getting this for a song. Our clan has treated the Fs worse than humans for six centuries. Once they got unsealed, I was sure they'd be out for our blood, but apparently they've fallen into Julius's gravity just like all the rest of the upper alphabet, because they're not demanding retribution. They're not even asking for an apology. All they want is a binding promise that we'll treat them 'equally.' A promise I have no idea how they'll enforce since it's a proven fact that most Heartstrikers treat their siblings like dirt."

That comment drew a laugh from the crowd, and David's smile widened. "You want to be treated like normal Heartstrikers? Fine." He extended his hand to Fredrick. "I swear on my fire to treat you with the exact same callous disregard I give to every other sibling who hasn't proven themselves useful. And since I'm the highest-ranking Heartstriker present with the exception of Conrad and Justin, I *also* swear on my fire to make all of our lesser siblings do the same on pain of my displeasure.

That way we won't have to sit here and wait for you to squeeze a separate oath out of every single dragon while the world crumbles around us." The crowd laughed again, and David's green eyes twinkled. "That good enough for you, prince of the Fs?"

Fredrick didn't answer at once. He was too busy replaying David's words in his head, frantically looking for the hook or double cross he *knew* had to be there. For once, though, the most political Heartstriker seemed to be playing him straight. From the way he was bouncing on his feet, David actually looked even more eager to get to the fight than Justin, which was out of character enough to make Fredrick extra leery.

"Why are you in such a hurry?"

"Because I have a lot of plans in the air, and I'd rather the world didn't end before they came to fruition," David said. "I'm also chairman of the Senate Armed Services committee, and I've already pulled every string I have convincing the president to scramble all of our forces to the DFZ's defense. That's a lot of political capital wasted if I'm not there for the victory photo op."

Fredrick sighed. There was the David he knew. In a way, though, his blatant maneuvering for power was reassuring, because it meant he was serious. If David saw Fredrick and the others as the means to his ends, he'd keep his promise to the letter, and he'd force every Heartstriker below him to do the same. That was as much as Fredrick could hope for, and he found himself reaching out for the older dragon's hand.

"We'll take it," he said as they shook.

"As you should," David said, squeezing Fredrick's fingers painfully before looking over his shoulder at Conrad. "Your turn. Quickly now."

"I will swear nothing," Conrad snarled, looking down his nose at Fredrick. "Knights do not give in to threats. But I will give you my word that if you fly with us against the enemy, I will treat you all as Heartstrikers. Nothing less, nothing more."

"Yeah, what he said," Justin piped up, standing as tall as he could at his older brother's side. "Now can we get going? At this rate, Julius will probably trip over something and kill the Leviathan by accident before we even get there, the lucky bastard."

Fredrick glanced at his siblings. When they nodded their agreement, he turned back to the knights. "We accept."

"About time," Justin growled, drawing his sword. "Take us to Detroit!"

Fredrick nodded and bent down to pick up his sword. When his hand wrapped around the hilt, though, David placed his elegant Italian leather shoe on the blade. "Not with that," he said when Fredrick glared at him. "I know how Chelsie's blade works, and if we have to wait for you to ferry the whole clan over by twos, this will take forever. I have a much better idea."

Fredrick snatched his sword out from under the older dragon's foot with a growl. "What?"

David lifted his phone again with a smirk, dragging his fingers through the invisible AR interface before raising the speaker to his ear. "Mother?" he said when the call picked up, his smirk transforming into a full-on grin as he met Fredrick's eyes. "It's me. I've got them."

Fredrick didn't need to hear Bethesda's cackle on the other end. He was already wincing, sliding his sword back into its loop on his belt as he hoped against hope that he hadn't just made a terrible mistake.

• • •

Julius paced nervously back and forth beside his ruined front porch. A few feet away, Amelia, the Qilin, Svena, Arkniss, the infamous Marlin Drake, and all the other heads of the newly arrived clans stood in a loose circle. In a concession to the now-cramped space, all of the dragons had donned their human forms, which just made it easier to see the angry impatience on their faces as they waited for the one clan that had not yet arrived.

"Where are they?" Julius hissed, pacing faster. "What is Fredrick *doing*?"

"Relax," said Bob, who was sitting on the cracked porch step, eating an apple he'd found who knew where. "They'll be here before you know it."

Julius looked at him hopefully. "Did you foresee that?"

"No," Bob said, biting a chunk out of the fruit with his sharp teeth. "I've been too busy searching the future for an exit ramp to worry about nonessential details like arrival times. But Fredrick is loyal to you to an unhealthy degree. If he told you he'd bring them, he'll make it happen. In fact, I bet we'll hear something…" He paused, mouth moving silently like he was counting in his head. "Now."

Sure enough, Bob's brick of a phone began to vibrate in his hands. Grinning, he offered the device to Julius, who snatched it up, slamming the antique to his ear with a rush of relief. "Fredrick!"

"Not quite," replied a cruel female voice.

As always, the sound made his stomach clench, and Julius closed his eyes with a silent curse. "What are you doing, Mother?"

"That's my question," Bethesda replied idly. "Planning a war without telling me, Julius? That's not very democratic. Aren't you the one who's always going on about how we're an equal council and no one should make decisions on their own?"

"This was an emergency," Julius said sharply. "And I was trying to bring you in. Fredrick said he would—"

"Fredrick's done *quite* enough," Bethesda snapped. "Fortunately for you, David's already handled everything. But we'll discuss your pet F's almost-treason later. For now, be an obedient child for once and hand me to Amelia."

Julius almost dropped the phone. "*You* want to talk to *Amelia?*" He glanced at his oldest sister, who looked as shocked as he was. "You've got to be kidding."

"Less talking, more doing," Bethesda replied, snapping her fingers— or maybe her teeth—into the phone. Unsure what else to do, Julius handed Bob's phone to Amelia. She snatched it up with a bloodthirsty smile, bearing all her teeth as she said in her sweetest voice, "Hello, Mother, this is your new god speaking."

Julius wasn't above blatantly eavesdropping on this conversation, but even his sharp ears couldn't hear what Bethesda said in reply to that. As best he could tell, she'd ignored it entirely and was now rattling off instructions very quickly. Utterly unacceptable instructions if the look on Amelia's face was anything to go by.

"Have you gone senile?" Amelia snarled into the phone. "Why, in *any* world, would I lift a claw to help you?"

"Because it helps you as well," Bethesda said, her smug voice finally loud enough for Julius to hear. "A mother knows her children, and you've always been more greedy than vindictive. Too greedy to throw away your chance for a grand display of power *and* a fast solution to your problem just to spite me."

She must have hit the nail on the head, because Amelia swore in several languages before hanging up the phone and tossing it back at Bob, who caught it without looking. Julius was opening his mouth to ask what was going on when his sister suddenly turned to him. "Do you know what a hype man is?"

Julius stared at her in bewilderment. "You mean the guys who whip up crowds at concerts? Yeah, but what does that have to do with—"

"Great," Amelia said, reaching up to tie back her thick, wavy black hair. "Get in there and start hyping."

"Hyping what?" he said. "What's going to—"

"Not going," she said, pushing curious dragons out of the way as she cleared a large spot on the gravel drive. "Coming, and in hot." Amelia spread her hands. "You'll see in a second. Just go tell the other big shots that Heartstriker is here."

That was going to be a hard sell considering Heartstriker was most definitely *not* here. But if this whatever-it-was was big enough to convince Amelia to work with Bethesda, it was too big for Julius to fight, so he threw up his hands and did as she asked, jogging over to the circle of fed-up looking clan heads.

"What is taking so long?" Svena snapped when he got close. "What's the Heartstriker doing? Taking a nap?"

"They're on their way right now," Julius said, hoping that was true. "My whole clan should be here in just a—"

A surge of power cut him off. Behind him, Amelia's magic clenched like a snapping jaw. This was followed by a giant *whoosh* of air as the Planeswalker threw up her hands to tear a gaping hole in the air directly above her head.

The portal was enormous, a perfect rectangle that spanned the entire width of the shelter created by the spiraling on-ramps. It happened so fast, Julius didn't even get a look at what was on the other side before a feathered dragoness in golden armor swept through.

She was unspeakably beautiful. As large as Conrad with rainbow-colored plumage brighter than a bird of paradise's, Bethesda the Heartstriker was famous for a reason. Her colors were so vibrant, she seemed to glow in the dim light of the cavern, an illusion that was flawlessly enhanced by the gleaming golden battle armor covering her chest, claws, and neck. Armor that was clearly mostly for show since her glorious, long-feathered tail had been left completely exposed, but at least her head was protected by the diadem of her transformed Fang.

Unlike Julius's sword, which formed a bone-colored crown at the front of his head when he was a dragon, Bethesda's encircled the back, catching the enormous crest of feathers that fell like a waterfall down her neck. The result looked a bit like a hairpiece, or an evil queen's high collar. Either way, between the plumage, the gold, the crown, and her own impressive size, his mother looked every inch the feathered goddess she'd once been worshiped as. Even Julius, who'd seen her like this before, had his breath stolen as she folded her huge wings to land in the wreckage of his house, crushing the last standing pieces of his home flat as she wrapped her tail around her feet like a colorful, smug cat.

"You can all stop worrying," Bethesda announced in the shocked silence. "The Heartstriker has arrived!"

"After everyone else," Svena snapped, glaring up at the dazzling dragoness. "Is this why you're late? Needed time to fluff your plumage?"

"My plumage doesn't require fluffing," Bethesda said, running her claws over her glossy rainbow feathers. "Unlike you sad snowflakes, I *always* look this good. But that's not the tone you should be taking with your savior, White Witch."

"*Mother*," Julius hissed, "stop it."

"Why should I stop telling the truth?" Bethesda asked innocently. "Heartstriker is now officially the greatest clan in the world! No other family has ever united the clans as Julius has, and no dragon has ever produced a *god*." She nodded pointedly at Amelia, who shrugged as if she couldn't argue with that. "Add in the fact that we now control two of the world's three seers, and there's no denying that Heartstriker is on top in every way." Her brilliant green eyes slid over to the Qilin. "What was that your mother said? 'Breeding will tell?'"

"Mother!" Julius snarled, but as usual, Bethesda ignored him, turning her triangular head to gaze out at the crowd of dragons watching her like she was the center act of a three-ring circus.

"Who's the broodmare now?" she crowed triumphantly. "You've all looked down on me and my children, but we'll see how your tune changes when *my* clan—the largest dragon army ever assembled—swoops in to save all of your scales." She lifted her head to the portal. "*Justin!*"

The moment she bellowed her second knight's name, Amelia's portal flickered like a slide projector flipping images, and Justin hopped down in human form with his Fang in his hands. He'd scarcely landed before all of Heartstriker came through after him. Unlike Bethesda, they were all human—the space couldn't possibly have held them otherwise—but it was still an incredible sight. Even Julius, who'd seen his whole family gathered just a few days ago, had never witnessed them like this. Every Heartstriker was armed and ready to fight, their faces grim as they moved to stand in formation around Bethesda. Fredrick led his siblings out last, hopping down with his hand on the hilt of his sword as he led the Fs to Julius's side.

Conrad came out last, and then the portal flipped again to Ian, who jumped down from the ruins of Heartstriker's throne room without a word. Conrad met him at the bottom, eying the assembled dragons warily as he escorted the final Council member to Bethesda's side. When everyone was through, Amelia closed her portal with a flourish and returned to her place in the leader's circle. When Ian motioned for Julius to come join him in their mother's shadow, though, the youngest Heartstriker missed the signal due to the palm he'd pressed over his face.

It wasn't that he begrudged his mother her gloating. Bethesda had been the butt of the dragon world's bawdy jokes for centuries. As horrible as she was, Julius couldn't say his mother didn't deserve a moment of glory now that the clan she'd taken so much heat for breeding was one-fourth of the world's entire dragon population. He did, however, wish she'd been more tactful about it. Lording victories over your enemies was one thing, but they were supposed to be coming together as allies, and the looks the other dragons were shooting her definitely didn't trend in that direction. Even the Qilin looked pissed, a very bad turn since Julius had been secretly counting on his continued good luck to help them do the impossible. He was trying to think of a way to stop his mother before she blew everything up in his face when she hopped off the house, transforming in midair to land beside him in a puff of bitter smoke and clattering of gold.

"There," she said, casting off her now comically oversized armor to reveal the equally glittery, human-sized gold mesh dress hidden beneath. "*Now* we can begin." She stuck her now sword-shaped Fang of the Heartstriker into the gold chain at her waist and turned to Julius. "What's the plan?"

"Why are you asking me?"

The question popped out before Julius realized how silly it was. He'd been at the center of this thing from the start, of course he'd be the logical person to question. But as much sense as it made… his mother *never* asked him for advice or input. She hardly spoke to him unless it was an order or an insult. To have her staring at him now like she expected competence threw Julius seriously off his game. Fortunately—or perhaps unfortunately—Amelia was there to back him up.

"Because you're the poor chump in the middle, Baby-J," the Planeswalker said, wrapping her arm around his shoulders. "I tie the dragons together, but you're the one with his claws in everything. The Merlins, the UN, the spirits, us—we're all here because of you. Also, your human's the one who came up with this plan, so unless you want to cede Marci to me—which I'd be *totally* cool with, by the way—that makes all of this your responsibility."

The gathered dragons nodded as though that were the only logical explanation, and Julius slumped in defeat. He didn't even bother trying to explain that Marci wasn't his human, because that never worked, and he didn't feel like wasting his breath again. Time and dragon attention spans were too short as it was, so since everyone was looking at him now anyway, Julius launched into a carefully pared-down explanation of their situation and the plan to fix it that he'd been rehearsing in his head since Marci left. He thought he had a pretty good wrap-up of everything, but by the time he was through, the dragons looked angrier than ever.

"Let me make sure I've got this straight," said Arkniss, who looked even more treacherous in his human form than his black-scaled dragon had been. "Algonquin got duped into screwing us all over, and now you want us to clean up her mess?"

"Yes," Julius said, nodding. "Because we'll all die if we don't."

"How like a spirit," the old dragon muttered, blowing out a line of acrid smoke. "And we're going to be working together with the Phoenix?" When Julius nodded again, Arkniss glanced over at General Jackson, who'd set up camp in the corner by Myron's unconscious body. "Strange bedfellows, indeed. But then, you Heartstrikers never were discriminating."

"What was that?" Bethesda asked, cupping a hand to her ear. "I couldn't hear you over the sound of my children saving your piebald hide."

"Considering some of those children are mine, I think I have a right to complain," Arkniss snapped. Then he gave her a smile. "Though I always did like your sharp tongue."

Julius's face went scarlet as his mother blew the black dragon a kiss, and Amelia rolled her eyes. "Can we save the inappropriate innuendo until after we get out of mortal peril?" she groaned. "If we have to wait around for all the 'your mom' jokes, the Leviathan's going to eat us before we get off the ground."

"I agree," said Marlin Drake, stepping forward, which made Julius step back.

It was a silly reaction. As leader of the clanless dragons, Marlin Drake had no family magic of his own. He was merely the head of a coalition of outcasts, most of whom had only banded together to keep stronger clans from hunting them down. The other dragons in the circle were far more powerful, but while Drake's pedigree was technically the lowest, he was still the most famous individual Julius had ever met in person.

As the first dragon to go public after the return of magic, Marlin Drake had rocketed to worldwide fame with countless movies and television shows. Sixty years later, he commanded his own media empire, running three major networks in addition to hosting what was still the world's highest-rated weekly talk show. Bethesda watched religiously and had been a regular guest on the program for decades. Even Julius, who tried his best to stay out of politics—draconic or human—had seen more episodes of *Saturday Night With Marlin Drake* than he liked to admit. But despite his mother's patronage, he'd never actually met the ludicrously famous First Dragon in Television. That made seeing him now surprisingly intimidating since Drake was even more charismatic in the flesh than he was on his show, a feat that didn't seem physically possible.

"It's Julius, right?" the handsome dragon said, holding out his hand with a well-timed toss of his television-perfect blond hair. "With a J?"

"I don't know what else you'd spell it with," Julius said nervously. "But I—"

"How wonderful to meet you," Drake interrupted, grabbing Julius's hand and shaking it vigorously. "And nice work bagging the first Merlin, by the way. You must have a serious eye for talent."

Julius's face began to heat. "I—"

"I'd love to have her on my show when this is over," Drake went on. "And you as well, since you're the point man on all this. Speaking of, how long do you think it'll be before your girl lands her banish? I've got a full helicopter camera crew ready to capture the whole thing for my exclusive report, but they're grounded at the moment due to magical interference, and I'd hate for them to miss the action."

"There's nothing for your humans to miss, you vain idiot," Svena snapped, stabbing her finger up at the towering, shadowy form of Ghost, who was still holding the barrier for them even though Marci was gone. "*No one* can fly right now, thanks to this mess. If it doesn't clear soon, we'll still be down here clicking our scales when Algonquin's End kills us all!"

"It'd better hurry up," Bethesda said irritably. "What's the good of gathering everyone together if we can't set a claw outside this dirt pit without getting crushed?" She looked down at the half-frozen mud coating her golden boots before turning her sneer on Julius. "Why did you live here again?"

Because she'd made him, and because it kept him away from her. "It was a good base," he said instead. "It still is." He nodded at the crowd of dragons surrounding them, none of whom were even pretending not to be listening. "We have every dragon in the world here now, and the Leviathan still hasn't noticed us. I think that's pretty impressive."

"Or telling," said She Who Sees, the dark-skinned dragoness whose extended family claimed most of the African continent. "He could be ignoring us because he knows we're not a threat." Her sharp black eyes flicked to Julius. "You said that thing was from beyond our plane. Are you sure we can fight it?"

"Actually, the bigger it gets, the more effective we become," Amelia said authoritatively. "Normally, the Leviathan *would* be outside of our ability to hurt physically. We've all tangled with it before in various scuffles over the DFZ, so I'm sure we all remember just how impossible those shadow tentacles were to fight. Now, though, it's using Algonquin's magic to shove itself into our plane. That means the Leviathan is covered in spirit magic, and we all know how well spirits burn."

The other dragons smirked appreciatively at that, and Julius let out a breath in silent thanks that Marci wasn't here. "The point is, we *can* damage it," he said. "Maybe not enough to defeat it, but that's not our job. All we have to do is keep the Nameless End from sucking up the last of Algonquin's water for the few hours it will take Marci to prepare her banishment."

"A few hours is a long time to fight something we cannot defeat," the Qilin said warily. "Especially when we cannot even take off yet." He lifted his golden head to the hole in the roof where the black tentacles were moving faster than ever. "It's gorging itself on her magic as we speak. By the time we can fly, it might already be too late."

"We can make it," Julius said forcefully. "All the spirits and mages have assured me that the magical fallout is dropping, and there's a *lot* of Algonquin left to drink. It doesn't matter if we only stop him from getting one bucket's worth of her water. So long as we keep that last gallon safe, the Nameless End can't fully take over Algonquin, and we still have a shot."

He hoped, anyway. This was Marci's plan, and he trusted her with his life, but even as he sold her strategy to the others, something about it still didn't sit right with Julius. No matter which way you cut the problem, Algonquin was always the one at the heart of it, and yet she was the one factor everyone seemed happy to ignore. Even Marci's solution was only to banish her magic. It didn't touch on the spirit herself. Considering Algonquin's despair was the cause of this entire crisis, that felt like a mistake. But while Julius was torn, none of the other dragons suffered his misgivings.

"Well, *I'm* looking forward to it," Svena said with a proud lift of her chin. "Algonquin shot my mothers out of the sky. Vengeance is overdue."

"Please," Bethesda said, rolling her green eyes. "You've been praying for your mothers to die for centuries so you could take over."

"That doesn't mean I can leave their deaths unanswered," Svena snapped. "Some of us still have honor."

Bethesda rolled her eyes again, and Julius reached up to rub his temples. "Whatever our reasons, the goal is clear. If Leviathan gets full control of the Great Lakes, everything is done for. We *must* protect Algonquin's remaining water at any cost, but the area we have to cover is huge, so communication will be key. We don't want to accidentally hit any of the UN forces that will be coming to help us."

"I think you mean getting hit *by* the UN," Arkniss said. "I've tangled with Emily Jackson before. The UN's Phoenix is a dragon slayer to her core. How can we be sure she won't shoot us down the moment our backs are turned?"

Considering that was exactly what she'd done to Marci, Julius had a hard time answering. But if he'd learned anything about Raven's construct, it was her steadfast dedication to results over personal feelings. She'd happily kill every dragon in the world to save one human life, but she'd just as happily work with them if that was what was needed to secure humanity's survival.

"So long as we're fighting together, I don't think we have to worry about betrayal from the UN side," he said. "General Jackson doesn't like or trust us, but she knows we're necessary to achieving her goal of protecting humanity. So long as that's true, I think she'll be a good ally."

"What about after?" the black dragon pressed. "The Phoenix can overlook, but she does not forget, nor forgive. She will tolerate our help while she needs us, but the moment the operation is done, those jets she's sending will turn on us, mark my words."

"We'll deal with that when the time comes," Julius said grimly. "But right now, we can't afford to be picky. We don't even know if we've got enough dragons to do our part properly. If we start mistrusting our human allies as well, this fight will be over before it begins."

No one seemed to like that, but no one argued with him, either. "We'll just have to hope for the best," Amelia said at last, shoulders slumping as she looked at Julius. "I'm glad you're taking point on the UN thing, Baby-J. You're the only one of us who knows how to play nice."

"He doesn't 'play' nice," Bethesda said, her voice disgusted. "He *is* nice."

"But that's to our advantage right now," Marlin Drake pointed out. "He's the right tool for the job."

"That doesn't make him any less embarrassing," Bethesda snapped, pressing a dramatic hand to her temple. "How did *I* end up with such a son?"

Julius knew better than to bother with that one. He was about to move the conversation on when Raven—who was normal bird-sized again—swooped out of the shadows to land on Amelia's shoulder.

"Finally," she said, grinning at her fellow spirit. "Are you here to clear us for takeoff?"

"Alas, I am not," Raven replied. "The ground convoys are moving thanks to absurd amounts of shielding, but flight is still too dangerous."

"Then why are you butting your beak in?" Amelia asked. "This is dragon business."

"Because you and I need to go," Raven replied, his voice dropping. "It's started."

Amelia's face turned deathly pale, and a heavy lump formed in Julius's stomach. "What does that mean?" he demanded. "What's started?"

"Nothing you can help with," Raven said, flapping into the air. "This isn't a matter for mortals. We'll handle it. You just focus on killing the bits you can reach."

Every dragon in the circle looked dangerously offended at being lumped in with mortals, but the bird spirit had already vanished, winking out of existence in front of Julius's eyes. Amelia followed suit, vanishing in a lick of flame.

With the Spirit of Dragons gone and everything on hold until they could fly, the rest of the circle broke up as well, the clan heads walking back to inform their dragons of the plan. Since Bethesda and Ian were already explaining the situation to the Heartstrikers, Julius took the opportunity to head for General Jackson so they could discuss how the UN and dragon forces were going to fight together, hopefully *without* anyone shooting anyone else in the back. This left Bob sitting forgotten and alone on the front porch step—the only part of the house that was still standing now that Bethesda had flattened it—slowly chewing his apple with his eyes closed and his pigeon on his shoulder, keeping him company as he searched and searched through the ocean of the future for the one drop where they lived.

CHAPTER NINE

Marci clung to Ghost's freezing back, looking nervously over her shoulder at the debris-scattered spiral of on-ramps that had once hidden their house, and now hid every dragon in the world. "Are you *sure* they'll be okay? We've never tried anything like this before. What if your shield goes down because you got too far away?"

"It will be fine," the Empty Wind said, sweeping them through the dark city on a gust of grave-cold wind. "The only reason I never did this before was because I didn't have the power. With the magic I have now, maintaining a barrier is so simple, I don't even have to think about it."

"Please think about it a little," Marci begged. "We're playing fast and loose enough as it is. The last thing we need is for our entire army to get crushed because we weren't paying attention."

Her spirit harrumphed, but she felt his magic shift through their connection, pushing more power behind them. "Satisfied?"

She nodded, grabbing Ghost's shoulders to pull herself up taller. She was riding on his back like a monkey with her feet planted on his hips and her hands gripping the freezing, ropey muscles on either side of his neck below his helmet. It was extremely undignified, but Marci far preferred it to being carried around in his arms like a fainting damsel. If nothing else, it was easier to see where they were going this way, not that she liked what she saw.

"Wow," Marci breathed, eyes growing wide.

Other than the streets immediately surrounding their house, the city was in ruins. She'd known it would be bad—she'd been standing on one of the buildings the DFZ had thrown at Algonquin, so it wasn't as if any of the destruction was new—but seeing the full extent of it lying still and dead under the dark of the Leviathan's shadow was gut wrenching. The famous double-layered city of Skyways and underpasses looked more like a pile of rubble. Everything—the superscrapers and the megafactories, the elegant treed boulevards by the water and the giant apartment bricks that held up downtown—was destroyed. Even the famous neon streets of the Underground were dark and empty, their long-hidden roads exposed under the broken Skyways, most of which had been wiped out completely, leaving lines of skeletal support pillars sticking up from the ruined city like jagged bones.

It *felt* dead too. A few fires still sputtered in the wreckage, but otherwise there was no light at all. Aside from their house, all the power in the city was out, leaving the ruins a broken jumble of muted blacks and grays beneath the stain of the Leviathan's shadow. Nothing moved in the dark, nothing made a sound. Even the seagulls were gone, leaving the banks of Lake St. Clair empty save for the corpses of thousands of dead fish. The stench was enough to make Marci retch even from this far away. She covered her nose with her arm, motioning for Ghost to take them west, toward the inland half of the city.

"I hope the spirit of the DFZ will be okay," she said as Ghost flew them over the pile of rubble that had once been Marci's favorite discount magical supplies warehouse. "I don't know how the city is going to come back from this."

"She'll be fine," the Empty Wind assured her. "She's a Mortal Spirit. An idea, not a place. So long as people remember the DFZ, she will live on, and she will rebuild. The only reason she hasn't started already is because she's been busy with the Leviathan."

"He certainly does dominate the conversation," Marci grumbled, glowering at the black shape that filled the sky high above their heads.

The Nameless End looked even bigger now that they were out in the open. As fast as Ghost had to be flying, if Marci didn't look at the ground, she wouldn't have known they were moving at all. But implacable as the enemy above them looked, Ghost's words gave her hope. When this was over, the DFZ would be the only place in the world ruled by a *Mortal* Spirit. A power that rose not of the land, but from the ideas and dreams of the humans that lived in it. Marci had already seen the DFZ move buildings like fingers and twist overpasses like vines during her fight with Algonquin. What could that power do when it came to rebuilding? Could she sprout new superscrapers from the ground? Lift the broken Skyways back into place like a surgeon setting a bone?

Marci didn't know, but she desperately wanted to see it. Reason number eighty thousand to beat the Leviathan and stay alive.

As expected of the aftermath from a fight between a city and a lake, the damage was largely concentrated along the water. Downtown and the other shore districts were an absolute mess, but the farther inland they flew, the less dire things looked. By the time they reached the tumbledown houses of the old University District at the border of Reclamation Land, the landscape below looked almost normal. Better than normal, actually, because the hazy, pea-soup magic leaking over the fence from Algonquin's spirit paradise was gone. True, it had been replaced by the even thicker magic of the crash, but that was already starting to feel natural. From the shimmer of Ghost's magic surrounding them, Marci knew the ambient magic must still be crazy high, but at least there was no more glowing snow rising from the ground.

"Looks like it's finally fading," she said as Ghost set them down. "How does it feel to you?"

"Thinner," the spirit reported. "Ten, maybe twenty more minutes, and we won't need a shield at all."

"That's good news," Marci said, glancing again at the Leviathan, which still filled the sky in every direction for miles. "If our counterattack doesn't get up in the air soon, there'll be nothing left to defend."

The Empty Wind nodded grimly before they both turned to walk up the broken driveway toward the slanting, ivy-covered, ranch-style brick house that had been Marci's first home in Detroit.

The place looked even worse now than it had then. The basement windows were still shot out from the fight with Bixby's goons, and the garden had been torn to pieces by the treads of Algonquin's anti-dragon taskforce tanks. The roof had collapsed in places, probably due to all the shaking from the DFZ's battle last night, but as battered and sad as it looked, the house was still standing, and in the broken, dusty, junk-piled windows, Marci could see the gleaming eyes of cats watching their every move.

"We always end up back here," Ghost said quietly.

"Because it's yours," Marci replied, stepping off the driveway and onto the grassy path that led to the basement stairs. "Of all the death-filled places in this city, this is where you rose. It's also where I was able to recharge you when your magic was almost gone. If there's anywhere in the city that's closest to your domain, this would be it."

Ghost nodded and followed her through the shot-off door into the basement, his glowing eyes watching the cats as they fled deeper into the ceiling-high piles of trash that filled the damp brick room. "I wish I could tell you why," he said as Marci pulled magic into the circle of her bracelet to give them some light. "But I don't actually remember why I picked this place. I don't remember much of anything from the beginning. All I know was that I was in darkness, and I was so angry. Angry, hungry, and alone, just like them."

He knelt down on the stained cement floor, holding out his hand to the scrawny, bony cats watching nervously from the mounds of trash piled against the walls. "We were all forgotten. No one wanted us. No one remembered. No one cared if we lived or died."

"Maybe that's why you rose here," Marci said. "They needed you."

"They needed a champion," Ghost agreed. "But I needed…" His voice fell off as he shook his head. "I don't know. I knew I needed something, but I had no idea who I was or what I was meant to do back then. Helping them made me feel like I had a purpose, though. Even when I was killing that poor, sick old woman, I remember feeling righteous. She was the one who'd brought them all here and forgotten them, who'd left them to die buried under garbage without even a name. I thought killing her would make it right, but…"

"But it didn't," Marci said, squatting down beside him. "The old lady's long gone, but this place is even worse off without her. Algonquin's DFZ has no animal control, no shelters other than what volunteers provide from the kindness of their hearts. Once their owner was gone, no one even knew the cats were here except for you." She smiled. "You remembered them."

"I always remember," the Empty Wind said, his eyes flashing blue as he rose to his feet. The wind rose with him, blowing away the pile of old advertisements and paper cups in front of them to reveal the corpse of a dead cat. From the look of it, the poor thing had been dead for at least a few days, but Ghost reached down to pet its rotting fur as if it were still alive and warm.

"I was made to remember," he said, running his frozen fingers along the small body. "Every person, every creature, every soul who dies with no one left to mourn them, I am there. No one is ever truly forgotten so long as I exist. That is my purpose. That is why they call to me."

"So answer them," Marci said, nodding at the piles of trash. "I can tell from the smell that there are dozens more dead cats in here. They're calling to you, right?"

"The dead always call," he said as his hands began to shake. "So many voices. They need so much."

"Then give it."

His head whipped toward her. "Now?"

Marci shrugged. "If not now, when? The world could end in half an hour. I promised when I gave you your name that I would help you, and that's what I'm doing." She smiled. "Do what you were made to do, Empty Wind. Help the forgotten. Remember the dead. Give them peace. Make this place your domain, somewhere the dead don't have to be alone, and maybe we'll both find what we're looking for."

The spirit's glowing eyes widened as he finally realized what she was trying to do. "Very clever," he rumbled. "But do you really believe this will work?"

"If not this, then nothing," Marci said. "But I *think* it will. Every time I've helped you help the dead, we've gotten closer, become a better team. I don't think that's coincidence. The whole idea of a Merlin is someone who helps a Mortal Spirit be their best self. I didn't technically become one until I passed through the Merlin Gate, but it was only through your steadfast friendship that I was able to reach the gate at all. We're clearly meant to be a pair on all levels, so it only makes sense that the way back to my job in the Merlin realm would be through helping you do yours. If nothing else, we'll do some good before the end, and that's never a waste."

"Helping the dead is never wasted," Ghost agreed as the wind picked up. "Their gratitude is forever, the only warmth I feel." The wind grew stronger as he spoke, whistling past the broken windows. This time, though, the gale did not disturb the trash. It blew *through* the piles, passing through the torn papers and broken bottles and piles of rotting clothes like water through soil, and everywhere it touched, the cats appeared.

They came in droves, packing the room just as they had when Ghost had been one of them. As Marci watched, he became one of them again, transforming into a giant white cat while his ghostly voice echoed through the howling magic.

Come with me.

All through the dark basement, lights appeared. They glittered like mist, coming together to form faint outlines of cats of all ages and sizes walking out of the trash toward Ghost. They dissolved again when they reached him, their ghostly shapes blown away by his wind, but they were not lost. They were still there, their faint magic becoming part of the vortex that swirled around the Empty Wind.

Marci couldn't begin to count how many dead cats her spirit raised. The basement was full of them, and still they kept coming, filtering through the brick walls from the garden and down through the ceiling from the floors above. With each one that joined the Empty Wind, the grim aura that had hung over the house since she'd first come here lessened. It was still freezing, and the basement certainly didn't smell any better, but a weight had most definitely been lifted. Even the living cats noticed it, their eyes growing less wary and fearful as the dead released their grip. Then, when the flow of ghostly shapes from the mountains of trash had slowed to a trickle, the Spirit of the Forgotten Dead turned to Marci.

He was hard to see through the hurricane of magic that was blowing around him, but Marci didn't need her eyes to know that Ghost was smiling. She could feel his happiness in her bones. The tide of joy flowing down their connection now was even stronger than the happiness she'd felt when he was playing in the magic. That had been mere giddiness.

This was the absolute satisfaction of finally doing what he'd always been meant to do.

Because of you.

The voice in her head was a multitude. A haunting gale of sounds, most of them not human, threaded together into joyful words. *Thank you, Merlin.*

"It was my pleasure," Marci replied with a sincere smile, squinting at the outline of her giant white cat of a spirit through the whirling magic. "So what now?"

She felt Ghost's invisible smile widen.

Jump.

Marci didn't hesitate. The moment the word formed in her head, she jumped, leaving her body behind her as her soul leaped into the gale of spirits to blow with them back to the realm of the Forgotten Dead, and the Sea of Magic that howled above it.

• • •

Marci's first impression when she entered the Sea of Magic as a living soul was panic. The magic here had always been chaotic, but what she'd seen before was nothing compared to this. Even safe inside Ghost's protection, the currents were strong enough to knock her around like a bug in a jar. She wasn't even sure which part of her body was her head and which were her feet anymore when a door suddenly appeared in front of her, the only fixed point in the moving, swirling, boiling madness.

She dove for it instinctively, nearly burning off her hand in her rush to get to the blessedly stable, normal-looking wood. The moment her fingers touched its surface, the Merlin Gate opened for her, and Marci tumbled inside, landing in a heap on the stone. She was still trying to stop the spinning in her head when a hand appeared under her nose.

"Bumpy entrance, huh?"

Marci looked up with a start to see Amelia standing over her, her face grim. "What are you doing here?" she asked, grabbing the dragon's hand. "You're supposed to be with Julius."

"I was," Amelia replied, hauling her up. "And I will be again, but this was kind of a crisis, so I bopped over. Shiro was going to kick me out on account of my whole 'not having a Merlin' thing, but now that you're here, you can vouch for me."

Marci nodded absently, too distracted by her surroundings to pay Amelia's explanation proper attention. She was certain she'd come in through the Merlin Gate, but this was *not* the stone courtyard at the foot of the green mountain where she'd entered last time. Everything looked so different, it took Marci several seconds to realize she was standing on top of the flat peak of the mountain... which was no longer a mountain at all, but a tiny island in the middle of a vast and terrifying black sea.

"What happened?" she cried, turning in a circle. The mountain, the forest, the stairs, even the *gate* was gone. The place where she'd come in was just a line scratched into the stone. Beyond that, there was nothing but sea. Not the beautiful blue expanse from before, but a huge, rough, terrifying, tar-black ocean full of giant waves that would have been washing them all under if not for Myron and the DFZ, who were frantically holding the water back with a shimmering barrier.

"Novalli!" Myron yelled over the crashing water. "Help us!"

Marci rushed to obey, grabbing a fistful of magic and slamming it into Myron's spellwork to help keep the ward in place. She was frantically trying to make sense of Myron's maze-like patterns so she would be more effective when the other mage ran over. "Not like that!" he yelled in her ear, grabbing her fingers and moving them to press against the faint green lines rather than the blue ones. "Green is always ground!"

Marci shifted her magic accordingly. "Like this?"

He nodded and ran back toward the center of the island. "Hold that in place while I link it into the rest of the circle."

"What circle?" Marci cried as a giant wave crashed into the magic she was struggling to hold up. "Everything's gone!"

"Not gone!" yelled another voice. "Just underwater."

She jumped at the sound, looking over her shoulder to see Shiro climbing out of the sea where the waves were sloshing under the edge of Myron's dome. The shikigami caretaker was absolutely drenched, his black-and-white robes hanging like soggy bedsheets from his slender body. Despite his bedraggled appearance, though, he looked extremely pleased with himself.

"I found this!" he said excitedly, running over to hand a small, battered-looking leaf to Myron. "It should be enough to serve as an anchor."

Myron snatched the leaf out of his hand with the barest nod of thanks. After staring at it for a moment, the mage turned the small piece of greenery upside down, placed it carefully on the ground, and stomped on it with all his might, grinding the green leaf into paste under the heel of his shoe. Marci was about to yell at him for being so rough with something Shiro had clearly gone to great lengths to obtain when the stone lit up with the glowing lines of Myron's labyrinth. As he finished grinding the leaf—and the spellwork baked into it by the ancient Merlins—into the pattern, the whole maze shifted and locked, shutting out the roar of the storm-tossed sea as though someone had just inverted a thick glass bowl over their heads.

"There," Myron said, his breathless voice painfully loud in the new silence. "That should keep us afloat for now."

"What is going on?" Marci demanded, letting go of the now-stable ward so she could face him properly. "Why is the Heart of the World underwater?"

"Why do you think?" Myron snapped. "You broke the seal and unleashed a thousand years of magic back into the world all at once! *Where did you think it was going to go?*"

Marci blinked in alarm. She'd been so busy dealing with the magical fallout in the real world, she hadn't even considered that the same thing might be happening on this side. Even so. "How was I supposed to know the mountain would sink?" she cried. "There's the same amount of magic now as there was a thousand years ago when this place was built. It's not my fault the Merlins made themselves a tiny island!"

"They didn't!" Shiro said angrily, pushing his dripping black hair away from his face. "It's never looked like this before!"

"How did it end up like this, then?" Myron demanded. "You told us the last time we were here that new magic accumulation over the drought was minimal!"

"It *was* minimal," Shiro said, pointing at the fifty-foot-tall waves that were crashing over the top of Myron's barrier. "This isn't new magic. I don't know what's happening, but I've never seen the Sea of Magic this high before."

"Neither have I," Raven said, finally coming out of his hiding place in the squat little tree at the mountain's center. "And I've been here a *long* time."

"Okay, so what's going on?" Marci asked.

"Not what," Raven said, hopping over to perch on her shoulder opposite Ghost, who was still a cat. "*Who.*"

He pointed a wing tip at the waves. Curious, Marci walked to the barrier and pressed her face against the magic, squinting through the glowing maze of Myron's labyrinth spellwork. No matter how hard she looked, though, she couldn't see a thing, which didn't make sense at all. The entire point of the Heart of the World was to translate the Sea of Magic into something humans could understand. It was a lens designed to let humans see the unseeable, but Marci couldn't see anything at all. The crystal-clear water she'd looked through last time was gone, replaced by murky tides every bit as dark and confusing as the mess outside.

"I don't get it," she said at last. "I can't see a thing."

"Neither can we," Amelia said, crossing her arms. "That's the problem. Remember what Raven said earlier about the Leviathan being in Algonquin's vessel? Well, turns out he didn't stop there. The entire Sea of Magic has been infiltrated."

Eyes wide, Marci turned to look again, and this time, she saw it. It wasn't the *water* that was dark—it was the things inside it. The once-bright ocean was filled with thick, black tangles. They stretched as far as Marci could see, bobbing with the waves and carpeting the sea floor in all directions. A few tendrils had actually crawled up to the edge of the Heart of the World's peak. They were tiny, no thicker than fine black hairs, but the deeper ones were as thick as buildings, and there were *tons* of them. Possibly millions, which explained how the sea had been pushed so high. It was full.

"What *are* they?" she asked, voice shaking. "Tentacles?"

"More like roots," Raven said grimly. "They started in Algonquin's vessel, but they've been spreading since she gave in."

"Is that why it's so stormy?" Marci asked. Then her face grew pale. "He's not attacking spirits, is he?"

"No," Amelia said. "If he were, we'd already be screwed. Bad as this looks, though, I've seen no evidence that he's eaten anything yet except Algonquin. The waves you're seeing were actually here before Leviathan started spreading." She grinned. "Turns out, you get a lot of sloshing when you dump a thousand years of magic in all at once."

"That is not 'sloshing,'" Myron snarled, stabbing his finger at the giant waves washing over his protective bubble. "*That* is the work of spirits, and it's all *her* fault."

He snapped his finger back to Marci, who sighed. "What are you blaming me for now?"

"If you didn't do so many irresponsible things, that wouldn't even be a question," Myron snapped, marching over to the giant stone seal at the center of the mountain-turned-island, or what was left of it. The circular slab that had been the seal on a thousand years of magic was cracked right down the middle, the stone blown away as though it had been blasted apart from the inside. But even broken, it was still a huge chunk of rock, and there was more than enough left for Myron to climb on top of.

"Come," he said, snapping his fingers at Marci. "You can't see them from the ground due to the waves, but come up here, and you'll see that I was always right."

Marci had never heard a less compelling reason to do anything, but Myron was clearly not going anywhere until she complied, so she sucked it up and climbed onto the cracked seal beside him. "There," she said, tilting her head so she wouldn't bump it on the zenith of the protective bubble over their heads. "I'm up. Now, what am I looking for?"

Myron pointed toward the horizon. Marci followed the motion with a sigh, squinting as she tried to see what he was so worked up about. But while it was much easier to see over the waves from up here, the Heart of the World's interpretation of the over-full Sea of Magic's chaos was still so rough, it took far longer than it should before Marci realized that the giant breakers peaking in the distance weren't actually waves. They were creatures. Huge, alien-looking monsters, and they were attacking each other.

Every direction Marci looked, giant *things* were breaching the stormy sea like killer whales, flinging themselves at each other in bloody confrontations. There were so many fights, the ocean looked like it was boiling, and those were just the battles that broke the surface. Now that she knew what to look for, Marci could see the creatures clashing below the water as well. Thousands of dark shapes silhouetted against the Leviathan's deeper blackness, trying their best to rip each other to shreds.

"Now I see why we had such a rough entrance," Ghost said, abandoning his fluffy white cat form to appear at her side as the faceless warrior he always turned into when things got serious. "They're at each other's throats."

"They who?" Marci asked desperately.

Her spirit looked at her, his glowing eyes terrified. "Everything."

"Everything, pah!" Myron scoffed, pointing at one particularly enormous shape on the horizon. "Those aren't normal spirits. Those are *Mortal* Spirits! The magic filled them, and now they're rising and going crazy just like everyone warned you they would!" His face turned scarlet. "We *told* you this would happen. *I* told you! But did you listen? *No!* You just dumped the magic out, and now everything's going to pieces!"

"You can't blame this on me!" Marci cried. "I wanted to let the magic out slowly, remember? Algonquin's the one who broke the seal and dumped it, and even she only did so by accident. If anyone's to blame, it's the Leviathan! He's the one who cracked the seal in the first place, and I bet all those roots he's put down are what's driving everything into a frenzy." She crossed her arms stubbornly over her chest. "I'm no spirit, but having a Nameless End shove his tentacles into your face sounds pretty panic-worthy."

"Actually, I believe Sir Myron is right," Shiro said, wringing the water from his robes. "This is more extreme than usual, but Mortal Spirits have always been dreadful. That's why we were willing to sacrifice all magic to stop them, but now they're back and bigger than ever." He looked out at the chaos. "Perhaps this is simply the new way of things."

"I don't think you can lay all the blame on the Spirits of Man this time," Raven cawed. "Humans have a flair for the dramatic that's truly terrifying when distilled into its purest form, but even Mortal Spirits can't cause this much chaos by themselves. Look again, and you'll see there are plenty of Spirits of the Land and Animals in the mix as well." He fluffed his feathers. "Today's madness is equal opportunity, it seems."

"Because the Leviathan is driving them to it," Marci said.

Raven shrugged. "Leviathan, Algonquin's betrayal, bumping elbows with crazed, newly raised Mortal Spirits. We're spoiled for choice on reasons to panic, which is why everyone seems to be doing it. This mess is a team effort."

"That's fitting," Marci said, hopping down off the broken seal. "Because it's going to take a team effort to get us out."

Myron gaped at her. "You can't be serious. You still want to go ahead with the banishment plan?"

"What other choice do we have?" she asked, pointing at the black roots that filled the water. "The world is ending, Myron. That's not hyperbole. Our reality will literally *cease to exist* if we don't do something."

"I know, but..." He dragged his hands through his graying hair. "I can't work miracles. When I told you earlier that I could fix the seal, I was counting on having access to all the spellwork covering the rest of the mountain, but I've got nothing to work now! Shiro had to risk his life swimming down to get me a leaf just so we wouldn't all be washed away." He pointed at the broken seal under his feet. "What am I supposed to patch this thing with? My hopes and dreams?"

"If that's what it takes," Marci said, smiling at him. "You're one of the greatest modern mages, Myron. You built a barrier against the raging Sea of Magic using nothing but labyrinths and a leaf. If anyone can make this work, you can."

Myron rolled his eyes. "I appreciate the pep talk, but I'm not just being melodramatic. I really *can't* do this without the rest of the Heart of the World. If we have to wait for Shiro to dive for every material I need, we'll be here all year."

"Then ask your spirit for help," Marci said, turning to the DFZ, who'd been oddly quiet this whole time. "Can you get him what he needs?"

"I don't know," the city spirit replied, her orange eyes glowing in the dark of her hood as she considered it. "I've never tried swimming before, but I should be able to handle the currents. Even when it's rough, the Sea of Magic is my world, and I'm pretty strong."

Myron whirled on her. "You mean you could have been helping me this whole time?" he cried. "Why didn't you?"

"Because you never asked me!" the DFZ yelled back, sounding so offended, Marci couldn't help but laugh.

"What did you expect?" she asked, trying her best not to let either of them see just how amused she was. "You tied yourself to the spirit of the *Detroit Free Zone*, Myron. That's not a place known for volunteering. If you want something in the city, you have to do it yourself or pay someone else to."

The city spirit's orange eyes flashed. "I like being paid."

Myron looked horrified. "You expect me to *pay* my own spirit? That's ridiculous!"

"Hey, I got here through a swirling vortex of dead cats," Marci said with a shrug. "Mortal Spirits are as ridiculous as the human desires that create them. Sometimes you've just gotta roll with it. That said, if you two are going to work together, you might want to try understanding how the DFZ does things instead of just giving her orders."

Myron scoffed. "Are you a relationship counselor now?"

"Nope," Marci said. "Just someone who's already had to learn this lesson and wants to spare you the trouble. Not that I don't enjoy watching you suffer, but repetition is inefficient, and we're crunched enough for time as it is." She grinned at the city spirit. "I don't care what it takes. Promise her ownership of the entire DFZ if you have to, but I want that circle up and ready to receive on time. The dragons and General Jackson's troops are probably in the air by now, and I don't want them in danger one second longer than necessary because you're bad at communicating."

"I'm *not* bad at communicating!" Myron cried. "I'm a professor! I've written fourteen books! I—" He cut off with a clench of his jaw. "You know, never mind. I've made a career out of doing the impossible. I'll do it again now. You'd do better to focus on holding up your end of this bargain, and speaking of." He folded his arms over his chest. "How *do* you intend to get enough magic to drop a hammer banish? I let you brush me off before because I didn't want a bunch of dragons asking questions, but now that it's just us, I need to know. You said you had a plan. What is it?"

"Oh, that's easy," Marci said. "I'm going to ask the spirits."

Everyone turned to stare at her.

"What?" Amelia said at last.

"I'm going to ask the spirits for help," Marci clarified. "They're sentient magic, and magic is what we need. I know they can give up their magic freely because they did it for Algonquin while she was trying to fill up the DFZ, and since they're all going to die too if this Leviathan thing goes south, I thought I'd ask them to pitch in."

"Let me get this straight," Myron said, rubbing the bridge of his nose. "You're going to ask a bunch of ancient spirits—many of whom see you, a Merlin, as the bringer of a different sort of apocalypse—to commit suicide in order to help you defeat Algonquin's weapon?"

"It's not suicide," Marci said irritably. "They'll just re-form in their domains once the banishment is complete. Most of them will be down for a week at the worst, and when they wake up, they'll still have a world to call home. That sounds like a good deal to me."

"It doesn't matter what you think," Raven said. "Algonquin's spent the last six decades teaching them that this was the only way. They've already made up their minds. You're not going to change that."

"Yes, I can," she said. "Because this goes beyond normal spirit politics. We're talking about an end even you immortals can't survive. I know Algonquin's poisoned the well, but 'work with me or we're all dead' is a pretty powerful argument."

"But you won't just be dealing with Spirits of the Land," Myron said, reaching into his pocket to pull out a small slip of paper, or the representation of his memory of a slip of paper since nothing was actually physical on this side. "I suspected you wouldn't have a proper grasp on this subject, so I did the math for just how much power it will take to hammer banish Algonquin's magic off the Leviathan before I left. Assuming the standard formula, the answer seems to be just shy of…" He trailed off, checking his equation one last time. "All of it."

Marci blinked. "All of what?"

"All the magic that currently exists on this plane," Myron clarified. "Give or take a few percent."

His Cambridge professor accent rendered every word perfectly, but Marci still couldn't understand what Myron was saying. "Wait, wait, wait," she said, putting up her hands. "You're seriously telling me that banishing the Leviathan is going to take *all* the magic there is?" When he nodded, she gaped at him. "How is that even possible? Algonquin's *five* lakes. She's not the Pacific Ocean!"

"If she were an ocean of any sort, we couldn't banish her at all," Myron said. "You said it yourself: hammer banishes work by using a blast of overwhelming power to completely disperse a spirit's magic. But the amount of power required to qualify as 'overwhelming' increases exponentially with the spirit's size. Algonquin's one of the largest spirits of the land. No one's ever used the hammer method on something her size before, let alone a spirit that's currently *inside* a separate extraplanar being." He held the paper out so Marci could see. "Frankly, some of these numbers are just guesses on my part. There's a chance we could swing everything we have, and it *still* wouldn't be enough."

She snatched the paper from his hand, but when she looked the figures over, she saw Myron was right. When she'd come up with this idea, she'd assumed the standard ten-to-one ratio for a hammer banish, which meant that if she could get just ten or twenty big spirits on board, it would be enough. But she'd forgotten about the exponential curve. Under that math, she needed to multiply every number by a power of ten. Once you did that, all the magic in the world started to look terrifyingly short.

"We can still do it," she said, hands shaking as she handed the paper back to Myron. "We're just going to need everyone now. But that's fine. So far as I know, *everyone* wants to live, so my argument still stands."

"And there are Mortal Spirits now as well," Ghost added. "Our kind is much more powerful than the land and untainted by Algonquin's hate."

"You are also mad and unpredictable," Shiro said angrily, pointing at the battles that thrashed the sea. "All the gods humanity learned to fear have risen. I sided with you before because you said you would do it slowly, and that you would find them all Merlins, but there's been no time for that. Those are all newborn powers, maddened spirits who don't yet know the destruction they are capable of. They don't even know their names yet! Forces like that cannot be reasoned with."

"Nothing can be reasoned with if you don't try," Marci snapped, marching back to the line on the ground that marked the temporary, un-submerged Merlin Gate. "I'm going."

Shiro stepped in front of her. "With respect, Merlin, that is suicide. The Sea of Magic is more treacherous than I have ever seen it. The chaos will rip you to shreds."

"It will not touch her," Ghost growled, moving closer to Marci's side. "You forget, construct. I am a face of death. Nothing shall touch my Merlin so long as she is in my shadow."

"But you're no longer the only god out there," Shiro pleaded, his face growing desperate. "No one has ever brought the Mortal Spirits to heel, and they are panicked now. They will not be reasonable."

"It's because they're panicked that this will work," Marci argued. "And I'm not trying to bring anyone to heel. I'm offering them a chance to save themselves, and no one fears death more than immortals."

"That may be true," Shiro admitted, his voice quivering. "But... we just got you back! This world—*I* have been without a proper Merlin for so long! Sir Myron is unquestionably skilled, but he doesn't have your understanding or vision for how the future can be better. I want to see the world you promised the last time you were here, and that can't happen if you're dead for real!"

"It won't happen if I don't go, either," Marci said, surprisingly touched. "Your support means a lot to me, Shiro, but I have to do this. Not because I'm the Merlin, but because I'm the only one who can do the job right now. I want to see that world too. I want to *live*, and I can't do that if Tentacle Face out there eats my plane. I'm ready to do whatever I have to to beat him, and I'm betting there's a lot of spirits who feel the same. We've never been able to unite before, but we've also never faced a truly universal threat. This is an existential crisis that threatens every sentient being in our reality. The enemy of my enemy may not be my friend, but that doesn't mean we can't come together and fight to survive, especially when the stakes are this high."

"You are right," Shiro said, lowering his eyes. "I was being selfish." He bowed deeply. "Forgive my disobedience, Merlin."

"Thank you for caring enough to try to stop me," Marci said, grabbing his shoulders to gently pull him back up. "But I've got this. Just hold down the fort, and make sure Myron doesn't get so caught up haggling with his spirit that he forgets to mend the seal, because when I come back, I'll probably be coming in hot. Also, Amelia and Raven are allowed to come and go as they please."

"I believe the Spirit of Dragons has already gone," Shiro said. "But I will not try to kick her out again." He lowered his head one more time. "Good luck, Merlin."

Marci smiled and turned away, sliding her hand into Ghost's freezing one as they stepped through the door into chaos once again.

CHAPTER TEN

General Jackson's truck convoy arrived with much fanfare. Ten UN armored personnel carriers rolled into the sheltered area below the ramps like soldiers charging the enemy line. Each one was covered with what had to be a million dollars' worth of glowing military-grade wards, which explained how they'd made the journey from the armory in Chicago through the still-dangerous magic levels. They slowed down when they hit the dirt to let the dragons get out of the way, but they didn't stop until they'd formed a protective circle around General Jackson, who hadn't even looked up yet from the makeshift war table she'd fashioned from the top half of Julius's front door.

When the APCs were in position, the bulletproof doors rolled open, and UN soldiers with ANTI-DRAGON TASK FORCE stamped in yellow letters across their augmented body armor poured out, much to the chagrin of the watching crowd.

"Are you serious?" Lao demanded, his eyes shining like blue fire as he placed himself between the soldiers and the Qilin. "You dare bring *dragon slayers* to our aid?"

"I'm the general of the Anti-Dragon Task Force," Emily replied dryly, her eyes still locked on the map of the Great Lakes region she'd sketched onto the cracked wood with one of Marci's sticks of casting chalk. "You go to war with the army you've got."

Lao growled low in his throat, but the general didn't even raise her head until the last officer hopped off the trucks, a young man with a confident air and reams of preprinted ward tape attached to holsters to his belt. The yellow band on his arm marked him as a battle mage, but

Emily looked much more excited about the sleek, cement block-sized augmented reality receiver he was carrying in his hands.

"Finally," she said, grabbing the receiver and setting it down on the door-table beside her. The officer handed her a smartphone in a Kevlar case next. Emily snatched it out of his hand, taking a quick picture of her hand-drawn map before swiping her fingers through the phone's augmented reality field to bring up an actual map in the air above it.

"Much better," she said, smiling at the glowing projection of the Great Lakes region. "Status report."

The battle mage saluted and started rattling off a bunch of jargon Julius didn't understand. It must not have been what the general wanted to hear, though, because her face—the only part of her body that wasn't currently made of scrap metal—grew dourer by the word.

"What's wrong?" Julius asked after she'd dismissed the soldier.

"Everything we already know, plus a bit more," Emily said, sweeping her hand through the AR to replace the floating map with a circular display of satellite images and magical readouts. "It seems the Leviathan is bigger than our original estimation. I don't know if Raven was wrong about his size or if he's grown in the last half hour, but we're going to be stretched even thinner than planned. The good news is that Canada, the US, and Mexico are all sending their air forces to help. Washington in particular is being extremely generous, though I think we can all guess why that is."

She glanced pointedly at David, who was busy schmoozing with the heads of two European clans. The senator smiled when he saw her looking and took his government-issued phone out of his pocket, wiggling it at her before sliding it back into place.

"The president of the US has preauthorized a nuclear strike and designated Senator Heartstriker as the man on the ground," Emily continued. "I don't intend to use it because I'd like to avoid having all of our forces and what remains of the DFZ vaporized, but it's good to know we've got an ace in our pocket."

"Would it even work, though?" Julius asked nervously, glancing up at the Leviathan. "Can you nuke something that big without destroying everything you're fighting to save?"

"We can damn well try," the general said grimly. "But if we have to launch a nuclear strike, we've already lost, so it's a moot point."

"It won't come to that," Julius assured her. "Marci's plan will work."

"It'd better," Emily grumbled. "Because all our other options are just different flavors of defeat."

Another soldier came up to them as she finished, an older woman wearing a bright-orange vest that read LOGISTICS and carrying a heavily armored metal box the size of a picnic basket. Emily grinned when she saw it, clearing the table so the soldier could set the box down. The woman was still saluting when Emily popped the locks and threw the box open, revealing an array of complicated-looking military gadgetry packed inside custom-cut black foam.

"Here," the general said, grabbing what looked like the world's most expensive black plastic headband and holding it out to Julius. "Put this on."

"What is it?" Julius asked, taking it from her.

"Coms rig," she replied, grabbing a second one to place over her own head. "It's got a full AR interface, a camera, a phone, and an old-fashioned radio, just in case things go *really* south. There's also GPS, though with the Leviathan blocking the satellites, that's probably useless." She pointed at the satellite pictures that showed nothing but a wall of black above the entire northern border of the Midwestern US. "It's also got military-grade mana-contacts that are better than anything on the civilian market, so it should work in your dragon form as well as your human one. Just make sure at least one side stays in contact with your skin at all times, and you'll have full AR sound and capability."

That sounded extremely useful, but... "Why are you giving it to *me?*"

"Because you're in charge," Emily said, looking at him as if she couldn't understand how that was a question. "I overheard your dragon powwow. It's clear you're the one the others are looking to as the leader of this assault."

"That's only because Amelia told them I was running things!" Julius said quickly, putting up his hands. "I'm not—"

"It doesn't matter how you came to be in charge," the general said brusquely. "You are, and to be frank, I'm delighted. Despite the bad blood between us, you've been extraordinarily fair and reliable. Those are rare qualities in a dragon, and priceless traits in an ally."

Julius was glad to hear it. He knew the others didn't share his sentiment, but the UN general was a good ally for them as well. Dragons were powerful but, as he'd recently discovered, not nearly as numerous as he'd been led to believe. If they were going to keep his promise and hold out until Marci was done, they needed all the help they could get.

"I'm always ready to make an ally," Julius said. "I've already told the others not to attack any of your planes, even by 'accident,' but I need you to make sure your soldiers do the same. If a dragon gets shot down, I can't guarantee this won't dissolve into a brawl."

"Don't worry," Emily said. "My people aren't stupid enough to pick a fight with this many dragons. So long as no one claws a jet out of the sky, we shouldn't have any problems."

She shot a sideways look at Fading Smoke as she said that, and Julius winced. "I'm picking up that you two have history," he said quietly. "Is that going to be an issue?"

"That depends on how much stock you're putting in Arkniss," Emily said, her mechanical eyes whirring as she refocused on Julius. "I know saying a dragon is untrustworthy is like saying the sky is blue, but Arkniss is special. A decade ago, my superiors in Copenhagen made a deal with him for safe access to airspace over the Mediterranean. He invited us to his fortress under the Rock of Gibraltar, signed the treaty, and then betrayed us before the ink was dry. All of my subordinates died, and I was taken captive and tortured for four months before Raven got me out." She looked down at the scrap-metal hands Raven had rigged up for her with a sigh. "Bastard cost me my last real limb."

"I'm sorry," Julius said, horrified.

The general shrugged. "Price of being a dragon slayer. Point is, Fading Smoke is not someone I trust with my soldiers. Normally, that wouldn't even need to be said, but since we're enemies of an enemy together, I feel it would compromise mission integrity if I didn't warn you."

"I'll make sure he's positioned as far from you as possible," Julius promised. "Thank you for telling me."

"Thank you for caring," she said, turning back to her maps. "I have to stay down here and coordinate UN forces, so I'll be counting on you to be my eyes in the sky. I'll be feeding you real-time positions for all human units, so make sure you keep that headpiece on at all times. I've instructed my pilots to obey any orders from you the same as they would from me, so don't be afraid to send in the jets yourself if you need them."

Julius swallowed. Being in charge of a dragon clan was one thing, but he was used to Heartstriker. Ordering military air strikes felt much scarier, somehow.

"Don't make that face," Emily said. "I know you're not a killer, because if you were, I'd be dead. But I like that in an ally. I know I can count on you not to waste my soldiers' lives." She lifted her head, giving him a sincere smile. "I'm glad you're the one I ended up with. We didn't get off to the best start, but if we die today, it's been an honor to work with you, Julius Heartstriker."

Julius had no idea how to reply to that. He felt obligated to say "You too" or something similar, but he couldn't, because even though she'd come back, he still hadn't forgiven the general for killing Marci. He didn't think he'd *ever* be able to look at her without that old hurt and anger coming up, but there was a practical, eyes-on-the-prize honor to Emily Jackson that he couldn't deny. She wasn't kind or compassionate, but Julius trusted her to fight for humanity's survival—and by extension, all of theirs—to the bitter, bitter end.

"Thank you," he said quietly.

The general nodded and turned back to her map, using her fingers to redraw the battle lines on the projected maps that she'd originally drawn in chalk on the door-turned-table. Duly dismissed, Julius stepped away to fiddle with his new piece of military hardware. The headpiece was easily the coolest gadget he'd ever used. The mana contacts barely needed to touch his skin to hook into his personal magic, and the AR interface was the fastest and most responsive he'd ever seen. He was poking through the floating menus when he felt something loom over him. That was all the warning he got before a giant arm wrapped around his neck.

"Ack!" he cried, hands flying up instinctively to fight off his attacker before he realized the arm belonged to his brother. "*Justin!*"

The knight of the Heartstrikers cackled in reply, lifting Julius off the ground with a wicked grin. "Look at you," he said, grinding the knuckles of his free hand into Julius's scalp. "Got the Phoenix herself eating out of your hand. I knew I'd make a dragon out of you someday!"

"Justin..." Julius gasped, slapping his hands against the vise of his brother's arm, which was still locked around his neck. "Air..."

Justin released him, and Julius doubled over, coughing as spots danced in front of his eyes. He was still trying to catch his breath when Justin slapped him on the back hard enough to send him sprawling on the ground.

"I always knew you'd pull it off," the knight said proudly as he yanked Julius back to his feet. "Everyone said your coup against Mother was a fluke, but I *knew* you had fire in you. You had a weird way of showing it, but you still beat the Qilin *and* kept our clan from getting conquered. I just got the whole story from Fredrick, and it was *awesome*. I can't wait to rub this in the rest of our clan's faces forever. They told me I was stupid for wanting to be your knight, but *who's looking stupid now?*"

He yelled that last part at the gathered group of Heartstrikers, who rolled their green eyes, and Julius winced. "Could you not?" he said, dusting himself off. "I still need them to listen to me, you know."

"Oh, they'll listen," Justin said confidently. "The White Witch and Amelia the Planeswalker just whistled up every living dragon to fight under your banner. *Everyone's* scared of them, and they're taking orders from *you*. That makes you the most important dragon in the world." He slapped Julius on the back again. "I *knew* you had it in you!"

There were so many things wrong with that statement, Julius didn't know where to begin, so he didn't bother. Arguing with his brother over facts was the same as banging your head against a wall: painful and ineffective. There was no point, anyway. If Justin was happy, that was good enough for Julius, so he dismissed the inaccuracies and accepted the compliment as it had been intended. "Thank you, Justin."

"I'm the one who should be grateful," Justin said, puffing out his chest. "You made me look amazing, and I wasn't even there! I should give you a boon for this."

"Please don't," Julius begged. "I've had enough trouble with debts to last me the rest of my life. The last thing I need is another..."

He trailed off. Justin went quiet as well, dropping a hand to the wrapped handle of his Fang of the Heartstriker as Marlin Drake left his knot of dragons and approached, a charming, hungry smile on his too-handsome face.

As soon as he got within striking distance, Justin put himself between the older dragon and Julius. "What do you want, clanless?"

"Just coming to pay my regards while we wait," Drake replied smoothly. "The Affiliated Clanless Dragons have always been steadfast allies of the Heartstriker. Bethesda's been a regular on my show for fifty years, you know."

"Yeah, we know," Justin snapped. "She makes us watch every time she's on. But I don't see what your famewhoring sellout of a dragon-and-pony show has to do with anything."

"*Justin*," Julius hissed, putting a hand on his brother's arm as he dropped his voice to a whisper. "We don't have enough allies to afford insulting one!"

"But he's the head of the *clanless*," Justin hissed back. "They'll take anyone who'll swear loyalty to Drake. Complete lack of standards. Don't believe me, check out who's lurking in his ranks."

Justin glanced at the mismatched knot of Marlin Drake's "clan" standing at the far edge of the cavern. Sure enough, the clanless dragons stood out from the rest of the room like platypuses among swans. All the other families were clearly cut from the same cloth with similar clothing and physical features. Even the Golden Empire's dragons—which were technically twenty different clans held together by a lucky golden claw—looked like a matched set. But the only uniting feature of the clanless dragons was that they were standing together. They came from every family, age, and type, including a few breeds Julius had never seen before. All of them looked scruffy and intimidated by the bigger powers surrounding them, but one dragon in particular seemed to be going out of his way to hide in the shadows, his green eyes glowing like a sulking cat's.

"Is that…" Julius squinted through the gloom, breathing in deep to catch the dragon's scent. When he found it, he grabbed Justin's arm. "That's *Gregory!*"

It didn't seem possible, but Julius's nose didn't lie. There was no question the dragon lurking at the urban cavern's edge was Gregory no-longer-Heartstriker. Just seeing him was enough to make Julius's long-healed injuries twinge as if they were fresh. The only reason he didn't panic was because Gregory looked just as freaked out as Julius felt. The banished dragon was practically cowering behind his fellow clanless, watching the Heartstrikers as though he expected them to come over and rip his head off at any second, which, given the way Justin was growling, was probably a legitimate fear.

"You dare bring a traitor into our midst?" the knight snarled, taking a menacing step toward Marlin Drake. "Some *ally.*"

"*I* didn't bring him," Drake replied. "He was called by the Planeswalker and summoned by the White Witch same as the rest of us. My only crime was vouching for him, but don't worry. I've heard all about the unpleasantness at Heartstriker Mountain, and I promise you personally that he will be no trouble." He looked over his shoulder at Gregory with a killing smile. "As a clanless dragon, he has nowhere else to go. Even Heartstriker's enemies would not shelter a traitor. I'm his only safe harbor, and I've made it very clear that my protection is strictly conditional on our continued good relations with your family." He turned back to Julius with a smile. "You won't even know he's here."

"I'll believe that when it happens," Julius grumbled. But annoyed as he was at this new complication, a very small part of him was happy that Gregory had found someone to take him in. Dragons were highly social creatures, and traitor or not, no one deserved to be alone.

"This has been a very humbling experience for him," Drake said, leaning around the still-growling Justin to lock his eyes on Julius. "He was actually the one who first told me your name. You're the head of Heartstriker now, aren't you?"

"I'm one of three heads," Julius corrected. "I share power with Bethesda and my brother Ian via a clan council."

"Dragons don't *share* power," Drake said dismissively. "On paper, perhaps, your rule is split, but I just saw every dragon in the world deferring to you, which tells me where the real power lies." He moved a little closer. "So how *did* it actually go down? Gregory was tragically short on the details, and Bethesda threatened to eat me when I asked her. I'd love to hear the whole story from the dragon who was in the middle of things."

He smiled eagerly, and Julius bit his lip. "We don't really have the time right now to—"

"Of course, of course," Drake said, moving closer still despite the increasing volume of Justin's growling. "You can tell me everything on my show when this is over. An exclusive interview with you and your Merlin, and your knight, of course." He flashed a smile at Justin, who seemed surprisingly mollified by the possibility of being on television despite badmouthing the whole idea earlier. But while his brother was looking pleased, Julius was starting to get annoyed.

"*If* we survive, I'll think about it," he said, moving away. "Right now, we have more important things to worry about."

"But right now might be our last chance to talk," Drake said, his sea-blue eyes gleaming dangerously. "I'm dying to know more about the runt of a J who rose from the bottom of his clan to become the leader who commands the respect of every important dragon in the world. The Qilin, Svena, the Planeswalker, even Bethesda's Shade all defer to you, and I find that fascinating. Not *surprising*, of course. Unlikely success is in your blood. After all…" His lips curled into a coy smile. "You are *my* son."

Julius jerked back so fast he nearly fell over. His face must have been a sight, because Marlin Drake's smirk turned into a laugh. "When we survive this, call me," he said, flipping a business card out of his sleeve and tucking it into the front pocket of Julius's jacket. "We'll do a whole series. 'The Unlikely Dragon Who Saved the World!' It'll be a sensation." He gave Julius a final wink and turned around. "Bring your Merlin girl as well. When I'm done, the two of you will be the talk of the world. I just hope you're ready to be famous."

He walked off with a wave, leaving Julius staring after him with his mouth hanging open.

"There he goes again," Justin said, shaking his head. "Leave it to the First Dragon in Television to turn our real life into a cheesy 'tune in next week' style cliffhanger."

Julius's head bobbed, but he was still too shocked to speak. It wasn't until Justin grabbed his arm and started dragging him back toward the other Heartstrikers that he finally blurted out, "Did you know?"

His brother stopped, confused. "Did I know what?"

"That!" Julius cried, pointing at Marlin Drake's back. "Did you know *he* was our father?"

"Of course I knew," Justin said. "Drake does the dad reveal whenever one of us gets famous enough to catch his attention. He pulled it on me back when I became the clan's knight at seventeen, though I never got invited to do an interview."

Julius stared at him. "You've known who our father was since we were seventeen, and you *never told me*?"

"You never asked!" Justin cried. "I'm not psychic! I don't know what you want. Even when you do tell me, it doesn't make sense half the time."

"I would think this would be obvious!" Julius cried back. "He's our *dad*!"

"All the more reason to keep it to myself," Justin snapped. "What was I supposed to say? 'Hey Julius, you seem to be having a good day, so let me ruin it by telling you that our father is a clanless reject whose only claim to power is being in charge of other clanless rejects. He's also a shameless huckster who made his fortune spilling dragon secrets for human entertainment, and our mother only slept with him so she'd have a regular spot on his talk show.'" Justin rolled his eyes. "Seriously, you were mopey enough as it was back then. I wasn't about to make it worse by telling you the truth."

If he'd been less upset, Julius would have been touched by Justin's thoughtfulness. Emotional sensitivity wasn't usually his brother's strong suit. But while hearing the logic behind the decision made him feel slightly less betrayed, he still couldn't believe Justin had kept this from him.

"We have to tell the other Js," he said angrily. "They deserve to know."

"I'm pretty sure they already do," Justin said. "Like I said, Drake does the dad reveal whenever one of us gets important, and unlike you, all of us became important a while ago."

Julius's shoulders slumped. "So I'm the last to know?"

His brother nodded. "None of us talked about it because who brags about a deadbeat dad? But we all knew. Honestly, I'm surprised you didn't figure it out sooner. Marlin Drake's a sea serpent, and his dragon form is all over his movie posters. Didn't you ever notice we all shared his coloration and head shape?"

"Blue and green aren't exactly uncommon Heartstriker colors," Julius said defensively. Then he thought of something else. "Wait, if our father's a sea serpent, why don't we have any water-related powers?" Having gills or something would have been *really useful* all those times he'd nearly drowned fighting Vann Jeger and Algonquin.

"Because like I said, he's a deadbeat," Justin growled. "Bethesda picked prime mates for her early clutches because she was breeding up her power base. By the time she got to us, though, she needed other things more than she needed strong dragons, so her standards for good matches started going downhill. Drake is only slightly older than the H's and the last surviving member of his clan, so it wasn't like he had a broad power base to start from. Even if he had been ancient and powerful, though, it's never gonna be a good mix when you're combining scaly sea serpents with *feathered dragons*." He huffed in disgust. "If we did get something good out of the match, I've never found it. I can't even go into the water in my true shape without looking like a drowned chicken."

Julius had never been crazy enough to try swimming as a dragon for that exact reason, but hearing they'd gotten nothing from their dad made him angry all over again. Worse, Marlin Drake hadn't even bothered to seek him out until Julius had something he wanted. Like a true dragon, he'd only cared about his son when Julius became useful, and even then, his caring was limited to how Julius could be used to his advantage.

"He and Bethesda deserve each other," Julius snarled, crossing his arms over his chest. "I'd rather have no father at all than another parent who only sees me as a tool."

"That's what children are to dragons," Justin said with a shrug. "You see, this is why I never told you. The rest of us could handle the truth, but you were always too soft. You wanted parents who loved you, but that just doesn't happen for us. Anyway, it's not like Drake matters. He's half our DNA, but he's not family. We are. We're Heartstrikers, *clan.* That's something Drake could never have given us, and who wants to be part of a stage show for humans, anyway?"

He finished with a grin, but Julius could only stare at his brother in awe. Their entire life, Justin had been his bully, the tormentor of his childhood. He'd hunted and harassed and irritated Julius more than any other J, and yet, of everyone in the family, Justin was the only one who'd always been there. Even when he was being a pompous, overbearing jerk about it, he'd always looked out for his little brother even at the risk of his own life. He could be an absolute pain, but Justin had been truer to Julius's idea of family than any other dragon, and though he'd always known it deep down, Julius loved him for it now more than ever.

"Thank you, brother," he whispered, stepping in to wrap his arms around Justin's chest.

"Yeah, yeah," Justin muttered, tolerating the hug for a good five seconds before pushing Julius away. "Don't get all mushy on me. You get a pass as the Nice Dragon, but some of us have actual reputations to maintain."

"You're the knight of the Nice Dragon," Julius pointed out. "Doesn't that buy you some slack?"

Justin's answer to that was an appalled look. But just as Julius was about to tease him again, the military com he'd just put on his head buzzed to life. General Jackson's face appeared in the AR in front of his face a moment later. "Canadian Command in Windsor says that magical levels have dropped enough to authorize flight," she said, her voice surprisingly loud despite the fact that the com unit had no supplemental speakers. "I'm clearing all air units for combat. Repeat, all air units are cleared for combat. Get up there and bring that bastard down."

"That's our cue," Julius said to Justin as all the UN forces began to scramble. "Ready?"

"Are you kidding?" Justin said, drawing his sword. Fire engulfed him before the blade was even out, replacing his towering human form with a bright-green-feathered dragon with the bone cage of his transformed Fang of the Heartstrikers locked over his jaws and a look of pure glee shining in his green eyes. The moment the change finished, Justin launched into the air, his Fang transforming the flames that flashed between his giant teeth into the magical green fire of the Quetzalcoatl as he flew straight up into the shadow of their enemy. Julius was still staring after when he realized no one else was flying.

"What are you waiting for?" he shouted, turning to the rest of the dragons. "The magic's down! It's time to fight back! *Go!*"

"You heard the small Heartstriker!" Svena called, striding out from the circle of her sisters with her whelps clinging to her shoulders like a living cloak of snowy down. "Fly, you idiots!"

She shed her human form as she spoke, revealing the beautiful white dragon underneath. Then, babies still clinging to her frosted scales, Svena launched herself into the air as well, shooting up through the hole in the Skyways with a single powerful beat of her frosted wings. Her sisters followed at once, as did everyone else. Within seconds, the air was full of flapping wings and scraping claws as all the dragons of the world took off en masse.

Julius was the last to go, waiting until the cavern was empty before shedding his own human mask to transform into his dragon. As always, the weight of his transformed Fang was surprisingly heavy on his head, but at least it gave him somewhere safe to tuck his com unit before he launched into the air as well, following the others into a sky that was already full of fire.

• • •

"And they're off," Bob said, rising from his seat on Julius's last remaining step. "Quite the spectacle, isn't it?"

He glanced at the Black Reach, who was standing beside him, but the construct's face was bleak. "I find no joy in watching the race I was made to protect fly to their almost-certain deaths."

"Thank you, Captain Bringdown," Bob said. "But loath as I am to undercut your doomsayer routine, death is no longer a foregone conclusion. We're in new territory, predictively speaking, and new territory means new opportunities."

"That is true," the Black Reach admitted. "But just because the cards have been reshuffled doesn't mean they've changed their faces. We're still up against the same unbeatable foe." He arched a narrow eyebrow at Bob. "Unless you've got something in mind that changes the fundamental fact that we are outmatched in every way, I fail to see how any of these newly created futures will turn out differently than the old ones."

"I always have something in mind," Bob said with a smile. "This is *my* plot, remember? I didn't make the Leviathan mess, but I orchestrated its current form." He nodded at the sky full of dragons. "This fight is taking place on *my* board with *my* pieces. If there's a way out of this, I already have everything I need to make it happen. I just have to find it."

"And then what?" the Black Reach said, shooting a dangerous look at the pigeon snoozing on Bob's shoulder. "Use *that* to ensure it? Sell all other futures for the latest version of the happy ending where you survive?"

"My lady's already done her part," Bob said, placing a hand on the pigeon's feathered back. "She helped me survive you. Now that the veil of my death has finally been lifted, I'm free to use my genius to find us a real way out of this. No cheating required."

"That sounds dangerously close to desperation," the Black Reach growled. "Hope is fine for others, Brohomir, but we seers must always embrace reality. If you let what you want to happen blind you to what *will* happen, you'll be just as unprepared for the end as they are."

Bob's jaw clenched. "Perhaps I am being overly optimistic, but the only other option is to prepare for defeat, and I never could stand losing. You're the one who taught me that even certain doom isn't certain until it actually happens, and if there's any seer who could find a way out of this, it's me. After all..." His lips curled into a smirk. "I'm the one who beat you."

The Black Reach didn't dignify that with a response. He just stood there silently, rolling Marci's Kosmolabe between his long-fingered hands as the dragons overhead began burning the Leviathan's tentacles to ash.

• • •

The sky was chaos.

Though it was technically thin enough to move through, the magic still clung to Julius like glue. Flying through it was like trying to swim through molasses, forcing him to fight with all his strength just to stay airborne. Even after he got the hang of it, it was still a struggle to keep from being sent spinning whenever the bigger dragons blew past him, sometimes *much* bigger.

So far as he could tell just by looking, the average dragon seemed to be in their mid-hundreds. This meant most of them weren't much bigger than Gregory, but some were enormous. The Daughters of the Three Sisters in particular filled the sky like a weather front, turning the ruined city into a snowy wonderland as they blasted the Leviathan's black tentacles with their frosted flame. Conrad dominated as the wing leader of the Heartstriker attack, his enormous size matched only by Bethesda herself, who kept to the center of the pack, shouting orders at her dragons from a safe distance. But as huge as the dragons were, they were nothing compared to the monster they fought.

The first time Julius had crawled up to look at him, the Leviathan's black body had filled the sky. Now, though, the Nameless End *was* the sky. Even this high up, Julius could see no end to him. Not even the memory of sunlight got past him now, leaving the city blacker than any night under his shadow. If it hadn't been for all the dragon fire going off, Julius wouldn't have been able to see at all. He had no idea how the human pilots were going to manage, but the military flew night missions all the time, so he assumed they must have a way. He just hoped whatever system they used saw well enough to avoid the dragons, because from some of the near misses going on above him, crashing into each other in the dark posed more danger right now than the Leviathan.

"Julius!"

General Jackson's voice was an explosion in his ear. Her face appeared in his AR a moment later, floating in the sky somewhere off to his left, but she wasn't looking at him. Her attention was on the screen behind her, which Julius could only see because she'd apparently patched him directly into her own AR.

"Satellites are up," she said. "We still can't see through the Leviathan, but from the heat map data, it looks like Lakes Superior and Ontario are already dry. I'm ordering a flyover to be sure, but you should go ahead and tell your dragons to focus on protecting what's left of Lakes Michigan, Erie, and Huron so we're not wasting our time defending already lost territory."

"Understood," Julius said, looking around at the dragons, who'd already fanned out over the DFZ at astonishing speed. "I'll spread the word."

"Roger," Emily said before her feed cut out.

Julius took a deep breath. Technically, less territory to defend was good considering how much they had to cover, but it was still disheartening to hear they'd already lost two of the five Great Lakes. What he could see of Lake Erie in the distance didn't look good, either. When he tried shouting to the others to spread the information, though, he realized within a few words that no one could hear him.

As the runt of his clan and a firm believer in staying out of trouble, Julius hadn't spent much time in his dragon form, and practically none in actual combat. His fight with Gregory had been relatively close quarters, so he'd never realized just how fast a voice—even a dragon's roaring one—fell off over distance. In the two minutes it had taken him to get up in the air and get the information from the general, the dragons had spread out over several square miles, much too far for his voice to carry. He was desperately trying to think of another way to get the word out when a laughing voice bubbled up in his fire.

Looks like you could use a divine intervention.

Julius almost sobbed with relief when his oldest sister materialized in front of him, her giant dragon body coalescing out of bright-orange-and-red flame that kept burning even after her red feathers had formed.

"Sorry to be fashionably late," Amelia said, spreading her wings to fly beside him. "I had some business on the other side. What's the deetz?"

"Leviathan's already eaten two lakes," Julius replied immediately. "We need to focus on defending Michigan, Erie, and Huron, but I can't—"

"Say no more," his sister replied, breathing a lick of fire as she cleared her throat. Then, without warning, she roared, shaking the air and filling his magic with her voice.

Listen up, worms! she bellowed. *Thanks to our late start, we're already down two lakes. Ontario and Superior are Leviathan food, so anyone headed there needs to pick another body of water. I'm not going to bother assigning you all positions because we don't have that kind of time, so if you're fighting and you find yourself competing with other dragons for targets, move somewhere else. Likewise, if you're having trouble covering your area, call for me, and I'll send someone your way. The humans will be sending us backup in—*

She glanced at Julius. "How long until we get jets?" she asked in her normal voice.

He frantically brought up the updated maps the general had shared to his AR. "Two minutes."

Two minutes, Amelia repeated, the words hammering thorough his fire. *Remember, those planes are friends, not food. If I catch any of you being idiots, I'll snuff your fire on the spot and send you to an idiot's death. Ignore the Leviathan's main body as well. Our target is the tentacles. As my brother Justin is already demonstrating*—she motioned at Justin's distinctive flame in the distance, and Julius's head was suddenly filled with the image of his brother blasting black appendages out of the sky with giant bursts of his green fire—*they burn pretty well, but don't get carried away and waste time trying to turn everything to ash. The only thing we're up here to do is keep the Leviathan from drinking any more water than he already has, so just focus on stopping the tentacles from reaching the ground, and we should be all good.*

Her voice faded from Julius's fire after that, leaving the actual Amelia smirking at him from behind a wreath of smoke. "That went well," she said brightly. "You've got a line to the Phoenix, right?" When Julius nodded, Amelia rubbed her claws together. "Excellent. You'll be my wingman. You feed me intel from the ground, I'll spread it to the troops in between bouts of being a fiery god of death."

"Sounds good to me," Julius said, looking nervously at the dozen tentacles he could see in the area immediately surrounding them. "We need all the firepower we can get."

"Firepower is my middle name," Amelia said, the words coming out in curls of smoke as fire licked at her fangs. "You might want to get behind me."

Julius dove at once, darting behind his giant sister seconds before a wave of fire exploded out of her mouth. It was so bright, it whited out Julius's vision. By the time he could see again, all the tentacles around them were ash, and Amelia was looking very pleased with herself.

"Not bad, not bad," she said, lifting her eyes to the giant above them. "I wonder if that would work on the big one?"

"But you just told us to ignore the Leviathan's main body," Julius reminded her. "And aren't you the one who said it couldn't be defeated?"

"Normally, yeah," Amelia said. "But as I just demonstrated, I'm a god now. Gods don't follow normal rules."

"Neither does he," Julius argued. "Remember what Raven said? The Leviathan is using Algonquin's magic as a cover to hide his true form from the plane. Underneath that, though, he's still a Nameless End. If you go inside, he could devour your magic."

His sister scoffed. "Who said anything about going inside? I'm just going to try and burn a hole in his belly. I bet that would slow the tentacle production rate." She grinned. "No way to know except to try."

The idea of getting any closer to the Leviathan than they already were made Julius's skin crawl. Even this close, he could already feel how alien it was. How hungry. But when he turned to tell his sister that he *really* didn't think this was a good idea, Amelia beat her wings, blasting him away.

The wind rolling off her flaming feathers was hot as a furnace and strong as a hurricane, and it got stronger with every flap. All of her was looking bigger, actually. Julius didn't know if she'd been hiding her true size this whole time or if she was simply whatever size she wanted to be now, but Amelia's fiery body was already twice as large as Justin's, her fiery wings spreading until they lit up the entire DFZ. With one flap, she rose a hundred feet, bringing her flaming body directly below the Leviathan's as she opened her mouth to unleash the brightest gout of dragon fire Julius had ever seen.

He almost turned away too late. Even after he closed his eyes, the blast left him blind, lighting up the dark city like an atomic noon. Amelia's fire was so powerful, the heat of it curled his feathers and made it hard to breathe even a hundred feet away. He couldn't see what it was doing to the Leviathan, but it seemed impossible that so much fire would have no effect. Then, just as his hopes were starting to rise, the light snuffed out, and his sister vanished, her fiery form going dark as dozens of black tentacles shot through the air where she'd been.

"Amelia!" Julius cried, dodging frantically as one of the spears shot past him. "*Amelia!*"

Don't be dramatic, scolded the voice in his fire. His sister reappeared beside him a few moments later, though in a much smaller form. Her feathers hadn't even finished firming up when Svena swept in.

"What was that?" the white dragon panted, lowering the temperature several degrees with her frosty breaths. "And did it work?"

"Testing the Leviathan's resistance," Amelia replied, her own breaths worryingly short. "And no." She glanced up at the Leviathan's black shell, which, despite her incredible display of firepower, looked just as glossy and impenetrable as it had before.

"I don't understand," Svena said, pushing back one of the whelps who'd crawled too far up her neck. "I felt that blast all the way to my core. You hit him with the combined force of all dragon fire. *Nothing* should be immune to that."

"I don't think he's immune," Amelia said. "I saw my attack do a little damage before he tried to spear me, but not nearly as much as I'd hoped, and I'm afraid that's kind of my fault."

"How do you figure that?" Julius asked.

"Being made of sentient magic, spirits aren't usually bothered by physical weapons," his sister explained. "For example, you couldn't hurt Algonquin with a sword. No matter how hard you hit, your blade would just go right through her while she laughed. The reason dragons have never had a problem with this particular defense is because we're magic too. We're fighting fire with fire, so to speak, except our fire is from a different plane. That's why spirits have always seen us as such an enormous threat despite our relatively small numbers. We have a weapon they can't easily counter: our dragon fire. Unfortunately, when I became the Spirit of Dragons and tied our fire into the magic of this plane, I might have... broken that."

"*What?*" Svena shrieked. "I noticed the tentacles were taking longer to burn than they should, but I thought that was just the Nameless End's influence. I didn't realize you'd broken our fundamental advantage!"

"Not on purpose!" Amelia cried. "And if I hadn't tied us all into the magic, we wouldn't be here to fight at all!"

"We might as well not be," Svena snapped, jerking her long claws back at the dragons flaming all around them. "Look at how slow everyone's going! We're all going to die up here because you neutered our fire!"

Julius didn't think the assault was going slowly at all. Maybe it wasn't up to Svena's standards, but tentacles were still turning to ash at a perfectly acceptable rate, and in any case, "It doesn't matter," he said, shoving his body between the two dragonesses, who were both getting dangerously smoky. "We were never planning to assault the Leviathan directly, and we can still burn the part that matters."

He pointed across the city at the bursts of light where Conrad was burning entire clusters of the Leviathan's tentacles. "Our only job is to stall that thing long enough for Marci to banish it, and our fire still works fine for that." He turned back to Svena. "We're still on target, so please go back to your sisters and help protect Lake Erie. Also," his voice grew pleading, "*please* put your children down somewhere safe. I know bringing whelps into battle is an ancient dragon tradition, but it's terrifying to watch."

"Terrifying for a weak dragon like you, perhaps," Svena said with a sniff. "But *my* children are strong. When we survive, they will treasure this memory. Anyway, there's nowhere else to put them. The ground is just as dangerous, so they might as well be with me."

Julius wasn't sure about that. Now that the attacks had started, the Leviathan was sending down more tentacles than ever, except this time, not all of them were going for the water. Several were aimed at the dragons, including one that was flying right at Svena's back. Before he could warn her, a blast of fire scorched the incoming attack out of the sky, and then Ian swooped down beside them.

At least, it smelled like Ian. Julius had never seen his brother's dragon, which was oddly dark with deep reddish-brown feathers like a falcon's. But there was no other Heartstriker with eyes that rich brown color, and if that wasn't a big enough tip-off, the angry, possessive way he was staring at Svena banished all doubt.

For several moments, Svena looked just as shocked as Julius felt. Then her eyes narrowed. "I don't recall asking for your help," she said icily.

"You didn't need it," Ian agreed, his voice as cold as hers. "But they did." He nodded at the whelps on Svena's back, who were staring at him with huge blue eyes. "You can easily survive a direct hit. They cannot. Therefore, considering the number of tentacles in the sky, I think the best tactical move would be to divide them between us. That way, if one of us goes down, all of our children won't be lost."

"How very practical," Svena said.

"Our entire relationship has been practical," Ian reminded her. "That's why I treasured you. I thought we understood each other. You were the one who changed."

"I did not change!" she snarled. "Your family took my rival and betrayed me! I had every right to be enraged!"

"But not without me," Ian said, getting closer. "I would have fought them with you, Svena, and I don't fear your rage. It's part of what attracted me to you in the first place. You should have known that and kept me close. Instead, you shut me out. That was your choice to make, but you have no right to keep my children from me."

Svena looked extremely distressed by that, and Amelia rolled her eyes. "Can't you two save the custody battle for when the world *isn't* ending?" she snapped, glaring at Svena. "Just take him with you and work it out on the battlefield or something. I don't care what you do so long as you do it on the move, because while you two were bickering, the rest of your clan was falling behind."

The cluster of white dragons in the distance *was* looking a bit harried, and Svena sighed. "Ian," she said primly. "Your idiot sister makes a good point. I admit I was hasty in my decisions before, but—"

"Hasty?" Ian growled. "You freaked out over assumed information, broke our treaties, stole my children, and locked me out in a magical apocalypse after I flew all the way to Siberia to talk to you!" He crossed his short forefeet in front of him. "I deserve an apology, but since part of the reason I admire you is because you never give those, I'll settle for full reinstatement as your consort and a life debt."

Amelia whooped with laughter as Svena's eyes grew wide. "Scale's on the other foot now, snowball!"

"Shut up, fire chicken," Svena snapped, but she really did look nervous as she watched Ian. Then, finally, she nodded, and the binding magic of the life debt landed on all of them like frozen teeth.

Ian sucked in a breath as the cold struck him, and his face split into a triumphant smile. "There," he said, reaching out to the whelps, who happily leaped to him, their little noses quivering as they sniffed his feathers. "That wasn't so hard, was it?"

"That was amazing!" Amelia cackled, grinning at Svena, who looked ready to blast her in the face again. "Svena giving a life debt to her lover! Now I *know* the world is ending."

Julius was feeling the same way, but not because of Svena and Ian. The whole time they'd been talking, he'd been watching the battle—both with his eyes and on the radar screen his com had picked up from the incoming jets. From what he could tell, their end of the fight was going as well as he could have hoped. Justin was having the time of his life blasting endless targets to his violent heart's content, Conrad was a powerhouse, and the Golden Emperor had all of Lake Michigan on lockdown, leading his dragons in such perfect harmony, it looked as if they'd choreographed the whole thing in advance.

But while the Golden Empire was hands down the best, they weren't alone. *All* the dragons were fighting together rather than with each other. Even Gregory was fighting. The clanless dragons were a little far away, but Julius had seen enough of Gregory's fire to know it anywhere, and it was pushing just as strong as the others. So far as he could see, *everyone* was doing their part, including the wing of planes that had just arrived over Lake Erie. The humans had just entered the fight, but already they were shooting down tentacles almost as fast as the dragons were, and—more importantly—*not* shooting dragons. It was incredible, the greatest display of unity he'd ever seen or heard of.

And it wasn't working.

No matter how fast they burned them, the Leviathan's tentacles always came back faster. Destroy one, and two more would pop up in its place, shooting down at the tiny pools of water like kamikaze bombers. For every one they caught before it touched the ground, another got through, sucking up gallons of water before their forces could destroy it. Julius knew their efforts had to be slowing down the Leviathan's consumption compared to when he'd been drinking unhindered, but he couldn't shake the horrifying feeling that they weren't actually making much of a difference, and what progress they were achieving was coming at a heavy cost.

As he'd seen with Amelia and Svena, the Leviathan's tentacles were no longer just going for water. Several were actively attacking dragons now, swatting them out of the air every time they left an opening. So far, everyone he'd seen get hit had come back up, but the damage was evident in their slowed wings and uneven flight. He'd come into this knowing it would be a battle of attrition, but as he watched it unfold, Julius became more and more worried that they were already on the losing end of it.

Please, he thought silently, turning toward the western edge of the city where he could still smell a hint of Marci's scent. *Please, Marci, hurry.*

He was still begging when a huge, slimy tentacle smacked him from behind, sending him spinning through the air.

CHAPTER ELEVEN

The Sea of Magic was even worse than Marci remembered.

It was still black, still nauseating, and still chaos, but there was just so much *more* of it. Even though her human eyes couldn't process it, Marci could *feel* the weight of all that power pushing down on them like they were being crushed at the bottom of the ocean. It was even more terrifying now than it had been when she'd been dead, because while her soul was definitely firmer this time around, the safety zone provided by her spirit was much, much smaller, pushed nearly to her skin by the pressure outside.

"What now?" Ghost said, his terrifying face set in a nervous frown as he stared at the swirling magic above them.

"Find some spirits," Marci said.

"That won't be hard. They're everywhere. But getting them to listen is another matter." His frown deepened. "I've never seen them so worked up, and I was here for the madness that broke out once we realized the Merlins were cutting off the magic."

"It gets harder, I'm afraid," Marci said. "You heard what Myron said. If we're going to make this thing work, we need *all* the spirits on board, and we need them fast. That means we can't do this one by one. We need to talk to everyone, preferably all at the same time."

"That's impossible," Ghost said immediately. "No one can talk to every spirit at once."

"Just hear me out," she said, flashing him a smile. "I've been doing some thinking about how you got me in here. One of the fundamental rules of all spirits is that they are strictly defined by their domains. Inside your area of influence, though, you're basically a god."

"Obviously," the Empty Wind said. "I couldn't have brought you here were it otherwise. But I fail to see how the Forgotten Dead can help us in this particular situation."

"You didn't see how they were going to get me over here, either," Marci reminded him. "But we made it work. I'm pretty sure we can make this work too." She waved her hand at the churning dark. "This is where our souls go when we die. From a human perspective, the Sea of Magic is basically the afterlife, and as a spirit of the dead, that makes it yours."

Ghost shifted uncomfortably. "I think that's a bit of a stretch."

"Of course it is," Marci said. "But that's what humans do. We think outside the box and stretch things to make them work. You're a human spirit, a *concept*. Unlike a lake, your borders are defined not by hard lines, but by human ideas. That makes you stretchy by definition." She grinned at him. "You've called yourself a face of death multiple times now, and *I* know this place is death because this is where I went when I died. If both of those are true, then you should have special powers here that other Mortal Spirits don't. Maybe even the power to make your voice heard to every other spirit inside it. I mean, you can speak to all the dead inside your wind, right?"

"I can," Ghost said cautiously. "But only speak. I can't make them do things."

"That's fine," Marci said. "Talking is all I want. We're not here to make anyone do anything, we only need to get their attention so we can explain the situation and hopefully convince them to act in their own best interest. Just give it a try. If it doesn't work, all we've lost is time spent yelling into the void."

Her spirit still looked deeply skeptical, but he must have had a lot of faith in her these days, because Ghost gave it his best. He set her down in front of the Merlin Gate with a bubble of magic to keep her from being swept away, and then he flew up above her, growing larger and larger until the dark of his body merged with the dark of everything else. Finally, when all she could see of him were two glowing eyes floating like stars in the blackness, Marci felt something shift.

That shouldn't have been cause for comment. Everything in this place was constantly moving, only this time, it was all moving together. Slowly, like water being pushed by the wind, all the swirling chaos began to flow in the same direction. It wasn't that the sea grew calmer, just that the violence had a new unity, the nauseating eddies and tangles flowing together like leaves blown on an icy wind Marci felt all the way to the core of her being.

It took a long time. The wind rose quickly, but the sea was enormous. Every time Marci thought they must have reached the end, Ghost's magic redoubled, and the gale grew larger, blowing into every crook and bend of the surging sea. Then, when his magic was stretched across more of the Sea of Magic than Marci had ever dreamed existed, the Empty Wind spoke.

I am Ghost, he said, the words howling through the dark in a thousand voices. *The Empty Wind, Spirit of the Forgotten Dead, bound Mortal Spirit of the first of the New Merlins, Marci Novalli. Algonquin has betrayed us, and the Nameless End is coming to devour all that exists. If you wish to remain eternal, come to the Merlin Gate and hear how we plan to survive. If you do not care, then stay where you are and learn how the deathless die.*

His voice was like thunder by the time he finished. It shook through the magic, making the whole sea tremble. When it was over, Ghost collapsed into himself, sinking back down through the chaos to land beside Marci in a heap.

"How was that?" he asked weakly.

"Fantastic," she assured him. "Just the right balance of threat and promise."

"Spirits need threats," he said, pushing back to his feet. "It's easy to bury your head when you can live through anything. If you want them to act, you have to tell them what is at stake. I just hope it worked."

"We'll know soon enough," Marci said, lifting her eyes to the dark, which was already growing crowded. It was hard to make out details through the swirling ink of the unfiltered magic, but there were definitely things around them now that hadn't been there before. Very *big* things, watching her from the shadows. She was trying to tilt her head back far enough to actually look at them when something spoke.

"Who are you?"

Chills ran down her spine. The voice sounded like a knife the size of a cruise ship rasping over a mountain. If Ghost hadn't been right behind her, Marci would have turned and run. But he *was* behind her, his cold, comforting weight reminding her that she was not alone, and that gave her the courage to step forward instead.

"My name is Marci Novalli," she said, speaking as loudly and clearly as she could. "Bound to the Empty Wind, Master of the Heart of the World, first Merlin since the return of magic, and I'm here to ask for your help."

She reached down to touch the ground at her feet. Thanks to the swirling dark, it looked as black as everything else here, but she knew from what she'd seen in the Heart of the World that the smooth, hard substance beneath her feet wasn't stone or congealed magic or anything else natural to this world. It was part of the Nameless End, one of the roots he'd set down, and it was everywhere.

"I'm sure you already know what this is," she said, scraping her nails across the hard, black substance. "Algonquin's Leviathan is a Nameless End, a devourer of worlds. He's eating her as I speak, and when he's finished, he'll have a foothold in our plane big enough to keep him rooted while he eats the rest of us. He's already dug in deep. If we don't want to die, we're going to have to work together to dig him out again before he ends us all."

Marci thought that was a pretty compelling argument, but the powers above her seemed unimpressed.

"Why should we fight for you?" asked a growling voice. Then, like the sun coming out from behind a cloud, a wolf appeared. Not a normal wolf, but a monster the size of a charter bus, its long tail lashing in anger.

"Why should we fight?" Wolf asked again, his yellow eyes flicking up to the much bigger spirits looming over him. "*They* are back, which means *our* world is already doomed. The mortal gods are even bigger than they were before. They will overrun us all!" He bared his bloody teeth. "Why should I fight for a future where I will be trampled?"

"You dare blame us!" cried the enormous, knife-scraping voice, and the magic above them jerked, forming into a painfully thin man covered head to toe in a long, red shroud. No, Marci realized, not a shroud. It was blood. The man was dripping with fresh blood as he stabbed his red hand at Wolf.

"This is your fault!" he cried. "We'd barely woken before you tried to tear us to pieces! I don't even know my name yet, and you had your mongrel teeth on my throat! Why should we be devoured because your Algonquin could not control her fear? We are spirits just as you are!"

"You are *monsters*!" Wolf roared. "Fear, impulse, panic, the worst of humanity's sins made flesh! All of this world's problems lie at *your* feet. If you could control yourselves, Algonquin would have never turned to the Leviathan!"

"You attacked us!" cried a rasping voice as a new figure appeared beside the bloody man. A bent old woman wrapped in animal hides with a bushel of stinging nettles clutched in her bare hands. "We did nothing but wake," the woman snarled, beating her nettles across the wolf's nose until it yelped. "You are what is wrong!"

"The *Leviathan* is what is wrong!" Marci cried, shoving herself between them. "I know you've all got a lot going on right now, but who's to blame won't matter when we're all dead. And make no mistake, we will *all* be dead if we don't act quickly." She turned to glare up at the giant wolf. "You're the spirit of wolves, right? What do you think is going to happen to all those wolves when Leviathan wins? Because I'll tell you right now, it'll be a lot worse than anything they can do."

She pointed at the red man and the old woman, but the giant wolf just snorted. "You know nothing, human. Your kind has already hunted mine to near extinction. Why should I tolerate your spirits as well?"

"I'm not asking you to tolerate them," Marci said. "I'm asking you to help yourself not die. We're not trying to solve thousands of years of conflict here. You guys have miles of legitimate reasons to be mad at each other, but if you let all that anger get in your way right now, there'll never be a chance to fix anything because we'll all be dead. So if you're cool with dying stupidly, go on your way. But if you want to hear my plan to save everything, stop yelling at each other for five minutes and *listen*."

That was not how one talked to gods, and Wolf's glare made sure Marci knew it. But for all his big talk, the animal spirit didn't leave, and Marci took that as her cue to keep going.

"I wouldn't have come out here if I didn't have a plan," she said, pointing over her shoulder at the looming pillar of the Heart of the World. "We didn't mean to let the magic out all at once like that, but having all of it active right now actually works in our favor. The Leviathan is a Nameless End, a scavenger who eats dying planes. But *our* plane is healthy, which means he's not supposed to be here. The only way he was able to stay is because Algonquin let him, and now he's using her magic to dig in deeper still. But the same thing that made his plan work is how we're going to beat it. By filling himself with magic like a spirit, he's picked up your vulnerabilities as well, specifically banishment."

"What is banishment?" asked the blood-covered man.

"Ignorant," Wolf sneered, causing all the Mortal Spirits to boil over in fury.

"We only woke a few hours ago!" cried the old woman.

"I remember nothing!" cried another, a giant shadow dripping with something she couldn't identify. "Even my name is gone!"

"We are lost, lost," moaned a third, who was so far back in the swirling void Marci couldn't even see its shape. "We have no anchors, no help."

"We'll get you help," Marci promised, giving the creature what she hoped was a reassuring smile. "I know things are crazy, but this is actually the beginning of a golden age. There are more humans now than ever before, including millions of mages. That means there are Merlins enough for all of you!"

"You don't have to be alone," Ghost added, putting his hands on her shoulders. "I, too, was alone when I woke, but Marci found me. She calmed my rage and helped me find my purpose. Now we work together to serve the Forgotten Dead, and I am content. You can be too. We are human spirits, and humans are not meant to be alone. We are born in darkness, but we don't have to remain there. The Merlins are here to help us."

"The Merlins betrayed us!"

The shout crashed through the dark like breaking ice, and Marci froze. She knew that voice. As long as she lived, she'd never be able to forget it. Sure enough, the tall spirit who appeared from the dark beside Wolf was the same blue-skinned, seaweed-bearded Viking she'd seen when they'd ripped the black bag off her head in that interrogation room what felt like forever ago. He no longer had a weapon in his hand, but there was no mistaking the piercing eyes and hate-filled sneer of Vann Jeger, spirit of the Geirangerfjord, the Death of Dragons.

"You've been played for a fool, cat," Vann Jeger said, sneering at Ghost. "The Merlins were the ones who sealed magic away to destroy your kind. She's banking on your ignorance now as well, because her 'plan' won't even work. She speaks of banishment as though it's the end, but she and her pet dragons did the same to me, and here I am." He pounded his fist against his massive chest. "I was banished by her hand for attempting to slay one of the dragon interlopers, but all she did was send me back to my vessel here. I was too weak to rise again at first, but when the magic came crashing down, I was refilled in an instant. The Leviathan will be no different." He bared his black teeth. "She thinks she can make fools of us all!"

"I'm not trying to fool anyone!" Marci cried, stomping forward to face him as anger overwhelmed her fear. "I never said banishment was permanent. I *said* it was a solution to the Leviathan problem, because while he's impersonating a spirit, he doesn't actually belong here. You had a fjord to go back home to. He doesn't. There is no Leviathan-shaped hole in the bottom of the Sea of Magic. If I banish him, all the magic he's stolen will go back to Algonquin. *She* will rise again. He will not. Without Algonquin's magic, he'll have nowhere to hide, and our plane will kick him out like it should have done at the beginning."

"A convenient technicality," Wolf growled. "But why should we trust you?" He nodded respectfully toward Vann Jeger. "The lord of the Geirangerfjord speaks the truth. You Merlins started this mess when you stole our magic. You sent us all to sleep so you could keep our world for yourselves. Now you come with talk of unity because you need our help. Why should we believe a word you say?"

Because she was *right*. Because they were *all* going to die if they didn't. Marci was dying to scream the truth in Wolf's stupid dog face, but as justified as her rant would be, that sort of anger was how they'd gotten into this mess in the first place. If this was going to work, then Marci had to actually make them listen, and you didn't get that by yelling. She was trying to figure out how she *could* get it when a black shape swooped over them.

"You can believe her because that's how she became Merlin," Raven said, flapping down to settle on Marci's shoulder.

Wolf snorted. "Why am I not surprised to see you take her side, carrion eater?"

"Because I'm always on the right side of history, deer-breath," Raven snapped back, turning his beady eyes to glare at the rest of the spirits hiding in Wolf's shadow. "I was there when this human became the new Merlin, and I can tell you that she did so by fighting for *us*. Sir Myron Rollins, whom I know you're all familiar with, wanted to seal everything up again. Marci's the one who stopped him. If it weren't for her, we'd all be stuck down here asleep again while the Leviathan ate our world at his leisure."

"And we're supposed to just believe you?" Vann Jeger growled. "Trust the trickster?"

"Yes," Raven said, fluffing his feathers. "Because unlike you lot, *I* didn't panic and surrender all of my authority to Algonquin. I kept my magic and thought for myself, which means I've been paying attention to this since it started. I've seen the Leviathan with my own eyes on this side and the other, and if you think there will be anything left of this world once he's done, you're all idiots."

Wolf scowled. "Algonquin said—"

"Algonquin sold us out!" Raven squawked. "You saw her beg for your magic. You knew how far she'd fallen. Now she's let her irrational hatred of Mortal Spirits do what nothing else in the universe could. She's let it kill her, and she's going to get the rest of us killed as well if we don't do something."

"And this Merlin knows how to stop that?" asked the red man.

"I think she does," Raven said, turning his head to peer at the Mortal Spirit. "You're awful rational for someone covered in blood. Which spirit are you?"

"I don't know," the man confessed, looking down at his gory hands. "I don't know how I got here or why I'm covered in blood. I don't even know if it's my blood or someone else's. I just…" His voice trailed off as his bloody hands began to shake, and then he raised them to cover his face. "*Help me.*"

The terrified sorrow in his voice overwhelmed even the metallic knife-scrape sound, and Marci's heart broke. "We will help," she promised. "As soon as this crisis is resolved, I'm going to start recruiting and training Merlins. One of them will be yours. Their entire job will be to help you. We can work it out together, all of us."

She turned back to the gathered spirits. "My ancestors made a huge mistake. We were afraid, and in our fear, we took what was not ours. We stole the magic and locked it away because we knew we could live without it and you couldn't. That was wrong, and on behalf of all the Merlins—past, future, and present—I am sorry."

Her words were met with silence. Not angry silence or dismissive silence. Shocked silence. As it stretched, Marci realized with a start that no human had probably ever apologized for the drought. Not before, not during, and not since. But while she was certain one apology wasn't going to be enough, the silence was the best reaction she'd gotten so far, so Marci kept going.

"I'm sorry," she said again, lowering her head. "I'd give those years back to you if I could, but all I can do is promise to learn from my ancestors' mistakes. They let fear push them into doing something incredibly stupid that hurt everyone. Now Algonquin's doing the same thing on an even bigger scale. She's let her hate of Mortal Spirits convince her to end *everything*, including us." She looked at Wolf. "I know you have good reasons to be angry. The bad blood between the land and animal spirits and the mortal ones stretches back farther than human civilization. It's impossible to reconcile something that big in one conversation, or even one lifetime, but if dragons and humans can work together for this, surely we can too. I'm not asking for peace or forgiveness. We can work on those later. All I'm asking right now is for you to help me ensure that there *is* a later, because the world won't make it another six hours without your help."

Marci held her breath as she finished. That had been her best shot. If an apology plus the threat of mutual annihilation didn't change their minds, nothing would. Even Raven seemed nervous, hopping foot to foot on her shoulder as they waited.

"I will help," said the bloody man, breaking the silence. "I have to survive, or I'll never find out why I'm like this."

"I'll help as well," said the woman with the nettles. "I don't know what I do yet, but I will aid you if I can, Marci the Merlin."

With that, all the Mortal Spirits began to nod. Some of them violently, some awkwardly, as if they still weren't sure what they were agreeing to. But while many of the Mortal Spirits clearly weren't all there yet, none of them walked away, which was good enough for her.

The other camp was less optimistic. Now that her eyes had gotten used to the dark, Marci could see just how much smaller the crowd of land and animal spirits was. They were still huge compared to her, but next to looming shadows of the Mortal Spirits, they looked tiny. Small and scared, their dark shapes huddled around Wolf and Vann Jeger, who were still the only two who'd come forward. But while the whispers from their group were angry, Algonquin must have been the only one who was truly willing to die to spite the Mortal Spirits, because a few minutes later, Wolf stepped forward.

"What do you need of us?"

It took everything Marci had not to collapse in relief. "Your magic."

It didn't seem possible, but Wolf looked even less pleased. "How much?"

There was no good way to say it, so Marci just spit it out.

"All of it."

The words were barely out of her mouth before every spirit balked.

"*All* our magic?" the bloody man cried. "But we just got it back!"

"We're not giving *all* of our magic to a mortal!" Vann Jeger yelled at the same time. "What guarantee do we have you won't keep it and start the drought all over again?"

"Come on," Marci snapped, glaring at him. "You, of *all* spirits, should know how much I like being a mage. Do you really think I'd give that up? Give up Ghost?" She scoffed. "No way. And yes, I really do need *all* of your magic. We're talking about banishing something as big as Algonquin. That takes world-class power, and in this world, that means you."

"But how will you use it?" the bloody man asked. "Where will we go?"

"The only circle big enough is the Heart of the World," Marci said apologetically. "I know you just got out of there, but I swear it'll only be for a moment. Once I've gathered your magic, I'll cast the banish and blow up the Leviathan, scattering Algonquin's power and everything else. Since you're all immortal spirits, you'll just fall back into your vessels to rise again once things calm down, but the Nameless End will be left high and dry. When that happens, our plane will shove him back out into the void between worlds, and we'll all be free."

The spirits began muttering again as they discussed this. Marci waited impatiently, biting her lip as the whispers dragged on and on. Then, as if he were just as fed up with waiting as she was, Vann Jeger threw up his arms and stomped over to Marci.

"No one ever won a battle putting off the inevitable," he said, his words breaking like ice as he put out his giant hand. "When this is done, you shall again be my sworn enemy, dragon lover, but for now..." He trailed off, staring up at the pillar of the Merlin Gate with a mix of hate and resignation. "Show me where to jump."

"Right this way," Marci said, turning around so he wouldn't see her triumphant smile. "Just let me see if Myron has the landing pad ready."

• • •

Myron did *not* have the landing pad ready. Marci wasn't sure how long she'd spent talking to the spirits—time flowed a bit wonky in the Sea of Magic, and it wasn't as though her soul had a watch—but it felt like enough time to patch up a circle. When she returned to the Heart of the World, though, Myron and the DFZ were still elbow-deep in preparations. Soggy bits of spellworked leaves and rocks were scattered everywhere, making the island mountaintop look like a yard after a big storm. When Marci nudged one of the branches aside so she'd have somewhere to stand, Myron shouted at her, stomping over to put the branch back exactly as it had been.

"Please tell me you're almost done," Marci groaned, squeezing her feet into the one bit of clear mountaintop left. "I've got every spirit in the world lined up to help, but it won't count for squat if they've got nowhere to go."

"Sorry to lag behind," Myron snarled. "But I'm doing my best to pull off the impossible here, and that's hard enough without you stomping all over my matrices."

"He's in a bad mood," the DFZ informed her. "His first attempt didn't work."

"If you want to be useful, get in here and help me hold all of this in place," Myron said, gesturing at the interlocking maze of wet leaves he'd layered over the top of the broken seal.

Marci tiptoed through the chaos and put her hands where he pointed. "How much longer do you—"

"It'll be done when it's done," he snapped as he laid down another layer. Sticks, this time. "I'm using the mountain's existing spellwork to save time, but it took forever to gather materials with everything being underwater. Shiro was helping, but then he had to go deal with the situation downstairs."

Marci frowned. "What's happening downstairs?"

"The Leviathan's tentacles are starting to creep into the base of the pillar," the DFZ said, handing another armload of sticks to Myron.

"Are you kidding?" Marci cried frantically. "This place was built to be a magical collection chamber! If he gets his slimy tendrils into the Heart of the World, he'll be able to suck all the power out of our plane like he's drinking it through a straw!"

"Why do you think I'm working so fast?" Myron said testily, nudging the last stick into position. "There, that's done. Now I just have to..." He spread his hands over the layer of leaves and twigs, closing his eyes as the green light began to rise from the maze of spellworked foliage. As it lit up, Marci felt the magic working through every part of the submerged mountain below, but it wasn't until the stone itself began to shift that she realized what Myron had done.

"Holy—" She backed away, eyes widening as the leaves and twigs began to burn themselves into the seal, forming a patch over the crack that had split the stone circle. "You reordered the mountain?!"

When they'd first arrived, one of the things that had blown Marci away most about the Heart of the World was how everything—the rocks, the trees, the leaves, the grass, even the pebbles—was crafted from spellwork. The whole place was a giant circle, the biggest spell ever made, and Myron had just made it bigger. He hadn't just taken spellwork from below and repurposed it. He'd woven his own school of labyrinth magic into the work of the ancient Merlins, adding new spellwork not just on top of, but *into* the finished matrix of an already functional circle. That was hard enough to do with normal spells, but Myron had done it on the most complicated magical artifice ever constructed. Even more impressive, he'd done it in hours rather than years, but the most amazing part of all was the fact that it *worked*.

The crack in the stone seal that had once held all the world's magic was healing in front of Marci's eyes, the labyrinth of leaves and twigs melting into the spellworked stone as though they'd always been part of it. When the green light finally faded, the stone circle at the center of the mountain was whole once again. Not perfect—the patch job was obvious—but it held together when Marci knocked on it, and she looked up at Myron in awe.

"That's impressive."

"I'm aware," Myron said, brushing off his hands with a superior smile. "I *am* the world's greatest mage."

Any other time, Marci would have rolled her eyes. This time, though, Myron had earned his bragging, and she applauded accordingly. "Bravo."

"Thank you," he said, looking around. "So where are these spirits you were boasting about?"

Now it was Marci's turn to show off. She walked to the line in the stone that served as the temporary Merlin Gate since the official entrance was underwater and grabbed hold of the magic that kept the barrier closed. The spellwork yielded easily to her now that she was officially a Merlin, allowing her to peel the bright air back like a curtain to reveal what was waiting in the chaos outside.

Raven flew through first, followed immediately by Vann Jeger. The bleeding man came in third, his bloodshot eyes wide as he looked around at the island in wonder.

"Is all of this yours?" he whispered to Marci.

"It's ours," she replied warmly, turning to Myron. "Did you remember to build an entrance into your seal?"

"Of course," Myron said as he gave the giant stone circle a shove. "Hop in."

Marci's jaw dropped. The very first time she'd come up here, she'd thought that the circular stone at the center of the mountain looked like the cap on a well. Now, she saw that she'd been right. The giant seal—which had always felt as solid as the mountain itself whenever Marci had touched it—moved easily when Myron pushed it, sliding aside like it was on tracks to reveal a shaft that went straight down into the stone below.

"It *was* a well," she said breathlessly.

"More like an access port," Myron replied. "You don't put water *into* a well. But this is by far the easiest way into the Heart of the World's holding chamber. So, as they say in your country"—he pointed down the deep, dark hole—"Geronimo."

"No Native American says that," Raven chirped as he hopped to the edge of the pit. "It is *big* down there, isn't it?"

"It held all the magic in the world at one point," Marci reminded him. "But I promise it won't be for long this time." She turned to the doorway where the other spirits were waiting. "We won't even put the seal back on. I just need you to lend me your magic for a few minutes, and then you'll all be returned to your vessels."

The dark shapes shuffled nervously, but Vann Jeger pushed his way to the front. "Enough coddling," he growled, shoving Raven aside. "I am not afraid." He glared down at Marci. "I am the immortal hunter, and I will be back to hunt you and your dragon again, in this life or the next. For now, though, I will do what must be done."

With that, he stepped off the edge, dissolving into water as he fell into the dark.

Marci held her breath, waiting for the splash at the bottom, but she didn't hear a thing. The spirit was simply gone, eaten by the mountain below.

"That was anticlimactic," Raven said, fluttering up so the other spirits could see him. "All right, you all saw where the Geirangerfjord went, so let's hop to! The world won't save itself."

"Who are you to give us orders, thief bird?" Wolf growled, pushing his way through the door. "If you're so sure, let's see you go in."

"I was about to," Raven said, fluffing his feathers as he landed at the edge of the pit. Then, as he was turning to go in, he paused to look up at Marci. "We're betting it all on you," he whispered. "Don't fail us, Merlin."

Marci opened her mouth to swear she would not, but Raven was already gone, the beat of his wings vanishing as he plunged into the dark.

After that, there was nothing else to be said. One by one, the spirits marched through the Merlin Gate, their huge forms shrinking to human scale so they could squeeze through the doorway and jump down the well inside. The bloody man went after Raven, then Wolf dove in, then the crone with the nettles, then a tree Marci didn't recognize, then something that looked like an eel with a man's face.

On and on they came like a silent parade of imaginary monsters. Some—the animals mostly—were easy to recognize, but most Marci couldn't have named if she'd tried. Word must have spread while she'd been waiting on Myron, because there were even more spirits waiting outside than she'd seen while she was pleading with them. Hundreds, thousands, maybe millions of spirits tromped through the door she held open. Every time Marci thought that must be all, more would appear, and as they jumped one by one into the holding circle that was the Merlin's mountain, the raging sea outside began to retreat.

It happened so gradually, Marci didn't notice the change at first, but after an hour of watching spirit after spirit disappear down the hole, she looked up to see that their tiny island was no longer tiny, or an island, but a mountain once again. Down below, the cliffs were back, and the tops of the green trees were visible beneath the churning water. Bit by bit, the sea fell, retreating down the Merlin's green mountain until she could see the white courtyard where they'd first entered, and then the Merlin Gate itself.

But it didn't stop there. As more spirits poured themselves into the Heart of the World, the Sea of Magic sank lower and lower. By the time her hands began to burn from holding open the door so long, the water was shallower than Marci had ever seen it, leaving the Leviathan's gnarled roots exposed like black worms across the seabed from horizon to horizon. She was trying to wrap her head around just how much of the Nameless End was down there when Shiro hauled himself up the now dry stairs looking like he'd just lost the fight of his life.

Marci handed the door to Ghost and ran to him. The shikigami fell over when she reached him, collapsing to the stone like a pile of wet cloth. "Are you okay?" she cried, rolling him onto his back.

"No," he gasped, grabbing her hands. "I kept him out of the Heart of the World, but…" His dark eyes met hers. "He is bigger than anything I could have imagined, Merlin. Bigger than all of us. What we see here, what he's done, it's just a fraction. He will crack this plane open and eat us whole. We cannot stop him."

"Don't say that," Marci said angrily. "We can still win."

"Nothing can win," Shiro said, shaking his head. "This pillar reaches to the very bottom of the Sea of Magic, its base anchored in the wall of our plane itself. When I went down to make sure he did not enter, I caught a glimpse of what waited outside." He started to tremble. "I *saw* him, Merlin. Saw what should never be seen. And now—" He cut off with a shudder, his hands desperate as they grasped hers. "No one can beat this. He is the end of all."

Marci cursed and looked back at the line of spirits, which seemed to be winding down at last. Below her, the pillar-shaped mountain of the Heart of the World stood as high and dry as a dock post at low tide, its spellwork stretched tight as a drum trying to hold all the spirits that had crammed themselves inside. There were still a few puddles left in the black-riddled seabed outside—spirits who'd been too afraid or stubborn to come—but for all intents and purposes, the magic of the world was *here*. The spirits had answered her call, and Marci had to believe that was enough.

"I don't doubt what you saw," she said, turning back to the guardian. "But you've been claiming things were impossible since I met you, yet here we are. I didn't come this far to fail now. We will beat this, Shiro. We will banish the Leviathan and take back our plane, and there's nothing anyone—not Algonquin, not the Black Reach, not even the End itself—can do to stop us."

"I hope you are right," Shiro said quietly. "I know you are not, but I hope."

Marci squeezed his shoulder and rose to her feet, turning around to see Myron standing between the Empty Wind and the DFZ, the only two spirits left.

"So," the mage said, looking down at the well, which was now filled to the brim with magic. "What now?"

"What do you mean 'what now?'" Marci asked angrily. "We hammer the Leviathan."

"That was the plan," Myron said nervously. "But now that we've got all the magic, someone has to actually *cast* the banish, and I'm not entirely sure how that's going to happen without one of us burning themselves to a crisp. We've got the most sophisticated casting circle ever constructed, but even the best spellwork still needs a mage to operate it, and no one's ever handled magic on this scale before."

Marci gaped at him. "Shouldn't you have brought this up *earlier?*"

"I did think about it," Myron said. "But to be perfectly honest, I didn't think we'd get this far. And if we did, I figured we'd just wing it since casting the banish is by far the easiest step of this endeavor. Now that I'm actually seeing just how much magic we're dealing with, though..." He trailed off with a shrug. "I have no idea how we're going to do this."

"I don't believe it," Marci groaned, sitting on the ground with a *thud.* "We finally built a hammer big enough to smash a Nameless End, and we can't pick it up."

"*You* can't pick it up," the DFZ said. "But we can."

Marci blinked. "Say again?"

The city flashed her a radiant smile. "I'm the city of mages, remember? My entire Skyway system was designed to be a magic gathering funnel for Algonquin. I might know a thing or two about casting big spells, and it seems to me that what we've got is a bandwidth problem. The power's there, but holding all of it even for the second it'll take to cast the banish will kill you. But what if you *didn't* have to hold it all at once? What if someone else could carry it for you? That way, all you'd have to do is point the magic in the right direction."

"That's impossible," Myron said. "Humans are the only ones who can move magic. Spellwork helps organize and focus, but no matter how fancy you get, sooner or later, someone has to actually *cast* the spell. That's why we don't have spell-casting machines. Without humanity, magic doesn't work."

"That's true," Marci said, pushing back to her feet. "But she's talking about holding magic, not casting it. Casting is just the act of pushing magic at a target, and you don't have to be able to hold all of something to push it. It just has to be connected, and there's nothing more connected than a Merlin and her spirit."

The DFZ nodded happily, and Marci turned to Ghost, who looked as excited as she felt. "Can you do it?"

"I won't know until I try," he said. "I'd call it a long shot, but you expanded my horizons just now when you showed me that the entire Sea of Magic is a realm of death. That's a lot of room to work with." He nodded. "I think I can do it."

"Better than I could," the DFZ said grumpily. "I'm just a city. He's a whole concept of mortality." She kicked one of the spellworked pebbles that still dotted the ground. "Stupid Algonquin, making the smallest spirit possible. *I'm* the city of mages! This should have been our gig!"

"I'm perfectly happy to let Novalli hog this spotlight," Myron said. "It was a good observation, though." He smiled at his spirit. "Perhaps we're not so badly matched after all."

The city snorted. "I wouldn't have accepted you if we were. But if the Empty Wind's going to play capacitor, my work here is done." She reached her hand out to Myron. He shook it gladly, giving his spirit a truly warm smile as she turned and began walking toward the well.

"Wait," Marci said as the DFZ neared the edge. "What are you doing?"

"My part," the spirit said. "Myron and I already talked about this, and we both agreed. I'm the DFZ, and that thing is right above me. Without my city, I'm nothing, so like everything else, I'm throwing my lot in with you." She glanced at Shiro, who was watching them with a shocked look on his face. "He says it's impossible, but mages do the impossible every day. I should know. My city is full of them." She grinned, pushing her hood back to look at Marci with her bright, orange eyes. "It's time to live up to your reputation, Marci Novalli. Pull it out of the bag one last time and save us all."

She stepped into the well as she finished, her body dissolving into the bright, neon-reflected water that flowed through the gutters of the wilder parts of the Underground. For a split-second, her magic glittered beautifully. Then, like all the rest, it was gone, sucked down into the Heart of the World as the spellwork groaned.

Marci watched to the end with a lump in her throat. "Are you sure about this, Myron?"

"It wasn't much of a choice, really," he said quietly. "If you succeed, she'll come right back. If you don't, we're all dead anyway, so I won't be around to regret my decision." His face grew sheepish. "Though if I may ask you a favor, Novalli, please don't mess this up. I just got to be a Merlin, and I'd very much like to spend some time here when I'm *not* in a panic to save the world, if it's all the same to you."

"I'll do my best," Marci promised, putting out her hand to Ghost. "Ready?"

A cold wind was her answer. No sooner had she touched her spirit than his body dissolved, his magic settling over her like armor.

Ready, he whispered.

Marci nodded and leaned down, pressing her hand against the spellwork Myron had so miraculously repaired. There was so much magic packed inside, it practically leaped into her hand. Marci pushed it back down again, closing her eyes until she was certain of what she meant to do.

It didn't take much. Boiled down, a hammer banish was just throwing magic at a spirit as hard as you could. You didn't even technically need spellwork for that, but Marci still sketched it out in her mind, using one of the rocks Myron had brought up to scratch the spellwork equation for the hardest, densest hammer she could imagine into the plastic of her bracelet. When Marci was certain she had every bit of the spell right, she reached down again, leaning hard on Ghost's wind as she plunged her hand into the condensed power of the world.

CHAPTER TWELVE

The fight against the Leviathan had been raging for just over an hour, but it already felt like a hundred.

The sky was full of fire. Everywhere Julius looked, dragons and jets and helicopters were shooting down the black tentacles that fell from the sky like streamers. There were actually more human aircraft than dragons now. They'd been arriving in a steady stream since the magic had dropped enough to let them fly, and not all of them were military. Between General Jackson and David, everything capable of flight for three hundred miles had been scrambled. The ones that couldn't shoot served as spotters, helping Julius direct the rest to places where the tentacles were getting through.

"South of the river! Canadian shore of Lake Erie!" a voice shouted in Julius's ear. "No one's here, and that thing's drinking the lake like a damn hose!"

"Copy," Julius replied, looking up at Amelia. "We need someone on the Erie north shore by the river."

"Working on it," his sister growled, hovering on her flaming wings as tentacles shot through her. She wasn't even bothering to burn them anymore. She was too busy coordinating the dragon half of the world's biggest, deadliest game of Whac-A-Mole, abusing her ability to turn into pure flame to avoid having to dodge the tentacles that were constantly sailing through the air.

Julius didn't have that luxury. He was still flesh and blood, which meant he spent most of his time dodging, blasting whatever he could while he frantically tried to keep track of everything that was going on and which locations needed help the most.

"Most" was key, because *everywhere* was in trouble. When they'd started this, he'd assumed that the Leviathan couldn't be everywhere at once. After an hour of fighting, though, Julius had decided there was no practical limit to the number of tentacles that thing could produce. They literally filled the sky at times, forcing the dragons to scramble out of the way as the black appendages crashed into the lake beds to suck up whatever water was left. The less-agile human vehicles weren't so lucky. They went down flaming when the tentacles got thick, the pilots' voices screaming in Julius's ears before their radios cut out.

It would have been horrific if he'd had time to process it, but there was no time for anything except the fight. They'd long since given up trying to stop every tentacle. At this point, it was simply a race to slow the Leviathan down enough for Marci to finish. He just hoped they could make it.

"Julius."

He snatched his eyes off his AR radar display as General Jackson's face appeared in the air to his left, looking more harried than he'd ever seen her. "We're losing too many units," she said. "We can't keep up like this, so I'm pulling two squads off Lake Michigan and authorizing a bombing run on the Leviathan's main body. I need you and the Planeswalker to pull someone in to cover their areas during the gap."

"I don't know if we *have* anyone else," Julius said, flitting to the side just in time to avoid being hit by the flaming end of a tentacle Justin had just chomped in half. "Why are you wasting time on a bombing run anyway? Amelia already blasted that thing with enough dragon fire to melt a battleship, and it did nothing."

"I know," the general snapped. "But we can't keep up with the tentacles and I'm running out of planes. If we don't start doing some damage back, this fight is going to be over in the next ten minutes."

Julius swallowed. He'd known things were dire, but he hadn't realized they were *that* bad. "I'll find someone to cover the gap," he promised. "Good luck."

But the general had already cut out. A few moments later, Julius saw the jets on his radar tracker peel off their pattern above Lake Michigan and start heading for the Leviathan.

"Fools," Amelia snorted when he told her. "If I couldn't burn it, no combination of metal and explosives has a chance."

"I said the same thing," Julius replied. "But while I agree it won't work, the general has a point. Every tentacle we burn pops right back up, but while the Leviathan doesn't seem to care, we're taking real damage." He glanced up at Justin, who was still bathing the sky in green fire despite the blood dripping through his feathers. "We can't keep on like this. If we're going to survive until Marci gets here, we have to find a way to start hurting it back."

"If you've got any suggestions, I'm all ears," Amelia said, the flames that made up her head flickering wildly as she watched the jets fly in. "Here we go."

That was the only warning Julius got before the bombardment began. He barely managed to cover his ears in time before a halo of white light filled the sky as multiple magical warheads struck the Leviathan's carapace. The force wave hit him a second later, sending him tumbling through the air. He caught himself with his wings just before he crashed into a toppled building, clutching the wreckage with his claws for balance as he watched, breathless, to see if the attack had had any effect.

When the smoke cleared, his heart sank. It was hard to see in the dark, but it didn't look as though the fighters' bombs had been any more effective than Amelia's fire. The bottom of the Leviathan was still a solid wall of shiny black, smooth and impenetrable.

For the first time since he'd taken off, Julius began to feel truly hopeless. They couldn't hurt it. They must have burned thousands of tentacles by now, and it didn't seem to have changed a thing. The lakes were almost gone. People were dead. Only a few dragons were down, but that number was bound to rise as more of the UN forces were destroyed or forced to drop out. It didn't matter how hard they fought—they were failing, and there was nothing he could do about it. If Marci didn't come through soon, they would all die up here. *He* would die, and he wouldn't even get to apologize to her for failing. He couldn't even tell her goodb—

"*Julius!*"

The yell came through his com, but it wasn't General Jackson. It wasn't even human. It was Bob, and he sounded frantic. Frantic good or frantic bad, though, Julius didn't know yet.

"Get back to Amelia," the seer said, raising his voice over General Jackson, who was screaming at him to give her back her com in the background. "Tell her to get everyone out of the sky."

"Why?" Julius asked, pushing off the ground as fast as he could. "What's going to happen?"

His oldest brother's face popped into his augmented vision just in time for Julius to see him grin. "Looks like your human came through."

That was all he had time to say before Emily Jackson wrestled her com out of his hands, but Julius wasn't watching his AR anymore. He was flying as hard as he could back to Amelia, whose fire was suddenly looking dimmer.

"Where did you go?" she panted, grabbing on to him as her body flickered. "I need your help. Something's happening to the magic. I can't—"

"It'll be okay," Julius said frantically. "Marci did it! Bob just called to say she's on her way. You need to tell everyone to get out of the sky *now*."

The radio in his ear was already full of chatter as Emily ordered all human troops to the ground, but Amelia was shaking her head. "That's what I'm trying to tell you. I'm not sure if I *can* tell everyone. The magic just suddenly started dropping like a stone. It feels like the drought all over again, except *way* worse because I'm the one drying up this time!"

It was true. Her flaming body was shrinking in front of his eyes. By the time she finished talking, she wasn't much bigger than he was, and her eyes were terrified. "Help me, Julius!"

"I've got you," he assured her, blowing a lick of flame. "You can shelter in my fire. I'll give you whatever you need, but you have to tell the others to get down. You're the only one who can talk to every dragon, and I don't think Bob would have warned me if it wasn't going to be bad."

Amelia nodded and vanished, her orange flames snuffing out only to reappear inside Julius's, making him gasp as a new power entered the fire that was the center of everything that made him a dragon.

Sorry, Amelia whispered in his mind. *You might want to go ahead and land, because this is going to hurt.*

Julius nodded and dove for a bit of open roadway below, but he'd barely made it ten feet before a wave of weakness knocked him out of the sky. There'd been no attack, no injury. Every muscle in his body had simply given up, leaving him limp as a ribbon as he plummeted through the air. He was trying to roll over so he'd at least land on his feet when a shout shook the sky above him.

"*Julius!*"

The roar was so loud it made his ears throb. Then giant sharp claws stabbed into his back as Justin snatched him out of the sky.

"Ow," Julius groaned.

"Better than hitting the ground," Justin snarled, the transformed Fang of the Heartstriker on his jaw punctuating each word with a plume of green fire. "What is *wrong* with you? I didn't see you get hit!"

Julius couldn't begin to explain what had happened with Amelia, mostly because he didn't fully understand it himself. Fortunately, Justin's questions seemed to be perfunctory, because he didn't even wait for Julius to answer before dropping him on the ground so he could take off again.

"Wait!" Julius cried after him. "Justin, come back! We need to stay on the ground!"

"But we're not done!" Justin yelled, blasting another tentacle out of the sky before swiveling his massive head to glare down at his little brother. "Just stay there. I'll be right—"

GET DOWN!

Justin jerked as the command hit him, his whole body seizing as if he'd been electrocuted. Julius wasn't much better. He was already on the ground, so there was no danger of falling, but the pain was still excruciating as Amelia grabbed his fire and twisted, forcing her will into the flames.

Everyone on the ground NOW, she roared, her voice shaking with effort before cutting out as fast as it had come up. Her presence vanished from Julius's fire at the same time, making him gasp in relief as the unnatural weakness faded, leaving only good old-fashioned normal pain behind. He was still trying to breathe through it when a tiny voice spoke beside him.

"Whew," it said. "Sorry about that. Dragons lost in battle lust are notoriously bad listeners, so I had to pull hard to make sure I had enough oomph to get through."

Julius blinked in confusion. The voice sounded like Amelia's, but it was so soft he could barely hear it. He couldn't see her either when he opened his eyes, then something poked his forefoot, and Julius looked down to see a tiny dragon made of fire standing on the ground beside him.

"Hi," it said. "Thanks for the boost."

He blinked at the little creature in wonder. "Amelia?"

The dragon was no larger than a kitten, but the annoyed look on her face was *definitely* his sister's.

"What is going on?" Justin demanded, setting down beside them. Then he spotted the little dragon. "What the—is that the *Planeswalker?*"

"Laugh at me and die," Amelia growled, giving the knight a killing look before scampering up Julius's leg to perch in the spot between his wing and his neck. "This isn't a form I wanted to revisit, but I didn't have much of a choice. Something's gone seriously haywire in the Sea of Magic. I don't know what Marci's doing over there, but it's *big.*" She cowered in Julius's feathers. "You might want to duck."

Julius swallowed. Now that she'd mentioned it, the world did feel a bit... empty. He'd been too busy to notice before, but now that he was paying attention, he could feel the lack of magic like dryness in the air. If the city hadn't been so saturated with the stuff only minutes before, Julius didn't think he could have maintained his dragon. He already felt uncomfortably heavy, like a fish out of water, and he wasn't the only one. Justin was actually gasping, his green eyes strained as he ripped the cage of his transformed Fang of the Heartstriker off his mouth.

"What is... going... *on?*"

As though in answer to his question, a cold wind rose, but not winter cold. This was the cold of the grave, and it was coming from the ground, rising up through the dirt like it was blowing in the world below. Under any other circumstances, it would have been the creepiest thing Julius had ever felt, but this time, the dry, death-scented air brought a giant smile to his face.

"It's Marci," he said, crouching low, as Amelia had suggested. He was reaching up to drag his gasping brother down as well when the wind doubled, filling the air with the cold anger of the forgotten dead.

• • •

Marci had never known she was so empty to be so full.

She was holding more magic than she'd ever felt in her life. Keeping it all contained felt like trying to carry the ocean in a thimble, and yet, thanks to Ghost, it worked. Everything she couldn't hold, the Empty Wind took, letting the magic pour into the abyss of his vessel, which was now floating below them.

Marci stopped, blinking in confusion, but that didn't change what she saw. With one blink, she was standing on the mountain in the Heart of the World. With the next, she was floating inside the yawning emptiness of the Empty Wind's domain, the same place he'd brought her when he'd eaten her during the fight with Myron and the DFZ at the Merlin Gate.

"What's happening?"

You're blending with me, her spirit replied, his voice as loud as hers in their shared head. *The magic is blurring the barriers, making you see as I see.*

"*This* is what you see?" Marci said, horrified. Every time she blinked, she saw something different: the dark, the mountain, her own unconscious body back in the DFZ, their crushed house far below the battle. Hundreds of images flicked past like slides on a sped-up reel. But while Marci found the chaos even more nauseating than the Sea of Magic, a cold part of her mind found the mishmash comforting, even inspiring. It was utterly confusing until Marci realized that bit wasn't part of *her* mind at all. It was Ghost. Her spirit was inside her thoughts in a way he'd never been before. Likewise, she could feel herself in him, blowing through the dark as the magic poured in.

"Wow," she whispered, flexing her hands, which weren't her hands at all, but his. A soldier's dark, sure fingers. "And it's the magic that's doing this?"

The magic is crushing us together, yes, he said. *But the fact that we're handling it is all us.* She felt his smile on her face. *Our bond is strong.*

"We are *awesome*," Marci agreed, searching through the confusion of images until she found one that looked down on the DFZ from high above. "There."

They moved together, sliding through the barrier, which was no longer much of a barrier at all. With so much focused magic near it, the wall between reality and the Sea of Magic was running like hot wax, sliding out of the way easily as Marci stepped out of the Heart of the World and into the high, cold air above the Leviathan.

"Wow," Marci said, looking over their shoulder at the melted hole in the world they'd left behind them. "It's just like when the DFZ was pulling in magic through Myron. We've blended worlds."

"We've done more than that," Ghost replied, turning their winds—because they *were* wind now, a freezing, grave-like wind that blotted out the sun and filled the air with memories—back to the Nameless End below. "The magic of the world, all the spirits and those who rely on them, the life of this plane itself has been shaped into one massive force. The only reason it hasn't blown itself to bits yet is because the Heart of the World is holding it. We're hooked into it now too, but if you want to bring it down on *him*"—he nodded at the dark expanse of the Leviathan—"you're going to have to grab that mass and swing it."

That was the part she'd been dreading. There was no turning back now, though, so Marci rubbed the memory of her hands together and reached through their connected magic to the flimsy shadow of her soul, which was still kneeling in the Heart of the World. Using her new double vision, she kept one eye on the Leviathan while the other focused on her spellwork, opening the dam to let the high-pressure magic surge out of Myron's circle into the banishment she'd scratched onto her bracelet.

Even merged with Ghost, the force nearly blew her apart. The moment she pushed the power into the spellwork, all that magic—that ocean in a thimble—became a living, pounding thing desperate to be free. Controlling it was like trying to hold a dragon with a hair, but every time Marci started to slip, Ghost was there to catch her, his winds shoring them both up. There was more here than any spirit, even a god, could hold, but Ghost and Marci together were greater than the sum of their parts. Somehow, they kept it together, Ghost containing the edges while Marci guided the magic through her spell, folding and winding and condensing the power just as she'd done with Amelia's flame when Svena had shoved it down her throat. On and on and on it went, until, at last, all the spirits who'd jumped down Myron's well were crushed into a ball that fit in Marci's hand.

And it was beautiful.

Short as their time was, Marci couldn't help but stop and stare. No mortal eyes had ever seen all the magic of the world together in one place. Given how dark the Sea of Magic normally appeared, she'd expected the spell to look like a black hole, but it didn't. It looked like a star. A shining orb of every color that glowed so bright it hurt to look at. It was heavy, too, dense enough to weigh down even their wind. If she held it for much longer, the weight would crush them against the Leviathan's back, but Marci didn't need to hold it. Thanks to the Empty Wind, they were already in position, which meant all she had to do was let go. So, with a triumphant smile, Marci opened her hands and let the magic drop, releasing the spell that was so simple, it had only one word.

Scatter.

True to its form, the banishment fell like a star, picking up speed with every inch until it was screaming through the air. When it hit the Leviathan, the entire world went silent, holding its breath as the condensed magic imploded in a blinding flash, blowing everything apart.

Including them.

The exploding magic crashed into them like a wall. One moment, Marci was flying as part of the Empty Wind. The next, she was scattered across the entire Great Lakes area. For a horrifying moment, that seemed to be the end, but then, as always, the Empty Wind caught her, hauling both of their magic back into the quiet safety of his black-and-white realm.

Marci snapped back together with a gasp. She was still a disembodied soul, but she was no longer in the Heart of the World. Instead, they were back in the basement of the cat house at the edge of town, standing over her unconscious body, which was being kept warm by a purring blanket of stray cats. Outside, the sky was white through the broken windows. Marci couldn't see more than that from this realm, though, so, without even waiting for Ghost to tell her how, she jumped back into her body.

It hurt a lot more than she'd expected. Not having died this time, Marci expected to just pop back up like Myron always seemed to. But even when you did it the nonlethal way, traveling to the afterlife on the Empty Wind still clearly had deathly overtures, because she woke up with the same horrible heaviness in her limbs as when Raven had taken her back the first time. She didn't have to claw her way out of her own grave, and the cats had kept her warm, but it was still horrifying. She was gasping the air back into her lungs when Ghost shouted in her head.

Marci!

His excited voice was surprisingly quiet. Softer than it had been in weeks. When Marci looked up to see why, the Empty Wind was a cat again, his fluffy white body smaller and more transparent than it had been since the time she'd accidentally almost snuffed him by taking him out of his domain. As dim as he looked, though, Ghost's glowing blue eyes were wide and excited as he hopped onto her chest. *Come see!*

Marci forced herself to her feet. On the way up, her body made it clear in no uncertain terms that moving was a *very* bad idea, but after all they'd just gone through, she wouldn't have missed this for anything. It hurt and made her sick, but she kept going, staggering through the blown-off basement door into the grass outside.

Into the sunlight.

She shielded her eyes at once. The winter afternoon sun was hazy with smoke, but after the Sea of Magic and the dark of the Leviathan's shadow, it felt as strong as a spotlight, primarily because it was *there*. The sky above their heads was empty. They'd done it.

"It worked," Marci said, her face splitting into a grin as she blinked frantically in the light. "*It worked!*"

The Leviathan was gone. Where he'd been, a fine mist of water was falling like rain, but other than that, there was no trace of him anywhere. He was simply *not there*. Banished, just as she'd promised.

"We did it!" she cried, grabbing Ghost so suddenly he yowled. "We banished a *Nameless End*! We saved the world! Do you have any idea how famous we'll be when this gets…"

Her voice trailed off as something clenched hard in the pit of her stomach. Now that she'd blasted all the magic back out into the world, she and Ghost were no longer blended into everything, but she'd have had to be deaf, dumb, and blind to miss the yank that had just happened at the pit of her soul.

"Ghost—"

I felt it too, he whispered, hopping up on her shoulder to look around. *But I don't know what—*

He was cut off by the *whoosh* of thousands of gallons of water suddenly being sucked back into the air. All around them, the rain that had been falling from the banished Leviathan was reversing. The water even left her clothes, the wetness pulling out of the cat-hair-covered fabric like someone was vacuuming it up. In the space of a few seconds, all the magic the banishment had scattered was back in place, and as it coalesced, the hazy sunlight vanished yet again as the Leviathan reappeared.

"No," Marci said, her eyes going wide. "*No!*"

This couldn't be happening. They'd won. The Leviathan had been *gone*. How was it back? How was this *possible*?

He must have re-formed, Ghost said quietly. *Banishments* are *only temporary.*

"Not *that* temporary!" Marci cried. "And re-formed where? He has no vessel! No home! How did he pull himself back together so—"

"*Marci!*"

The yell came from far away, and she looked up to see a small blue shape racing toward her across the city. A few seconds later, Julius landed panting beside them, his feathered face grim beneath the crown of his Fang. "Are you okay?"

"No!" Marci said angrily, stabbing her hand at the once-again black-ened sky. "That should have worked! *Why didn't it work?*"

"I was hoping you could tell me," Julius said, lowering his wings so she could climb onto his back. "Hop on. The others are waiting back at the house."

Marci didn't want to go back to the others. She wanted to return to the Heart of the World and figure out how things had gone so horribly wrong. There was no way she'd screwed up the banishment. It was a one-line spell, and she'd *seen* it work. But she wasn't sure how to go back, or if it was even possible anymore. Now that she'd stopped, Marci was starting to feel how tired she was. Ghost was exhausted too, his weari-ness pulling like a weight on her mind. Already, his transparent body was fading, leaving her spirit a small, sad, cold lump in her arms as she climbed onto Julius's back.

"The same thing happened to Amelia," he said as she carefully placed the sleeping cat on her lap. "Right before the banishment land-ed, she shrank down to nothing."

"Because I was using all the magic," Marci said glumly. "I balled the entire sea up and blasted it to pieces, and it didn't even work." She clenched her fists. "It should have worked!"

"It did," Julius said, taking off. "I saw him scatter just like you said he would. But then he put himself back together."

She slumped over with a groan, and he swiveled his triangular head back around to smile at her. "It's okay. You tried your best. No one's mad at you."

"*I'm* mad," Marci said, her body shaking. "We got robbed! Our ace in the hole just blew up in my face. *Literally.* Now what are we supposed to do?"

Julius's silence was answer enough as he flew them back through the destroyed city to their home.

· · ·

"I told you so," the Black Reach said.

"Save it," Bob muttered, pacing back and forth down the rut he'd worn in front of the wreckage of Julius's home.

"You knew this was coming as well as I did," the construct went on. "You knew the young Merlin's plan would fail, and yet you still encouraged—"

"Likely to fail," Bob said. "It was *likely* to fail, which isn't the same as *would* fail. There was still a chance."

"A small one," the Black Reach said. "Which you had no business betting all our lives on."

"I don't see you doing anything!" Bob snapped, startling his pigeon from her roost on his shoulder. "At least I'm trying to save us. Where are your grand plans?"

"Already made," the elder seer replied, holding up the glittering orb of the Kosmolabe.

Bob turned away in disgust. "Running away isn't a plan. It's just another form of defeat."

"You mean another way to survive," the Black Reach said, dropping his arm with a sigh. "I am sorry, Brohomir. I know how badly you want your happy ending. It was a big factor in why I decided to spare your life. We've always wanted the same future, but unlike you, I cannot be blinded by emotion. I must look only at what will be, and as much as everything else has changed, that one factor of the future that truly matters has not." He looked up at the Nameless End, which had just finished re-forming itself in the sky. "We were always doomed. From the moment Algonquin let it in, this plane was lost. You should be able to see that as clearly as I can now that you've lived past your death. Why can't you accept it?"

"Because I don't blindly accept failure!" Brohomir cried, whirling around to face him again. "'The future is never set until it's past.' *You* taught me that! I didn't spend centuries alienating everyone I loved trying to snatch my life from your jaws so I could lose now!"

The Black Reach's eyes narrowed. "Spoken like a prideful idiot. You're better than this, Brohomir. You know perfectly well that you can't bully the future. That's what made you a brilliant seer. Unlike Estella, you understood that draconic bravado means nothing to the cold, hard math of possibility. That hasn't changed just because you escaped your death."

"I know," Bob said, raking his fingers through his hair. "I know, I know, I *know*. It's just…"

He wanted things to be different. He'd thought for sure that the moment he cleared his death, he'd spot a way out, because that was what he did. He *always* found a way. Now, though, the vast, intertwining streams of possibility were drying up before his eyes. With every second that ticked by, the stream of the future got narrower and narrower, leaving fewer and fewer paths, none of which went anywhere good.

"There has to be a way out," he growled, resuming his pacing. "There *has* to be."

The Black Reach turned away with a bitter sigh. "I won't be part of this sad delusion. Baseless hopes are for the blind. We who can see must deal truthfully with what's in front of us, or what's the point of seeing at all?" He waved over his shoulder. "When you're ready to be a seer again, come and find me. I'll be waiting where I always am at the end."

Bob didn't want to think about endings, but everywhere he looked now, the end was all he saw. Thousands and thousands of roads all leading to the same deadly conclusion. But even with the inevitable staring him in the face, Bob kept searching, frantically rooting through the remaining possible futures for the chance he could grab to keep them all alive. It wasn't until Julius landed in front of him, though, that he finally found it. His final gamble, so beautiful he could cry.

It's a long shot, his End warned. *You've had bad luck with those lately.*

"True," he said, petting her head. "But you miss a hundred percent of the shots you don't take, and as the Black Reach just so kindly reminded me, we don't have much left to lose."

The Nameless End leaned into his touch. *Are you ready to trade, then? All long shots come in if I guarantee them.*

Bob thought a moment, looking down his chosen future as far he could, and then he shook his head. "Not yet. Julius has never let me down so far, and if this plays out the way I think it will, I'm going to need you more than ever before the end."

I'll be there, she promised. *I am an End, after all.*

"You are indeed," he said, kissing her on the neck as he turned to face his youngest brother, who'd just set his human down beside the suddenly conscious body of Sir Myron Rollins.

CHAPTER THIRTEEN

The first thing Marci did when Julius landed was look for Myron.
She spotted him immediately, sitting up from the ground where the
DFZ had left his body when she'd taken him to the other side. The city
spirit was nowhere to be seen, though. Just another sign that everything
had gone wrong.

"Myron!" she yelled, practically falling off Julius in her rush to get
to the other Merlin. "What happened? How did the Leviathan re-form
so fast?"

The older mage put his head in his hands, which were shaking so
badly his silver, maze-worked rings were rattling like bells. "It was the
roots. Shiro, Raven, and I thought they were there so Leviathan could
drink the other spirits as soon as he was done with Algonquin, but..." He
took a shuddering breath. "We were wrong. So wrong. The tendrils he
sank into the Sea of Magic weren't so he could consume it. He was holding on, making himself a foundation. When the hammer banish blew
him apart, he just dug in and pulled himself back together."

"That can't be," Marci said. "I watched him explode into water vapor."

"And I saw this," Myron snapped, looking up at her at last. "He was
ready, Marci, and why wouldn't he be? Algonquin's a spirit who's been
running the world's largest magical consumer goods corporation for
the past six decades. She has a private army of mages. Of *course* she
knows how banishments work! And if she knew, he knew. He was by her
side the entire time." His face grew bleak as he returned it to his hands.
"We should have known."

"What difference would that have made?" Marci said angrily. "Even if we'd suspected he was prepared for a banishment, there was no other way to break up his magic. This was our one real chance to beat him. We had to take it. No one could have predicted he'd survive. We hit him with *all the magic there is*. It doesn't get bigger than that!"

As she said them, Marci realized what those words really meant. They'd taken their best shot, and they'd failed. Not missed, not screwed up, not fallen so they could get up and try, try again. No. They'd hit the enemy head-on with everything they had, and it simply wasn't enough.

"We've lost," she said quietly.

"No, we haven't," Julius said. "We'll think of something else."

"Not this time." Marci shook her head. "It's over, Julius. Everyone went above and beyond anything we could have asked, and it wasn't enough. Even if I came up with something else to try, I don't think we have the oomph left to pull it off. Ghost is stuck as a cat, Myron's a wreck, I'm exhausted, and I don't even see Amelia—"

"I'm here," said a small voice, and Marci looked down to see a cat-sized dragon made of fire appear on the ground beside Julius's foot.

"Just like old times, huh?" the little dragon said with false cheerfulness. "I nipped back to the Sea of Magic to try and scrounge up enough power to get back to my old incredible self, but all that exploding really mixed things up. It's chaos over there. Even Raven's not up yet, and he's normally the first to get himself together."

"What about the dragons?" Julius asked. "Where are they?"

Amelia shrugged helplessly. "I don't know. Like I said, the magic's all scrambled, including mine. I can still feel their fires, so they're alive, but I can't pinpoint my own nose in this mess." She glanced up at the hole in the ceiling. "If I had to guess, though, I'd say they're feeling about as peppy as we are right now."

It *was* pretty quiet out there. Other than the Leviathan, there was nothing in the sky. No dragons, no planes, no helicopters. The entire counterattack had ceased, leaving the black monster hovering completely unopposed.

"They're probably taking cover," Julius said, breaking the grim silence. "Can't blame them, really. I told everyone from the start that we were only holding out until the banishment."

"Which didn't work," Marci said, her shoulders sinking as the reality of their situation landed hard. "I failed you."

"You didn't fail," Julius said. "You did everything right. It just didn't work."

"But I told you it would," she said, lowering her eyes as her vision grew blurry. "I promised that if you could just keep the Leviathan busy, I'd take care of everything. You all did your part, but I—" She stopped, scrubbing the tears off her cheeks. "I wasn't enough. I'm the Merlin. I had everything, all the magic in the world, and I still couldn't do it. Even if I had a plan B, we don't have the resources left to try it, and we're out of time. The lakes have to be almost dry now." She slumped forward, pressing her wet face against Julius's blue-feathered chest. "I'm sorry. I wasted all our time."

"You didn't waste anything," he said, leaning down to nuzzle her cheek with his soft nose. "You tried your best, we all did, but it's not done yet. We're still alive, and I mean to keep us that way."

Marci looked up at him. "*How?*"

She hadn't meant for the question to come out quite that disbelieving. Fortunately, Julius didn't look offended. "Because I *do* have a plan B," he said. "It was my plan A before everyone shot it down, but I see no reason not to try it now. It's not like we've got anything left to lose."

That was certainly true, but... "What plan are you talking about?"

He smiled down at her, his green eyes warm. "The one where we talk to Algonquin."

Marci stared at him for a good ten seconds before her tact ran out. "Tell me you're kidding."

"Why would I be kidding?" Julius asked, looking genuinely confused. "Algonquin's always been the heart of this problem. It only makes sense that she'd be the key to getting us out."

"B-But you *can't* be serious," Marci stuttered. "I know you've talked people into some truly crazy stuff, Julius, but Algonquin wouldn't even listen to her fellow spirits, and she *hates* dragons. You could make the best case in the world, and she still wouldn't listen."

He shrugged. "I'll never know if I don't try."

"She'll kill you," Marci snapped.

"She might," Julius said. "But I won't be any more dead than I'd be if I stayed here." He dug his claws into the ground. "We have to do *something*, Marci."

"Yeah, something that will work!" she cried. "Something not *insane!*"

"I don't think it's insane," he said. "Algonquin's not some evil over-lord. She's just a spirit who's hurt and upset and doing stupid things because of it. Look at it that way, and she's not so different from Ghost, and you talked him around."

"That was different."

"It wasn't," he said firmly. "We've always treated Algonquin as our enemy because that's how she treated us, but we aren't the root of her problem. Whatever convinced her to surrender to the Leviathan, it was bad enough that she was willing to abandon her fish and give up immortal life. That's not anger. That's desperation, and desperate people want to be helped. If we can figure out how to do that, give her a path out of this corner that doesn't involve the Leviathan, I'll bet you anything she'll take it. But we're never going to find out what that is if we don't talk to her. Maybe she'll listen, maybe she'll kill us all, but if it's over anyway, we might as well try." He leaned down, resting the flat of his feathered forehead against hers. "We haven't lost yet. I trusted you. Trust me."

Marci sighed. She still thought it was lunacy, but she couldn't say no to anything when he asked like that. "Okay," she grumbled. "I'm with you. How do we do this?"

"I have no idea," Julius said cheerfully. "But I'm pretty sure our first step is 'get to Algonquin.'"

"Right," Marci said. "Just get to the spirit who's inside the monster we can't even hurt and whose magic will eat us if we do somehow get inside."

"Maybe not immediately," Amelia said, tapping her little claws thoughtfully against her chin. "I've never actually seen a Nameless End eat a plane. Maybe it takes a while?"

"Great, we can be digested slowly." Marci glared up at the Leviathan. "I don't even see how we'd get in to *be* eaten. That thing's nothing but shell and eyes, no mouth or ears, no openings of any sort unless you want to crawl up a tentacle with the water."

"Could we portal inside?" Julius asked, glancing at Amelia. "Your magic is low, but Svena's should still be fine. Could she get us in?"

The little dragon thought about that for a moment, and then she shook her head. "No. Don't get me wrong. Princess Snowflake is the best teleportation expert alive. She can get you anywhere in the physical world if she knows where she's going, but that thing is ninety-nine point nine repeating percent magic. Metaphysically speaking, that makes teleporting into it the same as trying to teleport into another person's soul, and there's not a power in the world—dragon or otherwise—who can do that."

The group fell silent. Marci was wracking her brain for a solution that didn't leave them all doomed when she heard the crunch of shoes on gravel. Her first thought was Myron, because the step was far too light for Emily's metal body, but it wasn't Myron or Emily, or even a human.

It was Bob.

"*Please* tell me you're coming over because you've just spotted a brilliant way out of this mess," Amelia said, flapping up to her brother.

"Alas, we're not there yet," Bob said, holding out his arm so the little dragon could land on it. "But I might have a solution to your impenetrable Leviathan problem. First, though, you need to talk to General Jackson."

"Why?" Amelia asked.

"Because she's about to authorize a nuclear strike."

Julius's eyes went wide, and then he was gone, darting across the cavern faster than Marci had known he could go to tackle the general, who was still standing hunched over her makeshift war table.

"Get off me!" Emily Jackson snarled, shoving at Julius. The temporary body Raven had cobbled together for her must not have been a patch on her old one, though, because she couldn't even budge him. "I have to do this!"

Julius's answer to that was to grab her com unit and crush it with his claws. He crushed his own as well, shaking the sleek black headpiece off the crown of his transformed Fang and smashing it into plastic shards.

"Are you insane?" the general yelled. "It's over, Heartstriker! We tried, and we failed. Now we have to use whatever we have left to blow that thing out of the sky!"

"No!" Julius yelled back. "If you call in those missiles, everything in North America will die!"

"Better than losing the whole world!" Emily cried, her dark eyes wild. "I don't like it any more than you do, but this is the only weapon we've got left. We have no choice!"

"Incorrect," Bob said, crouching down beside her. "I'm the local expert on choices, and I can tell you that there are at least twenty left. More importantly, though, it won't work. The Leviathan is magic, not flesh. His tentacles were vulnerable to physical attack because they were disposable, but nuclear warheads won't bother his main body any more than your other attacks did. I've already seen how that future ends. If you authorize a launch, all you'll achieve is killing off the rest of us."

Marci wasn't actually sure if Emily believed that dragon seers saw the future, but she must have believed Bob now, because she slumped beneath Julius's hold. "Fine, fortuneteller," she said bitterly, relaxing into the dirt. "If you see so much, what do *you* suggest?"

"What I always suggest," Bob replied, placing a hand on Julius's head. "Listen to my brother." He glanced at the smaller dragon. "You want to talk to Algonquin, right?"

Julius nodded rapidly. "We don't know how to get to her, though," he said. "She's inside the Leviathan, and nothing we've tried can get through his shell. Even Amelia couldn't burn him."

"Hey, I burned him a little!" Amelia said defensively, scampering up Bob's arm to perch on his shoulder opposite his pigeon. "I could have burned him a lot more if I'd had my old fire, but now that our magic's hooked into the Sea of Magic, we're trapped in the same sinking boat as everyone else."

"Why?" Marci asked, genuinely curious. "I used to use Julius's magic all the time in my spells. It worked great. Why won't it work now?"

"Because we're not casting spells," Amelia explained. "Humans aren't picky, so I'm sure you've never noticed, but dragon fire is fundamentally different from any other type of magic on this plane. We came from an entirely different system! Our magic was basically alien, which was why we never really integrated into our new home. I fixed that when I became a spirit, but in order to fit our magic into the rules of this realm, I basically had to turn fire into water. That's great for us in the long term considering we have to exist in a *Sea* of Magic, but it's hard to burn a hole in something like the Leviathan when you've traded your flame thrower for a fire hose, you know?"

Marci wasn't quite sure that she did, but Bob was shaking his head. "Don't bemoan our fate yet," he said. "You might have changed our fundamental nature, but there's still one dragon whose fire isn't connected to yours."

Amelia blinked at him. "How is that possible? I'm the Spirit of Dragons. If it's a dragon, it's mine."

"Not this one," Bob said, smiling wider. "He's got a loophole, because, despite appearances, he's not actually a dragon."

He turned to point at the Black Reach standing alone in front of the tunnel that led out of the spiral of on-ramps, his tall body silhouetted by what was probably the last working streetlight in the DFZ, and Julius gasped. "Of course!" the dragon cried. "The Black Reach is a *construct*, a magical machine! He was built, not born, which means he's not under your control!"

"Are you sure about that?" Amelia asked, frowning. "My domain is pretty broad."

"Absolutely sure," Bob said, giving his sister a flat look. "Do you think I would have put myself through that melodrama with Julius earlier if you could have pulled the Black Reach's string to save me?"

"Good point," Amelia said, her voice growing excited as she launched off Bob's shoulder to flap toward the Black Reach. "Let's go get our super weapon!"

"I don't think he's going to help us if you call him that," Julius said as he hurried after her.

Marci followed right behind, looking suspiciously over her shoulder at Bob, who was watching the unfolding events play out like a director on opening night. "Are you sure about this?" she whispered, catching Julius's sleeve.

"No, but it's the best plan we've got," he said, looking down at her. "What's wrong?"

Marci shot another glare at the seer. "I just don't like how convenient it is. Bob's normally subtler about his tip-offs, but he practically gave us a quest to go talk to the Black Reach." She shook her head. "I don't like it. Smells like a plot."

"Of course it's a plot," Julius said, laughing. "He's a dragon seer. Plots are the air he breathes."

"That doesn't make them okay," Marci snapped. "Bob doesn't exactly have the greatest track record. He's already proven he's fine with killing both of us if that's what it takes to make his wheels turn. How do we know this time is different?"

"We don't," Julius said. "But…" He trailed off, coming to a stop so he could face her properly. "Bob did a lot of things I hate, but he also did things I'd never want to change. He used us and hurt us, yes, but he's also the reason we've made it as far as we have."

"But nothing we've tried has worked!" she cried. "The best plan I had bombed. Why didn't he warn us about that?"

"Probably because there was a chance it *wouldn't* bomb," Julius said. "And warning us might have made that future less likely."

"Why are you defending him?" Marci demanded. "He's done nothing but use us! Everything good that's ever come out of his plots for us has been a side effect, never the main purpose. His previous 'solution' for the Leviathan was to sell all of our futures to put us on rails without even asking where we'd like them to go. You hated that as much as any of us, so why are you okay with blindly trusting him now?"

"It's not blind trust to grab the only rope when you're drowning," Julius said firmly. "You're absolutely right. Bob *has* treated us horribly, but things aren't as simple as 'never trust again.' He did some very bad things, but I'm convinced he did them for good reasons. That doesn't excuse how he treated you or me or Chelsie or anyone else, but it doesn't make him the villain, either. He's just a dragon who had to make some hard choices, and while I don't agree with the solutions he came up with, the fact remains that he was always trying to save us."

"You mean save himself," she grumbled. "Don't forget why he started all of this. He admitted to your face that the only reason he picked you was to avoid being killed by the Black Reach."

"He also found us a way to save us from the Leviathan," Julius reminded her. "Maybe it wasn't the one we wanted, but he could have used the Final Future to save himself from the Black Reach, and he didn't. He used his one sure shot to make sure everyone else was safe and relied on plots to save his own future. If he'd failed and the Black Reach had killed him, we still would have been safe in the future he died to buy. We could *still* be safe." He nodded over her head at the pigeon perched on Bob's shoulder. "His salvation is still on the table. Always was. We were the ones who said no, and when we did, Bob respected that. He let us try to make our own fate, knowing the results weren't guaranteed."

"If Bob respects us so much, why does he seem fine with risking our lives?" Marci snapped. "He didn't have a problem with letting *me* die."

"I hate how he handled that," Julius said. "But I also think he would never have let that happen if he wasn't sure you'd come back." His lips curved into a soft smile. "I don't think Bob actually likes killing."

"How do you figure that?"

"Because I've never seen him do it," Julius said. "I'm sure a lot of his plots would have been much easier if certain pieces were permanently removed, but he never went there. He even tried to save Estella, and she was willing to destroy her entire clan to beat him. That has to mean something."

"I think you're being too nice," Marci grumbled. "Bob hasn't even apologized for how he treated you, but you already seem like you've forgiven everything."

"Maybe it is too nice," Julius said, smiling wider. "But it's what feels right to me. Trusting my gut has worked pretty well so far. I might as well stick with it until the end."

Marci was pretty sure this *was* the end, but there was no point in arguing. It'd be easier to kill the Leviathan with a spoon than to make Julius stop being kind. Even now, when his willingness to forgive and forget might be literally the death of them, she couldn't help but love him for it.

"All right," she said, reaching out to grab a fistful of his blue feathers. "We'll trust the manipulative seer, but I'm staying with you every step of the way. The moment I spot a trap, we're bailing."

Even as she said it, Marci knew that made no sense. You couldn't bail from the end of the world. But where any other dragon—including Amelia—would have mocked her mercilessly for that lapse of logic, Julius just leaned down to bump his nose against hers.

"I wouldn't have it any other way."

• • •

"*Finally*," Amelia said when Julius and Marci walked up. "What took you guys so long?" She narrowed her burning eyes at the Black Reach. "This cheapskate won't let me take a look at his fire."

"You'll have to get used to disappointment," the Black Reach said bitterly. "Unlike every other dragon, I am under no obligation to you, Planeswalker."

"You see?" she cried, turning back to her littlest brother. "Talk some sense into him, would you?"

"Why don't you go back and wait with Bob?" Julius suggested.

Amelia snorted. "Why would I do that?"

Because convincing the Black Reach to help them instead of running to another plane as he'd planned was going to be hard enough without his impatient sister wheedling them both. "Because I have something private I'd like to discuss with him," Julius said instead.

Amelia blew out a puff of smoke. "Fine," she said, flapping onto Marci's shoulder. "Who am I to interfere with the methods of Julius, Dragon Whisperer? Come on, Marci, let's leave him to do his thing."

Marci must have been serious about sticking with him, because her jaw tightened. Before she could tell Amelia to go by herself, though,

225

Julius gave her a pleading look. Amelia would *never* leave if she thought they were plotting without her. He didn't know how to explain that to Marci without words, though, so he just looked at her until, at last, she reluctantly let go of his feathers, walking backward so she could keep her eyes on him the whole way as she escorted Amelia back to Bob.

When they were out of earshot, Julius turned to find the Black Reach watching him. "That was neatly done," the construct said, looking him in the eyes, which he was actually tall enough to do. The Black Reach's human guise was big enough that he didn't even have to tilt his head back to see eye to eye with Julius's dragon. Smiling, Julius desperately hoped that was a sign he could convince the construct to see eye to eye with him on everything else.

"So," said Dragon Sees Eternity, reaching into his long sleeve to pull out the golden orb of the Kosmolabe. "Are you ready to go?"

"No," Julius said. "But surely you knew that."

"I did," the construct replied. "But by mentioning it, I've reminded you that there is another way out of this, thus giving you the chance to reconsider."

That was some slippery seer work, but Julius expected nothing less from the Construct of the Future. "I need your help. I want to talk to Algonquin so I can try to change her mind about all of this, but she's locked herself deep inside the Leviathan, and you're the only one whose fire might be able to burn a path to her. You don't have to go inside with us. We just need you to make us an opening. Please."

The Black Reach scowled. "Are you *sure* you don't want to reconsider my offer?"

"I'm sure," Julius said. "Can you do it?"

The eldest seer looked up at the black expanse of the Leviathan. "There's a high likelihood that I could burn a hole through the Nameless End's protective carapace, but the success of everything after that is significantly less probable."

"Any chance is good enough for me," Julius said happily. "I just need you to get us in. We can handle the rest. Bob wouldn't have sent me to you if he didn't think we had a shot."

"That's where you're wrong," the Black Reach said, his voice oddly bitter. "Brohomir is one of the greatest seers I've ever known, but this isn't like his plans for you before. Those were the careful machinations of a master seer executing his life's work. This is a desperate dragon grasping at straws."

"But there *is* a chance," Julius said. "It's not impossible."

"'Not impossible' isn't the same as 'possible,'" the construct reminded him. "There are chances for almost everything, but only a small subset of those actually go on to become fact. A proper seer knows to weed out the long shots, not bet on them, and as a *proper* seer, I cannot support your brother's delusions. The chance of you successfully convincing Algonquin to banish the Leviathan is so infinitesimally small, it's barely visible even to my eyes. Assuming she still possesses the ability to send the Nameless End away, the Lady of the Lakes has hated our kind since we came to this plane. She is the patron of Vann Jeger, the Death of Dragons, and the murderess of the Three Sisters. With the purge of the DFZ, she has been personally responsible for the deaths of more dragons than any other being in our history. No matter what logic you bring, what arguments you make, the most likely outcome is that she will not listen, and you will die."

He spoke this as though it were already past, but Julius knew better. "Is that what you see?" he demanded, digging his claws into the dirt. "When you look at the future, do you *see* Algonquin killing me?"

"No, but that is merely due to a technicality. Seers can only see the futures of those connected to them, and Algonquin is none of ours. Our inability to foresee her decisions is how we landed in this mess in the first place. If I'd known she was going to bring a Nameless End to our doorstep, I would have destroyed her myself long before the drought. But I did not know, because she was not mine to see. *You* are, of course, but once you enter that thing, your futures become very hard to follow. Even I cannot peer easily through a Nameless End."

"So if you can't see her and you can't see me, how do you *know* she'll kill me?" Julius asked.

"Because it can be no other way," the Black Reach snapped. "The future is never certain, but there are some things we can safely take as constants, and Algonquin's hatred is one of them. She didn't listen to you back in Reclamation Land. What makes you think she will hear you now?"

"Because *now* is different," Julius said. "Back then, she had all the power. Now she has none, because she's given it up to the Leviathan. All I want is to help her get it back, and it's a lot easier to listen to someone when they're saying what you want to hear."

"It will. Not. Work," the seer growled. "Just like Brohomir, you are allowing what you want to blind you to what is, and what *is* is over. The Nameless End has won. This plane is doomed. The only statistically likely chance of survival we have left is for you to accept my offer and flee to a new world before this one is devoured." He leaned in closer, dropping his voice to a whisper. "You refused me before because you said I was leaving too many behind, but thanks to your efforts, almost every dragon in the world is currently in the DFZ. If you agree to run with me right now, there's a very good chance we could get everyone gathered and through the portal before the planar barrier collapses. You could save them all that way, no long shots needed."

"But not Amelia," Julius said. "Spirits are tied to this plane, which means no Marci, either. She'd never leave Ghost behind."

"There would be sacrifices," the Black Reach admitted. "But for a much greater good."

"How good can it be if the only way to get there is by abandoning my friends and family?" Julius said angrily. "I'm *not* leaving them behind."

"So you would risk everyone?" the seer said. "Risk your brothers and sisters, all of your kind, to save the world's most arrogant dragon mage and a single human?"

"I'm not risking anyone," Julius snapped. "I'm refusing to let *you* sacrifice them to buy an easy out. I still believe we can do this. You're the one with doubts." He tilted his head. "Why are you making this my decision anyway? You already have the Kosmolabe. You could open that portal and run whenever you want, with or without me."

To his surprise, the Black Reach lowered his eyes. "I am not without fault," the construct admitted quietly. "I was built to guard the future of our species. A perfect seer, uncorrupted by the usual draconic appetites for conquest and domination. But steering the future cannot be done coldly. Guiding our kind to a better place requires a certain degree of optimism, and that leaves me as vulnerable to the beguilement of hope as any other dragon. Hope for the future is why I fell prey to Brohomir's plan, and why I still linger now. The course with the highest chance of success would have been to open the portal the moment it became clear that your Merlin's plan had failed, but I could not bring myself to do it, because I knew if I ran away then, the one dragon I wanted to bring most wouldn't be with me."

Julius's skin flushed beneath his feathers. "You don't mean me, do you?"

"Whom else could I mean?" the Black Reach asked, his ancient eyes pleading when he lifted them again. "You are the opportunity I've waited ten thousand years for, Julius Heartstriker. That's why Brohomir chose you. He knew you were the only one I couldn't kill, because killing you would mean killing my own hope. I'm certain you're the one who can push us to a better future. No dragon has ever gotten all the clans to work together, but you did so in under an hour. What other miracles could you work, given the time?"

"But that wasn't me!" Julius said. "Amelia got them here with threats!"

"But why did Amelia call them?" the Black Reach asked. "And why did Svena help her? Why did the Golden Emperor pledge his support to the Heartstrikers, his sworn enemies for the last six centuries? Why did the Daughters of Three Sisters, the clan who has hated yours more than any other, fly to your aid? That wasn't because of anyone's threats. That was you. *You* forged those bonds just as *you* took your clan from Bethesda's poison claws and made it into something better."

A smile broke over the construct's face. "Do you know how long I've waited for a dragon like you? How many times I've tried to engineer the situations Bob created simply by placing you in them? I've spent my entire existence trying and failing to make dragons act as they do when you're around, which is why I can't leave unless you come with me. Brohomir positioned you well, but *you* were always the one who chose the better path, and I would risk almost anything to let you keep going."

Julius was ready to sink into the ground by the time the seer finished. He'd never been praised so much, and it felt all wrong, like something terrible was going to happen if the Black Reach kept talking. That said, everything terrible had already happened, which was the only reason Julius was able to swallow his embarrassment and meet the Black Reach's gaze once more.

"If you're willing to risk that much for my sake, then help me," he said, voice shaking. "Dragons can live in any world, but we'd do best in this one. You called her arrogant, but Amelia became the Spirit of Dragons for the same reason you want to save me. She's also trying to make a better future. The *Planeswalker* sacrificed her ability to go to other planes so she could make us a home in this one. We've run from one plane already. Let's do better with this one. We can save this world, I know it. But only if you'll help."

The Black Reach looked away with a deep breath. "You ask more than you know," he whispered. "I stand by my claim that your endeavor is almost certainly doomed, but to be honest, I'm no longer sure that I care. I am sick of watching my charges stupidly repeating the same mistakes. If the duty built into me by your ancestors wasn't pushing me to save them at any cost, I'd help you in a heartbeat. I'd much rather dragonkind die here nobly defending their home than flee to another plane so they can kill each other pointlessly for another ten thousand years. But duty isn't the only reason I've held back. There's also this."

He placed a hand on his chest over the spot where the dragon fire burned when they were in human form. "The reason my fire is still able to burn the Leviathan is because it was never mine at all. I'm a construct. A magical creation, not a living thing, which means I can't make fire of my own. I survive on the magic your ancestors breathed into me before they opened the portal to this world. As I am now, that combined flame is enough to keep me running indefinitely. But if I spend it to create a path through the Leviathan, the magic I burn will be gone forever, and what is left might not be enough to keep me functional."

Julius stepped back. "You mean you'll die?"

"That depends on how much I have to use," the Black Reach said with a shrug. "If I use it all, then yes, I will cease to be. But even if I spend only a portion, what is left will almost certainly not be enough to allow me to continue my duties as guardian of the future, and as much as I wish to help you, that is a sacrifice I cannot make. I can bend the rules if I deem it necessary for the greater good, as I did with you and Brohomir, but I cannot abandon my duty entirely. Every seer tries to sell the future at some point. If I am not there to stop them, it won't matter if we save this world today, because sooner or later, one of our own seers will end it."

"You don't know that," Julius said. "We can always destroy ourselves, but that's the price of having choice: we have to choose correctly. I understand why my ancestors created you. They wanted someone to keep us from making the same mistakes they did. But by putting our future in your hands, they took the responsibility for it away from *us*, and that's no good. If dragonkind is ever to mature as a species, you can't make our decisions for us. Our future has to be our own to worry about and protect, not yours."

The Black Reach stared at him in horror. "You would have me abandon you," he said. "Give up the purpose for which I was created!"

"I want you to trust us to take care of ourselves," Julius said. "You've said a lot of very nice things about me, but to be honest, the only noteworthy thing I've done is convince dragons that they could do what they already longed to. I didn't make the Qilin choose happiness with Chelsie over suffering for his empire forever. He already desperately wanted to do that. All I did was convince him to go for it. Everything you want dragonkind to be is already inside us. It's our culture that tells us to dominate and be cruel, not our nature. There are *lots* of nice dragons in the world. I'm just the only one so far who's had a chance to show his true colors and live."

"Because of Brohomir," the Black Reach said. "If dragons really are as far along as you claim, why did it take the greatest seer in centuries to ensure your survival?"

"Because we're having to fight against our own stereotype," Julius said fiercely. "Against what venerable dragons like *you* are constantly telling us we are! If you really want to make a better dragonkind, start with that. Because the real problem isn't that seers are selling the future, it's that they feel that's the only way. They'd rather face you, their *death*, than compromise or work together or do any of the other things we're told from birth that we're weak and stupid for wanting. *That's* the mistake that must never be repeated! Not her." He pointed back at Bob's pigeon. "Amelia knew it too, which is why she tied herself to this plane. She was trying to buy us a chance to live long enough to mature past our megalomania stage. *That's* the sort of progress you should be fighting to save, not me. I'm just one dragon, but this plane and what we've already achieved coming together trying to save it is the best shot you're ever going to get at actually changing dragon culture. Our better future is already here! I just need you to help me make sure it doesn't end before it can begin."

The Black Reach sighed. "And by that I suppose you mean burn a hole in the Leviathan for you?"

"Only if you can do it without dying," Julius said quickly. "I believe in everything I just said, but it's still a long shot. Just because I'm willing to bet my life on that doesn't mean I want to burn up everyone else's last chance to run. No matter what happens, though, our entire species still came together today. That's a huge step in the right direction, one you can carry into any other world. Just don't let what we started today die, and I think you'll have a better future no matter how this ends. So if you can help me, I'd appreciate it, but if it'll cost you too much, go ahead and start evacuating as many dragons as you can. I'll just find another way in."

By the time he finished, the Black Reach looked almost angry. That wasn't what Julius had intended. He'd been trying his best to be reasonable, but when he opened his mouth to apologize for whatever he'd said wrong, the construct began to laugh.

"If I didn't know better, I'd swear Brohomir was feeding you lines," the Black Reach said, shaking his head. "You truly are a dragon of a different color, Julius Heartstriker. It will be my honor to light your way into the Leviathan."

"Wait, really?" Julius said, shocked. "You're sure it won't kill you?"

"I cannot say," the Black Reach said calmly, looking up at the Leviathan. "It will take a massive amount of fire to burn through the carapace the enemy has built from Algonquin's magic, and even more to keep the Nameless End from consuming you once you're inside. I have no idea if I have enough, but I know I am the only one who could. With the death of the Three Sisters, no dragon remains who is old enough to produce a flame that could challenge a power of this magnitude. But I am Dragon Sees Eternity, one of the two greatest creations of our old realm! Inside me burn the flames of all the ancient clan leaders, including those of your grandfather, the Quetzalcoatl. He was the wisest of all the great dragons, and you remind me very much of him. I believe he would have been proud to know his fire helped you now."

"But—"

"The decision is made," the construct said. "And we have very little time left. Now stand back. I will make you a path."

The words weren't out of his mouth before the Black Reach began to change, his human body fading as it had when he'd threatened Bob. This time, though, it wasn't just a claw that emerged from the shadows, but an entire dragon. The biggest Julius had ever seen.

"Whoa," he said, stumbling back.

He'd known for a long time now that Dragon Sees Eternity was big. He'd seen his brother, after all. Despite Amelia's all-clan roundup, Dragon Sees the Beginning was still the largest dragon Julius had seen by several orders of magnitude. At least, he had been until now. Julius wasn't sure if the twin constructs had started out unequal, or if ten thousand years of being the only thing keeping a plane from collapsing had shrunken Dragon Sees the Beginning, but as huge as the bone-white construct of the past had been, he was nothing compared to the dragon that appeared now.

Dragon Sees Eternity was as long as his name. Like his twin, his overlapping scales looked more like stone than anything organic, and each one was marked with a symbol in the ancient magical language of dragons that only experts like Svena could still read. But where Dragon Sees the Beginning had been white, Dragon Sees Eternity was as black as the void, his snaking body so enormous, Julius could no longer see the Leviathan behind him. He was trying to make sense of how something that big could even be alive when Marci ran up and grabbed his neck.

"Oh man," she said, clutching Ghost to her chest as she clambered onto Julius's back. "This is going to be *epic*!"

"I just hope it's fast," Amelia said, clinging to Bob's arm as the two of them walked over. "I don't know if you looked up during that enlightening conversation, Julius, but things are starting to get extra apocalyptic."

It *was* getting rather dark. "Are we the only ones going?" Julius asked, looking at Marci on his back.

"Yes," Bob said. "Or rather, there are plenty who *would* come, including me, but you're the only ones who *should*. You're going to Algonquin with a human Merlin, a dragon, and a Mortal Spirit. That's already a combo pack of her least favorite things. Let's not make it worse by piling on."

"I *really* wanted to go," Amelia said grumpily. "When else am I going to get a chance to see inside a Nameless End? But Bob convinced me that a Mortal Spirit who was also a dragon would be a bridge way too far, so I'm taking one for the team."

"Good call, Amelia," Marci said. "I'll tell you how it is."

"Make sure you take notes," the dragon spirit pleaded. "If we survive, I'll need a full report."

Marci crossed her heart and crouched down low on Julius's back, Ghost tucked safely under her arms. "Ready when you are."

"I'm ready," Julius said, looking up at the giant dragon floating above them. "But what do I do? Do I just fly up?"

"I have no idea," Bob confessed. "There are so many ways this goes wrong, we're down to picking the least bad. Whatever you choose, though, I'm sure it will be fine."

Julius swallowed. "That doesn't sound very seer-like."

"It's not," Bob agreed. "But I'm still confident, because it's *you*." He looked at Julius, his green eyes surprisingly serious. "You've only known me a short while, but I've known you almost my entire life. I've watched these last few months unfold in a million permutations, and in all those potential outcomes, even the tragic ones, you've never done less than your best. That's all I could ever ask of my cornerstone piece, and it's why I believe in you now. I *know* you, Julius. I don't have to see the future to know that so long as there's the tiniest chance of making this work, you'll find it. And if you don't, we'll all be dead, so I'll never know I was wrong. It's called being an optimist."

Julius would have called it crazy, but he never got to say so because Bob had already stepped back. "Time to go," he said, lifting his Magician's Fang. "Good luck!"

The seer hauled back as he finished, swinging his sword like a bat. The flat of the blade whacked Julius right across the middle, knocking the much smaller dragon high into the air just as the giant construct above them took a deep breath. The magic was so thick now, Julius could feel his feathers curling as the heat built and built and built. Finally, just when it seemed the air itself was about to combust, the construct of the future opened his mouth to release a gout of flame so huge and bright, it whited out the sky.

Julius went still so fast, he nearly fell out of the sky. The Black Reach's fire was the most beautiful he'd ever seen. It was burning hot, but in that heat were more colors than he'd known existed, including the Quetzalcoatl's famous green. If he hadn't been in danger of melting, he could have happily watched it forever, but the lovely plume of deadly fire was already flying away, arcing like a solar flare to crash into the black underbelly of the Nameless End.

"NOW, HEARTSTRIKER," Dragon Sees Eternity roared, his mouth dripping fire. "GO WITH THE FIRE *NOW!*"

Julius obeyed, pressing his wings tight to protect Marci as he shot into the geyser of fire like an arrow. As his vision went white, Julius closed his eyes, certain they were about to be burned to a crisp. There was just no way anything could survive fire this hot, and yet the magic didn't consume him. It lifted him, carrying his snaking body like a leaf in a stream up to the Leviathan and through, past the melting wall of black congealed magic and into a deeper dark.

CHAPTER FOURTEEN

After the chaos of the battle and their mad dive through the Black Reach's kaleidoscope of fire, the sudden stillness inside the Leviathan felt like someone had pulled a plug on the world. The hole they'd flown through closed immediately, leaving Julius gasping in the dark, but while nothing hurt, he couldn't see or feel his body, or anything else.

"Marci!" he called frantically, feeling around. "*Marci!*"

"I'm here," Marci said, her voice surprisingly close. "But I can't see you."

"I can't see you, either," Julius said, his voice confused and frustratingly disembodied. The Black Reach had said his fire would protect them inside as well, but he couldn't see a—

Light blossomed around him, making him jump. All over his body, the strange, thick darkness was boiling away to reveal a warm glow that came from below his feathers. It reached Marci a heartbeat later, revealing her face, and then her body in a slow unraveling as the light from his fire pushed back the dark. The change was primal and slow, but eventually it covered them both, surrounding them in a bubble of warm illumination that felt unspeakably old and fragile. The soft glow looked nothing like the brilliant multicolored fire outside, but it smelled strongly of the Black Reach, and when the flames crackled over Julius's skin, they spoke in his voice.

You don't have much time, the Black Reach's fire whispered. *I gave as much as I dared, but though he is not yet fully here, the Nameless End eats quickly. He will eat me too if you do not hurry.*

"Then we'd better get moving," Julius said, looking at the wall of liquid dark beyond the circle of the Black Reach's flickering protection. "Any idea where to start?"

Marci shrugged helplessly, and the Black Reach said nothing. In hindsight, Julius wasn't actually sure if he'd been talking to the construct himself, or if the words had been a message bottled up for him in the fire. Either way, it seemed they were alone in here for real now, assuming there was a "here" at all.

The inside of the Leviathan was empty in a way Julius had never felt. Even with the Black Reach's fire illuminating the space directly around them, Julius wouldn't have known there was a floor if his feet hadn't been planted on it. It had no texture or temperature, no feeling of any sort. It was just... nothing. He couldn't even smell the magic anymore, and the lack of it was making his dragon body feel heavier than ever. Much more of this, and he'd be forced back into his human shape whether he wanted it or not. Yet another timer they were going to have to beat to have a prayer of pulling this off. But just as Julius was wondering how one navigated through nothingness, his nose caught the faint scent of lake water.

His head shot up so fast Marci jumped. "I smell her," he said, breathing deeply. "That way."

He took a tentative step in the direction of the scent, pressing his foot down on the emptiness beneath them. But while there was no sensation at all—no movement, no solidity, not even the pressure of his own weight—he didn't fall into the blackness, which was good enough.

"What are we walking on?" Marci asked, tapping her shoe against the blackness. "Leviathan guts?"

"Who knows?" Julius said. "We're inside a Nameless End. Physics might not even apply here."

"If that's the case, why are we wasting time being cautious?" Marci asked, hopping back into position between his wings. "Let's fly!"

Flying when you couldn't see where you were going was a terrible idea. Technically, though, this entire journey was a terrible idea. Julius saw no point in being cautious now, so he spread his wings, pushing off the strange emptiness with his claws.

It was one of the oddest experiences of Julius's life. Flying through nothingness made even less sense than walking on it, but while he felt no wind under his feathers or lift in his wings, it did seem like he was going faster. It might well have been all in his head since, without landmarks or anything to judge distance by, actual relative speed was impossible to determine. But flapping made him feel like he was doing something, so Julius kept it up, pumping his wings as hard as he could as he followed the lake water scent like a bloodhound through the dark.

It took forever. Having just battled it, Julius was painfully aware of how huge the Leviathan was. He'd been flying at what felt like top speed for several minutes now, but the scent wasn't getting any closer. He was beginning to worry it *was* all in his head, and they weren't actually moving at all, when he spotted a spark of light in the distance.

The glow was as faint as a distant star. If everything else hadn't been so unrelentingly black, Julius would have missed it entirely. As they got closer, though, he realized the spot wasn't actually glowing. It was simply not dark—a small, muddy circle of cloudy, greenish-brown water no wider than a manhole cover. The puddle didn't even ripple when he landed beside it, and the scent of lake water was only moderately stronger than it had been at the beginning. He was lowering his snout to the surface to make sure this was the source of the smell he'd been chasing when a woman's hand shot out of the water and grabbed his nose.

Julius jumped backward, almost knocking Marci off as he frantically scrambled out of reach, but he needn't have bothered. Unlike every other time he'd encountered Algonquin, the hand that grabbed him now was as weak as the muddy water it appeared to be. It broke the moment he jerked away, falling back into the puddle with a tired, exasperated splash that warped into two wet words.

"Go away."

"No," Julius said, crouching at the pool's edge so Marci could climb down. "We went through a lot of trouble to get here, and we're not leaving until we speak with you."

Considering the finality of their situation, Julius fully expected Algonquin to tell him to sit there until they all died. To his surprise, though, the watery hand reemerged, followed by an arm, and then a body as Algonquin hauled herself out of the tiny puddle, her blank-mirror face still managing to glare somehow when it turned to reflect his own.

"Come to beg for your life, dragon?" she whispered, her once-roaring voice now as quiet as a spring rain. "I'm afraid you're too late. It's over. I've won."

"*Won?*" Marci cried, stepping forward with Ghost in her arms. "You fed us to a Nameless End! That's not you winning. That's *everyone* losing!"

"Typical human," Algonquin said. "Ignorant to the bitter end. But make no mistake, this will be *your* end, not ours."

"If you believe that, you're delusional," Marci said, her face furious. "I've been to the Sea of Magic, Algonquin. Your monster is getting ready to eat a lot more than just dragons and humans."

"But not forever." The spirit lifted her watery head proudly. "The End and I struck a deal. I give him myself, all current magic, every living thing, and the rest of our world down to the bedrock, and in return, he promised to leave the land when he moves on. It may be barren rock for a long time, but eventually, life will return. New spirits will rise from that barren ground, and the world will be reborn." Her murky water curled into something like a smile. "A new world, clean and pure. A world without *you.*"

Marci clenched her shaking fists, but Algonquin's words actually gave Julius hope. He'd known she wouldn't truly destroy the world. It went too hard against everything he'd heard about her, and what she'd said herself. Her dream had always been to return to the time when the Spirits of the Land were the *only* spirits. From that perspective, sacrificing herself to the Leviathan so he could eat their world down to the core made a twisted sort of sense. Spirits were eternal. So long as land existed in some form, they would always rise again. They could afford to wait the eons it would take things to recover, especially since, without humans or dragons, there'd be no competition getting in their way. Algonquin clearly saw herself as a martyr, trading her life for a better future for everyone. There was just one catch.

"Do you really believe he'll stop?"

Algonquin's head snapped toward him. "You have no right to question me, worm!" she cried, her muddy water boiling. "It is because of you and the humans that I was forced to do this!"

"We didn't force you to do anything," Julius said calmly. "You chose to make a deal with the Leviathan. But what assurance do you have that he's going to stop where he said he would? He's a Nameless *End*. That doesn't leave much room for compromise."

Algonquin tilted her head, distorting the reflection of Julius's face as her water rippled. "I remember you. You're the little Heartstriker from Reclamation Land. The one who talked too much."

"That's me," Julius said. "But this *needs* to be talked about. You're gambling everything on the word of a planar force whose existence revolves around doing the *one thing* he's promising you he won't. He could eat this entire plane the moment he finishes you off, and you wouldn't even know. How can you trust him?"

"A fine question from a dragon," the spirit said coldly. "Your kind has no concept of faith or obligation. But you're right. He *is* untrustworthy, but no more so than the rest of you. I'd rather gamble on his honor than put my faith in the humans and their Mortal Spirits. At least the Nameless End is honest about his desire to destroy."

She turned to Marci and Ghost as she said this, her reflective face throwing back a distorted image of their growing anger.

"How did you get this twisted?" Marci cried, clutching her spirit. "How can you trust a creature who *eats planes* over your fellow spirits? He's the inimical alien force here, not us! The magic that I use and that makes up Ghost is no different from the magic that fills your lakes. We're the same. Why can't you see that?"

"Because it's not true!" Algonquin cried, rising up in a fury. "I am the land! You are simply an out-of-control infection, and that thing you call *spirit*"—she threw out her hand toward Ghost so hard, the muddy water of her fingers splashed onto his white fur—"is nothing more than the power you've surrendered to your out-of-control emotions! If I'd done nothing, my kind would be yours to abuse and exploit just as you exploited our land while we slept." She flung her arm out at Marci next, pointing an accusing watery finger in the mage's face. "*You* pushed me to this! This is all *your fault!*"

She was shaking so hard by the time she finished, her face could no longer hold a reflection. Julius could practically see the two-headed monster of rage and fear consuming what little was left of the once great Lady of the Lakes in front of his eyes. But though she'd been his kind's greatest enemy since they'd come here, all he felt for her now was pity.

"This isn't you, Algonquin."

"*Shut up!*" she snarled. "You are the worst of all! The others are a cancer, but at least they are a failing of this world. You are nothing but a parasite. A freeloader, feeding on our power. You have no right to be here!"

"But I am here," Julius said firmly. "We're *all* here, Algonquin, because this is the world now. I'm sure you thought things were paradise back when your spirits were the only ones, but that time is gone. Even if your plan works, and the Nameless End *does* stop where he promised, your 'victory' will be a barren rock. Whatever rises from those ashes won't be the world you knew. It'll be something else entirely, a new land with new powers struggling desperately to survive on the burned crumbs of a once-beautiful world. That's what you're leaving for the future. *That's* what you're calling victory."

"*You think this is what I wanted?*" Algonquin roared, splashing cold water onto his feathers as she rose over him. "My plan was to muzzle the magic back to a level where Mortal Spirits wouldn't rise! I would have done it too, if not for them." She threw a line of cold water at Marci and Ghost, who jumped back. "They are the ones who ruined my paradise. This was *never* what I wanted, but it's all I have left!"

"That doesn't mean you have to take it!" Julius cried, rising up on his hind feet so he could look her in the face. "Just because you can't go back to how things were doesn't mean you have to destroy what we have now. There's nothing stopping us from making a new paradise except you. If you'd stop hating us for a moment and *listen*, we could—"

"Why should I listen?" she demanded. "What have dragons done for this world except take? What have humans done except defile the land and fill it with monsters?" Her water opened like fangs. "*I have every right to hate you!*"

"But what has that gotten you?" Marci asked.

The cloudy water jerked. "Excuse me?"

"No one can argue the damage humans have done," Marci said, hugging her glowing cat against her chest. "We've done terrible things, and you have every right to be mad about them, but hating something doesn't fix the problem. I've had a front-row seat for every one of your sketchy plans to stop the Mortal Spirits, and not a single one has made things better for you or the things you claim to care about. I was willing to work with you in Reclamation Land, but you wouldn't even listen to a compromise. You tried to use Ghost and me by force, and when that didn't work, you fed your precious Spirits of the Land into the chipper-shredder to get enough magic to raise the DFZ as a slave to Myron so he could be the first Merlin."

Her face grew furious. "Do you have any idea the *good* you could have done with that much power? How much better everything could have been if you'd used your magic to greet the confused, newborn Mortal Spirit of the DFZ in peace instead of stomping on her? The DFZ turned out to be amazing! She could have been an incredible ally if you hadn't treated her like a fighting dog, but you *did*. You were so busy hating us, you didn't even think about trying something different, and now you're doing it again. You've chosen over and over to be the villain, and now you've sided with this monster against your own world! Your Spirits of the Land, the ones you *claim* to be doing all of this for, they're so afraid of what you've done that they willingly gave their magic to *me* so I could try and stop it!"

Algonquin pulled back. "The banishment," she whispered. "That was their magic?"

"It was *everyone's* magic," Marci said. "Land, Animal, Mortal—they all volunteered because they were scared to death of what *you* did! But even though my banishment failed, I'm still happy I tried, because it proved what I've been saying all along."

"That I'm the enemy?" Algonquin said bitterly.

Marci shook her head. "That we're all the same." She looked down at Ghost in her arms. "You always talked about the Mortal Spirits like they were aliens, some kind of new invasion completely separate from other spirits, but they're not. Ghost's vessel might have been carved by humans instead of geology, but he protects the forgotten dead just like you protect your waters and your fish. If you need more proof, look at Raven. He figured out ages ago that the lines we drew to divide spirit types are nonsense, and he used that knowledge to become something *more*."

"Do not speak that traitor's name!" Algonquin snarled, her watery head turning as she searched the dark around them. "Where is he anyway? Lurking in the shadows for the right moment to swoop down and say something dramatic?"

"He's not here," Marci said, her face grim. "He gave up his magic just like everyone else to try to banish you before you destroyed everything. He hasn't risen again yet. At this rate, he might never do so."

For the first time since they'd arrived, Algonquin looked sad, her murky water drooping. Then she pulled herself back together. "It does not matter," she said. "Raven was always against me."

"*You* were against you," Marci said. "Raven was always the one trying to *save* you."

"He was a fool," Algonquin spat. "But it doesn't matter." She slipped back into her muddy pool. "Criticize me all you like, mortal, but it's too late. This world is already finished."

"But it's not!" Julius cried, grabbing the water with his claws. "That's why we risked so much to come here! Because we're all still alive, and so are you. You're not dead yet, Algonquin! There's still time to change your mind."

The pool of water scoffed. "And do what? Join you? Forget the wrongs I've suffered and embrace those who hate me just as much as I hate them?"

"It was you who made us enemies," Ghost said, his cold voice startlingly soft as he hopped out of Marci's arms. "The DFZ and I were not born hating you. You taught us to hate through your actions. You killed the hundreds of thousands of people whose anger woke me from my sleep. You enslaved the city you built. Those are *your* sins, Algonquin. Not ours."

"*Your* kind are the ones who taught mine to fear," the water spirit snapped. "You were so out of control, your own Merlins shut down the magic because they couldn't deal with you. Where's the callout for those sins, cat?"

"That's unfair," Marci argued. "You can't blame Ghost for what Mortal Spirits did before the drought any more than you can blame me for what human mages did a thousand years before I was born."

"So I should ignore them? Do nothing?" She pointed at the Empty Wind. "His kind trampled mine and turned the world into a hell. Do you expect me to forget that just because he did? He's as immortal as I am! The Empty Wind blew back then just as it does now, but unlike the Mortal Spirits, I did not wake ignorant. I learned from the past to act in the present before it ruined my future!"

Marci responded with something cutting, but Julius wasn't listening anymore. He didn't need to. The arguments might be different, but the dug-in anger he heard in their voices was the same as he'd heard all his life. Marci and the spirits were stuck in the same cycle of violence and revenge that Julius had been banging his head against ever since he'd found the courage to lift it. But as frustrating as that was, it gave him hope, because while he was an outsider when it came to spirit magic, this was a problem he knew as well as his own fire.

"It has to stop."

The spirits and Marci jumped in surprise at his voice, and then Algonquin's water hit him in the face like a slap.

"This is none of your affair," she snarled. "You do not get to speak here, dragon."

"It's because I'm a dragon that I *can* say this," Julius replied, shaking the water off his feathers. "I've seen the damage hate and vengeance do to everything they touch. Just look at what they've done to you." He looked pointedly down at the pathetic stretch of muddy water. "You were the Lady of the Great Lakes, the most powerful spirit in North America. Now you'd fit in a bucket."

The water shivered. "You *dare* mock me?"

"I'm not mocking you," he said. "I'm drawing your attention to the results of your actions. I understand why you did it. You saw your world changing, and you blamed the humans and the Mortal Spirits be- cause they were the face of that change, but not once did you stop and remember that you're a product of change as well. Your five lakes used to be one. Before the last ice age, they weren't there at all. The source was different, but as Marci already pointed out, you were born into this world the same as any other spirit. Or any dragon."

"You are *not* of our world," she spat.

"But I was born here," Julius said. "So was my mother and every other living dragon. The Three Sisters you killed were the last dragons born in our old world. The rest of us were made right here, same as the humans or any other animal. Now that Amelia has tied our magic to this plane, we really are native, and we're fighting now to protect our world just like you are."

"This is not your world," Algonquin rumbled, pointing at Ghost and Marci. "It's not their world, either. It's *my* world!"

"And in a few minutes, it'll be no one's world," Julius growled. "Don't you get it? You've been so busy fighting for what you think you lost, you can't even see what you're actually losing right now!"

"I lose nothing," Algonquin said, slapping her water against the blackness. "This is my chosen victory! I would rather die here alone than live on in a world where I am ruled by Mortal Spirits, defiled by humans, and plagued by dragons!"

"But that's just it!" Julius cried. "You're so convinced that change is your enemy, you've forgotten that *you can change, too.* Everything can! If you don't like how a tree is growing, you don't burn it to the ground. You help it—prune it, tie it, coax it in a different direction. The future's no different. As Ghost just said, Mortal Spirits didn't come out hating you. You taught them that, because the only one who's ever acted like it's our way or the highway is you. But the good news is that you can *change your mind.*"

"Impossible," Ghost growled. "She will never change. Her hate is too deep."

"Everything can change," Julius said. "Two months ago, I thought my clan would always be a nest of vipers, but this afternoon, I watched all of Heartstriker fight alongside clans we've been enemies with for centuries." He turned back to Algonquin. "If stubborn old dragons can change to survive, you can. I mean, you're water! All you *do* is change, so change now. Let the old grudges go. Look forward instead of backward. If you can't live in this world, then work with us to build one you *can* live in. But if you destroy everything now, then it's over for *everyone*, including the lakes you've fought so hard all this time to protect."

That last part was the most important. Julius had been taught from birth to see Algonquin as his enemy, but even when he'd lived in her shadow in the DFZ, he'd never doubted her dedication to her lakes. Everything she'd done, including this, was to protect the land and those who came from it, and that gave him hope. She'd made a lot of terrible choices, but anyone who could die for others could surely be convinced to live for them instead. Even the fact that she'd held on to the Leviathan for sixty years before using it was a sign that Algonquin wasn't an implacable enemy. She was just desperate and cornered, like Estella had been, or Chelsie.

Like himself.

When Marci had died, he could have done terrible things. Would have, if Chelsie hadn't stopped him. When she'd grabbed him, the line between tragedy and survival had come down to a single moment. One decision to bend instead of break. To keep moving forward instead of dying with his fangs in his enemy's throat. It was a choice that couldn't be forced, couldn't be demanded. It could only be asked, so that was what Julius did now, lowering his head respectfully before the Algonquin.

"Please," he said, bowing before the spirit who'd wanted him and all his kind dead for ten thousand years. "Don't give up yet. All of us are here right now because we're too stubborn to die. That's common ground, so let's stand on it. Let's be stubborn together. Let's fight and argue and refuse to give up until we've hammered out a world we can *all* live with. It might take a long time, and things might get worse before they get better, but if we just keep going, there's nothing that can stop us from getting where we want to be. All I'm asking is that you keep trying with us. *Please*, Algonquin."

A long silence fell when he finished, and then the lake spirit sighed. "You beg surprisingly well for a dragon."

"I'm not begging," Julius said, lifting his head. "I'm asking you to do what you know is right. It's not over. You can still fix this."

"No," she said, cowering in her puddle. "It was the only way. The Mortal Spirits—"

"What could Mortal Spirits do to you that's worse than what you've done to yourself?" Julius demanded. "I've seen your lakes, Algonquin! Your shores are dry. Your fish are dead. The Leviathan took every drop of water from them, and you let him. You were their spirit, their god, and you let them die."

"Stop," Algonquin whispered, sinking lower.

"I can't stop," Julius said angrily. "Not until you do. You've always claimed you were fighting to protect the land. Now's your chance to prove it. *Stop* this, Algonquin. Don't be the hammer that breaks the only home we have."

By the time he finished, Algonquin's muddy puddle was smaller than a dinner plate. When she didn't rise again, Julius was terrified they were too late, that the Leviathan had already finished her off. Then her water started to shake, and Julius understood. Algonquin wasn't being devoured. She was crying, weeping in ripples that quickly grew to waves.

"I *can't*," she sobbed. "Don't you see? It's too late. Even if I wanted to stop, I already let him in."

She lifted a watery hand as she finished, and Julius gasped. In the dark of the emptiness, Algonquin's water had looked muddy, but now that a bit of her was stretched out under the soft light of the Black Reach's fire, Julius saw the truth. Algonquin wasn't murky at all. Like always, her water was crystal clear. The off color was merely an illusion created by thousands of dark, tiny lines running through her body. The way they spread reminded Julius of roots, but there was nothing plant-like about the hungry way the black tips twitched and moved, crawling through Algonquin's water like predators as they ate her alive.

"There is no more choice," she whispered, pulling her arm back down. "He's in every drop of my magic now. When he's finished consuming all the water from my physical lakes, he will *be* me, and our world will be his."

The defeat in her voice made Julius tremble. Even Marci was shaking, her whole body wobbling as she dropped to her knees beside Algonquin's murky shallows. "There has to be a way to reverse it," she said. "It's still your water. What if we—"

"There is nothing," Algonquin said bitterly. "Everywhere I look, everything I touch, he's already there, and I'm so tired. I've fought for so long now, lost so many times. If I could go back and do things differently, maybe this wouldn't have been such a waste, but as Raven loved to croak at me, we can never go back. The past is gone, and soon, I will be too." The puddle sloshed resentfully. "I'm sure that brings you joy."

"How can you think that?" Julius asked, heartbroken. "What have I ever said that could make you believe this is anything but a tragedy for everyone?"

The water gurgled, sinking even lower into her shrinking pool. "You are truly the strangest dragon I've ever met," she said quietly. "I wish we'd had this conversation decades ago, back when it might have done some good. But now..."

She let out a long, watery sigh, and then she lifted her head, raising her mirrored face from the hand-sized splash of water that was all that was left of her. "I will not apologize. This isn't how I meant for things to end, but I only did what I thought I must to protect my world, and I will never be sorry for that."

Knowing she'd had the best intentions just made everything worse. At this point, Julius almost wished she'd died cursing them. The hate would have stung, but at least it would have been a clean ending, not this bitter, tragic mess. Looking at Algonquin, all he could think was that if only he'd been better, said something sooner, he could have prevented this. They'd spoken before, but he'd always been too distracted by other disasters to pay attention to *why* Algonquin was acting the way she was. If he'd taken the time, looked harder, maybe everything would have been different. Because she wasn't a monster. None of them were. Dragons, spirits, humans—they were all just flawed, floundering souls fumbling their way as best they could. Now they'd fumbled right off the cliff, and by the time Julius realized what was happening, it was too late.

That was what ate at him the most. Not the loss or the death, but the *waste*. The deep unfairness of fighting so hard only to discover you'd never had a chance. He couldn't stand it. He couldn't lose. Not after how hard they'd tried. Not after everything they'd been through.

And just like that, Julius came to a decision of his own. It took only a moment, barely a thought, but he must have spent way too much time with Bob lately, because Julius could have sworn he felt the future pivot toward a new direction as he raised his head to look at Algonquin again.

"If things had been different," he asked quietly, "if you could do everything over, knowing what you know now, would you work with us?"

The spirit's mirrored face flashed with annoyance, but the inevitability of their coming deaths must have been enough to defang even Algonquin's hatred, because in the end, she just shrugged what was left of her water. "Perhaps. I certainly wouldn't have given up like I did. I would never have run to you with open arms, but if I could go back and do it all again..." She thought a moment longer, and then her head bobbed. "I would have acted differently, yes."

That was all Julius needed to know. "Marci?"

She lifted her head hopelessly. "If you're looking to me for a solution, don't bother, 'cause I've got nothing."

"That's not why I'm looking at you," he said, leaning down to rest his feathered head on hers. "I love you."

Marci looked surprised by the sudden show of affection, which made Julius feel guilty for not telling her the truth sooner. If they'd had time, he could have gone on forever about how much meeting her had changed his life for the better and how important she was to him. But Algonquin's puddle was shrinking by the second, so he had to settle for a final deep breath, holding the air that smelled of Marci and magic in his mouth as long as he dared. Then, when he couldn't stall any longer, Julius turned to the lake spirit and lurched forward, sinking his teeth deep into what was left of Algonquin.

As runt of his clutch, Julius had never been much of a dragon. He was awful in a fight, couldn't cast spells, had terrible control of his fire, and generally failed at everything most dragons considered vital to survival. But while he was a disappointment in every traditional sense, there were two things Julius did very well: being fast and ignoring the instincts that ruled other dragons' lives, including, in this particular instance, the drive toward self-preservation.

He bit Algonquin like a striking viper, sinking his teeth into painfully cold water that tasted of fish and death. If he'd had a thought to spare for such luxuries, he would have been proud since this was probably the best hit any dragon had *ever* landed on the Lady of the Lakes, but his target wasn't actually the spirit. He was going for the tendrils that ran through her, the threads of the creature who was not from their world. *Those* were what Julius was eying when his jaws snapped down, devouring all that was left of Algonquin in one quick bite.

"*Dragon!*" The lake spirit's voice was a roar as she poured down his throat. "*What are you doing?*"

"Getting you another chance," Julius said, or tried to say. The black threads twisting down his throat hurt far more than he'd anticipated. Even with Marci screaming at him, he couldn't make a sound. Thankfully, everything else seemed to be working perfectly.

As cold and magical as she tasted, Algonquin's water flowed down his throat just like any other liquid. He could actually feel her spreading through his blood as she was absorbed into his body, the chill of her touch spidering through his brain as she panicked, which made him sad. He hadn't wanted to scare her, but if he'd explained what he intended to do before he did it, he'd have risked tipping the Leviathan off. He'd hoped to tell her the truth now, but eating the Leviathan's tendrils had hurt so much more than he'd expected. More than anything ever had, including the beating he'd gotten from Gregory. Painful as it was, though, he had to say *something*, because if Algonquin didn't understand what he was doing, it was all for nothing.

"I'm a dragon," he choked out at last. "Mostly water, like any other animal. But I'm also an outsider. A creature from another plane." He broke off, catching a few rapid breaths before forcing himself to continue. "The Black Reach's magic is still the pure fire of my ancestors. It's what's been keeping the Leviathan from eating us all this whole time. I figured if the fire could stop him from eating Marci and me, it could keep him from eating you too."

But he already ate me! Algonquin's voice cried in his mind. *Now he's in both of us!*

Julius grinned a bloody grin. "But you can *leave* me. The Leviathan can't get through the Black Reach's magic or he would have done it by now, but you're water. You can move through anything, and I've seen you use dragon blood before."

There was quite a lot of blood now. The smell of Marci had long since been overwhelmed by the rich, salty flush of dragon blood dripping down his teeth as the Leviathan's tendrils screamed and ripped him apart from the inside.

"Take it," Julius gasped, collapsing on the ground in the middle of the new pool that was forming on the ground. His pool, made of his blood. "I'm giving it to you."

The spirit in his head collapsed into stunned silence. Then, in a quiet, broken voice, she whispered, *Why?*

"Because I can," he whispered back, coughing. "There was never much chance of me getting out of this alive, but now you have a shot. Flow out through my blood, take Marci, and escape. I know you can move between any of your waters, and there should still be a few drops left in your lakes to run to."

"*No!*" Marci screamed in his ear, grabbing his head in her frantic hands. "*Don't you dare, Julius!*"

"I'll hold him here as long as I can," Julius went on, desperate to get the words out while he still could. "Go, Algonquin. I've bought you a second chance. Choose again. Choose differently." He smiled. "Choose us."

A coughing fit forced his eyes closed after that. When he got them open again, he was staring into the puddle of his blood, its surface shimmering in the reflected radiance of the Black Reach's fire. Inside his stomach, the bit of the Leviathan he'd swallowed was fighting harder than ever, ripping him to shreds from the inside as it fought to get back to Algonquin, but it was too late. The cold presence of the lake spirit had already flowed out of him, dripping into the red pool along with the rest of his blood. The liquid churned as she took hold of it, and then the shimmering liquid rose up, turning to look at him with a perfect reflection of his own face. A *clear* reflection, free of the tendrils that were desperately trying to eat through his body to get to her.

If he'd been any good with his fire, he might have been able to back-draft his flames down his throat and force the Leviathan's tendrils down again and buy more time, but Julius had always been rubbish at that sort of thing. Justin had always said his lack of ability in anything resembling dragon combat would get him killed one day. Too bad Julius wouldn't have a chance to tell his brother he'd been right.

He didn't want his last thought to be Justin's "I told you so," so Julius looked at Marci instead. It was easy since she was in front of him now, and looking angrier than he'd ever seen her as she screamed at him that he couldn't die. That she wouldn't let him. But as terrible as he felt doing this to her, a small, selfish, draconic part of Julius treasured that she cared enough to be so furious. He wanted to gather that love-driven anger up and hoard it like the precious gem it was, but he was so tired. He couldn't even lift his head anymore.

Marci started to cry then, which hurt even more than the Leviathan. Julius wanted to tell her he was sorry, that this was the only way he'd known to save things, but it was too late. Even a dragon's ability to heal wasn't enough to keep up with the thousands of cuts the Leviathan was making inside him. The best he could manage was to wheeze Marci's name before Algonquin rose from the now very large pool of his blood and yanked the mage into it, dragging them both down through the blood and hopefully into the safety of her lakes.

It would have to be hopefully, because Julius had no way to know for sure. The Leviathan had finally ground a hole in the Black Reach's protective fire. As the light faded, tendrils started coming at him from the outside as well, stabbing into his body like jagged knives from all directions. The bigger tentacles were just starting to appear when his heart finally stuttered to a stop, and Julius Heartstriker, youngest son of Bethesda, Founder of the Heartstriker Clan Council, Diplomat's Fang, and all-around Nice Dragon, finally did what most of his family had been telling him to do for the last twenty-five years.

He died.

CHAPTER FIFTEEN

Marci was drowning in bloody water, and she didn't even care. She fought the current dragging her down with everything she had, kicking and screaming out all the air in her lungs as she lunged for the dragon she could still barely see silhouetted by the fiery glow above her. She was still reaching for him when the fire vanished, and she burst gasping from a puddle of freezing water hidden in the wreckage by the base of Algonquin's Tower.

She immediately tried to dive again, screaming at Julius that she was coming back, and he'd better not be dead when she got there. She was throwing her body at the shallow water when a cold hand grabbed her wrist.

"Enough, mortal."

Marci's head shot up to see Algonquin standing over her. Her watery body was clear again, as blue and deep as her lake with no trace of the precious blood she'd taken them through to get here.

"Take me back!" Marci demanded, grabbing the spirit with both hands. "I have to save Julius!"

"You can't," Algonquin said, flowing around Marci's grip. "He's dead." Her voice began to quiver. "A dragon died for me."

She spoke the words in wonder, but Marci refused to hear them. The Lady of the Lakes was wrong. Julius couldn't be dead. It wasn't possible. She'd just gotten him back. *Nothing* was that unfair.

Marci.

She shoved Ghost's soft voice out of her mind, falling to her knees in the mud beside the puddle that was all that remained of Lake St. Clair.

253

She didn't want to listen to anyone. She didn't even care if she died anymore. Everything she wanted was with Julius. She just wanted to go back to where he was and—

Marci!

"Mortal!" Algonquin shouted at the same time, snatching Marci back into the water a split-second ahead of the tentacle that fell from the sky to consume the puddle they'd emerged from. They surfaced again a few moments later, popping out of another, even smaller puddle at the far edge of the lake.

"Hurry!" Algonquin cried as Marci coughed up water on the muddy lake bed. "We have to keep moving!"

But there was nowhere to run. The lake bed was a dry bowl around them, and the shadow of the Leviathan was directly overhead, its constantly roving tentacles turning as one to focus their hooked ends on the spirit cowering in her last inch of water.

"Algonquin."

It was like hearing an earthquake speak. The name vibrated in Marci's bones, making her whole body ache. Algonquin was shaking too, her water rippling in a million little spikes as the tentacles drew closer, coiling together into a single huge mass that fell around the two of them like a noose.

"Return," the Leviathan boomed. *"Now."*

Algonquin pulled her muddy water tight. "I will not."

"The time for rebellion is over," the Nameless End said. *"Your surrender was accepted. You have no more voice. No more power."* The black noose tightened. *"Return to me now."*

"I will not!" Algonquin cried, her watery voice ringing as she surged up from her last shore. "I am done being a fool! The victory you offered was nothing but defeat by another name. I'm ashamed it took me so long to see that, but I will correct that mistake now." She rose higher still, pulling everything that was left of her water from the mud and the dirt until she was a pillar of blue inside the ring of black. "I reject you, Leviathan! I revoke your name and your privilege in this world! You are no longer welcome in my waters! Be gone, devourer, and never return!"

She spoke the words like a banishment, but though they rang beautiful and clear through the still air, nothing happened. There was only silence, followed by a rumble that shook the ground as the Devourer of Worlds began to laugh.

"It is far too late for that. You were the greatest spirit of this land. Now, you are nothing but mud on the ground. Your water is already mine, great Algonquin, as is the name you gave me when you welcomed me in. You have no power over either anymore, just as you have no power over me."

Lying in the now bone-dry dirt, Marci sucked in a terrified breath. For all Julius's hopes that Algonquin was the key to winning this, the Nameless End still sounded like he had all the cards. But though the Leviathan was laughing at her, Algonquin stood defiant, her water shimmering in the dark of his shadow.

"That is where you are wrong," she said triumphantly. "You may have all the power, but so long as even the memory of them exists, these lakes are and shall forever be *mine*. Their water will *always* belong to me, and now that I am no longer shackled with your presence, I am free to call them home."

The world rumbled as she finished, forcing Marci to scramble to her feet as all the water left in the empty basins—the mud, the drips from the sodden water plants, the blood left in the rotting bodies of the fish—rose from its hiding places to answer its Lady's call. Each stream was tiny, barely more than a few drops, but together they made a torrent, swelling Algonquin's pillar until its swirling edges pushed right up against the ring of the Leviathan's tentacles.

"You are the one who has no power here, outsider!" Algonquin's voice cried from every drop. "Everything you've ever claimed was stolen from me. Now, you will *give it back!*"

Her cry ended with an explosion. High overhead, the black body of the Leviathan bulged and ruptured as millions of gallons of water— the entire contents of the Great Lakes—burst from its sides. The lakes poured out in a thousand deafening waterfalls, the white cascades slamming into the dry beds and filling the empty river. The roar of it was so loud, Marci couldn't hear herself think. Even Ghost's voice in her head was drowned out as the surging water refilling Lake St. Clair rushed up her body. But just as Marci's head was about to vanish under the churning tide, hard, cold hands grabbed her and yanked, lifting her body high above the waves as Algonquin's voice crashed through them.

"Now, Merlin!" the spirit cried, frantic and triumphant. "*Push!*"

For a terrifying second, Marci had no idea what that meant. Then she felt it. The water wasn't the only thing rising. Magic was building around Algonquin, and not just on this side. Through her connection to Ghost, Marci could feel the wave rising in the Sea of Magic as well. It swelled larger by the second, growing even larger than the lakes as millions of spirits—none of whom should have been up so soon—rose from their vessels once again to join with Algonquin, adding their rage to hers until the entire world yelled in one voice.

GET OUT!

It came from Ghost and from Algonquin, from Raven and Amelia, from every spirit of every sort. Even Marci screamed it as she grabbed the magic and shoved, adding her strength to the rest as the whole plane pushed in unison against the predator trying to eat it.

GET OUT!

The Nameless End roared in the sky, its tentacles digging into the ground as it fought to stay anchored, but without Algonquin's stolen water giving it weight, its roots were no longer strong enough. As Marci pushed and pushed, channeling magic until her soul felt like it was burning, she swore she could feel the plane itself twisting, the dimensional walls closing in on the crack the Nameless End had squeezed itself through. With each push, the hole grew smaller and smaller, and as it shrank, the End began to fade, its impenetrable body turning back to shadow, then to empty sky. Then, with a final deafening *pop*, the Leviathan's presence vanished entirely, and the planar barrier snapped back into place with a crack, healthy and strong and whole, as it always should have been.

The second it was over, all the roaring magic slid away. The waves on both sides slumped as all the powers drained back into their respective vessels. Marci slumped as well, her body sinking into the freezing, choppy water of the refilled Lake St. Clair before Ghost—back in his warrior form at last—caught her in a bear hug.

"We did it!" the spirit cried, spinning her up and out of the water on his newly restrengthened wind. "Can't you feel it, Marci? He's gone! The roots, the tendrils, even his stench, they're all *gone*!"

Her spirit's joy flooded her mind as he spoke, but Marci barely felt it. Now that it was over, her eyes were locked on the sky where the Leviathan had been. The *empty* sky, where the most important person in her life had just been lost forever.

Marci couldn't look at anything after that. She turned away with a sob, burying her face in the darkness of Ghost's chest, which was why she didn't see the tiny ribbon of blue tumbling down from behind the evening clouds, or the large dragon with feathers brighter than a bird of paradise's that flew up to catch it.

· · ·

Brohomir was flying faster than he'd ever gone in his life. He shot through the air where the Leviathan had been, wings pumping harder and harder as he raced to catch Julius's plummeting body before it hit the ground. If it hit, every chance of his future was gone, but if Bob could catch him...

He put on a burst of speed, folding his wings like a dart as he reached out with his claws to snatch his baby brother's body out of the air. Julius's bloody feathers began to crack and turn to ash the moment he touched them. Bob wasn't sure what that meant now that Amelia had tied their magic to this plane, but ash was never good. He'd set this whole thing up on the slimmest of long shots with none of his usual groundwork, but Julius had always been a lucky little dragon. He'd just have to hope the streak held.

"Now, my love," he whispered, pulling his brother's body against his much larger chest before Julius could crumble any further. "Do it now!"

I cannot.

The pigeon was hovering in front of him, but just like that first time, it was the Nameless End he saw in his mind, boundless and dark. Final.

Now as then, the words in his mind held the indelible weight of unavoidable end. This time, though, the sadness in her voice was personal.

I'm afraid you were a few seconds too late. The future you seek is now so unlikely, I'm afraid the price we agreed on will no longer be enough.

"Then I will pay more," Bob replied without hesitation, looking down at his brother. "Of all the dragons I've used, he deserved it least. I crushed his hopes, betrayed his trust at every turn, but through all of it, he never abandoned me. I will not abandon him now." He tightened his claws, closing his eyes as more of Julius's feathers cracked and fell to ash. "Whether we're buying futures or setting them up ourselves, someone always pays. I've avoided my bill for a long, long time, but this time, the most important time, it will be me."

With that, he offered it all, opening the entire breadth of the futures he'd seen to her, but the Nameless End shook her head.

It is not enough.

For the first time in his life, Brohomir began to despair. "No," he said, voice shaking. "It's all I have. It *has* to be enough."

I'm sorry, she said, *but you cannot buy the future you wish with what you have to offer.* Her beady eyes flashed. *At least, not alone.*

Bob jerked in surprise, but the Nameless End just cooed sweetly, swooping in to rub her head against the feathers of his neck. *You kept your promise, Brohomir of the Heartstrikers,* she whispered. *It was a good story. I have been handsomely rewarded for my gamble all those years ago. Now, I too will pay my portion to help you end it well.*

She swooped away, her little body floating on the wind until she was hovering right in front of his eyes, and as she flew, Bob's futures began to disappear. They vanished one by one, plucked like flowers by an invisible hand. Not all of them, just the ones he'd marked for sale back when he'd thought he was being fiendishly clever. It was still a lot, though not nearly enough, but just as he began to worry something was wrong, Bob realized her futures were fading too.

All the futures they'd shared, the thousands of years they could have lived together were disappearing one by one. Each loss felt like a cut, but when he instinctively reached out to stop her, Julius's body slipped from his grasp. He caught his brother again at once, cradling the little dragon protectively to his chest as the last of the futures—his and hers—vanished, leaving him facing the unknown for the first time since he was thirteen. He was still staring hopelessly at the abyss when he felt feathers brush against his face.

The price is paid, his End said, her voice huge in the way he'd experienced only once before. *The future is bought.* The brushing feathers moved closer as the pigeon gave him a final peck on the cheek. *Thank you for sharing your present with me.*

Then she was gone, her touch vanishing like the shadow it always had been, and in the place where she'd been was a short, golden chain.

Bob grabbed it out of the air with a snap of his teeth and shoved it into Julius. The golden links vanished the moment they touched his bloody feathers, and then Bob was knocked out of the sky as the new future forced its way into place. The sudden jolt caused even more of Julius's body to crumble to ash, but as he felt apart, Bob finally spotted what he'd been waiting for. In the center of Julius's chest, an ember was still glowing.

The last ember.

That was all Bob had time to make out before he opened his mouth and engulfed them both in fire. Not normal fire, but life's fire, the core of the flame that made him a dragon. He breathed as much as he could force out, breathed until his heart stuttered and his wings faltered. Then, just as the world started to go dark around him, he felt something flare.

That flash of hope was the last thing Bob saw before his fire ran out. Without even enough magic left to fly, he began to plummet, wrapping his wings around what was left of his brother as they crashed into the churning water of Lake St. Clair, which, much to Bob's surprise, rose up to catch them.

• • •

"*Bob!*"

The scream made Marci jump. She hadn't had the presence of mind for anything but weeping, but Ghost must have carried her to shore at some point, because when she looked up, they were standing on the wreckage-strewn beach where Algonquin's lake met her Reclamation Land. Marci was still trying to figure out what was going on when a shadow whooshed over her head, followed by Chelsie's black-feathered body as the enormous dragon landed in the sand right beside her.

"Marci, help me!" the dragon yelled, her green eyes frantic. "Algonquin just ate Bob!"

"What?" Marci said, blinking slowly as the absurdity of that statement pushed its way through her grief. "What do you mean she *ate* Bob?"

"I mean her water reached up and grabbed him out of the sky!" Chelsie snarled, the words coming out in dangerous puffs of smoke. "You were just talking to her. Make her cough him up *now*, or I'll…"

She trailed off, the smoke fading from her breath. Across the beach, the cloudy blue water in front of them was parting, the waves giving way to dry land as a woman made of water walked out to meet them. She moved slowly, dragging the lake water behind her like a train. It wasn't until Algonquin knelt in front of them, though, that Marci saw why. The spirit wasn't trailing water. She was carrying a dragon.

Bob's multicolored body was cradled in her water. He was curled up so tightly, his feathered tail was wrapped around his nose. He didn't move when the spirit released him, or when Chelsie charged toward him across the exposed lake bed. It wasn't until Marci ran over as well that the seer finally unclenched himself enough to reveal what he was cradling in his claws.

It was a fire. A sputtering yellow-and-green flame no bigger than a candle's. But despite its tiny size, the warmth it gave off was strong. Strong and familiar, a heat Marci would know anywhere.

Julius.

"What did you do?" Chelsie roared, her fangs dripping fire as she turned on Algonquin. "I swear, spirit, I will set your lakes afire if you—"

"It wasn't her," Bob gasped, coughing up water as he struggled to his feet. "It wasn't Algonquin, Chelsie."

"Then who did this?" his sister demanded.

Bob was still coughing too much to answer, so Algonquin spoke for him.

"Julius did."

The spirit spoke slowly, lifting her face to reveal a fall of water so sorrowful, there was no human expression that could match it. "He gave his life to save me, to give me a second chance." Her water dropped as she finished, and then Algonquin bowed, dipping so low before the flicker of Julius's fire, she nearly merged with the mud. "A mortal's life is the greatest treasure they possess. Being immortal, I have no death to give in return, but I..." Her beautiful voice began to shake. "I am sorry. For what I've done. For what I put all of you through. For my selfishness and anger, I am sorry."

The words were soft, but they darted through the quiet air like fish, because they weren't just for Julius. Algonquin was apologizing to her own banks and creatures, and to those watching beyond. Now that things were quiet, Marci could feel them all around. The little faces peeking from the grass and mud, the birds that landed in the reeds and trees and the deer that watched fearfully from the woods beyond—the Lady of the Lakes was apologizing to all of them. She might even have been apologizing to the dragons. If that was the case, though, it fell on deaf ears, because Chelsie was already rushing back to the shore where the Qilin was waiting with their daughter on his golden back.

"What's wrong?" he asked.

"I have to get Amelia," Chelsie said quickly, spreading her wings for takeoff. "She's the one who knows the most about preserving dragon fire. You stay with Bob. Don't let Julius go out before—"

A blast of wind cut her off, knocking Chelsie back to the beach. Even Marci was blown off her feet as a black shadow appeared above them. It happened so suddenly, her first horrible thought was that the Leviathan was back. When she looked up, though, she realized she was only partially right. It *was* a giant monster from another plane, just not the one they'd been fighting.

"*Brohomir!*"

"Oh dear," Bob said, closing his claws protectively around Julius's sputtering flame as he lifted his head to face the Black Reach, who was hovering above them like a weather front.

"*Ungrateful seer!*" the construct thundered, black smoke pouring from his mouth. "I showed you mercy! I gave you my fire! I spent uncounted thousands of years of my power to cover your wager, and *this* is how you repay me?"

"Well, technically, I didn't do it for you," Bob said. "You see—"

"Spare me your excuses," the Black Reach snarled. "There was one thing you could not do. *One thing*, and you stuck your snout right in it! I haven't even had a chance to look and see which futures you sold, but I *felt* you do it. You have committed the one crime I can never forgive, and now I have no choice but to kill you!" He slammed his tail into the lake, splashing water so high into the air, it froze. "Do you know what I went through to spare you? How hard it was to fight ten thousand years of programming to do what I felt was *actually* right? Why did you put me through all that if you were just going to betray me now?"

"Because I also had to do what was right," Bob said with a shrug. "And for the record, I don't regret it at all. Especially since you're not going to kill me this time, either."

"There, you are wrong," the Black Reach snarled, reaching out his charter-bus-sized claws. "There's no escape this time, Brohomir of the Heartstrikers. You've already done what can never be forgiven, and from the number of futures I can no longer see, you did it to the hilt. I don't know what you got in return, but it certainly wasn't your survival, because every future I see has your life ending right here."

"Then I'd suggest you look again," Bob said. "Because I know for a fact that you *can't* kill me."

The construct growled in frustration, but he must have been at least a little bit curious, because he asked, "And how is that?"

"Because you are the death of seers," Bob replied. "And I am no longer a seer."

The giant dragon froze. "What?"

"I'm no longer a seer," Bob repeated. "I still have my powers, but I gave up every future where I use them in exchange for *this*." He held up his claws, opening them just enough so the Black Reach could see the precious fire hidden inside.

The eldest seer squinted. "Is that Julius?"

"My littlest brother," Bob said, nodding. "He was the axis around which I built the machine that saved the world. We all owe him our futures, including you, but since I'm the one who set everything up, it only felt fair that I be the one to foot the bill this time around. The fact that this selfless act of brotherhood also conveniently puts me outside of your jurisdiction is merely a convenient coincidence."

"It is never coincidence with you," the Black Reach snarled, looming close. "You planned this."

"Actually, I planned a lot less than this," Bob said, his voice strangely thick. "My lady and I worked this cleverness out together, as we do all things. When the moment came, though, the price was higher than we expected, and I did not have enough. I would have given everything, I owed Julius that much, but my lady spotted me the difference." His voice began to shake. "An End sacrificed her one present to give us a chance at a better future. Surely you can appreciate the poetry in that?"

"There is no appreciation that can save you now," the Black Reach snarled. "Even if the only futures sold were your own and a Nameless End's, you still crossed the line, and for that you must die."

"Why?" Bob demanded. "Your purpose is to stop seers *before* they sell our futures. That's why you had to kill Estella even though her initial deal wasn't on our plane, because we both knew she'd never stop until I was dead. I'm a different case entirely. I *can't* sell a future ever again. I gave that power away to save my brother's life, so what would killing me accomplish?" He shrugged. "Nothing. I'm now the safest seer you could ever ask for, because I am now physically incapable of breaking your rules. If anything, you should be thanking me for this. Not only did I save your favorite dragon's life, but with me no longer able to meddle in the future and Chelsie's daughter not due to have her first vision until she hits puberty, I've bought you a decade of vacation. When was the last time you got that?"

He finished with a toothy grin, but the Black Reach looked unamused. "It doesn't matter if the ends were good, the means you employed go directly against my purpose. I cannot let that go without punishment."

"*Without punishment?*" Bob cried. "I gave up my powers! Do you know how good a seer I was? I beat Estella, who was *two thousand years* older than I was, at her own game! I orchestrated the plot that saved the world! I beat *you*! No one is *ever* going to top that, and I just gave it away!"

Chelsie rolled her eyes. "So much for modesty."

"It's the truth," Bob snapped. "I'm amazing, and you know it. By losing my powers now, I'm quitting at my peak. That's punishment enough for the entire world."

"Enough," the Black Reach growled, blowing out a cloud of smoke. "I don't have time for your antics. I used up more of my fire today than I have in the last ten thousand years combined. I should use more to punish you, but while you absolutely deserve to die, I have decided to postpone your execution."

It might have been Marci's imagination, but she would have sworn Bob shuddered in relief. "Good choice," he said when he'd recovered, though not nearly as casually as he'd probably meant. "Saw things my way, did you?"

"No," the Black Reach said, and then the enormous dragon faded away, leaving only the tall Chinese man wearing the same black silk robe he'd worn every time Marci had seen him.

"The decision is strictly practical," the now human—and very tired-looking—construct continued. "Right now, your magic is the only thing keeping Julius Heartstriker's fire burning. If I kill you, he will die as well, and I didn't just spend half my fire protecting his futures to lose them now. Even if I wait until he's stable to kill you, though, doing so will burn through too much of my remaining power, and I simply don't have the fire to spare. Already, my flames are critically low. I need to rest and re-group what little remains if I am to survive. That demands several quiet decades, and I'm sure those will be much easier to obtain if I'm only dealing with one new seer instead of two." He reached out to tap Bob on the snout. "Right now, the male incarnation of the dragon seers is still locked up in you, even if you can't use it. If I kill you, that power will be reborn into a new fire, which means I'll have to scramble all over again, and I just don't have that sort of energy."

"Now you really do sound like an old man," Bob said with a chuckle. "A venerable and wise one, who sees the world clearly through his lens of vast experience."

The construct rolled his eyes at the fawning recovery and stepped closer still, looking up at Bob's dripping dragon with the stoic finality of a judge pronouncing a verdict. "Brohomir of the Heartstrikers, consider yourself lucky. You are still sentenced to death, but for practical reasons, including the fact that you are currently not a risk to the futures of dragonkind, your execution is commuted until I recover. Or until you annoy me too much."

Bob's face split into a triumphant grin. "Nonsense. You'd get bored without me."

The Black Reach's eyes narrowed, and Bob quickly backed down. "Thank you for your mercy, great construct," he said meekly. "I should probably take Julius to Amelia now."

"That would be best," the Black Reach agreed, glancing at the dragons watching from the shore. "Any more coincidences I should know about before I go?"

"No," Bob said, looking worriedly at the tiny flame in his claws. "But if you could spare a teensy, tiny bit more of that fantastic fire, I think we might need it. Julius was always small, but this is a terrifyingly dim fire, even for a runt."

The Black Reach's scowl softened at that.

"I'll see what I can do."

CHAPTER SIXTEEN

Death was a gentler experience than Julius expected.

Growing up with daily threats, he'd always expected his end would be quick, brutal, and messy. But while being ripped apart from the inside had been all that and more, the actual dying part hadn't been so bad. Peaceful, almost, which was why Julius was very confused when he woke up to find himself lying in a hospital bed.

He jolted, his whole body going stiff just in time for him to realize it was his *human* body, which only made everything even weirder. He was positive he'd died as a dragon. Inside a Nameless End, no less. If he was going to wake up anywhere, it should be inside his own death, as Marci had described. He knew he wouldn't be lucky enough to get their house, as she had, but he'd certainly expected better than a human hospital, complete with mint-green walls and scratchy sheets.

At least it smelled nice. The whole room smelled of Marci's magic. Tons of it, actually, as though he were inside one of her casting circles. Not that he minded, of course, but it was still odd. Why was there so much magic? And why was his chest so heavy? Like there was a weight lying right in the middle of his—

Julius froze, eyes growing wide. Marci was sleeping on his chest. The *real* Marci, unless ghosts came with dark circles under their eyes and hospital scrubs. That did explain the overwhelming scent of magic, though. Everything around him—the sheets, the bed rails, the hospital's monitoring equipment, the walls, the door, the window—was covered in spellwork written in Marci's precise hand. From the overlapping marker stains on her fingers, she must have been at it for days, but Julius had no idea what it was all for. He was arguing with himself about whether he should wake her and ask or let her sleep since she looked so tired when he realized the two of them were not alone.

On the far side of the room, sprawled across a plastic hospital chair like he'd been dropped there from orbit, was Bob. He looked absolutely terrible. His face was gaunt, as though he'd been starving for weeks, and his skin looked like it hadn't seen the sun in months. But while his dark circles were even larger than Marci's, the seer's eyes were open, the bright-green glowing in the soft light from the window as he smiled at Julius.

"Welcome back."

That felt needlessly cryptic, but Julius was too worried about the state of his brother to mind. "What happened to you?" he whispered frantically.

"You did," Bob replied, hauling himself up in his chair. "You gave us quite the scare. I must have poured five hundred years of fire into you before your flame caught, and who knows how much Amelia used. Even after we got you going, your fire was so weak we had to have someone with you at all times to keep it from snuffing out. We eventually set up a rotation. That's what the spellwork was for. Marci and the other human, Myron, I think his name is, they figured out how to construct a system that would send concentrated dragon magic straight into you. Sort of like an IV, except for fire. Anyway, everyone's been through to take their turn—Chelsie, Justin, Conrad, Fredrick, Svena, Katya, the Qilin." He grinned. "You've got so many different magics in you, you're practically the draconic average at this point. Even Mother dropped in to do her share."

Julius's jaw dropped. "*Bethesda* came to help *me*?"

"It was the fashionable thing to do," Bob said. "You know her. If everyone's doing something, she has to have her piece. I'm sure you'll hear all about how she saved your life the next time she needs a favor."

He was sure he would. "But," Julius said, clutching his sheet, "I don't understand. I was *dead*. How did you—"

"Never underestimate a desperate dragon," Bob said with a wink. "I still had a Nameless End of my own, so I traded her all the futures where I use my abilities as a seer in exchange for one where you lived. Of course, that exchange only guaranteed that I'd save your fire. Keeping it going was another matter, but if you think I was going to let you go out after spending so much to save you, you're crazier than everyone says I am."

Julius stared at his brother in wonder. "You... you did that for me?" he whispered. "Gave up your—*Why?*"

"Because I owed you," Bob said, his voice uncharacteristically sincere. "You've suffered for my plans for a long time now, Julius. The least I could do was pick up the slack at the end. Anyway, I was done being a seer. Once you've beaten the Black Reach, where else is there to go? The challenge was gone, so I thought I'd give myself a handicap and try playing the game on your level for a while. You know, just for something different."

"But you're the Great Seer of the Heartstrikers!" Julius cried. "How can you just give that up?"

"Because I never asked to be it," his brother said with a shrug. "There's no pride in being what you were born to be. It's how you use your gifts that counts, and I don't need to see the future for that. Everything that makes me great was always up here." He tapped the side of his head. "Never forget, I was a genius long before I was a seer. If you think losing my vision of the future will make me any less good at manipulating dragons, you haven't been paying attention. And speaking of attention, I need to be going."

"Why?" Julius asked, alarmed. "What's about to happen?"

"Nothing I'm aware of," Bob said, pointing at his eyes. "Blind as a bat now, remember? But I haven't slept since you went down two weeks ago, and I'd very much like to break my streak. Also, the sleeping pill I slipped your mortal should be wearing off any minute now, and I don't think you want me in the room for *that.*"

He wiggled his eyebrows suggestively, and Julius's cheeks began to burn. Laughing at him, Bob rose from his chair and held out his arm for his pigeon, who hopped off Julius's vitals monitor with a happy coo. It was such a usual Bob thing to do, Julius didn't even realize it was wrong until his brother was almost out the door.

"Wait!"

Bob glanced over his shoulder, and Julius pointed to the bird-that-wasn't-a-bird. "If you're not a seer anymore, why do you still have your Nameless End?"

"*Julius!*" Bob cried, cupping a hand over his pigeon's head as though he were trying to shield her from such offensive speech. "What sort of dragon do you think I am? I would *never* use and leave a lady just because my plots were finished. I can't believe you'd say that."

"Sorry," Julius said quickly. "I didn't mean to insult your, um—"

"Consort," his brother said primly. "She is my consort, and you are being very rude. She gave up her futures to save you as well, I'll have you know."

"I-I didn't know that," Julius said, bowing his head respectfully to the pigeon. "Thank you."

The pigeon blinked at him, uncomprehending, but Bob looked placated. "I am exceedingly lucky I found her again," he said, pressing a kiss to her feathered head. "I had to bribe Amelia to open me a new portal into the space beyond reality so I could start us over since all our timelines in this reality were used up. But that's the lovely thing about the future: you can always make more of it. All it takes is a bit of effort, and the fact that she was waiting just outside for me didn't hurt, either."

The pigeon cooed happily at that, and Bob sighed, lovestruck. "Anyway, you owe your life to both of us. I expect you to show proper gratitude in a few days after I've slept this off. Our pick, your treat, and make sure you behave like a *gentleman* this time."

"Of course," Julius said, ducking his head to the pigeon again. "I'm sorry if I offended you, ma'am."

The pigeon nodded back to him, which seemed to please Bob greatly. "Splendid!" he said as he walked out the door. "See you soon."

"You too," Julius said quietly, staring after his eldest brother in bafflement. He was still trying to puzzle out if Bob had been really offended just now or if this whole exchange had been another of his ploys when Marci woke with a start, her eyes shooting wide as she turned her head to gape at him.

"Hi," Julius said, smiling awkwardly. "Um, I'm back?"

The words weren't even out of his mouth before she tackled him, sobbing and laughing and hugging him until he couldn't breathe. He hugged her back with all he had, closing his eyes as he breathed in her scent. Breathed in being *alive*.

Needless to say, he didn't worry about Bob again for a long time.

• • •

"Yeah, well, I always knew he'd pull through," Amelia said, taking a swig from her cocktail. "How could he not? He had me on his team, and I'm a god now, remember?"

"How can we forget?" Svena grumbled. "You remind us every five minutes. And it's not as though godhood is anything special these days." Her blue eyes slid pointedly to Raven, who was perched on the railing beside Ghost's cat and the giant rat that was the DFZ. "We are overrun with vermin."

They were sitting on the roof of the hospital Julius had been taken to, which turned out to be an Algonquin Corporation private hospital on the edge of Reclamation Land. Like everything else in the city, the modern steel-and-glass building had taken heavy damage during the fighting, but it was now as good as new thanks to the DFZ.

"Pro tip: it's not a good idea to call the god of the city you're currently in 'vermin,'" Amelia whispered loudly. "This building was on its side when we found it, but she set the whole place to rights in under ten minutes with a flick of her little pink tail. Imagine what she could do to a delicate snowflake like you."

"I'd like to see her try," Svena said with a sniff, though Julius couldn't help noticing the White Witch's retort was much quieter than usual. No one was stupid enough to point that out, though, for which Julius was profoundly grateful. He'd had enough conflict to last him a lifetime, and Svena was surprisingly pleasant to be around when she didn't have her hackles up. Pleasant and amazingly knowledgeable. The things she would casually mention about magic constantly blew his mind. He just wished Marci were around to hear them.

Now that all the Mortal Spirits were up, the new Merlin had her hands full. She was in the Sea of Magic right now with Myron for a big peace talk. Ghost, Raven, and the DFZ were with them as well, though somehow also here. Julius wasn't entirely sure how that worked, but apparently spirits could be in multiple places at once now. He'd tried using that to his advantage, asking Ghost about Marci when she wasn't here, but the cat's shoulder was as cold toward him as ever, and he hadn't gotten far.

That was probably for the best. Marci didn't need him distracting her while she was trying to convince the new Mortal Spirits to cooperate with the Merlin Council she and Myron were trying to found here in the DFZ. As she'd explained it to Julius, the idea was to locate, test, and train a whole bevy of suitable mages so that new Mortal Spirits could have their pick of certified not-crazy humans for their potential Merlins. Something certainly needed to be done. In the fourteen days Marci had spent by his side helping keep him alive, the new gods had been running amok all over the world. She'd left to help Myron calm things down the moment she was certain Julius wasn't going to expire on her. That was two days ago, nearly all of which she'd spent inside the Sea of Magic, but Julius was confident she could handle it. Meanwhile, he was relearning how to handle himself.

Not being a mage or fond of burning things, Julius had never paid much attention to his fire. Since he'd woken up, though, the emptiness in his chest had been a constant ache. His family and friends still dropped by regularly to make donations, so at least he wasn't flat on his back anymore, but he was still confined to a wheelchair. Amelia had assured him his flames would come back in time, but time was a fuzzy thing to a dragon who'd lived for thousands of years. Julius hadn't gotten her to specify yet whether they were on a schedule of months, years, or decades. There was nothing he could do about it, though, so he tried not to worry too much. His magic would recover eventually. What really mattered was that everyone was safe.

After the Leviathan vanished, UN troops had swarmed in to take control of the city. The people had started coming back a few days later, though most had been forced to turn right back around again since their homes were in ruins. Normally, damage on this scale would have taken years to repair, if it could be rebuilt at all. For them as for Julius, though, having a god on your side changed things. The DFZ wasn't just powerful—she *was* the city. She knew how every inch of it should be, and she could put things back to rights in minutes, raising the broken buildings with a flick of her hand. She'd already made a ton of progress, but the DFZ was a *big* city, and all of it needed work. She was also very busy with Myron, keeping the other Mortal Spirits from destroying things. Unlike Ghost, though, the DFZ always took time to pass Julius's messages along to Marci. Provided he paid her, of course.

"Julius?"

He looked up to see Amelia staring at him. "Are you okay?" she asked, cocking her head. "You're awful quiet."

"What else can he be?" Svena snapped. "You take up all the available air."

"I'm fine," Julius assured her.

"You sure?" his sister asked, her eyes sharp. "Because I can get you more fire if you need it."

"I'm fine," he said again. "Really."

She nodded and turned back to Svena, but her eyes kept darting back to him. The watchfulness ruined the rooftop's happy mood, and a few minutes later, Julius grabbed his wheels and turned his chair away. "I'm a little tired," he said. "I think I'll go downstairs and rest."

Amelia stood up at once. "I'll push you back down."

"That's okay. I've got it."

Now she looked *really* suspicious. "You sure?"

"I'm sure," Julius said, wheeling toward the elevator as fast as he could go.

He knew she meant well, but Amelia's hovering made him feel like an invalid. Even Svena's presence was only for show. She far preferred to spend her time with Ian, whom she'd immediately moved back in with the moment the DFZ had repaired their superscraper apartment building. But he'd noticed Amelia always seemed to have another dragon around whenever he was awake, and it was starting to get to him. Having so many people watching made him feel like a drain, especially since he knew Marci could have used Amelia's help. She hadn't figured out the trick to being in multiple places at once yet, but she was a spirit too. She should have been in that meeting in the Sea of Magic, but she'd insisted on staying here. Ostensibly because of Svena, but Julius didn't believe that for a second. As flighty as she could be, his sister took her position as the Spirit of Dragons very seriously. The only reason she'd skip out on something this big was because she didn't think Julius could be left alone, and that made him feel like a failure.

With a frustrated sigh, Julius took the elevator back down to his floor. With so few people in the city, they had the hospital mostly to themselves, which meant no one was around to see him get out of his chair and hobble the last few feet down the hall to his room. It was really too soon, but he was so tired of feeling useless. He was trying to open his door without falling over when a hand shot past his to grab the knob.

"Let me get that."

Julius jumped, coming dangerously close to losing his balance as he spun around to see Chelsie standing behind him. This in itself was nothing unusual—it was the Heartstriker family motto that Chelsie was *always* behind you—but the rest of her was a shock.

His sister looked *different*. Physically, she was the same—same lean body, same short black hair, same deadly aura—but she wasn't dressed in black combat armor and boots anymore. She was wearing normal clothes. *Colorful* clothes, including a purple sundress and a washed-out jean jacket that stopped just above her waist. Her feet were tied into pretty lace-up sandals with little straw flowers on the tips, and her toenails were painted the same green as her eyes. It was such a stark difference from how she usually looked, Julius didn't know what to say, which unfortunately meant he blurted out the first thing that came to his mind.

"Are you going undercover?"

"What? *No!* I just…" Her cheeks flushed as she looked down at her clothes. "I haven't gone shopping in a long time, okay? Modern women's clothing is… tricky." Her brows furrowed. "Is it weird?"

"No, no," he said at once. "You look great! It's just... really different."

"You're telling me," she said, opening the door to his room so they could go in. "But I always hated wearing armor. Now that I no longer have to, I thought I'd try something new."

"It looks lovely," he assured her, trying not to show how relieved he was to get back to his bed. "So why are you here?"

Chelsie shrugged. "Can't I just visit you?"

"Yes, but no one does that except Marci." Julius sighed. "Amelia called you, didn't she?"

"The moment you left the roof," his sister confirmed. "But that's actually very responsible of her. Your fire is still too low to be left unattended. Really, though, you should be flattered. The only other dragon she's ever been this on the ball for is Bob."

Julius *was* flattered, which was part of what made this so annoying. It was hard to be mad at your sister when she was only trying to help. "I'm just tired of being treated like I'm made of glass," Julius grumbled. "I feel fine."

Chelsie snorted. "You just collapsed in your bed after walking half a hallway."

"Says the dragon who didn't stop working after she got *stabbed*."

"That was different," Chelsie said sharply. "I had to do those things, but you're not like me. You're free, and we're only doing this because we care about you. I don't see how you have cause to complain."

"I know," Julius said, slumping into his pillows. "You're right. I'm sorry. But it's only been two days, and I'm already sick of it. I just feel so useless. Everyone else is up to their necks in important work, and I'm stuck here being a burden."

"You're not a burden," Chelsie said. "You carried us over a lot of hard ground, Julius. Let us carry you for a change. And not *all* of us are working." Her lips curled in a smile. "I didn't just happen to be in the area when Amelia put out the call for someone to check on you. I came to say goodbye."

"Goodbye?" Julius sat up with a start. "Why goodbye? What's wrong?"

"Nothing's wrong," Chelsie said. "I'm just going on vacation."

He gaped at her. "*You* are going on vacation?"

Chelsie's smile grew wider. "Crazy, huh? I didn't want to leave so soon, but Fredrick insisted. He and Frieda practically packed my bags for me. Bethesda's still enjoying the novelty of getting to be in the DFZ without hiding, so F-clutch has taken over Heartstriker Mountain. They're all there, including the baby. They said they needed Felicity to themselves for a whole week, some nonsense about teaching her F-clutch solidarity, so they kicked me out." She shrugged helplessly. "I'd be suspicious, but it's so transparent, there's no point. Especially since Fredrick already went through the trouble of getting Xian kicked out too."

"Wait, wait, wait," Julius said, putting up his hands. "Fredrick got the *Golden Emperor* kicked out of China?"

"Actually, I'm pretty sure that part was Xian's idea. I find it highly convenient that my children kicked me out at the exact same time as my ex's subjects suddenly decided he needed a week off."

Julius did too. "But you're still going, right?"

"Of course I'm going," she said. "I haven't been to the Bahamas in a century, and Xian's never been. It'll be nice."

He grinned. "Nice, huh?"

"Shut up," his sister snapped. "This doesn't mean anything. We're not back together, we're just… trying it out. A lot has changed, and we need to get to know each other again before anything can… you know…" She cut off with a growl. "Why am I even telling you this? Anyway, I just wanted you to know where I was in case you needed me. I still owe you a huge debt, so if you need help with anything, promise you'll call."

Julius crossed his heart. "I solemnly swear that I will not call you for any reason while you are vacationing in paradise with the Golden Emperor. Have fun. You deserve it."

"Whatever," Chelsie grumbled, her face red. "Just try not to let Justin throw anyone out of your window. I'll be back in time for the all-clan meeting next week."

"The what?"

"The all-clan meeting," she repeated, giving him a funny look. "Didn't they tell you?"

"No!" Julius cried. "No one tells me anything in here! What's the all-clan meeting?"

"Exactly what it sounds like," Chelsie said, leaning against his door. "The defense against the Leviathan was the first time all the dragon clans had been together in one place in ten thousand years. Miraculously, we got through the whole thing without killing each other, so Bethesda, Ian, Xian, Svena, and Marlin Drake banded together to organize a more formal meeting next week. They're even holding it in the DFZ since this is still the only neutral territory in the world, though that's sure to change now that Algonquin's no longer around to keep everyone away. Between you and me, I think a big reason Bethesda pushed for the meeting is because she intends to claim the DFZ for Heartstriker. Seeing how we control the rest of North America, I don't see how anyone could object to that, but they will."

"Of course they will," Julius said. "Even in ruins, the DFZ is one of the wealthiest, most magical cities in the world. No one's going to let Bethesda just walk in and take it. She could start a war."

"So make sure she doesn't," Chelsie replied, giving him a wry smile. "You're on the Council, and you wanted something useful to do."

Dealing with his mother was *not* on Julius's preferred list of jobs. He'd much rather have helped Marci, or Amelia, or General Jackson, or *literally anyone else*. But his sister was right. He was one of the heads of Heartstriker, and the fact that Ian and Bethesda had planned this meeting without him even knowing proved it was time to get back to work.

"I like the idea of using the DFZ as neutral territory," he said, thinking it through. "Has a human government claimed it yet? Because I know Algonquin's out." Even after her apology, the DFZ had made it *very* clear that the lake spirit was never to enter her city again.

"Not yet," Chelsie said. "Plenty have *tried*. Canada's pushing hard, and David's bending over backward to make the case for Detroit rejoining the US. So far, though, the DFZ isn't interested. It's hard to tell a sentient city that she has to listen to a bunch of humans. Myron had to step in to convince her to let the UN troops stay so they could continue their disaster relief. It's been a mess."

Julius scowled. He hadn't heard any of that, either. How much were the others keeping from him? But Chelsie's report had set an idea spinning in his head. An idea that was rapidly forming into a plan. "Thanks for bringing me into the loop, Chelsie. I really appreciate it."

"I knew you would. Just don't tell Amelia. She's got everyone on strict orders not to tell you anything upsetting, but I'm painfully familiar with your nosiness, so I figured I'd save us all the trouble and get everything out now."

"Thank you," he said again, reaching for his phone to do some research. "Tell Xian hello for me, and have fun on your vacation."

His sister smiled. "I think I will," she said, shutting the door behind her.

• • •

Chelsie *didn't* come back from the Bahamas in time for the all-clan meeting.

"Where is she?" Julius asked nervously as Fredrick sewed him into the stupidly expensive jacket his mother was making him wear. "She was supposed to be back this morning!"

"If she hasn't arrived yet, I don't think she's going to," Fredrick said, holding Julius's sleeve at the precise right length with one hand while he quickly stitched it in place with the other. "It seems the island has been besieged by freak magical storms. The airport and all forms of teleportation are shut down, and she and the Golden Emperor have been forced to take shelter in their hotel. Very unusual."

"There's nothing unusual about it," Marci said with a snort. "Sounds to me like Mr. Magical Good Fortune didn't want to leave his love nest to go to a meeting." She grinned. "Would a 'getting lucky' joke be out of place?"

"Considering I'm the one who sent them to paradise, I find it entirely appropriate," Fredrick said smugly. "This is actually going even better than I'd hoped."

"Yes, yes, it's great for *them*," Julius agreed. "But what are we going to do? It's a hard room in there, and I was counting on the Qilin's support." He nodded through the door into the hotel ballroom, which was packed to the gills with dragons. Delegations from every clan sat at tables that had been set up in a circle, and despite this supposedly being a peaceful summit, every one of them looked ready to kill. "We could use some good luck."

"You'll be fine," Marci said, rising up on her tiptoes to kiss his cheek. "Who needs luck when you've got friends in high places?"

She looked pointedly across the hall at Amelia, who was deep in conversation with the spirit of the DFZ. The city was dressed in her best glowing neon for the occasion, her beady eyes shining a bright, cheerful orange from beneath the shadow of her deep hood. Myron looked less happy standing beside her, but what mortal could feel comfortable in the presence of so many dragons? Except Marci, of course. She was used to it, and like everything else about her, Julius loved her for it.

"You're right," he said, taking a deep breath. "We'll be fine."

"*You'll* be fine," Marci said pointedly, handing him his cane. "We've got to go take our seats now. Knock 'em dead!"

Julius took the cane with a smile as Marci adjusted her long formal dress—which looked suspiciously like a wizard's robe—and hurried to follow Myron and the spirits into the meeting room, Ghost trotting along behind her like the cat he pretended to be. Julius was still watching her go when he felt a familiar murderous presence behind him.

"You're bringing *that* in, are you?"

Bethesda's voice was scathing, and Julius turned to find his mother decked in gold from head to toe, glaring down her nose at the cane he was using to keep himself upright. "Really, Julius! I know you're only a week into being miraculously raised from the dead, but if you hobble in there like an invalid, you're going to look weak."

"Not as weak as I'd look falling on my face," Julius pointed out. "I don't like it any more than you do, but until my fire finishes healing, it's what I've got."

"You could at least try to stand up straight," his mother scolded. "That way, the others might think it's an accessory instead of a necessity."

Julius didn't think there was any chance of that. Dragons had a sixth sense for weakness, and even after everyone's contributions, his fire was still little bigger than a hatchling's. Cane or no cane, he'd be outed the second they smelled him.

"Where's Ian?" he asked, changing the subject.

Bethesda's perfect red lips curled in disgust. "Where he always is these days, with Svena." She shook her lovely head. "Cementing alliances is well and good, but this is bordering on ridiculous. The ex-Daughters of the Three Sisters are up to their snouts in debt to our clan, *and* we've already gotten our clutch out of them. There's nothing left for Ian to charm out of the White Witch, so I don't know why he's still playing consort. We're on top! He should be gunning for new conquests, not wasting his time hanging around old ones."

"*I'm* happy for them," Julius said stubbornly. "They seem well matched." Not that he understood a relationship that seemed to be based on who could use the other better, but Svena and Ian were both dragon's dragons, and it seemed to work for them.

"Well, he'd better pull himself out of her icy clutches soon, because we're starting in two minutes," Bethesda said, checking her phone. She grimaced when she saw the time and shot Julius the closest thing she had to a nervous look. "The plan *is* still on, right? You haven't killed it or something stupid like that?"

"Why would I kill it?" Julius asked. "It was my plan."

"Yes, but I like it," his mother pointed out. "And you *always* destroy the things I like, so…"

"It's fine," he assured her.

"What's fine?" Justin asked, suddenly appearing at Julius's side.

"Everything," Julius said, smiling at his knight. As always, Justin was dressed like a modern knight in military-grade spellworked Kevlar with his Fang at his side. Conrad was wearing the same as he stepped into place beside Bethesda. The only one who didn't have a knight was Ian, but he didn't seem to mind when he finally appeared.

"About time," Bethesda snapped, eying his skewed suit and uncharacteristically rumpled hair, which was standing up in the back as though someone tall had been running her fingers through it. "Did you make sure Svena is still on our side?"

"It didn't come up," Ian said, neatening himself up in the hall mirror. "But I trust my consort to do what is best for our clan."

"Which one?" Bethesda growled. "This is the problem with letting you bat for two teams. I'm never sure where you stand."

"I stand where I always have," Ian said, tugging his silk tie straight. "With my own self-interest, and that's very well served by Julius's plan." His brown eyes flicked to his brother. "Shall we go in?"

"Any time," Julius said. "We're just waiting on Amelia."

Bethesda rolled her eyes. "No point in that. This is her first big meeting as the Spirit of Dragons. She's not going to make a normal entrance through the door. Just go in. It never pays to make dragons wait."

That was a good point, so Julius motioned for Justin to lead the way. Proud as an armored peacock, the knight shoved the doors open, letting the Heartstriker delegation into the elegant ballroom where the rest of dragonkind was already waiting.

After greeting nearly every dragon in the world as they'd come through Svena's portal, Julius hadn't been too worried about seeing them all again now. As they walked to Heartstriker's table at the front, though, he realized he'd drastically underestimated the situation. It was one thing to face all the clan heads when the world was about to end, but it was quite another to stand in front of them now. Back then, they'd had no choice but to listen. Now, things were far less certain.

Thankfully, he was saved by Amelia. As Bethesda had predicted, the Spirit of Dragons had been waiting to make her entrance. The moment the Heartstriker delegation was in place behind their table, completing the circle of the clans, she appeared behind the podium at the circle's apex with a swirl of fire. There was quite a lot of fire, actually. The normal dress she'd been wearing just a few minutes ago had been replaced with a gown of living flames, and a crown of fire in the shape of a dragon crouched on top of her head. Even her shoes were made of fire, scorching the elegant hotel carpet and all but ensuring they wouldn't be getting the deposit back.

She stood there for a moment, looking haughtily around the room as she waited for shocked silence to become reverent awe. When she was satisfied everyone was suitably impressed, Amelia began.

"Welcome," she said in a voice as sharp as fangs. "As you know, but I never get tired of saying, I am Amelia the Planeswalker, Spirit of Dragons and your benevolent god. These talks were not my idea, but I heartily approve of them and thus have agreed to bless you with the gift of my presence. Since I could swat any of you like flies, I will not take sides since that would be king making, and I'm not looking to be one of those micromanaging deities. I will not interfere with any decisions for the same reason. You're all free to act in your own best interests, as dragons should. However, since these are *peace* talks, I will incinerate anyone who attempts to break the truce. Those are the rules. Don't break them. Now that we're all on the same page, I'll pass the stand to my brother, Julius Heartstriker, who surprisingly didn't arrange this meeting today but has somehow managed to end up leading it. Take it away, Julius!"

She threw out a fire-wreathed hand toward him, and Julius winced as every dragon in the room turned to stare.

"Thank you, Amelia," he said awkwardly, hobbling to the podium as fast as he could. He paused when he got there, looking around the room as his sister stepped aside to give him space. What he saw wasn't very re-assuring. When he'd arrived this afternoon, he'd thought the ballroom his mother had booked in one of the nicest hotels on the just-restored riverfront was ridiculously huge for their purposes. Now, he was wishing she'd gotten a bigger one. Even in their elegantly dressed human forms, the circle of dragons filled the room. He couldn't even see Marci, Myron, and their spirits standing in the back through all the calculating scowls and measuring glances, but he knew they were there, and that gave him the courage he needed to begin.

"Thank you all for coming," he said, lifting his voice since no dragon would ever respect someone who needed a microphone. "The world has changed a great deal in the last three weeks. The human governments are in disarray from the influx of magic and the rise of Mortal Spirits. We have also changed, our fires bound to the magic of this plane by our own Spirit of Dragons. Thanks to her actions, we finally have a true home again, and now more than ever, we need to work together to ce-ment our future here."

He tightened his fingers on his cane. Here it went.

"For too long, we have acted like barbarians, fighting and brawling over land. That savagery has taken its toll. There are fewer dragons alive now than there have ever been, and that is our fault. No human hunter or vengeful spirit, even Algonquin, has hurt dragons more than we've hurt ourselves through our greed and shortsightedness. That is why, if we wish to live long enough to enjoy the new life expectancy my oldest sister's work has bought us, we dragons have to change. We proved we could work together when we defended the Great Lakes from Algonquin's Leviathan. Now, for our long-term survival, we have to do it again. If we don't wish to repeat the mistakes of our ancestors who destroyed their old home plane, we must come together as a species, if not in peace, then in alliance. It is my hope that, through these talks and the ones that will surely follow, the dragon clans of this world can surpass all who came before us by finding a way to coexist nonviolently for our mutual benefit."

He paused there, holding his breath, but to his amazement, most of the room was nodding. Some, like Fading Smoke, looked disgusted by the idea of stopping the killing, but the vast majority of the faces looking back at him were relieved. They were all tired, he realized. Tired of death, tired of dwindling numbers and fading power. That wasn't enough to bury all the centuries-old grudges, but it was enough to start, and Julius decided to push ahead.

"With this in mind," he went on, "as the first act of this all-clan meeting, I am taking the opportunity to formally claim the DFZ as my personal territory, effective immediately."

The room exploded.

"*What?*" cried Fading Smoke, almost knocking over his table as he surged to his feet. "You think Heartstriker can claim the richest prize in the world without a fight?"

Other clans were yelling similar things, then yelling at each other as the whole ballroom fell into one giant argument over who most deserved Algonquin's city. The noise of it was so loud, Julius couldn't hear himself think, but he made no move to calm things down, because that wasn't his place. It was hers.

"*SILENCE!*" the spirit of the DFZ roared, making the whole building shake.

Every dragon snapped their mouths shut, swiveling their heads back to the podium, where the spirit of the city had appeared beside Julius, her orange eyes shining like spotlights in her rage.

"I am not a corpse for you vultures to bicker over!" she snarled, baring her sharp teeth. "I am the DFZ, the living city! I can choose for myself which dragon is fit to manage your affairs within my borders, and I have chosen Julius Heartstriker. Of all of you, he is the only one who stood beside the Merlin to save me. He was the one who kept up hope when all other plans failed and the one who died so that the Lady of the Lakes could have a second chance and we could all survive. For these reasons and more, Julius Heartstriker is the only one of you I trust as the dragon of my city. I will accept no others."

She set her jaw stubbornly after that, glaring at the dragons as if she was hoping they'd be stupid enough to fight her on this. And sure enough, someone did.

"It's not your place to tell us whom to obey, *spirit*," Fading Smoke growled. "Why should we listen to you?"

"You don't have to," Bethesda said sweetly. "Even if you were stupid enough to ignore the will of the sentient city you're so eager to exploit, the DFZ belongs to Julius anyway. You were there same as the rest of us, Arkniss. You know perfectly well that my youngest son was the one giving the orders during the defense of the lakes, because you *obeyed* them. That fight and what he did after is the reason we're still here to bicker about this, which means the lands those actions won are Julius's by right of conquest. It's the same logic you used to claim your territory in Gibraltar, so unless you're willing to give your rock back to the dragons of North Africa, you have no ground to stand on."

"Bethesda is right," Svena said, her pale face shocked as though she couldn't believe those words had just come out of her mouth. "We all fought hard that day, but Julius Heartstriker was the one who led. Even I followed where he pointed, but none of us followed him into the final confrontation that defeated the Leviathan. For that alone, I back his claim. This city and all the Great Lakes belong to him."

"Why do you say to him?" Arkniss said, his dark eyes wary. "You mean they belong to Heartstriker."

"I am a Heartstriker," Julius said carefully. "But our clan lays claim to the whole of the Americas. Even we're not big enough to centrally manage all that land, which is why our clan has a long tradition of letting each dragon claim and run their own territory as they see fit. By claiming the DFZ, I am bringing it into Heartstriker's shared territory, but *I*—not Bethesda or anyone else elected to the Council in the years to come—will be the one who controls dragon affairs in the city."

When the other dragons started grumbling, Julius raised a finger. "Before you complain, this does not mean the rest of you will be cut off. As the dragon of the DFZ, my plan is to keep the city exactly what it is right now: neutral territory. I want to make this city a place where dragons of all clans can come together and talk without fear of being betrayed. Every one of you is welcome to work and profit and run whatever enterprises you wish inside my city. My only requirement is that you do so peacefully, no killing, no fighting, no clan wars. Furthermore, I also intend to offer myself as a neutral third party to mediate clan disputes so that they may be settled without the usual bloodshed."

"So that's your ploy, is it?" Arkniss snorted. "Play the peacekeeper? Make us come to you?"

"It's not a ploy," Julius said stubbornly. "It's a hope. We've lost so many powerful dragons to stupid clan drama, including my own grandfather, the Quetzalcoatl." His mother made a choking sound, which Julius ignored. "My goal is to stop that from happening again. It shouldn't be hard. We're dragons, the cleverest, sneakiest, most conniving creatures to ever live in this world. If we can't talk our way through a problem, then it can't be solved. We just need somewhere safe to do it, and that's what I mean to build." He thumped his cane on the burned carpet. "From this moment on, I am Julius, Dragon of the DFZ. Anyone who wishes to challenge me for that title may do so now."

He stopped, listening, but the room was silent. No one, not even Arkniss, said a word against him. Then, slowly, Lao, the Qilin's cousin who was filling in for the absent emperor, raised his hand. "The Golden Empire supports Julius Heartstriker's claim," he said calmly. "In this support, we honor our debt. Any who oppose him oppose us."

"Heartstriker supports him, of course," Ian said, speaking quickly before Bethesda could open her mouth and remind the other dragons in the room how much they hated her. "We feel that a neutral DFZ is in the best interest of all parties, and we will bring our full might against any who threaten it."

"We also support him," Svena said. "The youngest Heartstriker has long been an ally of my clan, and I can think of no better use of his skills than what he has proposed for this city." She flashed Julius a cold smile. "He is, after all, the dragon who tamed Heartstriker. I think we are all eager to see what other miracles he can perform."

The other clans seemed to like that, and Julius let out his breath at last. "Thank you all for your support," he said, trying not to sound as relieved as he felt. "And welcome to my territory. Now..." He smiled wide. "What can I help you with?"

• • •

"See that?" Bob said, passing his binoculars to the Black Reach, who was sitting beside him on the scaffolding surrounding the still-under-construction hotel directly across from the one the dragons were having their meeting in. "What did I tell you? He had it in the bag the whole time."

"You are no longer in a position to tell me anything," the construct replied sourly, though he did look through the binoculars. "You made a lucky guess."

"Luck has nothing to do with it," Bob said proudly. "That, old friend, was *skill*. I know all my assets, and Julius is the most reliable, especially for something like this." He sighed happily. "They'll be calling him 'Julius the Peacemaker' and flocking to him with their problems before the year is out, mark my words."

"Of course they will," the Black Reach said. "Because you'll be sending them, and spreading that ridiculous epitaph." He passed the binoculars back to Bob. "It's not actually predicting the future if you're setting everything up, you know."

"I don't care what you call it so long as it happens," Bob replied. "And neither should you. My little brother is in there building the future *you've* always wanted. You should be falling over yourself to help me help him."

"Who says I'm not?" the Black Reach said with a cryptic smile. "I'm here, aren't I? Despite that *thing* on your shoulder."

Bob went pale in horror, his hands shooting up to shield his pigeon roosting against his neck. "Don't listen to him, darling," he whispered. "He's just jealous you're with me."

The bird cooed in reply, and the oldest seer rose to his feet with a sigh. "Now that you've made your point, can we go? They're going to be in that meeting until midnight at least, and you promised me a local delicacy for dinner. Some sort of canine, I believe?"

"A coney dog," Bob said, popping to his feet as well. "Which isn't actually a dog, but you're still going to love it. And across the street, there's a place that serves chicken and waffles!"

The Black Reach looked troubled. "Why would anyone put chicken on a waffle?"

"Oh, my sweet, innocent child," Bob said, wrapping his arm around the taller seer's shoulders. "This is going to be the best vacation you've ever had."

The Black Reach sighed again, but he didn't resist as Bob dragged him down the scaffolding toward the service elevator, the pigeon fluttering along behind them in the cold winter air.

• • •

The meeting didn't get out until one in the morning. Julius was exhausted by ten. Given the state of his body, he really should have called it earlier, but the whole "get dragons to talk instead of killing each other" plan was working so well, he couldn't bring himself to stop. By the time the all-clan meeting adjourned, he'd helped resolve three clan wars—all of which were stupid—arranged a five-clan trade summit for next weekend, and gotten Svena and Amelia to agree to take on younger dragons as apprentices to help rekindle the dying art of formal dragon magic. All in all, it was a marvelous beginning, but the best part came at the end, when he hobbled out on his cane to find Marci waiting in the hotel lobby.

He hadn't expected to see her again tonight. The Merlin delegation was still fantastically busy. Getting them to come and support him for the first ten minutes had been tricky enough given their overlapping obligations, and he hadn't been offended when they'd ducked out the moment the actual clan politicking had started. He'd assumed they'd moved on to whatever world crisis was on the docket next, but when he stepped out, there she was, waiting for him by the elevators in the same lovely, long dress she'd worn to the meeting.

"Hey," she said.

"Hey yourself," he replied, hobbling over with a grin. "What are you doing here?"

She gave him a funny look. "What do you think? You just became the Dragon of Detroit. I'm here to help you celebrate!" Her look turned sly. "I might also have gotten us a room at the hotel since, you know, it's late and I thought you might be sick of the hospital."

He loved the way she thought. "You have no idea," he said, hitting the button to summon the elevator. "Thank you."

"You're welcome," she said, reaching out to take his hand. It wasn't until they got into the elevator, though, that Julius realized Ghost wasn't there. Not that she could ever really be separated from her spirit, but by their standards, this was alone.

Even three weeks after he'd confessed his feelings, that was still enough to turn his whole head red. "So," he said, loosening his collar against the sudden heat. "Anything big happen while I was in the meeting?"

"Actually, yes. Myron and I need to get serious about recruiting more Merlins to handle the flood of spirits, so we decided to go ahead and open up a formal headquarters in the DFZ."

His heart began to pound. "Here?"

"We can't exactly be anywhere else given Myron's spirit," Marci said with a shrug. "Personally, though, I think it's very fitting. The DFZ always was the city of mages. Now it can be that for real. We're actually meeting with what's left of Algonquin's city council tomorrow to discuss making the new Merlin Council a permanent part of the city's governing structure. The spirit of the DFZ isn't actually interested in running herself on a municipal level, but she doesn't want to cede power to humans she doesn't know, so we're trying to compromise with a joint government between the city's spirit and the elected officials. That way, we've got proper civil servants running all the normal stuff people need—trash, power grid, police, economic policies, and so forth—but the DFZ still has a say in how she's run without having to do something crazy like swallow up city hall, which she *has* threatened to do."

"I think that's a great idea," Julius said. "Anything will be an improvement over being left to fend for ourselves by Algonquin. Maybe we'll actually get laws this time."

"Don't count on *too* much order," Marci warned. "This is still the DFZ, and she values her freedoms. But I think we can strike a good balance between freedom of choice and cruel neglect." Her face darkened. "There are parts of the DFZ none of us want to see come back."

That was certainly true. "At least I won't have to worry about being hunted anymore," Julius said cheerfully. "The city can be my home for real now, and speaking of homes…" He turned to look at her. "If we're both going to be staying here for the long term, I'm thinking we should move in together."

Marci laughed. "But we've always lived together."

"I meant for real this time."

Her cheeks flushed as she realized what he was implying. "Oh," she said, reaching up to fiddle with her short brown hair. "Sure. I'd love to shack up with you."

"Actually," Julius said, moving closer. "I was hoping for something a bit more permanent."

He hadn't meant to say this so soon. He couldn't even kneel due to the stupid weakness in his legs. But Julius had learned his lesson many times now about putting things off, and it wasn't as if he would ever change his mind about Marci.

"I was hoping you would live with me forever."

By the time he finished, Marci's eyes were so wide, he could see the whites all the way around. "Wait," she said, voice shaking. "Is this what it sounds like?"

"I certainly hope so," Julius replied, leaning his cane against the elevator wall so he could wrap his arms around her. "Because I'd very much like you to marry me. If you can find the time."

"I have time right now," Marci said, whipping out her phone. "There's gotta be a twenty-four-hour license office somewhere in this city. I'll get us an appointment tonight and—"

Julius cut her off with a kiss, holding her tight until her body relaxed into his. "It can wait until tomorrow," he said when he finally pulled back. "I'm not going anywhere, and I'm not letting you go, either."

"Like I'd leave before I got you on lockdown," Marci said breathlessly, looking up at him with a lovingly dazed expression before she suddenly stopped. "Wait, is this all right? I've never heard of a dragon getting married. Do you guys even do that?"

"I have no idea," Julius confessed as the elevator stopped at their floor. "And I don't care. I've never been a proper dragon. Why start now? All I know is that I want to marry you, so that's what I'm going to do."

"Works for me," Marci said, dragging him off the elevator and down the hall, laughing the entire way.

EPILOGUE

20 years later.

Alicia Williams sat on the edge of her chair in the opulent golden lobby of Merlin Tower, nervously sorting through the notes the Merlin Council had posted for mages interested in internship positions. The other half of her AR interface was covered in her credentials: her honors certification from the University of Georgia School of Thaumaturgy, a list of her extracurricular activities and personal accomplishments, including the ward against mice she'd perfected for her local food bank and the results from the one MSAT where she'd gotten a perfect score on the spellwork portion of the test. Everything was strategically arranged to make her look like the best possible candidate. The trouble was, everyone here was already the best.

Merlin Tower in the DFZ was the home of the Merlin Council and the heart of everything magically important in the world. No one got here on anything less than their A-plus game, and while Alicia had been the best back in Atlanta, she was on the world stage now. She wasn't even sure which Merlin she was applying to intern under, but it didn't matter. Just working in this building would be enough to get her a full ride to any grad school she wanted. She'd already passed the weed-out test and the first-round interview. All she had to do now was ace this final meeting today, and the future was hers.

That should have been exciting, but it felt like there was a lead brick in her stomach when a man wearing a very nice suit called her name. Hands trembling, Alicia swiped through her AR to close it and stood up, clacking across the marble floor in her borrowed, slightly-too-big high heels to duck into the elevator he was holding open.

She expected the man to lead her to another waiting room, but the elevator took them straight to the top of the tower. When they reached the highest floor, her guide told her that the Merlin was waiting for her in the office at the end of the hall. Before Alicia could ask which hall—because there were two—the elevator doors closed, and the man was whisked away, leaving her alone.

Heart pounding, Alicia decided to try the right side first, creeping down the hallway that was lined with priceless magical artifacts, including a genuine spellworked leaf from the Heart of the World and a full labyrinth drawn and signed by Sir Myron Rollins himself. It was a jaw-dropping collection, and if she'd had more time, Alicia would have spent an hour taking pictures of all of it. But after the long wait downstairs, she didn't want to delay any longer, so she hurried through the hall of wonders to the door at the end, a solid wooden panel with no sign or nameplate beside it.

Taking a deep breath, Alicia raised her hand and knocked. When nothing happened, she was sure she'd chosen the wrong hallway. For all she knew, she was knocking on a closet. But just as she turned to try the other side, a woman's voice said, "Enter."

Swallowing, Alicia opened the door and poked her head inside. "Sorry to bother you," she said quickly. "I'm here to interview for the internship position..."

Her voice trailed off. The door hadn't opened into an office—it had opened into another world. After a few stunned moments, Alicia could acknowledge that was probably an exaggeration, but the room she was looking into still must have taken up half the top of Merlin Tower.

The ceiling was all glass. So were the walls, leaving nothing between the furniture and the glittering city below, the superscrapers and the lake beyond shining like gems in the bright morning sunlight. As always, the landscape was moving, the roads reworking themselves through the buildings like rivulets before her eyes, but that was to be expected in the Living City. Thankfully, big buildings like Merlin Tower only shifted occasionally. As she'd discovered on the harrowing drive from the airport, the smaller ones moved constantly, rearranging themselves according to the spirit of the DFZ's ever-changing whims.

As the home of the DFZ's human partner, Merlin Tower was the tallest tower in the city. It was only to be expected that the view from the top would be unparalleled, but what really surprised Alicia was that the rest of the room was equally as impressive. Everywhere she looked, the office was packed with casting tables and state-of-the-art workspaces. Wooden shelves held packs of casting chalk and markers in every color and type. Another corner was packed with special lamps that synthesized moonlight, sunlight, and starlight on demand, and there was an entire ten-foot square of slate on the floor for drawing casting circles. There was so much going on, Alicia didn't even see the woman with gray-streaked brown hair sitting at the cluttered desk in the middle until she stood up.

"Ah," the woman said, reaching out to nudge the large cat bed perched on the edge of her desk to a less precarious position. "You must be here about the job."

Speechless, Alicia could only nod. The job listing hadn't said whom she'd be working for, but the woman in front of her was one every mage in the world knew. Even with her graying hair in a bun and a piece of casting chalk stuck behind her ear, there was no question that this was Marci Novalli, the First Merlin, Archmage of the Merlin Council, and three-time winner of the Nobel Prize in Magic.

"Well, come in," Merlin Novalli said, her lips curling into a grin. "I don't bite, though he might." She pointed at the glowing cat Alicia could now see curled in a ball on the cat bed. "You'll have to excuse him. Ghost isn't a morning spirit."

Alicia obediently stepped inside, her eyes so wide they hurt. That was the Empty Wind. She was standing in the same room as an honest-to-god Mortal Spirit. The *first* Mortal Spirit! And the first Merlin! She was actually here, with them!

And she still hadn't said anything.

"Merlin Novalli," she said, almost tripping over herself as she rushed forward to offer the woman her hand. "Thank you so much for meeting with me. I can't tell you what an honor it is to be in your presence."

"Oh, I like you," Novalli said, shaking her hand with a wink. "But lovely as this is, I'm afraid we're on a schedule, so I'll have to make it quick." She reached down to tap the mana contacts on her desk's glass top, and a glowing AR display appeared in front of her with Alicia's face displayed front and center. "My secretary—the man who led you up— already sent me your information, and I'm very impressed. You've got a marvelous record all around, but I was particularly intrigued by your focus on wards." She glanced at Alicia through the floating display. "How do you feel about last-minute trips?"

"I… think they're exciting?" Alicia said nervously, unsure where this was going.

The Merlin nodded as if that was a satisfactory answer. "Who owns the magic of the world?"

"No one," Alicia answered promptly. "Magic is a natural resource to be shared by all."

"On a scale of one to ten, how important do you rate your personal safety?"

She bit her lip. "I suppose that would depend on the situation. Ten normally, but mages challenge the laws of the universe on a daily basis, so safety is never guaranteed."

The Merlin grinned. "I see you've read my books."

"With respect, Archmage, everyone's read your books," Alicia said. "You're required reading in most magical programs."

Her face lit up. "Am I? That's marvelous!" She went back to the AR. "Final question. If you were warding a nuclear power plant to keep out a Spirit of Apocalypse while still letting in workers, would you try to target *all* spirits, or would you use the emotional modifier variable to try to keep out only the malevolent ones?"

Alicia didn't even need to think about that. "Neither," she said promptly. "A ward against all spirits isn't specific enough to be reliably enforced, and the emotional modifier variable is too easy for an intelligent creature like a spirit to get around."

"Fair enough," the Merlin said, crossing her arms over her chest. "How would you do it, then?"

Alicia considered the question carefully. "If I was trying to keep out a Spirit of Apocalypse, I would use a double layer. The outer ward would be heavy, but as standard as possible, whatever the corporate mages normally put on the reactor. Inside of that, though, I'd place a second, inner ward with an emotional modifier variable set to detect for glee, because that's what I think a spirit of Apocalypse would feel after getting through a wall into somewhere he shouldn't."

The Merlin was scowling when she finished, then she bent over her desk to start scribbling on a pad of spellworked paper. "A double trap," she said. "That's a good idea. But how would you—"

The click of a door cut her off, and they both looked up to see a handsome young man with black hair and an infectious smile stick his head in. "I hope I'm not interrupting."

"Only mildly," the Merlin said. "I'm just interviewing my new apprentice."

Alicia's eyes flew wide. "Apprentice?"

"She means intern," the man said kindly, turning his blinding smile on her.

"I'm the Archmage of the Merlin Council," Marci Novalli said without looking up from her work. "Who ever heard of the archmage's intern? It's stupid. She's an apprentice."

The man shrugged helplessly. "I don't care what you call her so long as we're still on for breakfast. I'm starving."

"I'll be out in a second," Marci promised. "This won't take long."

The man grinned at her and left, stopping at the door to wink at Alicia. "Good luck."

Alicia nodded, too distracted by his inhumanly-bright green eyes to answer properly. "Um," she said when he was gone. "Was that a Heartstriker?"

"That was my husband," the Archmage said proudly.

The gasp popped out before Alicia could stop it. "*That* was Julius the Peacemaker?" She hadn't meant to sound so shocked, but unlike Marci Novalli, the dragon looked nothing like his pictures, or even like a dragon. He barely looked old enough to drink. "But he seems so... young."

"I know," Marci groaned. "That's the problem with marrying immortals. They inevitably make you look ancient. But Myron's already hard at work on making himself immortal, and I mean to piggyback on that the moment he succeeds." She finished her spellwork with a flourish and handed the paper to Alicia. "Was this what you were thinking?"

Alicia looked over the formulas carefully and handed it back with a nod. "Yes, exactly."

"Wonderful," Marci said. "You've got the job. When can you start?"

"Um, I don't know," Alicia said, too shocked to even say thank you. "I only flew in for the interview on a red-eye this morning. I don't even have a place to stay in the city yet." She bit her lip. "Tomorrow?"

"How about right now?" Marci said, walking away from her desk and across her bright office toward a door set in the only wall that wasn't all windows. "I've got to go to breakfast with Julius before he eats me, but I need to get that double ward of yours in position by this afternoon, or we're in trouble. Email me your details, and we'll take care of finding you a place to stay. In the meanwhile, we've got a very not-nice Mortal Spirit on the loose and not a lot of time to fix it, so why don't you come meet the rest of the team, and we'll get you started."

"The rest of the team," Alicia repeated, heart pounding. "You mean…you mean I'm in?"

"I said you got the job, didn't I?" Marci flashed a grin over her shoulder as she opened the door, which led to another door. A heavy, wooden one, its surface battered by age. It was a door Alicia had seen countless times in textbooks and movies but never thought she'd see in person.

"Oh my god," she whispered, practically vibrating in excitement. "Is that the Merlin Gate?"

"The one and only," Marci replied as her smile grew even wider. "You wouldn't believe what I had to go through to get this shortcut set up, but miracles happen when you're friends with both of the world's greatest dragon mages. It's the only stable portal to the Sea of Magic in existence." Her grin turned sly. "Want to go inside?"

Alicia had never wanted anything more in her life. "Yes, please."

Marci laughed and threw open the door, filling the room with the scent of magic. "Welcome to the jungle," she said as she stepped inside. "I just hope you weren't kidding about that personal-safety requirement."

Alicia was too excited to answer. She just bounded through the door, leaping after the Merlin—*her* Merlin now—and into a shining world she'd never seen.

THANK YOU FOR READING!

Thank you for reading *Last Dragon Standing*, and extra special thanks to all of you for sticking with me to the end! If you enjoyed the story, I hope you'll consider leaving a review. Reviews, good and bad, are vital to any author's career, and I would be extremely appreciative if you'd consider writing one for me.

Last Dragon Standing is the final book in Julius's series, but it's not the last you'll see of the Heartstriker dragons! I'm already working on a trilogy set in the new DFZ slated for 2019, so I hope you'll all join me for more adventures in the years to come. If that's too long to wait, I've got a lot of non-DFZ books coming out in 2018, including my officially licensed *Attack on Titan* YA novel, *Garrison Girl* coming in August from Quirk Books, and a new secret project that should be dropping soon!

If you want to be the first to know when I put out anything new, sign up for my New Release Mailing List at www.rachelaaron.net. List members are always the first to know about everything I do *and* they get exclusive bonus content like the list-only Heartstriker short story, *Mother of the Year.* Joining is free, and I promise never to spam you, so come join us!

If you need more books *right now*, you can always check out one of my completed series! Just flip to the next page or visit www.rachelaaron.net for my full bibliography, large shots of my covers, links to reviews, and free sample chapters. If you want to know more about me IRL, follow me on Twitter @Rachel_Aaron or like my Facebook page at facebook. com/RachelAaronAuthor for updates on all of my books, blog posts, and appearances.

Again, thank you so, *so* much for reading! I couldn't do this without you. You are the best fans an author could ask for!

Yours always and sincerely,
Rachel Aaron

WANT MORE BOOKS BY RACHEL AARON? CHECK OUT THESE COMPLETED SERIES!

THE LEGEND OF ELI MONPRESS

The Spirit Thief
The Spirit Rebellion
The Spirit Eater
The Legend of Eli Monpress (omnibus edition
of the first three books)
The Spirit War
Spirit's End

"Fast and fun, *The Spirit Thief* introduces a fascinating new world and a complex magical system based on cooperation with the spirits who reside in all living objects. Aaron's characters are fully fleshed and possess complex personalities, motivations, and back-stories that are only gradually revealed. Fans of Scott Lynch's *Lies of Locke Lamora* (2006) will be thrilled with Eli Monpress. Highly recommended for all fantasy readers." - **Booklist, Starred Review**

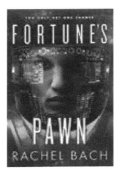

PARADOX
(written as Rachel Bach)

Fortune's Pawn
Honor's Knight
Heaven's Queen

"*Firefly*-esque in its concept of a rogue-ish spaceship family...
The narrative never quite goes where you expect it to, in a
good way... Devi is a badass with a heart." - **Locus Magazine**

"If you liked *Star Wars*, if you like our books, and if
you are waiting for *Guardians of the Galaxy* to hit the
theaters, this is your book." - **Ilona Andrews**

"I JUST LOVED IT! Perfect light sci-fi. If you like
space stuff that isn't that complicated but highly entertaining,
I give two thumbs up!" - **Felicia Day**

**To find out more about Rachel and read
samples of all her books, visit
www.rachelaaron.net!**

ABOUT THE AUTHOR

Rachel Aaron is the author of thirteen novels as well as the bestselling nonfiction writing book, *2k to 10k: Writing Faster, Writing Better, and Writing More of What You Love,* which has helped thousands of authors double their daily word counts. When she's not holed up in her writing cave, Rachel lives a nerdy, bookish life in Athens, GA, with her perpetual motion son, long suffering husband, and grumpy old lady dog. To learn more about Rachel, her work, or to find a complete list of her interviews and podcasts, please visit rachelaaron.net!

Cover Illustration by Tia Rambaran, Cover Design by Rachel Aaron, Editing provided by Red Adept Editing.

As always, this book would not have been nearly as good without my amazing beta readers. Thank you so, so much to Michele Fry, Jodie Martin, Kevin Swearingen, Eva Bunge, Beth Bisgaard, Christina Vlinder, Judith Smith, Rob Aaron, Hisham El-far, and the ever amazing Laligin. Y'all are the BEST!

12410878R00170

Printed in Great Britain
by Amazon